# Gentle Author

## Michael Eisele

Other books by Michael Eisele:
Without Tears And Other Tales
Twelve O'Clock Sharp
Odour Of Rectitude
Obeah
Rufe In Der Nacht (In German)

# Contents

Page

# Sleight Of Hand

*N*orbert Pfister glanced longingly at his sword hanging nearby on a wall. Twenty years ago he would have settled the hash of the ruffian who had entered his lonely cabin without a knock. A leap, followed by a hoot, both hands at the sword, he would have charged the intruder and chased him around the stump. But now in his seventies, sapped by the good life, he had lost the will, and no less the strength to make that move. He just sat there as if glued to his chair, acknowledging silently that diplomacy was the only available weapon.

Nevertheless, he instinctively reached for a nondescript object lying on a sideboard. It was done with the juggler's speed and dexterity; it also disappeared quicker than the intruder's eye could see, who didn't blink nor bat an eye while this happened. Pfister spoke first:

"What's up, young fellow?" he asked in a jocular fashion.

"You are up, old man, up the creek that is," the interloper snarled menacingly.

Pfister couldn't decide offhand whether to chuckle or frown. The youngster's unexpected as much as unwelcome appearance had a comical side to it, but just the same, prudence was advisable. His cabin, somewhat remote, was entirely hidden from view. Besides, the high season hadn't begun yet, when the surrounding cottages became occupied. In other words, help could not be readily obtained.

Upon closer observation Pfister gained an impression that the youngster looked familiar, and also lacked mental balance.

A nasty foreboding sneaked up his spine. He realised that this ill-mannered, unconventional visitor did not just stumble in; far from it, judging by the way he entered his peaceful abode. A bit more force and, by golly, the door would have flown off its hinges, Pfister surmised. No, this lumbering youngster did not just saunter about, whereby he came upon his cabin fortuitously; neither had he made the journey to pay his respect.

A peculiar ambience surrounded the gawky youth, evidently plagued by contradictory sentiments. One side of him inferred youthful tractability, the other foreshadowed inherent meanness. Right or wrong, Pfister concluded that his visitor was under the hypnotic influence of someone wishing him harm.

"Stall this overblown ruffian, whoever he is, sidetrack the lout till John Toby shows up," an inner voice urged.

He hurled imprecation at his neighbour's tardiness; silently, mind you, because he wanted to save his breath to pump this oddity in his living room.

"Is there anything in particular you want?" Pfister inquired while directing an eye towards his neighbour's cottage.

The fellow appeared to be unsure what to say. He stood there glowering from the depth of his being with a snare on his lips, yet fear in his eyes. Undoubtedly, the youngster possessed a resemblance with someone he could not place. His bearing bespoke disquieting news. It implied malfunction of his upper storey to begin with, but worst of all, he appeared to be enjoined to do something which he deplored. Odd to say, his mien, aggrieved and mischievous, was brightened by eyes that wanted to smile; but not presently, far from it.

"My father sent me," he hissed.

"Your father, who is he?"

"You should know, Randolph Gruber."

There, no wonder the youngster looked familiar.

"Have you got a message?"

"Yes."

"Well, what is it?"

"This."

Saying so he produced a sturdy rope with a noose at one end. Pfister's head bound up, he had the answer in a flash. The fellow is either a lunatic or an amateurish prankster. He knew Randolph Gruber like a brother, they spent many years together on the road, criss-crosssing Canada from Halifax to Victoria. They were known as the 'Dreadnaughts', magicians and jugglers whom no one could excel in speed and accuracy. Their extraordinary skills were gained in the school of hard knocks. Indeed, he and Gruber were a team that outperformed anyone in the trade. They abruptly parted over twenty years ago, under a cloud of hostility and nagging fear of each other. Their acts required utmost concentration, but most of all a sure hand guided by a sympathetic heart and peace of mind.

The apple of discord was Sylvia Steiner, a woman no longer young, but still girded with the girdle of Aphrodite. The short of it was this: Although courted avidly by both friends, Pfister won her hand. They married, and divorced before the end of the year. That happened about twenty years ago. The friends, who became bitter rivals and enemies, lost track of each other. After the divorce Pfister wandered eastward and finally put up stakes at Lac Archambeau, near St. Donat, Quebec.

The youngster's behaviour baffled him thoroughly, even more so when he spoke again:

"I have come to settle a score."

With one eye scanning the lake, the other trying to take the young fellow's measure, Pfister burst out:

"You what?"

"You heard me," he was told with a pained grimace that elicited the older man's pity rather than dread.

Yet these sentiments dissipated quickly upon sensing an undertone of villainy in his unwelcome visitor. Another disconcerting realisation gripped him: The fellow was but an automaton, programmed to do mischief. Humour him, an inner voice cautioned, stall this overgrown oddity till Toby arrives. Appeasement appeared to be the only option, placation and delay, since this errant son obviously laboured under serious delusions. He seemed set to do harm, thus prudence must be exercised. For he, Pfister, could never pit his weak physique against this almost elephantine hulk, in the blush of youth to boot.

"What is your name?"

"Viktor."

"Viktor Gruber?"

"Yes."

"You want to get even, I don't understand," Pfister chortled uneasily.

He soon did. He felt compelled to clutch his throat and neck when he observed Viktor's eyes wander from tree to tree outside. As he fingered the running knot of the noose, an eerie glint lit up his face. Pfister's consternation grew by the second, questions arose for which answers were wanting. Was this queer stranger really Randolph's son? Did he indeed commission him to take revenge for a trifling matter that took place twenty years ago? Or was the youngster mentally challenged, no doubt prone to buffoonery? But how did he find him who lived the life of a recluse?"

"Viktor, what do you actually want?"

Instead of a reply the youngster called out:

"Aha, that's the one."

"What are you talking about?"

"The branch from where you shall hang."

Pfister was about to make a snap remark and order him to be gone, or else, but something held him back. As he sized up the interloper icy shivers ran up his spine; he realised that Viktor was dead serious. No doubt he intended to string him up. Where the deuce was Toby? Thoughts raced through his mind that created a jumble in his head.

Two things became crystal clear: This wayward ruffian, whoever he was, had nibbled from the insane root. Besides, he was enjoined by someone, quite likely his father, to do him in. Resistance appeared to be a pipe dream, not worth a fig. This young giant could pick him up with one hand while laying the noose around his neck with the other. Carrying him outside, slinging the rope over a sturdy limb and hoisting him up, would be child's play for these muscular arms and sinewy hands. Calling for help? What good would that do in this remote spot. In any case his enfeebled body, plagued by asthmatic lungs, could hardly raise much of an alarm. Just as despondence stretched its tentacles towards him, surging hope lifted his spirit. He suddenly knew what had to be done. Like Hobson's juice it was this or nothing; act promptly or become a swinging corpse.

"Alright, Viktor, I am ready to bite the bullet, but first tell me why your father, whom I once knew and loved like my own kin, wants my demise. What made him sore enough to have me lynched?"

"You betrayed him."

"I did? In what way?"

"You left him to die, up in the Monashee Mountains."

"I did no such thing; in fact, I have no clue where this place is."

"Ha ha ha, father told me all about you. He warned me to be on guard, he drummed certain facts into my head."

"Like what?"

"That you are an artful quibbler and the prince of liars."

"I see, I see, what else did your father tell you?"

"I haven't the time to reel off the entire litany of your transgressions, but what really sticks in my father's craw is your attempt to seduce my mother."

"Your mother? But – but I have never met her," Pfister protested loudly against his better judgement.

His conviction grew that Randolph either had an axe to grind or, like the son, had gone completely off the rails.

"Who is your mother?"

"She died recently."

"I regret to hear it, but anyway, what is her name?"

"Name? Sylvia Gruber."

"Hm, and her maiden name?"

Viktor stared at him nonplussed, the question seemingly taxed his mental acumen. Well, the time had arrived to bring matters to a head. A last glance up the shore convinced Pfister that his distant neighbour is not coming, thus he was completely on his own. Straining every muscle in his body, training a steady eye on his would-be executioner, he spoke deliberately:

"Your father told you all that?"

"Plus much more, but as I said I feel no inclination to rattle on."

With these words Viktor, holding up the noose, was about to approach. He should have opened his eyes wider prior to making the first step. What would he have seen? An astounding transformation, surely not experienced every day. Pfister, meek and irresolute a moment ago, took on an aspect of a veritable fire-eater. He saw himself on the streets of Victoria, surrounded by awed spectators, who were stunned by the lightning speed and deadly accuracy shown them. The steely eyes that neither blinked nor changed their line of vision one iota, should have rung the alarm in the youngster's mind.

"Your father told you everything, you say?"

"He did."

"You are wrong, my boy," Pfister expelled through clenched teeth.

Surprised, Viktor stiffened.

"What are you saying, old man?"

"That your father did not tell you everything."

"Oh, what did he leave out?"

"A crucial fact."

"Tell me what."

"This."

Did young Viktor see Pfister's hand move? Probably not. Did he feel the naked steel pierce his heart? No one will ever know, because he collapsed and died without uttering another word. Norbert Pfister rose with surprising alacrity; work needed to be done. As he removed the finely honed, handmade stiletto, his face lit up in a satisfied grin, as if to say:

"There now, the old dog has not forgotten the tricks of his youth."

Twenty minutes later he arrived at John Toby's place.

"John, what's up, I was expecting you."

"Sorry, buddy, I was just about to leave."

Observing his friend and neighbour closer, he added:

"You look chipper this morning."

Nodding silently, Pfister just smiled. They spent a pleasant hour together, then Pfister rowed back to his castle, as he called it.

Shortly after he entered the police station in St. Donat. The facts, according to Pfister, were these:

"I impatiently awaited my neighbour, John Toby, who for some reason had not yet shown up. Being on tenterhooks, I finally rowed to his cottage. What time? Around eight o'clock in the morning. Be more exact, you request? Sorry, I wouldn't even try. You must understand that Toby, as much as myself, keep no clocks in the house, nor watches on our bodies. Sun, moon, and stars satisfy our needs."

Dr Meunier estimated that death occurred between nine o'clock and eleven in the morning. The cause? Instant heart failure, due to a knife wound or some other sharp object that penetrated the heart. The type of wound puzzled the doctor, for which reason he consulted Dr Marteau of nearby Ste. Agathe. Two things bothered them: The accuracy as much as the depth of the incision. The ensuing police investigation led nowhere. Sergeant Kusinef grilled Pfister mercilessly, but no light was shed on the case; it remained unsolved.

Two weeks later a registered letter reached Pfister, written on official looking paper, baring the name Stanley Webster, attorney at law. Its contents is given below:

Dear Mr Norbert Pfister.

I am the executor of the estate of Sylvia Gruber, nee Steiner, whose last will and testament names you as her sole heir. She died four weeks ago. A codicil exists, dated recently, confirming the original legacy, which Mr Randolph Gruber, the testatrix's husband of eighteen years is contesting. A hearing will take place July 15th at 9 A.M. at the Palais de Justice in Montreal. Your presence is required.

Pfister read the letter three times before the truth began to dawn on him. He knew of course that Sylvia was in line for a sizeable inheritance, but it swayed him not one iota, he couldn't bide her for all the gold of California. Thinking about the legacy brought a smile to his lips. Sylvia's inherent perversity, which he couldn't help admiring at times, clearly reared its head. Spite she loved next to contrariness. Having the last laugh at a man she most likely deceived and despised, must have eased her journey to the realm of the majority.

Pfister drew a deep sigh as he conjured up the image of the woman he once loved, but could never cherish.

"Yes, Sylvia, you must have laughed in your sleeve, thinking about how you were killing two birds with one stone. Depriving your husband of the means to live out his life in comfort, independent of you, surely brought wrinkles of merriment to your brow. Burdening me with the gold of Tolosa must have made you chuckle with glee, for you instinctively understood that it would unleash the dogs of discord."

One thing puzzled him: Why she left Viktor, the son, out of her legacy. Which fact he didn't belabour, however, since it might just have been one of her outlandish notions which abounded in that woman, who could unlock the remotest chambers of love and loathing in a man's heart.

Pfister could well imagine his erstwhile friend's and partner's irritation. Thunderstruck, and no less dismayed, seething with rage at his wife's presumed treachery, boiling with animosity towards him, he devised a plan to do away with him by proxy; using his son, in other words. Pfister knew about Gruber's grasping tendencies, whom he called Vulture Hopkins to his face. Often did he hear Randolph say he wouldn't be plagued by qualms to kill for gain, provided it were substantial and entailed no risk; like this undertaking for instance. Viktor appeared to have been the ideal executor of a scheme that could not fail to provide Gruber with the coveted life of Riley. Viktor, evidently impressionable and tractable, plus endowed with a brutish nature, not to mention his undeniable lunacy, was induced by subliminal persuasion to perform a righteous duty. He did, and died into the bargain.

Why had Gruber not apprised his son of his erstwhile partner's deadly skills, capable of endangering, if not thwarting, his mission? Was it an oversight, intentionally withheld, or just omitted out of indifference? Gruber could not possible have forgotten his extraordinary ability with knifes, darts, and arrows; it had made them famous beyond Canada's borders. Their reputation in those years bordered on legendry. Some people called him, Pfister, a latter-day Tell. Others referred to him as Egil's son. All were awed by his extraordinary dexterity in throwing knifes. It was said that he could hit a fly thirty feet away, and penetrate a solid oak board three inches thick with his finely honed stiletto. It seemed like child's play to him. What awed spectators most was the lightning speed exhibited at such demonstrations. The keenest eyes were unable to perceive the stiletto till its aim was found.

Why was Viktor not informed and cautioned to act with circumspection? The boy had no inkling concerning the risk involved. His father most likely breathed not a word about his deadly skill with a blade that never missed its target, nor ever bent or glanced from a surface. The youngster behaved like a cat dallying with a mouse that had not the ghost of a chance to escape. The truth hit Pfister with a force that made him tremble. Randolph had planned it well. He proceeded with ingenuity, no mistake about it. Should Viktor succeed in his imposed mission, so be it; Randolph would become the major beneficiary of Sylvia's fortune, whereas Viktor's share, as directed by law, must surely be placed under his tutelage, considering the circumstances. Thus he, the father, could manage it at his discretion; meaning to his advantage. In case the son bungled the assignment, became a victim of his, Pfister's unfailingly fatal steel in other words, what then? Thinking about it brought an appreciative smile to his lips:

"I have to hand it to you, old buddy, you are holding the trump cards," he murmured. "If I claim the legacy which you evidently have challenged, that will open the proverbial can of worms," Pfister granted.

In what way? Oh, quite simple, he concluded. Gruber's inevitable deposition with the authorities will most likely lead to his indictment, and ultimate journey upriver. Pfister sat down and wrote a letter addressed to Stanley Webster, attorney of law.

Dear Mr Webster:

I have received your communication concerning the legacy of Mrs Sylvia Gruber, nee Steiner. Please be advised that I assert no right concerning this bequest. This is my final and only decision.

"Let sleeping dogs lie," he reminded himself, while signing and sealing the envelope.

# The Banker

ismal days had arrived in Calgary. After a short heat wave temperatures dropped overnight, a mixture of hail and snow fell.

When James Wilmot looked outside, he instinctively recoiled. The lawns, green yesterday, had turned white.

"Oh well," he shrugged his shoulders in his inimitable fashion, implying that it could have been worse.

"Imagine," he said to himself, "if this had occurred a week earlier during the Calgary Stampede festival. So far, so good," Wilmot surmised, then whistled as he spruced himself up.

He possessed a devil-fetch-the-hindmost disposition, a happy-go-lucky fellow, whose star was once more in the ascendant. Riches were on the way. His cantankerous pal had sent word that he was about to sell their gold, and a bank draft for his half-share could be expected.

"Relax, wrest a smile from your stiff lips, mon brave," Hector Langevin quipped in his communication. He just couldn't refrain from alluding to his pal's starchiness, deemed comical to a Québecois.

"The total will surely amount to sixty thousand dollars," Wilmot was informed.

Despite the cold wind blowing from the foothills, he opened a window and announced to the world:

"Fortunatos, you old rascal, I have found your purse again."

His thoughts lingered for a while with the man he never rightly puzzled out. Although they had worked and gallivanted together on and off for fifteen years, he failed to fathom the

mercurial chap from Rimouski. There were times when Wilmot
doubted that they hailed from the same planet. Though
unpredictable like a bear with a sore head, Langevin possessed
one sterling quality: Honesty, unwavering integrity that never
failed. Yet, after two weeks had passed and neither his pal nor
the promised draft arrived, Wilmot began to pace the floor and
tap it with one or the other foot. Misgiving began to rear its
ugly head. Notions of dupery crossed his mind, inklings of
treachery rattled his nerves.

"Am I being swindled?" Wilmot asked himself, while
staring at the walls in anticipation of an answer.

The shock of his life was soon to come. The Calgary
Herald, which Wilmot only perused when want sat at his
doorsteps, revealed surprising news. There it was in black and
white. John Coles, the bank manager in Revelstoke, had been
abducted. Hector Langevin, a prospector from Rimouski, is a
major suspect. Langevin's features were described in detail, his
quaint accent received particular attention.

"Anyone knowing his whereabouts, or anything at all about
him, is requested to contact his local RCMP detachment," the
editor advised.

After Wilmot recovered from a growing astonishment, he
had a good laugh, then hurled imprecations at the newspaper
staff, from the publisher down to the printer and packer. What a
bunch of numskulls, laying a kidnapping at the door of a man
who, though quarrelsome by nature, could not hurt a fly. Just
imagining the lean, almost diminutive figure toting a well-fed,
sluggish banker up those steep mountains, would surely make a
croaker double up from laughter. No doubt that old, ornery
Frenchy could turn into a ball of fury, spitting darts and barbs
that pierces one's sensibilities, Wilmot granted. But they left no
scars, since they were neither dipped in malevolence, nor were
they meant to hurt.

"It's my Latin blood," Hector explained sheepishly after he
had vented his spleen.

Wilmot, every inch an Anglo-Saxon, treated these antics, as
he called Langevin's outbreaks, with sniffs and frowns. To be
sure, this condescension contained more than a tinge of
bravado, but it soothed his nerves. For, if the truth be known,

amid pristine surroundings, consecrated by a silence not found anywhere else, even whispered utterances suddenly made can sound intimidating. Yes, Hector Langevin can be a source of vexation at times, but being violent? Wilmot denied such notion vehemently. Knowing him even remotely could not in one's wildest dreams conjure up the idea of Hector carrying someone off, least of all a bank manager, to redeem him for ransom, or as a lark. No, the story in the newspaper was a canard, intended to divert the reader's attention from the lingering foul weather. Well, James Wilmot decided to read them the riot act, right this morning.

A knock at the door interrupted his pondering. Since he didn't respond quickly, a more insistent rap followed.

"Yes, yes, I'm coming," he cried.

The door, as always, had been locked and barred, for he lived in an unsavoury neighbourhood. Two policemen stood outside. Two eyes glared at him rebukingly, the other two accusingly.

"Sergeant Gardiner," the older one introduced himself while showing a badge. Pointing at his companion, who also displayed an insignia, he added:

"This is constable Burton. May we come in?"

It was a superfluous request since both were inside already.

"How can I help you, sergeant?" Wilmot asked, while trying to conceal his annoyance at the disturbance.

Two pairs of eyes were fixed at him. The constable poised a notebook and pen.

"You are James Wilmot," the sergeant stated.

"I am."

"You know Hector Langevin," the constable declared.

"Yes. Why do you ask?"

Instead of giving an explanation, the sergeant posed another query:

"Do you know his whereabouts?"

Hearing the tocsins ring, Wilmot faced the officers squarely:

"If you don't tell me what this is about, I shall utter not another word," he advised.

The sergeant glanced at the constable, seeking assurance no doubt, before he said more. Pointing a finger at the Calgary Herald on the table, he remarked:

"You have read the article, I presume."

"Yes, but I believe it's a Mother Goose tale."

"Far from it. We are in possession of conclusive evidence that your friend has more than a hand in Mr Coles' disappearance," the sergeant intimated.

"He is not exactly my friend," Wilmot objected.

"Didn't you prospect with him?" the constable fell in.

"Quite so. But while we emptied more than the traditional sack of flour together, we never grew close."

Eyeing alternatively sergeant Gardiner and constable Burton, Wilmot commented:

"I presume a warrant for his arrest has been issued."

The innocent query caused undue consternation among the officers, who squinted, pursed their lips, and creased their brows in annoyance. Seemingly vexed on account of Wilmot's aplomb, they left abruptly.

The first inkling of being shadowed manifested itself a day later. The weather improved overnight, not a single cloud marred the sky anymore. The sun, as if anxious to make up for the recent misery, shone with a winsome glow that brightened people's countenances and lightened their steps. Wilmot, though endowed with an optimistic disposition, began to fret. Not on account of the authority's sniffing about; far from it, but because his enthusiasm had played him a trick again. Upon receipt of Hector's welcome message, he betook himself to Calgary's major bookstores, where he spent, if not his last dollar, but close to it.

"Blast the rashness," Wilmot inveighed, for it increasingly played the deuce with his life, hurling him from one predicament onto the doorsteps of another. Yes, this overconfidence must be seized by the bridle.

"Next time, next time," he consoled himself on the way to the nearby post office.

It was his second trip today. He entered the building on the wings of hope, but left in the talons of despair. The clerk behind the counter, who recognised him from afar, shook his head suggestively:

"Nothing yet," he remarked with a compassionate grin.

"Has all the mail been sorted?" Wilmot inquired.

"Down to the last postcard," he was told.

On the way back, dispirited, in a contemplative mood, Wilmot's nagging presentiment of being observed, strengthened. Strange to say, the notion honed his mettle and put spring in his steps. He momentarily forgot his troubles; examining passers-by diverted his attention. He seized them up from the corner of his eyes, searching for telltale signs inherent to sleuthes. With the mien of a slyboots he looked in every direction. At times he stopped in front of a show window, pretending to be absorbed in the merchandise within. It provided an opportunity to cast oblique glances at approaching pedestrians. Most of the men, women too for that matter, were dismissed with a deprecating snort.

"Phooey, one look tells me that none of them has the making of a secret agent. That fellow there? Pshaw, I bet he couldn't trace a skunk in broad daylight, let alone track an old stager like myself," he muttered.

Kidnapping, Wilmot knew, being a serious delict, fell under the jurisdiction of the Royal Mounted Police. Well, Canada's pride and glory suffered from an illusion if they thought that he would lead them to his pal Hector Langevin.

"They can shadow me till the crack of doom, I shall not go near Hector," although he could well imagine where he can be found.

It turned out to be a hollow promise, necessity trumped integrity. Want, mingling with suspicion, at first whispered insinuatingly, but soon the sibilations turned into a roar, drowning out his good intentions. Wilmot's pockets were empty to the seams; in fact, he was in deep water. He sold what he could, and pawned the rest for trifles, then started to plan.

Now as then Wilmot had scruples about Hector's imputed escapade. He thanked his guiding star for having kept mum about their latest windfall, as much as their stamping grounds. Windfall? Wilmot couldn't help wondering, for it looked increasingly like a pipe dream. But no, he reassured himself, Hector will deliver, he always does.

So it went. One moment he felt consumed by doubts, the next he soared on the wings of confidence. Finally reality, which no force on earth can subvert, made itself known. Realising that he shall never see a red cent unless confronting Hector, he decided to visit the Selkirk wilderness once more.

This took place at a time when Canada gained a toehold in the world of sophistication. It eagerly shed the label of hewers of wood and drawers of water, or at least made a strenuous attempt to do so. In many parts of the country it was deemed to be an epithet. From the Atlantic Ocean to the windswept plains, people welcomed the breeze that bore tidings of progression. But the ardour to embrace the vaunted new era grew dimmer beyond the Great Lakes. The desire for change lessened as the Rocky Mountains loomed up. It had a difficult time to cross the Great Divide, for entrenched habits died slowly in that vast wilderness, where a remnant of adventurers and loners clung tenaciously to the independent life of their forebears.

Wilmot proceeded with utmost circumspection. Guided by an assumption of being shadowed, he altered his appearance. Growing a beard proved easy for a hirsute man, dying his hair took but an hour. He left his dwelling under cover of darkness by means of the fire escape, then boarded the first train travelling westward. The thought to be recognised never entered his mind, after viewing himself in a full-length mirror. The sight instinctively made him shrink back, he could barely suppress a cry of dismay.

Revelstoke, reputed to be a rough town in those days, which term the local police smugly acknowledged, bristled with excitement. Special RCMP forces had arrived from Vancouver, who combed mountains and valleys with scant success. They weren't rewarded with a whiff nor trace of the putative abductor's whereabouts. Guides, proclaiming that they not merely were acquainted with Langevin, but knew the places he frequented, offered their services free of charge. Yet, curious to say, when they arrived at these selected cabins and lean-tos, the wanted man could not be found. Prospectors, who camped there, vowed not to have seen Frenchy for ages. After a while the authorities caught on; they were led on a wild chase. Indeed, that was the case, for none of the old-timers had a grain of sympathy for banks, and even less for the police. Besides, they were a puckish lot; guiding these self-important, overweight detectives over cliffs and steep ravines, tickled their fancies.

Wilmot arrived in Revelstoke shortly before sundown. As he scanned the surrounding mountain peaks, someone called out mockingly:

"Halloo, there, going to a masquerade?"

It was Nat Morgan who owned several claims at the other side of Carnes Creek. Wilmot pretended not to see or hear him.

"What's the matter, old boy, did the cat get your tongue?" Morgan hooted.

Feeling secure in his disguise, Wilmot responded condescendingly:

"I don't know what you mean."

"Cut the cackle, James, I got something to tell you. Meet me in ten minutes at the Regent Inn, room 12."

Nat Morgan had recognised him, at first sight to boot. Small wonder, Wilmot granted, after all they had prospected together along Silver Tip Creek, right up to the falls. Besides, did they not drink to each other's health in every bar in town? He never did warm up to Nat the griper, as he was known throughout the Columbias. His brand of subtlety found scant approval with anyone, least of all with him, who deemed his occasional partner a regular crosspatch.

On the way to the hotel Wilmot was beset by doubts. Meeting Morgan at the railway station seemed ominous. Was he expecting him? Just fortuitously loitering about, or did his presence presage of something more serious? No matter what, prudence must be employed, Wilmot decided.

"Come in, James, come in," Morgan invited at the first knock.

Smirking from ear to ear he queried:

"Why the get-up, old boy?"

Wilmot, astir with suspicion, replied evasively:

"Ascribe it to a man's foibles. Don't forget I'm approaching a whimsical age."

The flippant reply earned him a censorious look.

"Anyway, Nat, what is it you want to tell me?"

"Hector left a message for you."

"Let's hear it."

"A strange one, I must say."

"Well?"

"Look under Murray's Rock."

"Just that?"

"Nothing else."

Wilmot smiled, he understood. On the way out he paused, then turned around. Looking Morgan full in the face, he asked:

"Nat, how did you know I was on that train?"

Did Morgan squint to see better in the waning daylight? Had he cleared his throat involuntarily or out of embarrassment? His reply had a husky ring to it:

"I didn't, I just happened to be around."

Wilmot, suppressing an urge to mention the RCMP's visit in Calgary, left the room. He would have liked to dwell on the fact that no one but Langevin knew his whereabouts, but an inner voice bid him to keep quiet.

The following day Coles, the banker, showed up; hale in body and sound in mind, albeit worn out and strangely fidgety. The police appeared at his doorsteps in a twinkle. Sergeant Brewster, with a local constable in tow, made many queries, some of which seemed to vex the banker, whereas others elicited smirks and chuckles. What emerged was this:

Coles decided to go on a camping trip over the weekend. His wife, who visited relatives in Nova Scotia, had not been expected to return soon. Monday was a bank holiday, thus the extended free time lend itself for the short excursion.

"I am embarrassed to tell you what happened."

Turning towards Webb, he continued:

"You might recall, constable, that on Saturday afternoon it started to rain with a vengeance, hence limiting one's vision considerably. Hoping to find a suitable spot to pitch my tent, I kept on walking. Soon I lost all sense of direction, besides getting soaked to the skin. Thoroughly disoriented, I set up camp under a large tree. When the rain stopped, my consternation started in earnest, since the chosen spot, in fact the entire surrounding proved to be totally unfamiliar to me. In other words, I had no idea where I was. But as you can see, I ultimately found my way back."

Heaving a deep sigh, acquiring a rueful demeanour, Coles declared:

"I sincerely regret the inconvenience caused you."

The words were meant to end the interview, but the sergeant haboured different thoughts. He had no intention to leave, nor was he inclined to close the file. Still fairly young, educated beyond a sergeant's requirements, he possessed a good measure of intuition. The staid, somewhat haughty bank manager bewildered him; he seemed to gloss over vital information, his whole story deemed him incongruous.

To begin with, Coles gave no impression to be partial to the wilderness. Quite the contrary; he exuded an aura of a man about town. Furthermore, his caustic deportment baffled and annoyed the officers. His replies to queries were accompanied by huffs, clicks of the tongue, and impatient gestures. He burst out:

"I don't understand what you are leading up to."

Cocking his head, frowning at the officers, he mocked:

"You are not insinuating that this – this rustic, what's his name again, marched me up the mountains at gun point?"

Noticing their noncommittal bearing, he chortled derisively:

"Forgive my merriment, I find that screamingly funny."

The policemen glanced at each other. Constable Webb pulled a notebook from his pocket, in which he slowly leafed.

"Last Friday you had an altercation with Hector Langevin."

"You might call it that if you wish."

"Langevin uttered a threat."

"He might have, I don't remember," followed a surly reply.

Sergeant Brewster drew himself up, he spoke deliberately:

"Mr Coles, I wish to impress upon you a simple fact."

"Which is?"

More acrimony could not have been crammed into these words. The sharp reply that lay on the sergeant's tongue was stifled by a sudden commotion outside the manager's office. Frantic cries were heard, angry voices resounded in the bank's vestibule. The manager's office door flew open. Despite someone's attempt to hold him back, James Wilmot stormed in.

"Hector is dead, I found him in a ravine at the bottom of Silver Tip Falls," he shouted.

The announcement affected everyone like a bolt from the blue. The police officers bridled involuntarily. Brad Tilley, the senior bank clerk, gasped audibly, as if seized by forebodings he could not name. Turning from his superior to the snow-covered Mount Begbie, he resembled a man buffeted by grim notions.

"What now, what now," he muttered repeatedly.

Wilmot, ignoring questions hurled at him from all sides, fixed his eyes on the police officers.

"Get some horses, I will lead you to the spot," he urged.

Sergeant Brewster took charge, his voice acquired an imperiousness not divined in a soft-spoken man:

"Constable, I suppose there are outfitters in town?" he inquired.

"Yes, several."

"Well, fall to it, procure two horses and a sumpter," he commanded.

When they stepped outside, the sergeant asked Wilmot:

"How far is it to that place?"

"Two hours on horseback, at a fair clip."

Pulling out his watch, Brewster queried:

"When does darkness set in?"

"Before ten o'clock."

"Hm, it's now three o'clock, if we get there by six o'clock, we should be back by nightfall."

They found Langevin, or rather his corpse, at the location indicated. After conducting the required examinations, taking pictures from every angle plus drawing up sketches, they loaded the body onto the sumpter and rode back to town. The following coroner's inquest, required by law, resulted in the verdict: Death by misadventure.

In the meantime Wilmot had returned to the cabin above Silver Tip Falls, which Fred Murray, a noted trailblazer of the area, had built over fifty years ago. One of the numerous ledges nearby was christened Murray's Rock by him and Langevin.

An opening in the solid rock below served them as a message centre. A large stone closed the cap inconspicuously and perfectly. No one not privy to the hiding place would give it a second glance. The opening was also used to deposit valuables within. To Wilmot's surprise the cage was empty. Searching high and low, inside and around the cabin, he found neither the gold nor a single message. Brooding over misfortunes could not be considered as one of his faults, lamenting even less. He rolled up his sleeves and went to work on the claim, owned by him and Langevin.

Hector had kept the facility in shipshape. To his joy he also found the larder chock-full. Stripping off the image of a future man about town, he threw himself at the work, or rather tried to. The recent events played havoc with his attention. Like a moth flutters around a light, his thoughts hovered around Hector's fate. What happened deemed him an enigma shrouded in mystery. The fatal tumble perplexed him as much as the empty cache, if not more. For a nimbler man more sure-footed could hardly have been imagined.

Wilmot sighed while reminiscing. How often had he marvelled at Hector's bodily poise, which roused his envy. Mountain goat, he called him, dall sheep on two feet. How could he slip and fall? Yes, Wilmot had difficulty concentrating on the business at hand; understandably so. The matter of the missing gold stirred his emotions to a degree that numbed his senses and weakened his mettle. After all, they had toiled ceaselessly for a long time to accumulate what they had.

He, Wilmot, wanted to sell when the value of gold started to rise; but not Hector, who sniffed at the notion. He ran the whole gamut of eloquence to prevent it. Now, with gold selling for over seven hundred dollars an ounce, it eluded his grasp. What made Hector change his plans? Something must have occurred that compelled him to deviate from his intention as mentioned in his wire; sending a bank draft, in other words. Yes, Hector could be whimsical at times, but not fickle. Changing his mind on the spur of the moment? Not that mulish Québecois, Wilmot had to admit, whose obduracy caused no small amount of dissension between them.

One morning, while sluicing avidly, a realisation hit him. Stopping instantly what he was doing, Wilmot strode towards the cabin, which he entered with feverish haste. He suddenly knew were the gold was. Hector's message conveyed by Nat Morgan, deemed cryptic till now, became plain as a pikestaff. Morgan had either misunderstood or misquoted Hector's message, which most likely was: "Don't look under Murray's Rock," implying that his share of the gold will be hidden elsewhere; namely, in a dugout covered by a trap door. Sure enough, under a pile of small rocks Wilmot found not one, but two pouches half full with gold nuggets.

"How strange," he murmured while shaking his head.

His joy and relieve can well be imagined, although both received a damper, when harrowing questions arose that demanded an answer. What induced Hector to change his mind about the bank draft? Furthermore, why did he not leave his, Wilmot's share, at the usual spot? Beyond that, what's the purpose of two pouches if one could easily have contained the contents of both? Shrugging his shoulders he remarked:

"Why worry? Care kills the cat."

Wilmot decided to pull up stakes, sell his share of the claim, and shuffle along. It was not meant to be; not immediately anyway.

When he spread the word and posted 'for sale' cards in places frequented by miners, prospectors, and disgruntled fortune seekers, he learned that Brad Tilley, second in line at the Toronto Dominion Bank, had quit his job, and moved back to the coast. Wilmot vaguely knew the man, who had prospected with Langevin for a stint. Their association must have been steeped in discord, judging by Hector's odd demeanour in connection with Tilley. Invariably loquacious like an oracle, he became close as a clam when inquiries were made about Tilley. The faintest allusion to the banker's assistant kindled a choking rage in the otherwise gentle Québecois. Something untoward must have happened between them that gnawed at Hector's mind.

Wilmot decided to cash in his gold. When he entered the Toronto Dominion Bank, Coles, the manager, raised his eyebrows disapprovingly; he seemed not enthused to see him.

Nevertheless, his mien softened when he learned the purpose of his visit. They had dealt with each other before, usually with tempers on edge, and tongues dipped in acrimony. Yet strange to say, after each concluded transaction they cordially shook hands, both seemingly glad to deal with someone of their own breed; crusty and straight forward, and no less petulant respective Coles, the banker.

Hardly had the door been closed when the bank manager snapped:

"Well?"

"I want to sell my gold."

Who or what admonished Wilmot not to produce the nuggets when Coles barked: "Let's see it," he could not have said.

Ignoring the brusque request, Wilmot digressed:

"What's the price today?" he queried.

A snort and a sniff by Coles expressed his sentiment to a tee. Consulting a chart, he advised:

"Between seven hundred and seven hundred and fifty dollars per ounce, depending on the assay."

Wilmot, still disinclined to open his packsack slung over his shoulder, used a subterfuge:

"I will fetch it. Can I return in an hour?"

Coles nodded assent, and Wilmot left.

He decided to have a snort or two at the bar across the street. There he met no other than Hal Jerome, the town's uncrowned King of Whispers.

"Do you know the latest news?" Wilmot was asked.

"No," he answered not exactly friendly.

Assuming a heralding mien, inclining his head towards Wilmot, he said in an undertone:

"Brad Tilley has been arrested."

"That's no skin off my nose."

"Maybe so. Wouldn't you like to know why?"

"Not especially."

"For fobbing off fool's gold as the real thing."

"It's been done before," Wilmot intimated with a deprecating wave of the hand.

"Has it? Not from your claim, old boy."

"What are you saying?" Wilmot demanded to know.

"Exactly what you heard," Jerome replied somewhat miffed.

Wilmot almost hurled himself out of his chair, for another piece of the puzzle fell into place. Hector's unaccountable fascination with pyrite came to his mind.

"Save it," his partner repeatedly urged.

"What on earth for?"

"I need every mite, you will soon find out why."

"Time to go back to the bank." Wilmot told Jerome.

Coles appeared to be waiting for him. With the new assistant in tow, he invited Wilmot to his private rooms. After the contents of the bags were carefully examined, weighed, registered, and receipts were signed and issued, the banker remarked:

"Why the two pouches? One would have been enough by the looks of it."

"That's a question only Hector Langevin can answer," Wilmot declared not exactly respectfully.

Out in the street he met Luc Besancour, an old-timer like himself. He never prospected with him, since he found the fellow lazy and argumentative. Besides, his mangled English jarred on Wilmot's nerves. Listening for a while to his rapid-fire double Dutch could induce a native English speaker to bewail the hour of his birth. Repeated inquiries what he was trying to say rendered Luc outright bellicose. Thus, when Besancour invited him to hoist a few, Wilmot, alleging a pressing appointment, politely reclined. He wished to be alone, for he felt an irresistible urge to mull things over. Langevin's preoccupation with pyrite smacked of eccentricity, as did his peculiar disposition towards Brad Tilley, his erstwhile helper and apprentice, whom he evidently loathed.

Deep in thought, pondering about a seemingly unsolvable riddle, Wilmot unwittingly approached the police building. When he looked up and noticed where he was, he told himself:

"I should go in and have a chat with constable Webb."

In the hope to elicit more information about the latest events, he crossed the threshold. Once inside, his conscience

stirred, he felt it incumbent upon him to tell all he knew; from
Hector's wire to Morgan's message and Tilley's exclamations.

Constable Webb received him cordially, but with little joy.
He looked weary, like a man taxed to the limits of his physical
and mental strength.

"What's up, James?" he inquired in a tired voice.

"Can I talk to you in private?"

Webb tried to suppress a frown, then took him to a
conference room.

"Take a seat," he invited Wilmot, who looked around the
large room with eyes dimmed by dismay.

He instinctively shrunk back as he surveyed the windowless
chamber. He abhorred being in a closed-in area, where neither
shrubs, trees, or open spaces can be seen. Nevertheless, he
related all he knew. Halfway through his report, as it were,
constable Webb became wide-awake. The boredom of a
moment ago evaporated almost visibly, his mental alertness
returned.

"Let me make some notes," he suggested.

As he opened a communal notebook, something appeared to
be dawning on him. Resting his crossed arms on the table, he
leaned forward and said frowningly:

"Why did you not speak up at the coroner's inquest?"

Why indeed, Wilmot thought, but now as then found no
ready explanation, except this: A sibylline whisper bid me to
clam up. He dared not admit that a hunch guided his actions, a
premonition fanned by Hector's fascination with worthless
pyrites. Then a question was sprung at him:

"By the way, James, did you or Langevin ever mine or
hoard fool's gold?"

Touched to the quick, Wilmot started up. On the spur of the
moment he almost burst out:

"Hector made me do it."

Yet he managed to curtail the impulse, for tocsins were
ringing again. Inexplicable as it may sound, Wilmot, trustful
since birth, preferred to lie rather to be true to himself.

"We did not," he answered gruffer than intended.

Then he inquired:

"Why are you asking?"

"Brad Tilley has been indicted."

"What's the charge?"

"Fraud. He palmed off pyrites as high grade gold."

"I never trusted that fellow," Wilmot remarked.

"Here is the clincher. He maintains that Hector Langevin put him up to it."

Wilmot's repudiation sounded hollow, his denial lacked force. Thoroughly confused, he left the precinct.

Once outside he neither perceived the bright sunshine, nor did he feel the warm afternoon breeze that made the leaves rustle invitingly. The snow-capped mountains bore no enticement, he did not marvel at the untamed wilderness all around him. With a bowed head, muttering to himself, he shuffled towards the bank.

John Coles, the manager, appeared to be in a jovial mood, outright expansive, he deemed Wilmot. All seemed in order; cash and bank draft for the balance was handed him without further ado.

"Sit down, Mr Wilmot, let's chat for a bit," Coles suggested.

Shrugging his shoulders, Wilmot took a chair. Assuming a compassionate mien, the banker intimated:

"Isn't it a pity what happened to Brad Tilley?"

Receiving no prompt response, he queried:

"You know Brad, don't you?"

"Vaguely, and to my regret, if I may add."

No, he never liked that spindly fellow, who reminded him of a long-necked goitrous bird of prey. He must have done Hector a vile turn, thus unleashing that latent penchant for retaliation in the Québecois.

Feigning ignorance, Wilmot inquired:

"What did happen to him?"

"Hm, I thought the whole town knew that he is facing fraud charges."

"Well, I'm out in the sticks, as you probable know."

"Quite so, quite so."

A moment silence ensued, which was interrupted by Coles:

"Funny, your dislike for Tilley was shared by Langevin, as manifested itself right here."

"Hector visited the bank?" Wilmot asked.

"Yes. He stormed in just before closing time. It happened on the Friday preceding the bank holiday. Phew, what a queer fellow, who had a chip on his shoulders. The moment he crossed our threshold, he seemed to spoil for a fight."

"Ah, Hector's bark was always worse than his bite," Wilmot chuckled.

"Well, you may have a point there, but let me continue. He brandished two pouches similar to yours. Yes, yes, brandishing is the right word. He said that they were chock-full with high grade gold nuggets."

"Was he – was he under the influence?" Wilmot felt compelled to ask, for the banker's description seemed inconsistent with his partner's wonted deportment.

"Perhaps, but we didn't think so."

"We?" interrupted Wilmot.

"Yes. I am referring to Tilley and myself."

"Brad Tilley was present, you say?"

"Langevin insisted on it, he wanted him to witness the transaction, which was not an undue request, I may add."

Wilmot's response made the banker raise his eyebrows.

"What do you know," his visitor said under his breath.

"Anyway, Brad and I had a difficult time to appease Langevin. Besides, we weren't quite sure what he wanted, outside of provoking us."

Wilmot started to sense a connection between Hector's visit at the bank and his change of plans. Coles had more to say:

"You know, I never figured Langevin's weird behaviour out, even today I am unable to separate fancy from facts."

"What happened finally?"

"He kept inveighing against us, threatening both with abduction and horsewhipping should we not accede to his wishes, which were never revealed. Mind you, we would have gladly dickered about the gold, if offered, but nothing of the sort was proposed. What finally happened is quickly said. He grabbed both bags, which he had deposited on my desk, then walked out in a huff."

Wilmot had heard enough; he took his leave. As he reached for the door handle, the banker said something that made him spin around.

"What did you just say?" he cried out.

"I just repeated Langevin's last words before he stomped out."

"Would you care to repeat them?"

Chuckling, the banker did:

" 'You will be safe under Murray's Rock.' "

Mistaking Wilmot's stare for signs of incomprehension, Coles explained:

"Langevin lifted each pouch to his lips and gave it a hearty smack while promising:

" 'You will be safe under Murrays Rock till Tuesday.' "

Without uttering another word, Wilmot hurried outside.

The fog around the mystery of the pyrite began to lift. Hector's masterful performance at the bank, it was nothing else Wilmot decided, served an ulterior motive. It was meant to disclose the fact that he possessed a considerable fortune in gold nuggets, which would be hidden till Tuesday, in a cache known to Tilley. It was a veiled invitation, cleverly directed at Tilley, to acquire that presumable hoard of gold. What a clever ruse! That vulture without a beak fell for it; hook, line, and sinker. But why did Hector resort to such machinations, surely meant to entrap his erstwhile helper?

What happened wasn't so difficult to reconstruct. Hector entered the bank in a feigned state of confusion, brandishing two bags supposedly stuffed with gold nuggets. Arguments ensued, brought on by Hector's inimical behaviour, which frustrated intended transactions. In a huff his partner stomped out, after he inadvertently, so to speak, blabbed about what should have remained unsaid.

Well, old comrade, you might have just dished out deserved dessert to your enemy, but at the same time you hoisted your own petard. Wilmot imagined what happened. After baiting his erstwhile helper with putative riches, Hector deposited the two pouches in the cache under Murray's Rock, no doubt cognisant to Tilley. Knowing his partner's inclination to gloat, he must have been laying in wait for him. In his eagerness to revel in

Tilley's anticipated misery, once he started to sell the stolen fool's gold, he must have become careless, slipped, and fell to his death.

Did Tilley witness Langevin's tumble? More than likely. That would explain the strange agitation at the bank, as much as his exclamation:

"What now, what now?"

Yes, it all started to make sense, albeit not in every detail, but the substance jibed.

Much later, back in Calgary, James Wilmot learned that Brad Tilley received a long jail sentence for aggravated fraud. Wilmot chuckled, Hector could rest in peace, his goal had been met.

# The Calgary Yodeller

*F*ritz Abram was at it again, finding fault that is, with everyone and everything, except himself. His present predicament, one of many, he attributed to nothing less than lack of appreciation by his fellow men. How else could a first-rate tradesman, certified and experienced in several occupations, be in want amid plenty. Calgary in those days revelled in an unprecedented construction boom. One could hear words by employment managers to the effect that skilled workers are painfully scarce. So much so, that any warm body with a whiff of qualification would do. Yet he, a seasoned craftsman, was still unemployed after pounding the pavement for fully three weeks. Something appeared to be amiss here which needed rectification.

For the past week he spent an early hour in a small park, ringed with several benches. The one at the end, hidden from view, had been chosen by him as the ideal spot to ponder. There he sat just now, catechising himself about his failure to find suitable work. Of course he glossed over a crucial point; the meaning of suitable. Therein hung a story, which he dared not tell, nor wished to be told. Whenever he looked up, Abram was visibly annoyed, chagrin mirrored in his face. A man steeped in discontent wants to be surrounded by inactivity and misery. Seeing in the near distance a host of looming tower cranes, swinging constantly while lifting heavy loads, made him wince. Hearing the rhythmic thuds of falling pile-driving hammers bothered him no less. The bustle grated on his nerves, or rather stung his conscience. He felt challenged and imposed upon.

Fritz Abram approached that stage in life where resignation stretches its tentacles towards the man endowed with more imagination than initiative. Sitting there, grousing about his unfair circumstances, he invited vindication, his loyal companion, for a debate.

"Who is at fault?" he murmured.

"Not you," whispered the obliging harridan, "not you, Fritz."

"Blame fate which cannot be circumvented," Abram consoled himself, rather tried to, albeit with little success, because his growling stomach drowned out the sibylline encouragement.

"Time to be on my way," he said to himself.

As he rose with a deep sigh, a most peculiar sound became audible, which made him stop in his tracks.

"What the dickens," he involuntarily exclaimed, while he searched for the source of the noise.

There it was again. Prolonged, piercing outcries that resembled a yodel, rent the air. They weren't exactly that, Abram realised, but shouts of irrepressible glee, which opened the sluice gates of nostalgia in his heart. Before his mind's eye appeared the green alpine pastures with grazing cows, whose bells around their necks produced a soporific serenity no sleeping draught could ever match. The yodeller, dressed like an alpine herdsman, came into view. Abram had to repress an urge to rush over and embrace him. He was glad he didn't, considering subsequent events.

Shooing the clouds of nostalgia from his eyes, he ducked behind a cluster of bushes. Something arcane took place not far from him. The yodeller stopped in front of the odd house, skirting a well-kept crescent, then bowed while making a half-turn, and let go with one of his inimitable cries of joy that in the alpine region is called Juchzer.

After the pseudo-Tyrolean, an apparition from a distant world, had made the rounds, he started anew. This time, however, his odd serenade took place at the front door of the houses selected. When a woman appeared and glanced in every direction before she slipped something into his haversack, Abram blinked instinctively. When this repeated itself at another and another house, he gaped in astonishment. Upon reaching the end of his rounds, the gyrating yodeller disappeared from Abram's view. The entire presentation lasted about ten minutes. Baffled, no less amused, Abram walked towards the inner city.

On the next morning the yodeller arrived at the same hour and expelled these odd, yet heart-warming cries of joy, in front of the same houses. Abram observed the lusty performer till he vanished behind a cluster of bushes. Shaking his head in disbelief, he started to muse. Vague images rose before his eyes; some made him chuckle, others creased his brow. What significance, if any, had these theatrics? Abram concluded that there was more to it than met the eye. Curiosity made his heart flutter, an inexplicable uneasiness disrupted his equanimity on account of weird notions that gradually took a foothold. What did these women slip into the entertainer's pouch? Matronly everyone appeared to be, refined, and seemingly in comfortable circumstances. Dared he think the unthinkable? Could it be that they were love letters or, perish the thought, invitations for an assignation? Who knows, he conjectured between snickers and chuckles.

It wouldn't be so exceptional that lovelorn women, living in the lap of luxury, wither in the climate of their men's indifference towards them. After all the yodeller's laughing face and rakish demeanour, can captivate a woman of any age, Abram allowed.

"Time to be on my way," he reminded himself.

It took every ounce of willpower to make the first steps towards the thumping, clattering downtown core. But necessity urged him on, because short commons would soon be his lot, he realised. Waving a deprecating hand in the direction of the wealth exuding houses, Abram murmured:

"Let sleeping dogs lie."

That proved to be easier said than done.

Fritz Abram's life, while not particularly eventful, nevertheless was beset by ups and downs; in fact, he seemed forever weighing anchor on a tossed up sea for no other reason than courting disaster. Yet he always got by, albeit by the skin of his teeth at times. He appeared to be the darling of a fate who loves reckless men that like to walk near a precipice.

Thoroughly annoyed by the din around him due to omnipresent construction, irritated by the buoyant spirit and purposeful strides of people, Abram slouched along. Idle men, vexed by indecision, loath activity, which distracts one's moping plus engenders feelings of guilt.

Hurling silent imprecations at the invidious bustle, Abram walked on. When the post office came in sight, he steered towards it and entered unwittingly. A pleasant surprise awaited him there. When the clerk handed him an envelope, which he opened with an uneasy frown, Abram almost let go with a shout of joy; he was in luck's way once more. Mortimer Wagner, a long forgotten acquaintance, had found him to settle an old debt.

"Saved by the bell," he murmured.

It wasn't a great sum, but to a hungry soul even bitter things look sweet. Well, well, he granted, exercising good judgement, curbing corporal desires, Mortimer's draft should tide him over for two months.

Back on the street Abram's slouch was gone; his mien cleared up. Humming a tune he strode briskly towards his meagre dwelling. For an instant he felt tempted to send out a yodel or two in the direction of the looming Rockies, but prudently desisted. First, he had most likely unlearned the intricacies of that heart-stirring warble; second, the sombre, mirthless environment stifled the least desire to dispatch greetings of the pristine mountains belonging to another world.

In his dwelling Abram paced the floor while contemplating what to do next. At every turn he swathed himself with another layer of hypocrisy, for he knew very well what would happen. Ever since he witnessed the strange presentation he felt an impulse to investigate. But sanctimony, the cat's paw of villainy, required a show of affection. He would have bridled at the thought of giving a name to his intentions, which in simple English are called spying. The first step towards another witch's circle had been made. Fritz Abram, the man who knew so much yet did so little, once again put his foot in it. He should have done something more sensible, like seeking work, for instance.

"Be quiet," he admonished his grumbling conscience. "First I must fulfill a duty."

That assertion rang hollow even to himself when broached. But repeating it made it more plausible. What amused him initially, then roused his curiosity, now fuelled his sense of duty. Yes, he told himself, there is skulduggery involved, which I feel obliged to expose.

Next morning Abram positioned himself at the same spot as before. He had taken certain precautions about his appearance. Besides wearing nondescript clothing and a run-of-the-mill hat, he sported dark glasses. As anticipated, the yodeller showed up punctually. He went through the same hoops as yesterday, but this time the odd display occurred at the entrances of houses not visited previously. Again, mature women, well-groomed, exuding an air of affluence, stepped out, peered left and right, then, after slipping something in his haversack, scurried back inside. When he reached the end of the crescent, still beaming from ear to ear, he stepped through an opening in the hedges.

Nothing further happened for several minutes. Abram, on pins and needles, decided to take a closer look; furtively, of course, for he didn't want to be caught snooping. As he neared the gap in the fence where a small gate swung on its hinges, he heard someone coming. Retreating hastily, ducking behind nearby bushes, he stood there motionless till the yodeller had passed him. What he saw made him gasp; the rakish entertainer had undergone an astounding transformation; the sight struck him dumb. For an instant Abram questioned his senses and doubted his vision. He removed his sunglasses and passed a hand over both eyes as if trying to remove obscuring scales. It was the yodeller, no two ways about it, judging by his countenance and bearing. True, the singular change from a lusty warbler to a staid businessman, in the twinkling of an eye to boot, could have very well unsettled a loyal disciple of Zeno, the Stoic. But stranger things have happened, Abram granted. Besides, looking at these events rationally might quickly penetrate the shroud of mystery. Changing one's clothes behind a hedge required no magic wand. Altering one's deportment,

especially if compelled by a powerful motive, hardly counted
as a remarkable feat. Actors do it all the time, some with a flair
matching the yodeller's. Why the mummery Abram couldn't
have guessed. But thoroughly intrigued now, he instinctively
kept at the man's heels, till he entered a house a bit set back
from the street. A sign over the door read: Kristian Lauber,
numismatist. Hm, that's worth a chuckle or two, Abram
granted, then conjectured that smuggler or trickster would be a
more appropriate label. Before he walked away, Abram
perused the shingle closer.

Business hours: 9A.M – 4 P.M was written below the name
and occupation. As he tried to shut out the conscience-
tweaking construction noise, Abram was beset by peculiar
notions. The man who had journeyed thousand of miles to
replenish his empty pockets, momentarily spurned the idea of
toiling for paltry returns.

"Balmy days are beckoning," he informed the Rockies
looming at the western sky.

Thumbing a nose at the swinging cranes imprecating against
the bustle that made him self-conscious, he stepped onto the
path, subliminally mind you, leading to a field of easy pickings.
He neither saw Jonathan's arrows, nor heard Cassandra's cries.

Buoyed in body and soul, pulsating with excitement, Abram
quickened his steps. They were not directed towards the inner
city however, where jobs were begging for applicants, but back
to the little park. The midday sun of Calgary, indifferent to
groans and lamentations, had attained a fiery glow. But Abram
paid no heed, even hell's own blazes could not have deterred
the man on a mission. Like St. Hilarion of days past, he was
going to sniff out sins; not to take them upon himself but to
wangle a life of easy street.

Detached reasoning had never been Fritz Abram's long suit,
perception even less. The adage, as the fool thinks so the bell
clinks, could have been expressly coined for him. True, he was
blessed with qualities that could make worthies blanch with
envy, but drawing conclusions wasn't one of them. Granted, he
could be quick on the trigger, yet wanting in aim at times.
Getting his hands at some of the objects, consisting of valuable
gems he reckoned, given to the yodeller, must be brought about

by hook or crook. But by what means? Spontaneously Abram slowed down, then stopped. Yes, by what stratagem, he mused. As mentioned he wasn't slow-witted, merely prone to fly off on a tangent.

Spurred by need, prodded by curiosity, he weighed the circumstances. A plan must be devised, bold, but also effective. Abram continued on his way to the little park where a disturbing sight made him bridle. Someone sat on his favoured bench. A woman, dressed up to the nines, appeared to expect company. Offhand he disliked her alluring look, and resented her presence. Disdaining the other benches, unoccupied and somewhat distant from the interloper, he prepared to turn away when footsteps could be heard. In a twinkle he scampered behind a cluster of bushes. A man approached whom Abram instantly recognised. Kristian Lauber waved at the woman who rose to greet him. They had much to say to each other, judging by gesticulations and a torrent of words.

Abram was all ears when fragments of their conversation revealed that they spoke in the dialect of his homeland. That gave him the idea to impersonate Lauber and collect these valuables in his stead. Surprising to say a physical likeness existed between them. Granted, it couldn't be compared to the Dormio brothers who were alike as two peas, but barring close scrutiny, one could be confounded with the other. Especially in that traditional costume. Language should entail no difficulties; Lauber's peculiar gyrations when yodelling could easily be imitated, Abram decided. Simulating that singular Jauchzer? Not to worry. A bit of practice should rekindle the skills of one's youth, Abram consoled himself as he buckled down to work. Lauber's presence of course had to be dealt with, but not immediately, he concluded.

Acquiring a Tyrolean habit proved to be anything but a trifle. They were available alright, for someone in clover that is. To purchase an outfit more than stretched his purse. Short term rental turned out to be beyond his reach for lack of a credit rating. Yet a man licked by the flames of greed, intoxicated with images of fame, does not throw in the towel readily; he stole a costume. Uttering those stirring shouts while twisting in the yodeller's fashion, Abram learned quickly. After he had witnessed the fellow's performance a few times more, he felt confident to imitate it. Of course the matter of Kristian Lauber's presence must be considered, Abram realised all along. Pondering helped little; he was up a stump, a high one to boot. The numismatist, bogus from head to toe in Abram's opinion, now as before made the rounds. Every morning at seven o'clock he showed up, then yodelled at the entrance of certain houses. Unfailingly a matron, well-groomed, exuding an aura of prosperity and old-world grace rushed out. She looked this way, glanced over her shoulders while turning slowly, then slipped something in his haversack. Abram chuckled. Why the ruse? he thought, for that it surely was from start to finish. Whom were they trying to mislead, and why? Admitted, a chance observer might be taken in by these antics. But not Fritz Abram who had a nose for skulduggery which he could smell from a hundred strides distance.

Revealing sentiments, Abram granted, but of little use for a man who needed food on the table and a warm bed, which he was apt to forgo very soon, unless he replenished his empty pockets. But how? Kristian Lauber loomed large before his eyes, and quickly swelled like a mazikeen ass that couldn't be circumvented.

Unwittingly Abram reached the centre of town. The construction din as always bothered him to no end. Every blow of a pile hammer deemed him an assault on his conscience. The bustle around him grated on his nerves; he considered it an effrontery aimed at himself, especially the buoyant demeanour of passers-by.

He looked weary this morning, no amount of silent or wordy encouragement on his part succeeded to throw off the lead from his feet, or the weight on his mind placed there by that harridan guilt. The man, envied on account of his jauntiness, would have made friends snicker at the sight of him now. Shuffling through the streets of noisy Calgary, vindication, his loyal apologist, whispered in both ears, or rather tried to. But Abram, hungry and discouraged, listened with one ear only, the other heard the tocsin ring; he stood at the proverbial crossroads. Entering either one was unpalatable to him, but necessity carried the day.

"I must find work," he admonished.

"Today," he muttered.

By three o'clock he had a promising interview with the employment manager of a large construction company. Two days later he commenced work. Luck had not forsaken him.

"Fortune, as often before, favours her own again," he chuckled, while putting the contract in his pocket.

The position offered not only paid well, but also included free accommodation for six months. It was a godsend, considering that his rent had to be paid within the week, or he would be out on the street. The pleasant surprise when he learned about it was a moment to remember. The world took on a lovely hue. Even the manager's face, framed in pomposity, lacking animation in Abram's eyes, acquired an air of cheeriness; just for an instant, however. In a twinkling the old, studied mask returned. Just the same, his next words sounded like music in Abram's ears.

"Do you have a place to stay?" he was asked.

"No," he answered truthfully.

Did the prim manager's mask twitch when he noticed the other's glimmer of hope, or was he choking on his self-imposed importance?

Abram didn't care, especially since he was soon in clover again. Good food graced his chin, mellow wine tickled his palate, a warm, comfortable bed lightened his dreams. Yet he couldn't leave well enough alone; his eyes mirrored the lustre of diamonds, his mind succumbed to the lure of easy street. The rigid routine, even less the semblance of discipline, didn't agree with his freewheeling make-up. But necessity curbed his roving nature for the time being. As mentioned Fritz Abram, the eternal rainbow chaser, grew restless; temptation and impatience, the bane of his life, gained control over him.

Two weeks later he was back on the bench in the little park, where he lingered for hours on Saturday and Sunday morning. Nothing unusual happened. Scurrying from bush to bush, ears pricked up, eyes strained, he couldn't detect a trace of the yodeller. Abram concluded that on weekends no transactions took place; certainly not in the morning.

At his place of work problems began to arise; he saw the writing on the wall, which he knew by heart. He also realised that he had acquired the moniker Panjandrum, a misnomer if ever there existed one. Putting on airs? Not Fritz Abram, who was just not a mixer; besides, he kept his own counsel. Yes, he could envision discord licking its chops. To be fair he had forsworn a hundred times to suppress his penchant for aloofness, but again he seemed to have failed, judging by the rising animosity at the place of work; it was in the blood. Wherever he went he soon became a mote in the eyes of others. Shrugging his shoulders he chuckled:

"Why worry, as long as my work is satisfactory I shall be alright."

Just the same he made an effort to ingratiate himself with his co-workers. Yet subconsciously, below the threshold of awareness, Abram's true nature had jostled to the surface. His disdain for fellowship, which never did warm the cockles of his heart, became apparent. It upset his colleagues; they felt patronised. The bosses were not enamoured with the new man's lack of team spirit, nor his lofty attitude. Besides, they felt slighted, made light of in other words.

Abram had found ease once more. The steady, ample income, coupled with comfortable rent-free accommodation, lifted not only his spirit, but also revived his bruised sense of worth. He whistled and hummed again. His surrounding acquired an aspect of contentment. Calgary, in late summer, can be delightful. Nights are cool, sunny days, no longer sweltering, beckon to be outside. People's strides become more measured; they turn inward, covet less and reflect on the wonders of nature and life. Even the ubiquitous construction noise appears to grow hesitant, less intrusive, and clamorous. Kristian Lauber, the scheming yodeller, fell into oblivion. True, his existence made itself felt now and then, but rather fleetingly, and no less shadowy. Then fortuity came into play, it set Abram on a rocky path.

Came Saturday he could be seen strolling along the streets of downtown Calgary. Whereas hitherto the sights and sounds annoyed him, today they were a source of elation. Why he halted his steps in front of the public library he could not have said, even less why he entered the building. There he met Hertha Emery, the office supervisor of the firm he worked for. She was the proverbial enigma wrapped in layers of riddles; to him in any case. A married woman, no longer young, she possessed a most contradictory disposition. She pretended to be lady touch-me-not, but acted like Jezebel of old; not in word or deed mind you, but with signals that everyone understood. She always dressed to the nines, carefully accentuating her buxomness that made men ogle and women wrinkle their brows. No doubt Hertha Emery savoured the attention, which was stoked with discreet make-up and studied postures; not to mention her come-hither demeanour directed at every male nearby.

Here is a paradox. Although she craved men's homage, be it silent or expressed, she scorned their very shadows. Strange to say Abram's indifference to her allurement upset her to the core. It was a mote in both eyes, and a thorn in her side. She made an attempt to inveigle him with promising glances and hints, not exactly immodest, but neither entirely chaste. His putative stance of the pure knight honed her womanly wiles. When Abram avoided her like the devil avoids holy water, so it deemed her anyway, she started to be concerned. Consequently she looked in the mirror with increasing concern etched on her brow, and questions directed at her reflection:

"Am I losing my seductive power? Is age creeping up on me perhaps? No" she told her image, "that fellow is a man in name only, don't fret about him."

But she did.

Their accidental encounter on that sunny afternoon revived Abram's interest in an affair he had forsworn to forget. Necessity dictated as much, yet dreams, forbidden or encouraged, haunt the man who has shaken the tree of imagination. The Calgary yodeller, never completely effaced from his mind, loomed like a spectre at the sight of Hertha, as she wished to be called. Why, we shall soon find out. She was surprised when he didn't sidle off as expected, but approached her with glee in his eyes, and bounce in his steps.

"I am glad to see you, Mrs Emery," he sang out.

"Hertha," she corrected.

His face fell for an instant, then lifted and brightened.

"Ah, I understand. Forgive me, it's my European upbringing."

Hertha Emery nodded and smiled. One side of her esteemed a courtly deportment in men, the other, however, was touched by embarrassment. Startled by this unwonted attention, she eyed him suspiciously, while wondering what this stuck-up German was up to. Involuntarily her hands, under intensive scrutiny by Abram, moved behind her back. For an awful moment she thought they weren't up to snuff.

"May I invite you to a cup of coffee, Mrs – Hertha, I mean."

Quite intrigued by now, she reluctantly consented. As they walked towards a nearby restaurant, she couldn't help being self-conscious. Abram appeared to be fascinated with her hands.

Conversation flowed easily since his interests were broad, albeit of somewhat limping knowledge. Hertha Emery could hardly be called a fount of wisdom, but her instinct was in fine fettle. She quickly recognised the source of the new-found esteem for her; it was the ring on her finger. She let him talk. While pretending to be all ears, smiling, nodding or chuckling periodically, her left hand moved absentmindedly closer towards Abram, whose eyes spoke louder than words. No doubt the ring on her finger, adorned with a lustrous, finely shaped diamond, fascinated Abram more than her Saturday make-up.

"I like your ring," he said.

"Oh?"

She looked at it with a mien of someone surprised that it even existed.

"It's beautiful. A diamond, I suppose."

"Quite so," she assured him.

"A heirloom, I dare say."

"Not at all, I bought it recently for a song," she replied, then added:

"The bargains one can obtain from that fellow are beyond belief."

The conversation started to slacken, something weighed on Abram's mind which he couldn't cast off. The ring on Hertha

Emery's finger seemed to spellbind him; he simply was unable to avert his eyes from that sparkling gem. Apparently unmindful of Abram's fascination, she moved her hand in this and that direction, thereby causing the diamond to emit dazzling sparks. Why a knowing smile hovered around her lips, only she knew. Why she sported a smug demeanour, reminiscent of a predator who had cornered its prey, Abram couldn't have guessed had he noticed it. Suppressing an innate reserve, he inquired:

"You spoke of that fellow, who might he be?"

"Kristian Lauber, a compatriot of yours."

"The yodeller?" he almost exclaimed, but managed to bite his tongue.

She said something else:

"You know, sometimes I thing he is a fence."

"Of stolen gems," he stated matter of factly.

"I'm only kidding," she hastened to say.

As mentioned, Hertha Emery, while not setting the Bow River ablaze with mental acuity, possessed surprising powers of perception, certainly matched by dissimulation. No less was she blessed with more than a pinch of inventiveness. No mistake, she had a penchant, well known to friends and acquaintances, for impromptu storytelling.

Now as then Hertha harboured a deep resentment for Abram. This sudden about-face, suspect to begin with, swayed her not in the least, she told herself. One thing was clear: The diamond ring furnished the spur for this out of the blue ingratiation. The imp was squeezing out of the bottle. Mrs Emery's smile broadened; more so when she noticed his remarkable reaction upon hearing the name of Kristian Lauber.

Hostility can hone or dull one's mind; in any case it usually heightens vigilance, like in the case of Mrs Emery, who felt slighted. From the moment when Abram hailed her with unwonted eagerness, her senses, nourished by a desire to harm the man who disdained her feminine allure, were on the alert. Had Abram not be gripped by excitement he might have noticed the telltale signs of mischief on her face, not to mention a blush indicative of malicious joy. Needless to say she sensed his discomposure, and no less the grounds for it; namely, Lauber, the jeweller; therein hung a tale, she realised.

"Do you know Kristian Lauber?" she asked.

"Don't squirm now," she nearly exhorted, but she bit her tongue.

"I don't recall hearing his name," he lied.

She took measure of him with mocking eyes and furrowed brow; she had heard and seen enough, the time had arrived for the next move.

As mentioned, Hertha Emery had a knack to invent fanciful and false occurrences on the spur of the moment. They were usually meant to set the listener's mind agog, or induce them to become imprudent, like now for instance. Abram's strange fascination with her ring, and the barely suppressed interest in Kristian Lauber, set that peculiar penchant in motion. Mrs Emery considered the inventive storytelling on short notice a net to entangle Abram with, in the hope to learn his secret. Why? It might supply the grist for her mill to get back at the man who gave the cold shoulder to her feminine charms, and more so disdained her provocative built, which in her opinion no man should treat with equanimity. Casting a sideways glance at Abram, she said:

"Remember, Fritz, what I implied a moment ago, half-heartedly, mind you?"

"Tell me," he requested.

"I insinuated with a chuckle that Lauber might be a fence."

"For stolen gems," he emphasised.

"Well, I snickered at the notion."

"So you did. What's the inference?"

She hemmed and hawed, then screwed up her face like someone at the horns of a dilemma, before she answered:

"A few months ago a daring robbery took place. One of the city's biggest and most reputable jewellery store was looted."

Abram's reaction, though anticipated to be noticeable, surpassed her expectations. Like a man being hot-footed he jumped up and spread his arms wide.

"Aha, aha," he cried.

Seeing people turning their heads, she tried to calm him down:

"Take it easy, Fritz, let me go on."

"Please do."

Despite a tingling of discomfort on account of his outburst, she couldn't help smiling. What caused this unseemly impetuosity she could not fathom, yet she divined an Achilles' heel in the man she wished to harm. Did Abram notice the glint in her eyes? Did he discern the snugness of her face? Probably not, since his eyes and ears were riveted at her lips.

"I tell you it was the boldest heist known to Calgarians. In broad daylight a sole man entered the store at noon, overpowered the two clerks, blindfolded them, and tied each one to her desk."

Abram, visibly on pins and needles, his imagination afire, posed a question:

"Was he armed?"

"Yes."

"Masked, I take it?"

"Masked and disguised by a most peculiar costume," she advised with a significant grin.

Hardly had she uttered the last syllable, when Abram blurted out:

"Peculiar costume? Hm, let me guess. Of Tyrolean design perhaps? "

Seemingly stunned, Hertha inquired:

"How did you know since this was never made public?"

"It was a wild guess, nothing else."

Abram wished Mrs Emery a nice day before he left on the double.

Outside in the bright sunshine and afternoon heat, Abram hurried towards the little park above the Bow River. Recurring thoughts about what he had just heard occupied his mind. He divined the circumstances surrounding Lauber, the yodeller, and those refined women of a certain age, exuding an aura of smiling contentment, usually found in virtuous womanhood. Could they be in the know, or were they being duped by scheming husbands whose will they obeyed? Pangs of regret assailed him on account of the precipitant departure. He should have lingered and asked some pertinent questions. Had the thief been apprehended, for instance. The thought elicited an involuntary snicker. Had he not seen, just this morning, the perpetrator gyrating up and down the crescent, yodelling like an Alpine herdsman unable to repress his animal spirit? A voice whispered from somewhere:

"Fritz, how can a man, a larcener to boot, of necessity imbued with stealth and deception, emit such soul-stirring sounds? Waving these vexing interruptions aside, Abram proceeded on his way.

He stopped abruptly; there was the voice again. If the robber wore a Tyrolean outfit, would he not compromise himself by flaunting it still? he countered with a shrug and the explanation that Lauber, an odd fish, if not a crank, probably enjoyed playing with fire. Deciding to be more attentive to Hertha Emery, possibly flirting with her a bit, he hurried along again. One thing he must find out: Whether a reward had been offered for information leading to the culprit's apprehension and prosecution.

When he arrived at his destination all was quiet, except the rushing river. The small grounds, traversed by a gravel footpath, possessed a quality not readily describable. The few benches skirting the park were usually unoccupied. The place permeated a tranquillity which, strange to say, repulsed more people than it attracted. Situated not far from the city's hubbub, yet somewhat secluded, it soothed one's nerves while resting one's body; provided anxiety, the fiend that never rests, is not present. As in the case of Abram who sought out the peaceful spot not to repose, but to give full rein to feelings that simultaneously made him exult in joy, and moan in misery. He had vowed many times in the past to stave off the impulse to chase chimeras, those tricksters that never keep their promises. But as then and now the battle was lost before it began. An enigmatic force, presiding over him since early youth, demanded that he unravel the mystery of the Calgary yodeller.

On the way back he felt irresistibly drawn towards Lauber's premises, where he was met by a surprise; the sign had been removed, the place appeared to be forsaken.

"The blackguard may have taken to his heels," Abram murmured as he walked up the few treads. "Should I knock and confront the fellow, fluster him with probing questions and knowing glances perhaps? Rather not," he decided as he retraced his steps.

Sunday turned out to be another pleasant day; not for Fritz Abram however. He was in a dither, so much so that he cursed himself, the world, and with special venom Hertha Emery. Why did she flaunt the ring before his eyes? For what reason did she relate that incongruous incident, unsolicited mind you, of a robbery that took place months ago? Did she have an ulterior motive? Was it meant to be entertaining or to attract attention? The devil fetch the reason, Abram exclaimed. Her narrative, innocent or otherwise, had lit the candle for that dratted compulsion to search for Noplace, an addiction he thought to have laid to rest.

"Tomorrow I will be a bit late," he told his superior, Bertram Austin.

"How late?" Mr Austin asked with raised eyebrows.

He was a stickler for steadiness and punctuality. Abram calculated quickly and silently. The yodeller unfailingly started his rounds at seven o'clock in the morning, which ended about a half hour later. Therefore, adding the time to reach the office, it seemed reasonable to commit himself:

"Two hours," he assured the chief.

"We shall expect you then."

The yodeller didn't show up, certainly not on time. When the Old City Hall tower clock struck nine times, Abram set out to his place of work. Not however, before he cast a long look around. The eerie silence deemed him a harbinger of evil tidings. The rest of the day proved to be sheer agony for him. Riven by contradictory sentiments, namely, sense and temptation, he couldn't concentrate on the work. Try as he may his thoughts wandered involuntarily from Lauber, the numismatist and part-time yodeller, to the women who moved in obscure ways. Hertha Emery, rather the information she so eagerly imparted, also occupied his mind; more so, since he obtained no corroboration about this robbery. In view of his intentions, latent at the moment, to imitate Lauber's antics, inquiries were made prudently, but so far unsuccessfully. They were invariably met with shrugs and pat responses:

"Never heard of it."

"Which jeweller are you referring to?"

Hm, Hertha hadn't revealed that part, which he forgot to elicit from her. Anyway, he had not seen her yesterday, nor today till now.

At noontime he went for a walk at the riverbank. Shunning people as much as possible he pondered with all his ability. Leaving well enough alone never entered his mind. What initially could be termed curiosity, kindled his inherent spirit of adventure and became now an obsession. He felt an irrepressible urge to get to the bottom of these capers, that surely served a purpose; a shady one to boot. Like the Magnetic Mountain that drew the nails out of approaching ships, the puzzling crescent unpicked the last stitches of his foresight.

Then the inevitable happened; he lost his job. That wasn't all. Of course he also forfeited the use of the company's apartment. After repeated tardiness and remissness in his duties, not mentioning ignored admonitions plus a final warning, he got his walking papers.

Once more he was on the road, chasing a rainbow that cannot possibly be caught. Anyway, he quickly had to find a place to stay, which proved rather easy with money in your pocket, plus a sympathetic presence. Finding work might be more cumbersome considering the unbecoming performance at his last job. Well, he would cross the bridge when he got to it. First he must unriddle the riddle of the Calgary yodeller. At the risk to pound the pavement again he sat for five days on the same bench from seven o'clock till nine o'clock in the morning, waiting for the show to begin, as he did right now. The yodeller did not show up, nor were the women, his presumed partners in crime, unduly astir.

While sitting there, eyes riveted at the crescent, both ears to the ground, vindication started to toy with his mind. He knew the script, but recited it again anyway. What harm had been done by forfeiting an income derived from sheer drudgery, bordering on slavery? Especially since it freed him to pursue a path leading onto easy street. From the wings of hope all looks rosy, even the notion that by replicating the yodeller's escapades riches can be gained.

"I will chance it," he encouraged himself.

He practically ran towards the newly rented rooms, a dive really, if the truth be told. Hardly had the door closed behind him when Abram darted to the hiding place where the Tyrolean costume lay. Soon he gaped in surprise; it didn't fit anymore. From the leather breeches to the ornate sash and alpine jacket, nothing could be donned. Only the hat still fitted. Nonplussed, to say the least, Abram sat down. Had the outfit shrunk, did he gain weight, or was he getting delusional? Jumping up he cried:

"No! and no! again. I distinctly recall that the breeches, and no less the jacket, were three sizes too large."

Becoming elephantine in several short weeks seemed incredible. But that is the only explanation, he deduced with a wrinkled brow. Since no full size mirror could be found in the apartment, Abram went looking for a store window wherein to mirror himself. True enough, he looked the same as always, he assured his reflection. It wasn't true, but as the fools thinks the bell clinks.

Abram, not duped easily as a rule but blinded by what he deemed a mission, had entered the sublime gate of make-believe. He conveniently glossed over some facts: The Tyrolean costume was not too large, he remembered or should have remembered, praising his sure eye for selecting, stealing that is, the right size. He also forgot, wanted to forget, that his regular clothes flapping around his body three months ago, felt more and more like a straitjacket.

When he got back he tried on the costume again, or rather made an attempt to do so. The leather breeches stubbornly refused to close around the waist; the jacket proved easier to get into than out of it. What now? Making alterations himself was out of the question; the mere thought made him recoil, for he was all thumbs in matters of tailoring. Giving up the whole idea? Not for a king's ransom, Abram advised the bare walls. Looking at his watch he murmured:

"Still time to find a tailor."

Gathering up the garments he took to his feet. He found a small shop across the bridge. It took some talking to reach an agreement with the proprietor.

"Tomorrow? Impossible," he assured the prospective customer.

Well, little did the tailor know about Abram's ability to persuade. An agreement was finally reached; the garment would be ready by tomorrow afternoon. Body measurements were quickly taken. After giving a false name plus a fictitious address and telephone number, Abram left in high spirits.

The elation proved to be of short duration. When he arrived at the tailor's shop the following day there were more people expecting him than just the tailor. Though not imbued with St. Hilarion's gift of smell, Abram felt an urge to turn around and flee at full speed. An odour of danger filled the little place. Before he could make a move however, one of the men present stepped up and shut the door.

"We are RCMP officers."

Showing his badge he advised:

"Sergeant Chris Parker."

Another fellow, surly looking, radiating grimness from head to toe, introduced himself:

"Corporal Angus Moore."

A small, wizened man past middle age stared ahead but never said a word. Fritz Abram realised instinctively that the ball had struck under the line. His presence of mind did not forsake him; the past had taught him a valuable lesson: Say little or nothing to the police, play dumb, and deny – deny. Pointing at the costume the sergeant asked:

"Are you the owner of this?"

Abram's five wits came into play at the speed of light.

"Not really."

"But didn't you bring it in for alterations?" the corporal queried none too friendly.

"True enough, but it belongs to someone else."

"Yes, to me," the man in the corner chimed in.

Meeting Abram's inquiring stare he introduced himself:

"I am Philip Molnar of Molnar's Party Rentals, were you, hm, somebody broke in and stole that costume."

Abram was about to protest. Before he bridled up in studied indignation Mr Molnar silenced him with a wave of the hand. He was a whimsical fellow, from the school of hard knocks, who did not always play the game. He grasped the situation quicker than anyone else in the room.

"Why not be pragmatic," he suggested.

Both the sergeant as much as the corporal cast questioning glances at him. Mr Molnar expounded:

"Provided I get my costume back in good repair, plus receive the full rental fee, I am willing to let bygones be bygones."

"You wouldn't press charges in other words," the sergeant inquired, frowning his best, while the corporal looked daggers at no one in particular.

"No," came an unequivocal reply.

The tailor spoke up:

"I need to be paid for my time and trouble too."

The policemen put their heads together in an adjoining room. They shared an opinion that the crown attorney would be reluctant to lay charges. Besides, they also understood that their man is anything but a sacrificial lamb; he knows the ropes they concluded.

When the sergeant with his corporal in tow returned, he nodded. Abram paid, albeit reluctantly, with an aggrieved air befitting a man being wronged. He lingered, something seemed to hold him back. Philip Molnar, endowed with more than a smidgen of insight, inquired with a smile:

"I can see that there is something on your mind."

"Yes."

"Well?"

Abram, turning full to the tailor, queried him:

"How did this come about?"

"Simple, I lost or mislaid your measurements."

"You could have gotten them again from me," Abram blurted out without thinking.

"Noticing the reproving stares, he tried to palliate his daft remark:

"Alright, alright, tell me what happened."

The tailor, more amused than annoyed, glanced at the grinning Molnar.

"What happened? Hm, you should ask. Since it is difficult to talk with a bogus customer I contacted the pertinent rental places listed in the book. The rest you can figure out yourself."

Abram knew what the clock had struck; he left without a salute or another word.

Quite dejected he stepped out onto the streets of Calgary. Although twilight approached, the roar of the city that never rests, in those days anyway, had hardly subsided. Yes, he had to leave, the town was getting too familiar, thus losing its magic.

On the next day he boarded the Trans-Canada train rolling eastward. Glace Bay in Cape Breton Island was booming, he had heard. Well, he would give the place the once-over.

# The Loafer

*H*allo, governor, how is life treating you today?" Alex Darby asked the man who sat at the foot of a clock tower amid the town square of Basseterre.

At the same time he handed him a five dollar note. The fellow, draped in misery, past middle age, took it without uttering a word. But his scowl left no doubt about his sentiments. He looked daggers at his friendly benefactor whom he evidently loathed. Darby's companion, a close business associate and friend, couldn't restrain a growing curiosity.

"You seem to know this fellow," he intimated as a matter of fact.

Darby, being in a roguish mood, feigned ignorance:

"To whom are you referring?" he queried with raised eyebrows.

"Don't play possum with me, Alex, since the day we arrived you handed a fiver to this – this loafer. So, what's up?"

"I just feel sorry for him, nothing more, nothing less."

Whether Sandy Muir believed or disbelieved his friend, he did not say. Yet his frown and pout spoke more than words. Being an unobtrusive man, he let it go at that. Anyway, they were pressed for time; a scheduled meeting at the nearby bank should have been in full swing by now. Money was the issue; lots of it. They had applied for a loan to finance the construction of a luxury hotel at Frigate Bay. Prospects weren't exactly rosy, for in those days the island of St. Kitts attracted few visitors of means.

"That will change," Darby assured the bankers.

"Quite soon to boot," seconded Muir.

Their avowals, however, fell on deaf ears, for a banker's judgement is not influenced by euphoria or suppositions. Muir, as much as Darby, partners in the venture, were on tenterhooks. While not chewing their nails, they certainly walked on a path of thorns and thistles.

"An answer will be given shortly," they were told at the end of the meeting. But shortly in the Caribbean has not the same connotation as in Toronto or Montreal, as the applicants soon learned.

It was a short walk from the hotel to town, pleasant and relaxing. Darby never missed an opportunity to stroll along the edge of the bay, listening to the gentle falling surf while savouring the view; so he said, but Muir knew better. He sensed what attracted his friend. It was the town square, especially the man seemingly rooted to the clock tower's pedestal. Not that the square, or circle rather, wasn't a worthwhile sight; far from it. One look at the ornate, small tower amid stately palms and flowering shrubs would have calmed the hearts of calamity howlers. Several times when he perceived Darby to be relaxed, after imbibing a bit, Muir was on the verge of broaching the subject that evidently caused his friend a measure of distress. He appeared to be in the throes of emotions, which no amount of dissimulation was able to conceal. Surely a connection existed between him and that likeness of Anker's, 'The Drunkard,' who seemingly sat at the same spot day in and day out.

Muir had reached a saturation of discomfort about his partner's obsession with that man at the tower. He was unable to suppress the notion that he went near him reluctantly, yet go he must. What compelled him to approach that loiterer with the mien of someone being dragged to the gallows, remained a mystery.

This loafer, as Muir had christened him, plainly haunted his friend. He concluded that a dreadful event linked their past, which he didn't wish to be reminded of, whereas the other, the helpless loafer, could not remember; it looked on the face of it. At the sight of Darby his countenance turned into a mask of hate at times, whereas on other occasions he considered him with knitted brow and blinking eyes, as if trying to place his benefactor. But that vicious grin which curled his lips never left his face while pocketing the proffered money.

The bank's decision arrived two weeks later; as feared they were not interested. Lack of private funds constituted one of the reasons for the negative reply; the island's location, being off the beaten track, also weighed heavily in their disfavour.

"Well, that's the end of our dreams," lamented Muir.

"Not really, Sandy, not by a long shot," consoled Darby.

"Anyway, we might as well go back to Canada," suggested Muir, who had hoped against hope to take root in this charming island.

He liked the unconventional way of life here, even more the free-spirited people in a land with few fences, and no garish signs. No doubt, Darby also felt pangs of disappointment, yet strange to say, it rendered him more upbeat than since the day of arrival. They decided to remain in the island as tourists for another week.

The following day the chief of police, Frank Gilbert, paid them a visit. After introducing himself, while shaking their hands heartily, he partook in trivial conversation before he got down to business.

"Gentlemen, I harbour no desire to prevaricate, I came to make an inquiry," he intimated, then added gallantly:

"Of course paying my respects bears equal weight."

"What is it about?" queried Muir, who sensed the reason of the chief's errand.

"I hope it's nothing criminal," Darby remarked.

"Not really, but vexing nevertheless. To come to the point. It concerns a vagrant who, how shall I say, took up quarters at the town square."

"Oh, him! Has he broken any laws?" Darby wanted to know.

"In a sense, yes. While not overtly soliciting, a case could be made for loitering."

"Well, what's wrong with deportation?" Muir suggested.

"Not a bad idea, sir, not bad at all, once we find out his name and country of origin."

"Does he not give it?" Muir inquired.

"No. If asked he just stares at one as if expecting the information from others."

Turning to Darby the chief commented:

"Perhaps you could help us."

"In what way, chief?" came a startled response.

"Don't misunderstand me, sir, we are anxious to be rid of the fellow. He has no visible means of support; in short, he is a nuisance and an eyesore."

"So tell me how I can help," Darby prodded somewhat defensively.

"Constable Pringle, who is in charge of this case, thinks you might know the man."

"What notion, I don't. I may have run across him somewhere, but I certainly couldn't place the chap."

"How about you, sir?" chief Gilbert asked Muir.

"Never laid eyes on him till I stepped onto the island."

"In that case I shall be on my way. Here is my card, should you hear anything of interest please contact me."

After shaking hands in his chivalrous way, the chief walked onto the terrace, where he stopped for a moment. Knitting his brow like a man who just remembered something, facing the partners who had followed him, he shook his head slowly.

"Do you know what we find strange?"

"No, what?" they questioned in unison.

"His gradual metamorphosis from a smiling hail-fellow-well-met to a growling malcontent. Constable Pringle swears that he is plucking up courage to commit a terrible misdeed."

With these words chief Gilbert turned and went his way.

The following morning Darby rose early. He walked out onto the terrace, still deserted at this hour, which afforded a view in three directions. Not far away lay Basseterre where people started to move about at the first signs of dawn. Across the narrow strait rose the mountains of Nevis out of the waning darkness. Below, along the bay, Fishermen's Wharf became alive. Men were pointing the bows of their boats seaward, women and children waved as they set out to the open sea.

Darby felt ill at ease; he could neither sit nor stand still. For some reason Gilbert's parting words weighed heavily on his mind; they sounded ominous, plus directed at him. Since the

partners were booked to return home two days hence, he
decided to visit the bank once more. It so happened that the
facility was situated within the town square, called locally the
circus, in whose midst of course stood the clock tower.

"Where to?" Muir called after him.

Trying to conceal a twinge of annoyance, Darby pretended
not to have heard. Muir, who knew how the wind blew, raised
his voice:

"Slow down, Alex, I'm coming with you."

As they walked towards Basseterre, the sun ascended
rapidly, in contrast to Darby's disposition who, despite
pretending to be in fine fettle, behaved like someone going to
his own funeral. He slackened his pace repeatedly, looked
nervously from here to there, creased his brow, and cleared his
throat. The loafer, as anticipated, sat at his wonted spot. Yet
how different he looked it flashed through Muir's mind. He
gave the impression of a man ready to strike. Muir attempted to
hold Darby back.

"Don't take another step," he murmured while stretching
out an arm to stop him.

But Darby thrust it aside, then strode up to the glowering
loafer, who meanwhile had risen from his perch. Muir
remembered crying out, or thought he did:

"Alex, stop!"

Then everything happened so fast that Darby had neither
time to utter his customary greetings, nor proffer any money. A
formidable dagger in hand, the loiterer staggered towards
Darby while snarling:

"You – you..."

Gasping for breath, expelling a loud shriek, he slumped
onto the pavement. People quickly gathered around the
writhing man, who bled profusely from an apparent head
wound. Seemingly from nowhere a policeman arrived, who
looked accusingly at Darby, before he started to clear the area.
When Muir looked at his friend, he gasped in disbelief; the
familiar countenance had become a diabolic mask where
triumph, hate, and remorse fought for supremacy. The loafer
died shortly after.

Darby and Muir, each separately, made statements at the police station. Chief Gilbert was not pleased, he repeatedly muttered:

"This is a fine kettle of fish, it is, it is."

The doctor's certificate listed haemorrhage of the brain as cause of death, thus rendering a coroner's inquest unnecessary. The authorities asked the partners to delay their departure till some formalities were cleared up, or at least until the stricken fellow was laid to rest.

On the way back to the hotel the friends spoke not a word; both were in a sombre mood. Muir made several half-hearted attempts to speak, judging by his hemming and hawing, but he remained silent. He either didn't know what to say or felt too embarrassed to voice what lay on his tongue. Darby cast furtive glances at his friend, as if expecting a question.

The heat became oppressive, heavy clouds hovered around Mount Misery, ready to burst any moment. Finally Darby broke the silence:

"What are you thinking, Sandy?"

"That you and the loafer had met before."

Darby nodded assent.

"So we have, Sandy, so we have."

Halting his steps for an instant, gazing pensively across the bay, he murmured:

"I will tell you everything, the whole lamentable truth, at the hotel."

They sat down on the terrace at a somewhat remote table. Before he started to narrate, Darby posed a question:

"You know the meaning of claustrophobia, no doubt?"

"I do, it connotes fear of being closed in."

"Morbid fear, if I may add."

Darby leaned back and sighed:

"The man's name, whom you call the loafer, is Marcel Sardis. I knew him well; in fact, we were partners in a construction company five years ago."

"Where is the connection, Alex?"

"You mean between irrational dread of being closed in and Marcel Sardis?"

"Well, yes."

"He suffered from it in an unimaginable degree. But let me continue. Our construction company operated out of Montreal, although most of our projects were located in northern Quebec, above the tree line."

"Ungava Peninsula?" Muir suggested.

"Yes, chiefly in Fort Chimo and along Ungava Bay."

When Darby noticed his friend's reproachful mien, he raised both hands appeasingly:

"Yes, Sandy, I lied, for good reasons as will soon become apparent."

Darby spoke in a husky voice, words fell reluctantly from his lips. Muir couldn't help thinking that he was beating about the bush, trying to garner momentum perhaps, to say what should be left unsaid.

"Alex, this erstwhile partner of yours, what was his name again?"

"Marcel Sardis."

"He appeared to be emotionally disturbed."

"Quite so. He lost his mind after spending some time inside one of those windowless construction trailers. Remember, he suffered from acute claustrophobia."

"How did that happen?"

"Someone locked him in."

"Erroneously, I guess."

When Muir received no reply, he posed a question:

"Alex, why do you think this fellow attacked you?"

"As I mentioned a moment ago, he was madder than a March hare."

They returned to their respective home towns; Muir to Ottawa, Darby to Montreal.

Shortly after a complication arose with their property in St. Kitts. They met at Darby's favourite restaurant at the Lachine waterfront to discuss it.

Autumn had approached, the leaves gradually acquired a profusion of colours only nature can produce. They rustled different now in the light breeze that caressed one's cheeks. The sun had lost its sting; people grew pensive, their hitherto raucous and obtrusive voices took on a subdued tone. An atmosphere of pleasing renunciation lay in the air; thoughts about the coming winter, severe and long, seemed still far away.

As they sat there, silent for a moment, watching the ships gliding along the Great Lakes Waterway some distance out on the lake, Muir felt a chill running up his back. The growling monster suspicion bared its teeth, ready to pounce. In a flash he knew what ought to be done; their short partnership, never a bed of roses, must be terminated. The man opposite him imbued him with abhorrence. He, a true blue, never cottoned to Darby, their natures were too contrary to eschew conflict. His partner's fickleness was a bone of contention, even more his moral turpitude. The episode in St. Kitts was the last straw, it made the scales fall from his eyes.

No one but Darby had locked that partner of his in, knowing full well it would unhinge him, which it eventually did. Worse than that, prolonged panic transformed the man into an inanimate object. From the beginning of their association he judged Darby to be callous, but not out-and-out cruel, as manifested itself. Why did he make him privy to this dastardly deed, which surely was neither a prank nor accident? No, he intended to inflict misery; the motive is not an issue here. To make matters worse, he later turned the knife, as it were, in the wound he had created, when he encountered his victim again in St. Kitts, most likely by chance. Wrapped in the cloak of altruism, he continued to torment that hapless fellow. He knew quite well that his proximity was like a red rag to Sardis.

What an odious man Darby turned out to be, outright dangerous to one's psyche; thus laying a distance between him and Darby became more imperative by the day, to avoid being tarred with the same brush.

Darby interrupted Muir's musing.

"Here is a copy of the missive, Sandy."

"I have also received one. It just confirms what we suspected. The option lapses at the end of the month."

"Unless renewed," Darby commented.

"On different terms, of course."

"Quite so, Sandy, quite so."

Muir neither asked, nor cared a whit about the new conditions, since he had resolved to end the partnership. Not all the wealth of Croesus could have induced him to continue their association. Darby considered his partner with the leering eyes of a Mephistopheles.

"So what do you say?"

"I am bowing out."

In a twinkle the leer changed to triumph. Darby resembled a man whose hopes had become true.

"You are quitting in other words. Let's dot i's and cross our t's. What are you bowing out from?"

"The option plus the partnership," came a curt reply.

Darby quickly lowered his eyes to conceal his joy.

The papers were drawn up, signed, and sealed prior to Muir's return to Ottawa. He heaved a deep sigh, a surge of contentment lit up his countenance; he felt young again.

Time passed, spring lay in the air, or rather soared on the wings of anticipation. The ice on the banks of the Ottawa River had disappeared; the Rideau Canal became alive again with boats, laughter, and shouts. The tulips had not yet pierced the cold ground, but wanderers in the parks swore they could hear a whisper, saying: "soon – soon."

Ottawa, while endowed with beauty and a measure of splendour, was haunted by two opposing solitudes. The all-pervasive shadows of lingering Anglicism, haughty and unforgiving towards anyone different from them, dampened the high spirit of the Québecoises, albeit not too seriously. Muir could never savour the charm of Canada's capital without a twinge of guilt and regret.

One morning, as he walked leisurely along the Rideau Canal, he met Bill Worsely, a schoolmate of his university days. They went to the nearest Brasserie. Worsely knew much to relate, for he had recently spent some time in St. Kitts. While exchanging views about that serene lovely island, the conversation drifted to the loafer, a subject seemingly close to Worsely's heart.

"I got your name from the local police."

"Oh, am I wanted?"

Worsely chuckled involuntarily:

"No, no, you are mentioned in connection with Lance Peyton, who had a fatal accident seemingly in front of your eyes."

"Lance Peyton? Never heard of him."

"Of course you did."

With these words Worsely retrieved an envelope from his pocket that contained several pictures showing the loafer on his perch under the tower clock.

"That's Marcel Sardis, Bill" Muir declared with a knowing smile.

It earned him an oblique glance, a pout, and raised eyebrows.

"Sandy, I have known Lance Peyton, a native Trinidadian, over twenty years. According to the police, plus numerous witnesses, he is the man who for months sat there and attacked constable Pringle with a knife."

Noticing Muir's flabbergasted demeanour, Worsely asked:

"Is something wrong, Sandy?"

"I don't understand, I don't understand," Muir murmured, then inquired:

"Did I hear right, he made an attack upon the constable?"

"I am surprised to hear you say that, since the incident took place before your very eyes, as stated in the police report."

"Why would he lunge at the constable, with a knife to boot?"

"That can be explained in a twinkle. The authorities were desperately trying to deport Peyton, but being ignorant about his country of origin, or even his name, they were stymied."

When Muir signalled incomprehension, Worsely raised a hand appeasingly, while chuckling:

"Patience, cry the lepers, I shall explain. Constable Pringle, goaded by ambition, I deduce, endeavoured to achieve wherein his higher-ups failed."

"Meaning?"

"He took it upon himself to importune Peyton relentlessly, hoping he would reveal his identity under duress, or just pack up and leave."

"Did you say that Peyton was a native of Trinidad?"

"Born, raised, and living there all his life, with the exception of course of the short sojourn in St. Kitts."

"Hm, I thought he was a Canadian."

"I doubt that he ever set foot onto our shores."

Neither man spoke for a while. Worsely's eyes wandered form the falls, where the Rideau River empties into the Ottawa River, to the nearby Parliament Building, whose dignified splendour made him avert his eyes. Across the broad, turbulent river one could see the Gatineau Hills on the Quebec side. His mind gradually drifted into the realms of melancholy. One side of him pined for the place of his birth and youth, the other yearned to be back in Trinidad, where folks are gay and words are true. In a dreamy mood now, he turned towards Muir to share his sentiment. Yet he desisted, because his pal was also lost in thought. Casting a glance at the Parliament's tower clock, he rose:

"Time to get back, Sandy, I am glad to have met you again. Let's keep in touch."

Before he reached the door, he turned and walked back to Muir.

"Alex Darby was your partner, I understand."

"Was, but never will be again."

"Well, my dear chap, you should have stuck with him."

"Oh, why?"

"He is the bigwig in St. Kitts now, and rich beyond dreams. Anyway, I must leave."

A few months later Muir learned that Cascade Developers from Montreal, who owned a substantial tract at Frigate Bay, had ambitious plans, a fact that surfaced about a year ago. Darby must have got wind of these future intentions, therefore taking an option on adjacent properties seemed advisable. Lacking the funds to do it, he came to him. Darby did mention Cascade Developers to make the transaction more attractive, no doubt, but he concealed more than he revealed, as it turned out.

Muir had no illusion about what had happened. Darby, a schemer beyond comparison, treacherous like a latter-day Ganelon, deceived him all the way. In retrospect Muir had to acknowledge that his partner stoked the flames of dissension; wilfully and purposefully. He pursued only one aim: To irreversibly spoil his appetite to continue their association. Well, he succeeded in a most dramatic way. Peyton's demise offered the opportunity. Though disgusted by Darby's shenanigans, he couldn't help admiring his ready wit. An unsavoury rascal with redeeming attributes one could safely call him. When a breach opened, he jumped in with both feet, and lightening speed to boot. Being cognisant of the fact that the loafer's identity was unknown, he promptly invented a name for him, plus a fictitious incident, meant to impel him, his ethical associate, to turn away in disgust; dissolve the partnership in other words. Give the devil his due, Muir conceded, it was a fantastic plan, conceived on the spur of the moment.

# Gentle Author

*P*hilip Rawlins threw down his pen in disgust. A scowl, seldom absent lately, darkened his brow. He wasn't getting anywhere with this novel started almost a year ago, yet scarcely half finished. Though swamped with ideas he was unable to set them on paper. Like many writers he went through periods of stagnation in the past which, however, neither lingered, nor were difficult to overcome.

This time, apathy, a writer's nemesis, tarried with grim resolve. Panic gripped him at the thought of a prolonged lull, or, heavens forbid, cessation of his writing skills.

"What happened to me?" he moaned under his breath.

Were the humours of his body drying up? Had he exhausted the mysterious forces that keep the creative juices flowing? His books, though not selling well, were almost universally acclaimed by the literati from Halifax to Vancouver.

Rawlins, though in a vexing bind presently, had not lost his equitable, congenial nature; not yet completely that is. The gentle author he was dubbed. Indeed, a more descriptive moniker could hardly have been invented. But this appellation stood on the verge of turning into a misnomer, for Rawlins grew increasingly edgy and quarrelsome.

Leslie, his wife, as always felt the sting of her husband's vexation piercing her heart that beat for both of them. Philip's plight, which he attempted to conceal, engendered a peevishness she had never experienced before. In the past these impasses were transitory, moreover, far less onerous. Philip, it appeared, was embroiled in a full-blown skirmish with inertia, which he called a writer's block. She knew better, but kept her own counsel.

"I see it, it's an approaching juggernaut that will crush me," he moaned one day in her presence.

"Not if I can help it," she countered.

Something had to be done. The albatross around his, and her neck for that matter, must be flung back into the sea.

The next day she contacted Kevin Strand, Philip's best friend, who was the librarian at the local library. They met at his office where he spent most of his waking hours.

"I know the solution," Strand interjected when Leslie paused in her lament.

"You do?"

"Yes. Let's send him up to my cabin for a spell, you know the place."

She did, and that's why she pulled a face. Noticing her lack of enthusiasm, Strand expounded with gusto:

"That's the spot were an effete author can rejuvenate his inherent qualities. I tell you, Leslie, in less than a week amid nature in the raw, old Philip will write like an angel again. Don't forget now I, as much as my staff, are anxiously awaiting his next book."

Against her better judgement she persuaded Philip to pack his things and head for the mountains. Autumn neared its end; soon the entire region would be under layers of snow. When he asked her to come along, she steadfastly refused.

"No, no, you must be alone for a while," she insisted.

In a way he welcomed the refusal, since he feared that her presence might unduly distract him. Her offer to visit him received ardent endorsement.

Well, it never came about; events, both quirky and unthinkable, precluded it. Rawlins, it should be remembered, stood in the midst of losing his winsome nature, which all who knew him attested to. Dubbed the gentle author, his forbearance even his enemies acknowledged, as much as his kindly disposition. His voice, it was said, hinted at a lovely frame of mind.

Rawlins, who made a pledge to his wife not to return without the completed novel, set out on a gusty November day. He was abundantly provided with necessities to last all winter. His writing kit, named thus jokingly, consisted of an oversized trunk crammed with a writer's needs.

The solitude high above Maple Lake appalled him initially. No other buildings were in sight, nor traces of human beings besides himself. Piles of firewood skirted the outside walls of the cabin, sufficient Rawlins reckoned, to last a whole year. He sure felt oppressed by the absence of accustomed clamour and bustle associated with civilisation; not long, however. Within days he began to anticipate and relish the feral cries of the wilderness, which reverberated from summit to summit, traversed valleys and lingered over grasslands. They soon became music to his ears and balm to his heart; in fact, his mettle rose at the sound of the coyotes' eerie calls, thereby stimulating his imagination, and setting the poised pen into furious notion.

In the middle of the night, wakened by these exuberant souls' singsong, forgetting his temporal grievances, he jumped out of bed, and scantily clad rushed to his desk. Cheered on by the untamed voices outside, he wrote without a pause. The novel progressed beyond his wildest dreams.

"Leslie, my dear, the pledge I made shall be fulfilled," he announced to the soaring hawks above.

Then came the snow which fell for three days and nights. Silently it descended, blanketing the uplands with layers of winter's delight. Afterwards a ghostly stillness settled over the land. The bears had wandered to higher elevations; coyotes, possibly stunned by the sudden change, remained mute; the soaring hawks had disappeared. Never in his life did Rawlins feel so isolated and lonesome.

A month later a man stepped inside the Lumby police station.

"I need to see the sergeant," he announced.

"Not possible," the receptionist advised, then added:

"Can a constable help you?"

Constable Oliver barely flinched at the man's words:

"I want to report a death."

"What's your name, sir?"

"Philip Rawlins."

"And where is the dead person?"

"Come with me and I will show you."

On the way to the cabin Rawlins behaved like a mute at Roman funerals, he barely uttered a word. Resisting constable Oliver's attempts to extract further information, he just said:

"First I will show you the corpse, then I will tell you all I know."

One look sufficed to recognise the man on the floor.

"Why, that's Kevin Strand, the librarian," constable Oliver exclaimed.

"It is," Rawlins confirmed.

A second glance told the officer that Strand was stone dead.

"What happened?"

"Search me, I found him stretched out like this when I came in."

Without a moment's hesitation the policeman radioed for assistance. Pulling out a pad, poising his pen, constable Oliver remarked:

"I need your statement."

"Kevin Strand, my friend, owns this cabin, which he made available to me so I could finish my novel in peace. Late this morning, returning from a long walk, I found Kevin laying on the floor, just as you see him. The rest you know."

"Have you moved anything?"

"Neither Kevin nor another object."

Clouds of suspicion quickly gathered around Rawlins, the police declared him the most likely suspect.

"Bring me a motive," the crown attorney demanded.

"We will, we will," the stuff sergeant promised, yet ultimately had to confess abysmal failure.

"Any dalliances?" the crown attorney inquired.

"You mean between Rawlins's wife and Strand? Not a chance! That woman is the embodiment of conjugal fidelity."

"I'm afraid we are stumped," conceded the crown attorney.

So they were by the looks of it. But constable Oliver did not throw in the towel yet. He reckoned that Rawlins, a brawny man, choked the last breath out of his slightly build friend's body. It could hardly have been otherwise, he possessed the strength, and no less the opportunity. Kevin Strand, a congenial man, had neither enemies nor detractors endeavouring to do harm. Besides, why would anyone tramp all the way to the inhospitable upland, seen by heaven knows whom, to perform a deed more conveniently done in town? It made no sense; less if taken into account the fact that a perpetrator required prior knowledge of Strand's whereabouts. No, this homicide had to be committed on the spur of the moment, possibly triggered by an altercation. But, Oliver sighed, how does one explain the absence of fingerprints? In any case the crown attorney steadfastly refused to lay charges based on circumstantial evidence alone; especially in view of Rawlins sterling reputation as a man of peace, who would rather extend a hand in friendship than raise it in anger.

Time passed, spring arrived, the sun climbed higher every day, presaging the arrival of another hot summer. Rawlins, who went to the mountains on the wings of hope, had returned amid clouds of despair; in fact, he appeared to be dispirited in mind, and worn out in body. He hadn't written a line since he came back. Some mornings, contrary to his habit, he lingered in bed, to his wife's dismay. Almost every day now he sat for hours in the garden staring into space. Trying to engage him in conversation proved futile, no matter how strenuously his wife tried. Her solicitous inquiries about his state of health were answered indignantly, accompanied by withering looks.

Leslie showed forbearance despite an inability to make head or tail of her husband's demeanour. A debilitating grief seemed to gnaw at his soul, which she attributed to the recent death of his friend.

A week later Philip took to his bed.

"I'm not feeling well," he announced.

Leslie, alarmed by now, summoned a doctor.

"Just ennui, spring fever," Dr Brandon diagnosed.

It proved to be something far more serious, she soon found out.

A few days later, sitting beside his wife in the blooming garden, Philip asked:

"Leslie, were you ever lonely?"

"What a question, of course I was."

When she looked at him inquiringly, he said no more. If Leslie deemed her husband's singular remark upsetting, she betrayed no sign of it. For an instant her pulse had accelerated, hoping that Philip was about to unburden his mind. Nothing of the sort happened. After that attempt he clammed up again and moaned occasionally as before.

Seeing a soul in anguish is not a pretty sight, especially if the afflicted being is a part of oneself. Something terrible must have happened in the cabin, so horrible to seal Philip's lips, whom Kevin's enigmatic and gruesome death seemed to have unhinged. Did he perchance have something to do with his friend's death? Perish the thought! not Philip, her gentle husband, who during their long marriage showed not the slightest trace of anger, or even raised his voice. True, she was not so credulous to attempt confuting certain realities. Instances were known of people acting contrary to their ingrained natures, be it out of fear, in a state of intoxication, or temporary derangement, also known as anger.

Fear of Kevin, his friend and mentor, deserved no consideration; they got along famously. Acting in an alcoholic frenzy? That notion she pooh-poohed. Philip drank nothing stronger than fruit juices. Flying into a rage, though inconceivable, then grappling whereby the weaker Kevin got the shorter end? Hm, possible, but remote. It could have been an accident in other words, ending in a regrettable disaster.

Leslie's conjectures, flimsy as they were, hit another snag. What the dickens could have triggered such ungovernable wrath in two calm men? At the end of her tether she resolved to take the bull by the horns and confront Philip. They could not continue to live in never-ending tension.

What she learned sounded absolutely incredulous, to a degree that she refused to lend credence to his weird narration; in fact, she questioned his sanity. Thinking about it afterwards made her shiver and cringe in fear. Several times she felt inclined to grab her husband by the collar, shake him with all her woman's strength and scream in his face:

"Tell me the truth, Philip, tell me what really happened."

She neither resorted to such drastic steps, nor did Philip

show signs of saying more. They lived beside each other like flotsam and jetsam, gradually drifting apart in a sea of resentment. In her growing despondency, Leslie considered talking to the police who after all, so it seemed, found no culpability with Philip. Their report, if released, might halt Philip's castigation and prevent her tumble into a slough of despair. Philip's so-called confession to her, besides being morbid, offended her sensibility. He told her everything while sitting at the dinner table, pecking at their food, trying to avoid each other's eyes.

"Leslie, do you remember being asked whether you had experienced loneliness in your life?"

"I recall answering in the affirmative," she replied, while instinctively recoiling.

The yearned for moment had arrived, she realised, desired, yet equally dreaded.

"I thought like you, till those days I spent up in the cabin, where the meaning of melancholy was brought home to me. After the snowstorm stopped, a deathlike silence descended over the land.

"What about the voices of the wilderness you wrote so glowingly about?"

"They died with the last snowflake that touched the ground. Cold air pushed down from the mountains, causing a dense vapour to rise as it settled on the warmer snow. Not a sound pierced that thick fog; I couldn't see trees thirty feet away. You implied that you know the pangs of lonesomeness. Maybe so, Leslie, but I doubt that it came near the feeling of desolation I endured in that cabin. It culminated in sheer torment, possibly self-induced, but nevertheless present day and night. The world seemed to have forsaken me, my soul shrunk, phocensian despair started to set in."

Philip paused, his face was marred by a haunted expression as if hateful memories had caught up with him. Leslie, though loath to hear more, showed a willingness to listen, for she realised that reviving ghosts of the past can be beneficial. She said nothing, though her eyes were overflowing with solicitude.

Philip, although weak in body and confused in mind, continued his singular narration.

"Within a weak the fog lifted, but cloudy conditions remained; so did the gnawing solitude. All life around me seemed to have died; melancholy spread out its pall. I felt entombed between walls of distress inexorably closing in."

Philip suddenly leaned back; his glassy stare softened, a smile lit up his countenance.

"One morning, while sitting at the desk, my mind as usually wading through the bog of misery, preying for mercy, I heard a whirr behind me. In the next instant a beetle landed on the desk. It wasn't much to look at, yet, laugh if you like, a godsend nevertheless."

Leslie, confounded by her husband's ramblings, had an odd notion that his soundness of mind started crumbling. He went on:

"Between that beetle and me sprang up a friendship, as happens with lost souls. The bug's presence, remember he was no beauty, lightened my days and soothed the nights. Gone were interminable hours of dispirited brooding, as much as sleepless tossing and turning in bed. In the morning, as soon as I sat down, there it was; my pricked ears perceived the sound that stirred the cockles of my heart.

"That beetle, I tell you, Leslie, had a habit of crawling, strutting I thought, back and forth in front of my eyes, stopping at times, and you know what?"

Seeing his wife shaking her head, he burst out:

"He twitched his feelers in a playful way. I swear to you that insect was talking to me. I not only grew accustomed to the little beast but pined for his proximity. Thank God! I was no longer alone. Needless to say the manuscript galloped forward by leaps and bounds."

As Philip talked, Leslie grew restive. His seemingly aimless narration not only puzzled but increasingly vexed her. Why? Because of the silent accusation directed at her. True, words to that effect were not uttered, yet his eyes revealed that for mysterious reasons he held her accountable for their distress. She wanted to protest, but he cut her short.

"Meanwhile the weather had changed; sunny skies during the day, and starlit nights were the norm. My little friend got real cosy with me, crawling over my hands and crossing the pad I wrote on. This continued for more than two weeks, till Kevin arrived."

Philip, leaning back, stared contemplatively at his wife, signifying irresolution whether to say more.

"What happened then?" Leslie asked.

A deep sigh escaped his breast, resembling a groan wrung from the depth of a stricken soul.

"It was the first cold day following a prolonged thaw, which rendered the snow firm enough to walk on without sinking. Despite the bone-numbing cold I went for a long walk. Barely had I returned who but Kevin should show up.

" 'What a surprise,' I cried. I was still dressed for outdoors when we shook hands."

Philip paused again, choked with emotions he could barely control.

"What happened next I cannot rightly explain. A fearful cry rent the air in that small cabin. Whence it came I could not even guess. Another scream, muffled and desperate, assailed my ears; it sounded like: 'Philip, Philip.' "

As if waking from a trance, gasping for air Philip moaned:

"As I regained a semblance of composure, I saw my hands clasping Kevin's throat."

Bewildered, Leslie exclaimed:

"But why, Philip, why?"

"He killed my friend."

"You are not referring to that beetle."

"Who else? While still shaking my hand, Kevin suddenly lurched forward, picked up one of those rustic paperweights with which he swatted like a man gone wild. I recall his triumphant cry:

" 'Ah, one less of those stinking bugs. Oh, how I...'

"The remaining words remained stuck in his throat, gripped by my vicelike hands. The rest you know. I made my way down to the valley towards the police station. Not, however, before throwing the gloves in the fire, and cleaning up the mess on the desk."

Leslie was stunned, but she quickly regained her composure; in fact, a broad smile spread over her face.

Surprised, also somewhat annoyed, her husband snapped:

"What's so funny?"

"I am reminiscing."

"About what?"

"Your vile manners, which always annoyed me, but no more."

Seeing his quizzical stare, she chuckled:

"Just think if you had obeyed accepted mores; in other words taken off your gloves before greeting Kevin. Tell me, where would we be now?"

# A Bet

"Come, my dear, come quickly, and admire my new home," her father wrote.

Susi Fowler frowned as she placed the short letter on the mantelpiece. The invitation reached her at a most unpropitious moment. To tell the truth, signs of annoyance flitted across her face, for she found it increasingly discomfiting to exercise filial obligations. To be a dutiful daughter had become burdensome to her. Since the mother's death her father, never easy to associate with, had grown outright bearish and reclusive. One day he left the house of her birth, never to return. He left a message behind, short and crisp:

"I want to be alone, I shall be in touch."

She didn't hear from him for almost two months, when he proudly invited her to be a guest in his new abode. The abode turned out to be a humble cabin in the middle of nowhere. So it went. His next dwelling consisted of a shack, then a ramshackle lean-to, and finally a tent. Susi had to come and admire every new home, as her father called them. To her chagrin he embraced solitude, then isolation till finally he became a regular hermit crab; meaning he would seek shelter in any empty shell. Thus she ignored his latest message, as much as the repeated reminders. But conscience has sharp teeth, it can cause one's heart to bleed. She saw herself on the horns of a dilemma. Obligation urged to comply with her father's wishes; aversion, egged on by vindication, allowed her to resist.

Her father's predilection for solitude she reluctantly accepted; his disdain for society's mores, although not welcomed, caused her no lost sleep. The apple of discord between them sprung from his willingness to embrace poverty and paltriness. She perceived such inclinations as a personal effrontery. There were times when she seriously considered marriage for the sole reason to change her name. Only ingrained misogamy prevented such a step.

Another invitation arrived along with a sketch and pictures. Also a more extensive description of the property was given in her father's inimitable style. Looking at the pictures, reading the alluring lines, she didn't know whether to pout or laugh.

"There we go again, another pie in the sky," she muttered.

She did not for one instant believe that this rather picturesque place was in any way connected with her impecunious, gone to seed father. Being a wag, he must have photographed an eye-pleasing lot with a quaint house, which he designated as his latest acquisition.

"Susi, my dear girl, the view alone is worth a king's ransom," he declared.

Then he waxed on:

"The charming house is surrounded by luxuriant grounds, a garden vying with Eden, plus mature trees seldom found in an arboretum."

Plagued by remorse on account of her undaughterly sentiments and attitude, she decided to pay her father another visit.

"Humour him," she said to herself, "it might be the last mirage accorded an ageing man."

It proved to be a chore to find the place; even on most maps, Lery, the town mentioned by her father, was not shown. With the pictures in hand, eyes peeled, and the pertinacity of a bloodhound, Susi searched for hours without success. True enough, she came several times upon the property depicted in the pictures, but she dared not to announce herself.

When she heard shouts of joy and saw a man approach with raised hands, she almost took to her heels. Why? Her father, it was he alright, hadn't looked so chipper and youthful in twenty years. After cordial greetings, the father and no less the daughter weren't the gushing types, Susi surveyed the house, which exuded a certain quaintness, despite the need for repairs.

It certainly looked solid in every respect. The view, she had to agree, raised one's spirit.

"Are you renting this place, father?"

"No."

She never thought he did, but seeing him in such a fettle she didn't want to sour his mood. Yet irked by his mocking bearing, she blurted out what lay on her tongue:

"I guess you are the caretaker."

"I am the owner," he stated with unwonted dignity.

Looking at him with eyes signifying reproach, but no less indulgence, she scolded:

"Come now, father, quit this fiddle-faddle."

With one sweep of the hand he produced a document, which he tapped vigorously.

"Here, convince yourself," he requested.

Glancing at it briefly, Susi stammered:

"But – but, it's impossible."

"Well, the title is in my name, clear and final, he countered.

"Yes," she reluctantly admitted after perusing the impressive looking folder with more solicitude.

Eyeing him suspiciously, Susi objected:

"Father, you are not earnestly claiming that this is your property?"

"I am."

"Is this on the up and up?"

"Absolutely."

Sensing that he was serious, Susi chuckled appreciatively.

"Father, how did you manoeuvre this?"

Winking mischievously, he feigned ignorance.

"Manoeuvre, Susi? I wonder what you might be referring to."

"So do I, please tell me."

"I won a bet, these premises were the stake."

Susi protested:

"But you had nothing to offer in return."

"There, my dear, you are mistaken."

Anticipating further remonstrations, he posed a question:

"You have heard of clairvoyance, I presume?"

"More often than once, chiefly from you."

"Well, it's a gift that very few possess," he explained.

Susi shrugged her shoulders:

"Maybe so, but I don't see the connection," she intimated.

"You will in a moment. It's this: I made a prediction that came true."

"Well, let's hear it," she urged again.

"Do you know Bruce Larsit?" he asked.

"I have never heard of him," she replied somewhat testily.

"He is the most conceited man between here and eternity, and no less bullet-headed. I can safely say that his high-handedness reeks to heaven. To make matters worse, he is also rich."

"That's a dangerous combination," Susi admitted.

Then she asked:

"Is this his house?"

"Was, Susi, was. Let me continue. Once Bruce Larsit makes a statement one better seconds it with amen – amen, or get out of his sight permanently."

Susi grimaced in annoyance.

"You made a bet?"

"Yes."

"Tell me about it," she urged.

Feeling impelled to haste he heaved a deep sigh.

"Be patient, Susi, preliminaries are essential in order to comprehend what occurred. I must acquaint you with Bruce Larsit prior to saying another word about the actual transaction."

Shaking his head in dismay, Bertram Fowler declared:

"You cannot imagine how vainglorious this man is; his ego swells out like a mazikeen donkey at the slightest contradiction. What else happens, you ask? He saws the air with both hands, stomps on the floor, and pounds the table with clenched fists and, by Jove, he roars like a wounded bull till one agrees with him unreservedly."

"Sounds scary. Wouldn't one better avoid a man like that?" Susi suggested.

Her father considered her with that crafty look she knew so well, and resented from the bottom of her heart.

"Hm, hm, I wonder," he remarked cryptically.

"What was the bet?" Susi queried.

"That Harry Larsit, Bruce's uncle, will die within the year."

Bridling involuntarily the daughter burst out:

"You are not serious!"

Nodding several times in affirmation, Bertram Fowler explained:

"I know it sounds weird, but listen to this: One day we got embroiled in an argument, in a mild dispute that ended in a regular row."

"Oh, about what?"

"Doctors, health, and medicine."

Susi shrunk back as if bitten by a tarantula. The mere allusion to such matters made her queasy, it conjured up unpleasant memories.

"You will recall my struggle with pharmacomania."

"Vividly," she replied.

How could she forget her father's epic battle with the mania to take drugs, legal or otherwise; especially his own concoctions, whose ingredients were never divulged, that proved to be the most addictive and nearly fatal. He won the fight, but got saddled with a virulent antipathy to sickness, whether real or imagined.

"Anyway, back to our argument. Bruce said something that stung me to the quick."

"What was it?"

"That thanks to medicine his uncle Harry maintained the physic of a young athlete and the health of an immortal."

Bertram Fowler snorted:

" 'Fiddlesticks!' I hurled in his face, 'Harry is on his last legs, he will die within the year.' "

"You know him then?" Susi interrupted.

"Harry? I knew him quite well."

"You speak in the past, father, is he no longer alive?"

"He died within the year," she was told.

"So you won the bet, how amazing."

Her father chuckled, an impish grin framed his countenance.

"Amazing, you say? Maybe not."

"How is that to be taken?" Susi wondered.

Her father explained:

"Harry always looked sick to me, he exuded an aura which I know so well."

Susi nodded, for she too remembered her father's dazed look and strange complexion when he went through his ordeal. Bertram Fowler continued:

"Hardly had I uttered my prediction, made chiefly out of defiance, I admit, when Bruce turned into a regular fire-eater.

" 'Did I hear right?' he yelled at the top of his voice.

"I should mention that by now both of us were three sheets in the wind.

" 'You did,' I repeated, 'Harry will not live another year.'

"Leaning halfway across the table, acquiring the mien of a slyboots, he taunted:

" 'Want to bet on it?'

"I was about to exclaim no, when something flashed through my mind."

"What, father?"

Pursing his lips, signalling uncertainty by spreading both hands, he explained:

"I couldn't have couched it in words then, nor am I able to do so now, but I managed to swallow the rejection which lay on my lips."

Observing his daughter intensely, attempting to glean from her face the meaning of his action, he intimated:

"Perhaps I intended subconsciously to put something over on Bruce Larsit or, who knows, I might have sensed an opportunity not to be sniffed at. To conclude, I advised Bruce that I possessed nothing worthwhile to put up as stake, thus laying a wager was out of the question. Did my objection deter Bruce Larsit? Not in your dreams. He snapped his fingers at the notion, jumped up and rummaged for pen and paper, then pooh-poohing my objections with the words:

" 'Save your breath to cool your porridge,' he started to write.

"The gist of it was this: He bet with me that his uncle Harry would live much longer than another year. Should he die within a year from today, Bertram Fowler shall obtain free of any encumbrances the following property."

"This, in other words," Susi remarked.

"Exactly. Anyway, I left while Larsit was still crowing about uncle Harry's redoubtable strength and youthful fitness. For an instant I felt tempted to appraise him of a compelling reality."

"But you didn't, I presume," Susi remarked for no particular reason, yet the expression on her face made a silent request – tell me, father.

"Telltale signs were clearly visible to me at the moment I laid eyes on Harry. Those dark bluish rings around his eyes spoke volumes. The waxy skin presaged of life's tissues on their last leg; the whole man appeared to be a puffed-up shell, bare of vital innards."

"In other words, he looked ill," interrupted Susi.

"That's an understatement. Subsequent encounters taught me that the man was fated to depart this life in a short while. His pretence to be a virile man's man, while misleading Bruce Larsit, deceived me not for one minute. I could see with one eye that uncle Harry was destined to die."

"Within a year," suggested Susi with a wry smile.

Her father made no reply, he pretended to be engrossed with a freighter appearing out on the lake.

"Well, father, you wagered wisely, especially since you had nothing to loose," she remarked.

Bertram Fowler's head came up slowly, deep wrinkles appeared on his forehead, which he tried to wipe away with the back of his hand. Dark shadows flitted across his face, a heartfelt moan escaped from his breast. Yet he said not another word.

On the way back Susi couldn't banish contradictory thoughts. On the one hand she felt elated on account of her father's good fortune, whereas on the other hand a premonition cast a pall over her joy. To her chagrin she had learned to distrust her father. Since the mother's death he appeared to have changed. The former staid, easygoing man turned gradually into a desultory, artful dodger. She possessed a keen insight into human nature, which to be sure was dimmed by indulgence towards a wayward father, who increasingly displayed traits she never divined while her mother was among them.

Yes, her father puzzled, and no less perturbed her. How a man's character should be transformed so suddenly, she found difficult to fathom. As mentioned, Susi Fowler was not an obtuse woman, and no less a cowering Griselda. Like Menander, she dared calling a fig a fig, and a spade a spade. Looking beyond the border of sentimentality a disturbing fact obtruded itself. Her revered father was never the man she made him out to be. Inherent traits of wretchedness were kept in check by his wife's, her mother's, presence. After her death the veils lifted exposing the true man.

Just as Susi fell asleep that night a lurking countenance rose lifelike before her, dripping with guilt, sighing with relief, like someone who had avoided a disaster by the skin of his teeth. It was her father, Susi realised, as she bolted upright.

Bertram Fowler did not tell his daughter the truth; he uttered a barefaced lie. When Larsit challenged him to bet on his uncle's destiny, he squirmed not a second. This is what happened:

When Bruce Larsit dared him with the words:

"You want to bet on it?" he didn't plead penury, meaning lack of a stake; quite the contrary, he jumped at the chance.

"With pleasure, Bruce," he responded.

"What's your stake against my property you like so much?"

"Down at the crossing?"

"The very same," Larsit confirmed.

He owned several pieces of real estate along the lake. Some, like the one in Fowler's possession, were nicely appointed, plus fully furnished. The grounds, neglected in part, were expansive and a gardener's dream. Fowler was in full swing. Without a moments reflection he was prepared to gamble away the house and home in Montreal were Susi was born, and which she cherished with every fibre of her heart. Although the property was in his name, he had bequeathed it to her some time ago in his will.

Sitting outside wrapped in silence, he felt a chill move up his spine, while thinking about his close shave. It was a narrow escape alright, from eternal shame and never-ending remorse. How could he have endured his daughter's sad eyes, filled with silent reproach upon learning about his treachery? Was he not duty-bound to help matters along when Harry Larsit showed no signs of satisfying the terms of the bet as proposed by him, Bertram Fowler that is? The clock kept ticking, weeks flew by, months passed quickly, the year's end drew near. The wrinkles on his darkened brow deepened; more and more, the clammy hands of desperation were closing around his neck. He approached Bruce Larsit several times in the manner of a supplicant, to rescind their foolhardy agreement, but he was rudely rebuffed. Tapping his breast pocket playfully, Fowler was reminded:

"A covenant is a covenant; besides, I always wanted to acquire a property in Montreal, especially in Westmount."

The last time, about four weeks before the end of the term, when Fowler ate humble pie, Bruce Larsit hooted:

"What do you know, our know-all is getting cold feet, in midsummer to boot. Courage, old chap, quit whining, soon you will get your comeuppance. Yes, me hearty, it might teach you not to be so cocksure next time, you prig."

When it became certain that Bruce had no intention to relent, notions of flight gained momentum; even death seemed preferable to being stuck in this morass fed by humiliation and guilt. Thoughts of Susi were seldom far from his mind; he began to resent her. To his everlasting disgrace he prayed for her demise. Harry Larsit he hated with a choking intensity, he watched him with the eyes of an assassin ready to pounce. Observing him stealthily, even openly, presented no difficulties, since Harry, the feigner, as Fowler called him now, lived nearby. No doubt, that man knew the ins and outs of dissimulation, one had to admit. Though visibly racked by excruciating pain, he managed to convey an aspect of a man sound in mind and blessed with youthful vigour. Albeit only to undiscerning clodhoppers like Bruce Larsit. He, Bertram Fowler, could not for an instant have been thus deceived. Harry, the uncle, suffered from an incurable disease that hauled him towards an early grave. Bruce of course, now as then sang about the uncle's health:

"Strong as a horse, sound as a fiddle, that describes uncle Harry. Ha ha ha, what a dolt you are, Fowler," he called out at the sight of him.

Strange, Fowler thought, a man pretending to see through a millstone, and hear the grass grow, divined not an iota of his uncle's malignant tumours, that gnawed away his vitals at an alarming rate. Signs of inner decay were omnipresent in the man deemed bursting with vitality. The enormous bags under his eyes, lauded by Bruce as a mark of manliness, told a story of its own; as did the facial skin which gradually changed from a varnished appearance to wattled pastiness. No doubt the end was near, but by the looks of it the day of reckoning drew even closer. In three weeks Fowler would face certain disgrace, unless a miracle occurred. That conclusion was reached after a visit with uncle Harry one morning, who to his dismay greeted him with an exuberance unseemly for a man who must be hearing the deathwatch in the walls.

Later that day he walked to the lake's edge where he sat down to ponder. The sun slowly dipped towards the horizon. Soon a peaceful glow, strangely encouraging, spread over the land. In the following twilight freighters moved ghostlike, deep in the water, westward to the Great Lakes. Others, returning from the inland, more buoyant now, were heading towards the open sea. It always intrigued Fowler to observe these huge cargo ships enliven the lake, especially at dusk and dawn; not today, however. The dreamy frame of mind refused to make itself felt, nor did the cooling breeze that started to ripple the water, catch his attention. Serious concerns creased his brow. What could Harry Larsit's chipper demeanour portent? Calling to mind his unwonted verbosity, the words dripping with mockery surely aimed at him, made Fowler cringe. Even his gestures, strangely angular and abrupt, expressed silent taunts and undisguised rebuke, Fowler conjectured. Was Mr Larsit, he always addressed him thus, cognisant of that confounded bet he stood to lose unless a miracle occurred, which increasingly looked like hope against hope?

Meanwhile darkness had set in; lights from the opposite shore cast weird reflections onto the water. Fowler wrangled with contradictory images, which his mind could neither disentangle nor banish. But one thing stuck clearly in his mind: The property in Montreal, Susi's ancestral home, may not be compromised.

"But it is, it is!" a voice from somewhere lamented.

"No!" he cried out, then jumped up, turned and walked towards the house.

As he approached the stairs Fowler's head bound up at the realisation of Bruce's arcane behaviour concerning the agreement; he bridled. Why have it notarised? Beyond that, how come his, Fowler's, signature needed not to be witnessed by a notary? The more he attempted to probe, the less sense it made. Then it flashed through his mind that he hadn't looked at the name of the notary, which surely must be imprinted on the seal. He rushed inside and opened a drawer where the covenant lay. What he saw made him gasp involuntarily.

"Edward Larsit, justice of the peace" he read aloud more often than once.

Slowly the truth started to sink in. Edward Larsit of course was Bruce's father, who most certainly would have balked at such a harebrained agreement. Authenticating it? From what he knew about the old diehard, not even the threat of torture could have induced him to affix his stamp to a fraudulent document. Two names were mentioned, but only one person presented himself for the signature as attested.

As mentioned, curious thoughts began to obtrude themselves onto Fowler's mind. While still holding the affidavit in his hands, he looked at Susi's picture on the wall.

"Have no fear, daughter, your beloved home will be yours forever," he promised.

The bet was off; under the circumstances Bruce would not dare to register a claim. A heartfelt sigh escaped from his breast which soon groaned under the weight of an incubus that grew from hour to hour. Its name was covetousness, the fiend that cannot be tamed. Despite an ingrained habit to retire early, Fowler still walked around the shabby house, a shack really, rented for a song from Bruce Larsit, long after midnight. Sleep, he knew, was out of the question, for he realised that a mind beset by indecision, trying to appease a heart stuffed with avarice, finds neither rest nor ease; especially if he is unable to muffle the buzz of promise in his ears.

"If the bet is off, your ardent wish to take possession of that house on the lakefront is not worth another thought," he repeatedly told himself.

Fowler did everything but pray that night, to find a way out of this seemingly blind alley. By the first glow of dawn he stroked his chin with hands that no longer twitched. Hope approached, not soaringly mind you, but at a steady pace. He concluded that something can be wangled out of Bruce Larsit; what and how still had to be worked out. He surmised as follows:

Bruce had usurped his father's authority by using his seal surreptitiously. He committed a criminal offence that could be attested to by him. That's what must have happened, for no notary in the province would have affixed a seal bearing his name and signature to a document that might send him up the river; certainly not Edward Larsit, reputed to be a pillar of probity. Fowler concluded that Bruce Larsit never for one instant intended to honour the terms of the spurious covenant. But having once acceded to the bet, though foolhardy from first to last, he had to go the full distance. Like most vainglorious men he couldn't let well enough alone. Fowler had been thunderstruck when Larsit showed up the following morning with that neatly typed official looking contract, signed and stamped, yet possessing neither teeth nor claws, since his own signature was missing.

"How silly of me to bestow credence to a bogus covenant," Fowler spoke aloud.

In the afternoon he strolled to Roger's Brasserie, which he seldom visited for good reasons. First and foremost, he could ill afford to drink or eat there; second, he found the ambience wanting. It was a rather noisy place, frequented by locals from Kahnawake to Beauhornois. Barely had he stuck his head inside when someone waved at him:

"Have one on me," a man vaguely familiar called out.

He seemed to be in fine spirits, and a bit the worse for liquor.

"Have a seat," the man said with a smirk that put Fowler on guard.

More so when he cocked his head in a meaningful way.

"Aren't you our neighbourhood lawyer?" Fowler asked.

"So I am, so I am."

Extending a hand, he announced:

"Maître Charlevois at your service, Mr Fowler.

"Oh, you know me?"

"By name only till now," replied the lawyer.

They talked about this, that, and everything, except what seemingly lay on the lawyer's tongue. Maître Charlevois wants to tell me something, Fowler couldn't help thinking, but professional ethics bid him to desist. Yet liquor of course loosens the tongue and drowns timidity; potvalour jostles to the surface and elbows discretion aside.

"How are you getting on with your landlord?"

Surprised, and no less wary, Fowler asked:

"Bruce Larsit?"

"The same," Maître Charlevois replied with a knowing grin.

"Oh, quite well," intimated Fowler.

The admission earned him a sideways glance. Pursing his lips, frowning as if taking umbrage at what he heard, the lawyer's next words came as a bombshell:

"One more guilty verdict seals that fellow's fate. He will be a lifer at Archambault."

Fowler's head came up in surprise.

"I don't understand."

"You heard about the American maxim: Three strikes and you are out?"

"Vaguely, but I'm not quite sure what it means."

"After three convictions the book will be thrown at you. Our own, Canada's, precept is somewhat different."

"In what way?"

"After the forth conviction a felon loses the right to a parole."

Cocking his head while creasing his brow, Fowler queried:

"What's the relevance here?"

Maître Charlevois recoiled. He wiped his forehead, stood up, bowed almost imperceptible and left the tavern.

That chance encounter set the bee in Fowler's bonnet again. Weird notions entered his mind; ideas sired by greed and hatched by thoughts unthinkable, yet strangely alluring. How

should one interpret Maître Charlevois' arcane remarks? Were
they made randomly or purposefully? Fowler pondered. Did
the lawyer insinuate that Bruce Larsit had a criminal record
three times over, or was the wish father to the thoughts? Then
again Charlevois, who evidently haboured ill feelings towards
Larsit, might have intended to tell him something under the
rose, but changed his mind at the last moment.

Well, the target day arrived, then passed without a stir.
Bruce's uncle still walked among the living; in fact, he looked
healthier and younger than a year ago. Fowler clutched his
brow whenever their path crossed, especially since Harry
smirked or chuckled unfailingly:

"Hem – ahem, ahoy there, Bertram, old chap, you look
green around the gills. Something bothering you?"

Fowler, though entertaining several notions about the man's
behaviour, could not define it. Bruce, as expected, undertook
no steps to claim the stake of the bet. Fowler, resigned to a
continued existence in the ramshackle hut, was about to bury
the entire affair, when it reared its head again with a roar.

Bruce Larsit couldn't leave well enough alone. A Lord Strut
he was, the title fit him like a glove. But Fowler would never
have imputed the local hero, deemed a latter-day Croesus, with
vindictiveness. To his utter surprise and dismay an official
notice arrived which terminated the tenancy. Reasons stated,
while surely contrived, complied with the tenancy act. Fowler
was stunned, he pounded on the walls and stomped on the
floor.

"What now," he cried, while raising a fist in the direction of
Larsit's home.

His present accommodation, paltry to be sure, nevertheless
served his needs; especially in view of the nominal rent, that
was all he could afford.

Enraged, stung by despair, Fowler decided to confront
Bruce on the spot. Like a challenged bull he stormed onto the
street, then turning on his heels he returned to the house with a
wily smile on his lips. At sixes and sevens a moment ago, he
started to disentangle his thoughts as he rowed towards a
cluster of islands about two miles distant. Rowing soothed his
nerves, the ripple on the water cleared his mind from the fog of

uncertainty. He moored the small boot at one of the uninhabited islands, where he sat down to ponder. It was his favoured spot, which he had christened the Meditation Rocks.

After an hour long undisturbed musing, Fowler rowed back. When he arrived at his shack he knew what needed to be done.

"Relax, Bertram, the fates are smiling, you are not on the highroad to Needham yet," he promised himself.

"Maître Charlevois, I came to consult you about a ticklish matter. Let me be frank. My scant means don't permit me to pay a regular fee," Fowler indicated.

The wary lawyer peered at him steadily; suspicion dimmed one eye, the other darkened with distrust.

"He knows more than he is willing to admit," it flashed through Fowler's mind.

"Never mind the fee for now, I usually grand half an hour free of charge," Charlevois advised.

"Here we go, Maître, I'm in a regular pickle, thus legal advice would be appreciated."

"Well?" encouraged the lawyer.

With the words:

"Take a look," he handed him the notice of cancellation.

"Hm, it appears to be quite in order, a challenge might be futile," the attorney advised.

How much should he tell Maître Charlevois, who more than likely was in the know anyway? Considering Bruce Larsit's penchant to brag and tattle, the whole affair might be one of Polichinelle's secrets already; meaning that every man, woman, and child within five miles spoke about it in stage whispers.

Fowler commenced to explain, or tried to rather, when the lawyer fell in:

"Quit beating about the bush, Mr Fowler, I am an officer of the court, what you tell me goes no further than this room."

Embarrassed by the reprimand, Fowler muddled on till the lawyer, visibly annoyed now, interrupted again:

"Let me rephrase. You have incriminating evidence against Bruce Larsit which you intend to trade for favours, is that it?"

"Sort of," admitted Fowler.

"What do you want from me?"

Seeing Fowler hesitate, casting a glance at the clock on the wall, he urged brusquely:

"Let's hear it."

Somewhat cowed, feeling like an unwelcome visitor, Fowler inquired:

"The other day at Roger's Brasserie you implied that Bruce Larsit has a criminal record."

"So I did, but shouldn't have," the lawyer remarked with an expression in his face that gave the lie to his words.

"Anyway, it's piper's news that our celebrated nabob had two convictions against him, plus presently serves a suspended sentence for fraud."

Eyeing his prospective client with undisguised disapproval, Maître Charlevois hastened to add:

"If you are privy to a crime committed by Larsit, I strongly suggest that you report it to the police, who will be glad to investigate."

Maître Charlevois, who was nobody's fool, sensed where the wind blew.

"It is incumbent upon me to advise you that blackmail is a federal offence," the attorney said.

Fowler had heard enough; he took his leave and went straight to Bruce Larsit's home.

"Bruce, I shall come to the point," Fowler growled more than he spoke.

"About the notice? It's irreversible."

"So be it, so be it. But my visit serves another purpose."

"Does it now? If it concerns that daft bet, I neither want to talk nor hear about it."

Fowler prepared to leave. He stroked his chin and pursed his lips, as if undecided whether to say what lay on his tongue.

"Before I leave, you ought to know that I must perform a painful duty," he informed the other.

Larsit shrugged his shoulders and raised his eyebrows as if to say: Why tell me? Yet something made him change his attitude; he turned a shade or two paler.

"What is it about?" he queried.

Fowler told him. Not everything mind you, but enough to make Larsit aware of his intention which was nothing less than obtaining the property put in pledge.

Bruce Larsit became fidgety while his entire demeanour changed. An observer could have sworn that the man, brash a moment ago, shrunk within himself. But a village boss neither quails easily, nor lays down arms without a display of bravado, and an attempt of browbeating. He snarled:

"Bertram, I called you a dolt before, but regrettably I must update that assessment by several degrees."

Stretching himself to his full height, he thundered:

"Do I understand right, you wish to trade my property for your silence?"

"That's it in a nutshell."

For an instant Fowler feared for his safety. Larsit behaved like a howling, whirling dervish out of all bounds. He was roundly cursed, blatantly slandered and, yes, obliquely threatened. Yet despite the bluster one had an inkling that Bruce overplayed his hand, plus that he was aware of it. Lines of worry creased his brow, glimmers of fear shone from his eyes. Yet he swaggered on till Fowler began feeling sorry for the man burdened with the cross hubris, which he could not cast off. Finally he told him roughly to shut up.

"Think it over, I expect an answer within the week."

On his way out Fowler said over his shoulder:

"You know of course that I am in possession of the original agreement, signed and stamped by your father. Need I say more?"

Larsit reared up. Crying:

"Impossible, impossible," he ran into an adjacent room, where he rummaged through drawers.

Then a shout of despair rang out which made Fowler, who was out on the street already, hastening his steps.

Two hours later Larsit appeared at Fowler's threshold.

"Let's talk," he said.

"Yes, let's talk," Fowler concurred.

Larsit looked decidedly worried, he must have put two plus two together. But once a Bluff Hal, always a Bluff Hal.

"Where is the original of that covenant?" Larsit barked.

"In trust with a notary in Montreal. Here is a copy."

With these words he pointed to a folded sheet of paper on the table. As Larsit reached for it with a victorious grin, Fowler chuckled:

"It's of little use to you."

So it was, the original alone could have saved him from a dire fate, or the loss of one of his properties. When Bruce demanded to know how the original covenant came into his hands, Fowler acted surprised:

"You gave it to me," he chuckled.

That wasn't exactly true.

"You left it here," would have been a more accurate reply.

It took a while, plus a great deal of wangling to reach an agreement whose content was as follows:

Bruce Larsit consented to a title transfer which contained two encumbrances: One, no mortgages, liens or other charges were allowed during Fowler's holding; two, clear title shall revert back to Bruce Larsit upon Fowler's death or legal disappearance.

On the same day, almost simultaneously of the title transfer, notary Frechette handed the envelope, containing the original of the covenant, to Larsit.

Autumn arrived, the maple trees, green for almost five months, rapidly changed their colour. Birds of passage flocked together; their sudden whizzing sounds raised many a head. Daylight diminished, nights grew longer and cooler. Sailboats, till recently omnipresent from sunrise to sunset, soothing to the eyes, uplifting the spirit, gradually disappeared. The wind picked up, carrying a chill in its wake; soughing in the trees it made the water rise in swells and waves at times. The mood of the people began to change; they vicariously perceived the tidings of chillier and darker months. Ships were still plying the Seaway, slower now it deemed the beholder, as if guided by a more contemplative captain.

Two weeks later two policemen appeared at Susi Fowler's home. At the sight of the sombre officers, Susi's heart leaped to her throat:

"My father," she instinctively gasped.

"Yes, madam, Bertram Fowler died yesterday."

"But that's impossible, he was hale a few weeks ago."

"He drowned on Lac Saint-Louis while rowing in a small boat."

Susi, perplexed, and no less incredulous, asked many questions, which the policemen were reluctant to answer.

"There will be a postmortem, madam, till then we cannot say much," she was advised.

Susi attended the hearing, which she left deeply upset. The facts:

Bertram Fowler was rowing, as often before, in a small boat on the lake, which was swamped, then capsized and sank. The water, neither calm nor tossed up, could have been called frigid. The boat, readily retrieved, had no floatation in its compartments, nor could any life jackets be detected. Witnesses attested to the condition of the weather which, as mentioned, was not severe. One of them swore that he saw a powerboat passing repeatedly the little dory at high speed. There was no physical damage detected on the rowboat. The verdict? Death caused by a fluke accident.

When Susi Fowler tried to claim her father's putative property, she received a shock upon learning certain facts. When she met Bruce Larsit and saw a large speedboat moored below, she fled in horror. Voicing her suspicion at the police station, the sergeant showed empathy, but little interest.

"We realise that it was a peculiar accident, but believe me, madam, it happens all the time," he averred.

# Lack Of Compassion

*T*his was the straw that broke the camel's back. Helga, his wife, a professional hypochondriac in his eyes, went too far. First she used a cane to walk, then crutches. But noticing her husband's yawning indifference, she resorted to a walker; a small collapsible cage used by sufferers from arthritis, which had just reached the market.

"You don't want me to move about, is that it?" she quipped when her husband snickered.

Seeing his rebuking frown, she defended her action:

"Am I responsible for my condition?" she yelled at him.

Lucky for him he suppressed the words rushing to his lips:

"You sure are."

"Besides, Dr Vanstrom insists that I make no move without it," the wife countered.

"Dr Vanstrom doesn't know Adam from Eve," Brooks offered angrily.

Their married life, a bed of roses once, had become a resting place strewn with thorns and thistles; in fact, they were gradually drifting towards the proverbial vale of tears. One blamed the other for their misery, which a friendly smile now and then would have chased over hills and dales.

In the passing years Helga Brooks turned into a veritable Niobe; the personification of female sorrow in other words, exposed to the iniquities of an unfeeling husband. Keith Brooks did not share these sentiments, to him Helga nourished ailments for the sole purpose to vex and punish him. The notion, seemingly preposterous, nevertheless took deeper and deeper roots. True, his perceived apathy regarding her suffering, annoyed her considerable, yet that was not the main source of their discord; by no means. The driving thorn in the wife's side was his innermost self, his intrinsic character to be exact. Helga felt unappreciated, insufficiently cherished, perhaps fallaciously so, yet easily imaginable considering Keith's impassive nature. While not exactly a stoic, Brooks inclined towards aloofness which offended her feminine sensibilities. Helga Brooks deemed herself a modern-day Griselda; meek, virtuous, and patient, who bore her husband's harsh treatment with charitable smiles.

Nothing could have been further from the truth. She was a petty tyrant before he met her, to which attribute could be added combativeness. Keith, her husband, took scant umbrage at these peculiarities, which he overtly treated with banter, and covertly hoped she would learn to curtail. But during the last year, Helga, a picture of health by any standard till then, drifted from one ailment to the next. She consulted every other physician in town till she finally ended up in the clutches of Dr Vanstrom. From thereon Helga's hypochondria acquired symptoms of lameness. Soon the day arrived when Brooks' indulgence started to wane. He could no longer conceal a growing contempt for his wife's slide into a world of morbidity. Even more disturbing deemed him Helga's slavish obedience shown a doctor who might well peddle ambulatory aids. Strange to say, as the husband demurred louder, the wife's ailments grew graver. Her latest complaints, so deemed by Brooks, but called afflictions by Helga, cumulated in acute arthritis. When her husband withdrew to that dreaded tower of aloofness, she became an invalid, thus creating the need for a walker.

One afternoon an ambulance could be heard kilometres away, which drove up to the house occupied by Keith and Helga Brooks. A terrible accident had occurred there, the medics were told, near fatal, someone advised. Helga Brooks lay at the bottom of a stairway with broken limbs sustained by a tumble, and a hoarse throat from screaming. Helga survived, albeit in a state of partial paralysis. Keith Brooks ended up with two years behind bars. The charge: Unprovoked assault upon a handicapped person, his wife. Brooks pleaded guilty without the benefit of a lawyer. Helga, seemingly in shock, suffering from amnesia, professed that she remembered her husband, frightening enraged, approach her in a menacing manner.

"Where were you?"

"Standing at the top of the stairway, holding on for dear life to my walker. What happened next I cannot remember," she informed the police, who knitted their brows at some of the evidence, yet calculated that an indictment would be warranted.

The crown attorney proceeded reluctantly, however, only after perusing Evelyn Prat's declarations. She was Mrs Brooks' friend and neighbour who had much to impart. It appeared that she was the victim's sounding board, used to amplify the husband's transgressions, especially his vociferous objections to her use of essential walking aids. To everybody's surprise Brooks pleaded guilty as charged, after having piled denials upon denials for so long.

"Yes, I wrested that accursed cage from her hands," he admitted. "Why, you ask?"

Staring at the crown attorney, he said:

"Because she didn't need it."

Considering the judge with a rueful smile, he added:

"My wife never needed ambulatory aids, until now."

Although these comments were voiced in a deliberate manner with unshakeable conviction, they caused no stir.

"The accused is trying to salve his conscience," glances exchanged between the judge and the crown attorney appeared to be saying.

The prison chaplain, Father Currie, was known as a fire-eater. Some inmates, tough to the core, found him too aggressive, others shrunk back from his scathing wit. None dared to stare him into silence when he thundered about decency and Christian duty. All showed the white feather when his dander was up. No doubt, Father Currie spoke and looked daggers when the need arose. But all knew he possessed an honest heart. He mingled among the prisoners regardless of his or her unsavoury reputation. With the Lord's prayer on his lips, the fighter's resolve in his heart, he stepped into their cells, always alone.

After the initial visit with Brooks, Father Currie didn't know what to think. Invariably he sized up every inmate at the first encounter. Not this time, however, he admitted frowningly. As he left Brooks' cell, somewhat at sea, it must be said, he mumbled to himself. His vaunted ability to judge someone's character with unfailing accuracy had sustained a kink. Father Currie, though wearing the cloth with humility, could never wrestle down the sin – vanity.

"Give me ten minutes with a man, and I shall tell you who he is," was one of his pet sayings.

But not this time. The prisoner in cell forty-two had him stumped. His distinguished manners, unexpected in a criminal, threw him off guard, his lordly air even more. On his way out the Father knocked at the superintendent's door.

"The inmate in cell forty-two, who is he?" he queried.

"Hm, forty-two – forty-two, there now. His name is Keith Brooks," he read from a card index.

"What is he in for?"

"Unprovoked attack on his invalid wife," the superintendent advised.

Staring at him in disbelief, Father Currie bridled instinctively, yet he managed to keep his composure. Thanking the superintendent, he took his leave.

Throughout the day Brooks' image rose before his eyes; it followed him like a ghost, intending to cause mischief. It did in a way; in fact, the spectre touched the Father at the sensitive spot; his ego, but no less his conscience. The prisoner in cell forty-two gnawed at his peace of mind, he had a creeping suspicion that an innocent man languished in jail that must be helped.

Father Currie announced himself at the police headquarters.

"Could I have a word with the chief?" he requested in his authoritative manner.

"May I know who is calling?" the desk sergeant asked.

"Father Currie, the local prison chaplain."

Chief Frank, a man of few words, and not a smidgen of affection, wanted to know:

"What can I do for you, Father?"

"As the sergeant might have mentioned, I am the prison chaplain."

"He did."

Father Currie, a bit taken aback by the chief's brusqueness, tried to be more ingratiating.

"Would I be deemed prying, or not minding my own business, if I ask some questions?"

The chief made a wry face.

"It all depends," he intimated.

"There is an inmate at the provincial prison who, how shall I say, occupies my mind."

"In what way?"

"I think he is innocent."

The chief chuckled.

"Hm, that's quite an assertion."

He was about to fob off the Father with fair words, when he changed his mind. A roguish expression flitted across his face that seemed to say:

"Why not have a bit of fun."

"What makes you think so, Father?" Frank queried in a light-hearted tone.

"Instinct, intuition."

"Oh?"

Chief Frank somehow managed to wrap the monosyllable in layers of condescension, and swathe it in sarcasm. Undeterred, Father Currie, looking squarely at Frank, said:

"His name is Keith Brooks."

The chief, who took office recently, perked up.

"Did you say Keith Brooks?"

"I did."

"What does he look like?"

Father Currie described him in that inimitable style of his, which could be compared to an artist's deft strokes with a brush that created portraits close to life.

"That should give you an idea. Added his standoffishness, and the penchant towards eloquence, well, there you have him."

The chief, opening the door, called out:

"Catherine, would you bring me the records pertaining to Keith Brooks."

A few minutes later the secretary advised:

"The file is closed, chief."

"Oh well, find it anyway," he requested.

Turning to Father Currie with a considerable warmer attitude, he remarked:

"Father, thanks for the information, I shall be in touch."

Later on Frank visited the jail.

"It's been a long time, Keith," were his words of greeting.

"Yes, it has been, Richard."

"I read your file."

"Hasn't it collected dust already?"

"So it had, but I blew it off."

The two men observed each other with set lips, searching in their faces for signs that were no longer there. Time, the merciful healer or relentless punisher, had left indelible traces on their countenances.

"Keith, what happened?"

"You read my file, that's what happened."

"Why did you plead guilty?"

"Because I am guilty."

Did Frank sniff at Brooks admission or just make an inadvertent sound?

"You and I know, Keith, that the indictment was built on sand."

"I am not a jurist, Richard," came a curt reply.

Taken aback by the unfriendly response, Frank lowered his head. When he raised it again, he saw a man whose demeanour could hardly have been called alluring. Richard Frank, a man who rose from the ranks, refused to be fobbed off easily. He made another attempt to breach that inexplicable wall of obduracy.

"Keith, I have a good mind to reopen your case."

"Count me out."

Baffled, no less irritated, the chief queried:

"Will you apply for parole at least?"

"I don't intent to," came a blunt reply, accompanied by a glance implying that he wished to be left alone.

Frank, though thick-skinned, could take a braod hint as much as the next person; especially from Keith Brooks whom he remembered from their years in the Arctic, where in his official capacity he needed to deal with people of all walks of life in various conditions. He encountered Inuits as pigheaded as they come, fought with inebriated women who weren't exactly compliant when sober, that had turned mulish beyond description. Yet never had he met anyone instilled with a bulldog tenacity like Keith Brooks. Realising that his well-meant interference would stoke the embers of contrariness, the chief took his leave.

When Frank got back to his office he made some inquiries which put his mind at rest. Keith would be released within two months, since he most likely will earn a remission of his sentence. The chief shrugged his shoulders:

"Best to forget about that stiff-necked troublemaker," he told himself.

He couldn't help chuckling while reminiscing. They were younger then of course, much younger considering the crucial period in their lives. Ah, how different things seemed then, fifteen years ago, when one's inside did not quail at the whiff of adversity. He and Brooks were more than a few times at sword's points which, however, was never dipped in acrimony. He, the senior police officer in Frobisher Bay, a fast growing town just below the Arctic Circle, was forced to issue several citations against the freewheeling hotel keeper, who scoffed:

"Come now, officer, you imbibe, I'm no slouch when it comes to honouring Bacchus, so what's wrong with the natives having a few?"

"It's against the law, that's what's wrong. For the last time, quit serving them liquor."

A few weeks later they went through the same rigmarole again.

The day of Brooks discharge approached; he had earned a one third remission of his sentence. The superintendent had always praised Brooks to the skies:

"I wish all inmates were as exemplary as the prisoner in cell forty-two," he exclaimed with evident relish.

However, such eulogies should be taken with a pinch of salt, for recalcitrance in prisoners is silently prayed for, since it constitutes the guards' reason for being.

Father Currie made his last visit.

"Well, Mr Brooks, good luck," he wished the man whom he had labelled an enigma wrapped in a riddle. An embarrassed silence ensued which made the Father ill at ease. Brooks appeared on the verge of saying something. After hemming and hawing a bit, he blurted out:

"Come tomorrow my penal register will be erased, but will my offence be forgiven?"

"You mean your attack on your wife?"

Brooks observed Father Currie with doleful eyes; a merciful smile stole to his lips.

"Father, I never attacked Helga," he declared in a sympathetic tone, not exactly devoid of complacency.

Yet it sounded convincing to the priest, who for some time had harboured similar sentiments. Brooks hadn't unburdened his mind yet; he shifted this way or that, then said more:

"Father, can I talk with you in confidence?"

Stung by the question, the priest assured Brooks with a tinge of acerbity:

"You know very well that my lips are sealed."

"Quite so, but I'm not alluding to a confession."

"It makes no difference, I am sworn to silence."

Eyeing the Father with a mixture of anxiety and hope, Brooks inquired haltingly:

"Can I tell you what happened?"

Receiving no immediate encouragement, he declared:

"I must tell someone."

"If it eases your conscience you have my attention," the priest informed Brooks.

"My wife and I spent many blissful years together, till she started to quarrel with fate."

Seeing the Father's inquiring look, Brooks hastened to add:

"I cannot describe it in any other way, my wife declined rapidly in body and mind."

Father Currie perked up, his interest was awakened:

"Can you explain, Mr Brooks?"

"I shall try, rather I must in order to retain my sanity. Believe me, Father, witnessing my wife's descend into a world of despair made me sad and angry. Consider for a moment a woman, high spirited and adventurous whose laughter once filled the house, turning into an embittered scold, bemoaning a cruel destiny, of her own making I dare say."

"That's a harsh depiction," Father Currie protested.

"Harsh? By no means considering the facts. You see, Father, Helga rapidly entered the slough of hypochondria. Symptoms of every ailment under the sun, mostly imagined in my estimation, seemed to haunt her. The woman, once a picture of health, radiating good will from every pore, quickly turned into a regular bedlam, assailed by physical suffering and mental anguish, for which I lacked sympathy."

"Did she consult a doctor?" Father Currie wanted to know.

Brooks grimaced while turning sideways, as if trying to evade a slap in the face.

"Dozens, I venture to say, yet to no avail. My once sprightly wife, brimming with optimism, tumbled, fled I say, from one ailment to the next. To my chagrin she started to use ambulatory aids. First a stick, then crutches, and finally that execrable cage, called a walker."

"I suspect you questioned the necessity of them?"

"With every fiber of my heart."

Casting a mirthless glance at the priest, Brooks declared:

"As subsequent occurrences manifested themselves, my instinct was right."

"It was?"

"Yes, but let me continue. The time arrived when Helga moved not an inch without that infernal contraption; she almost slept with it."

Father Currie, blessed with infinite patience and compassion, bridled at Brooks' next words:

"It was all a swindle, a consummate fraud meant to punish me."

"For what?" Father Currie expelled.

"Search me, Father. Perhaps it's in a woman's blood, I cannot think otherwise. Shall I go on?"

Father Currie, his brow deeply creased, bewildered by Brooks' lengthy preamble, seemingly reaching a dead end, replied resignedly:

"Please do."

"One day I finished work early. On the way home twinges of remorse  touched my heart. I decided to surprise Helga with flowers and a kiss."

The priest nodded approvingly, while his face lit up.

"I approached the house silently, then unlocked and opened the door with deft hands, so quietly that not a sound could be heard. Imbued with kind feelings, yes, even love I hadn't felt for some time, I entered the house. As I tiptoed into an alcove to hang my coat, I heard footsteps upstairs. Wondering who that could be, I instinctively shrunk back."

Brooks fell silent. Visibly shaken, trying to collect his thoughts, he stared at the priest with a tormented expression. The following words sounded strained, as if beyond belief:

"When I craned my neck to see better, I froze to the ground. Father, you could have knocked me down with a feather upon beholding what took place before my eyes."

Lifting his head, observing the priest with wide-open eyes, Brooks asked:

"Have you ever imagined something vividly for some time, yet when actually perceived you were shocked out of your wits?"

Father Currie nodded assent:

"Yes, yes," he intimated.

"There was Helga, walking, skipping I should say, from room to room on the upper floor, without the help of a cane, crutches or walker. Overjoyed at the sight, I stepped forth and cried:

" 'Helga, Helga, you can walk. I knew you could, I knew it.' "

As Brooks paused for breath, Father Currie grew impatient, the languor of a moment ago had blown over, he was all ears now. An odd smile stole around Brooks' lips as he continued:

"What happened next defies description. Helga stiffened. Expelling a Melusina scream, she leaped up and grasped the walker nearby, which she lifted over her head, then flung it with such force to make her lose a foothold. In short, Helga tumbled to the bottom of the stairs, where she came to rest with broken limbs."

Stunned, Father Currie was undecided whether to console or chide Brooks. Confused, yet believing every word uttered by Brooks, he stared at the bare walls. While trying to regain his composure, a dozen notions raced through his mind; some weird, others worthy of consideration. Old age had honed his perception. Long ago he learned not to look with eyes alone, but also with one's heart. Truth, he realised, is a fickle dame; reality, he knew, can have many shades, and so has guilt. Weighing one thought against another, reflecting about this or that, one question lay heavy on his tongue; it must be asked, the Father decided.

"I have no wish to be indelicate, but tell me, why did you plead guilty in court?"

"Hm, why indeed," Brooks wondered.

He was not given to psychological musings, nor did he seek a profound meaning behind every event. Yet his wife's naked hatred shown him that afternoon changed his life. It made him feel degraded, but also reflective. Then one day an awful truth dawned on him.

"You see, Father, I soon realised that such fierce revulsion does not thrive in one breast alone."

"In other words, you felt responsible for her resentment," the Father suggested.

"Exactly. I concluded that my aloofness was a fertile soil for Helga's grievances. Added my lack of compassion drove her into the arms of despair, thus stirring up resentment. Yes, Helga felt hatred for me, but fate she hated most, even more so now, I venture to say."

Father Currie, visibly at sea, evidently not quite comprehending what he is being told, least of all the reason for it, inquired with little gusto:

"Were you admitting guilt for no other reason than atonement?"

"Perhaps, Father, perhaps," came an evasive answer.

Father Currie was about to pose another question when he considered Brooks closer. A puzzled expression darkened his

broad, kindly face. He blinked, then blinked again, and finally
gasped. What he saw made him shrink back. The bland
countenance of a moment ago underwent a perplexing change.
Brooks' features acquired a sardonic aspect, a host of imps
danced on his knitted brow; so it deemed the baffled priest,
who acknowledged a disquieting reality: The man sitting
opposite him accepted the penalty for a crime he did not
commit for other reasons than mere atonement. No doubt he
suffered pangs of guilt and nips of remorse on account of the
shabby treatment accorded his wife; but that was not the
deciding motive, the priest realised.

A chill crawled up his spine while he glanced from the exit
to Brooks, who imbued him with wonderment and sudden
anxiety. A notion gripped the priest that made him shudder.
Father Currie understood. Brooks, guided by morbid
sentiments, professed guilt in the hope to punish Helga. There
is no other explanation, he granted. Brooks intended to requite
imagined or real grief caused him by his wife. Of course, as so
often happens, the scheme backfired; it turned out to be a pipe
dream. The expected suspended sentence, most likely promised
by the prosecution for their case was weak, if not flimsy,
proved to be nothing but a trap; he received the maximum
penalty, plus a scathing reprimand from the judge.

How Brooks must have fretted when it became evident that
he had hoisted his own petard. But why did he refuse to reopen
the case and walk away a free man? Why, indeed, as Brooks
himself wondered a moment ago. Furthermore, how does one
explain his refusal to apply for parole, which to a model
prisoner like him would probably have been granted.

Father Currie sighed, he divined what words could not
express. Brooks' sufferings, though resented, yet self-imposed,
nourished a baser instinct. It stoked the flames of hate,
especially for his wife. How entangled the human mind can
get, the Father thought as he took his leave.

# Sun Cheng

"Sun Cheng must go, my patience is running out," Clyde Pringle announced to his companions.

He was the leader of the scientific crew, commissioned to record the movements and behaviour of polar bears who lingered about Churchill, Manitoba, till the ice formed up on Hudson Bay. Winter was rapidly setting in. The whales had left their breeding grounds in the estuary of the Churchill River; they were on the way to the Arctic Ocean.

The three scientists, plus Sun Cheng, cook and factotum, had taken up quarters in a forsaken army barrack on a lonely isthmus, some distance from Churchill.

Pringle gave it no rest. For undisclosed reasons he resented Cheng with all his might. He took umbrage at everything the man from Manchuria did; from the way he walked, talked or performed his duties. Pringle's colleagues, Simon Hogan and Hugo Pyles, felt unpleasantly affected by his constant fault-finding with Cheng who, in their estimation, was an asset to them.

"The boss is overdoing it," Hogan complained.

"Yes, he is behaving like a regular Mrs Grundy," agreed Pyles. "Nag, nag, all day. Cheng this, Cheng that. No matter what the poor man does, it's wrong in the eyes of our leader," Pyles lamented. Then added:

"You know, Simon, I'm beginning to worry."

Hogan dismissed such sentiments with a frown and a wave of the hand. He was the youngest of the three, not counting Sun

Cheng, whose age no oracle could have guessed, thus also the most unwary. Yet he too had reservations about the new leader's puzzling, inimical one could say, attitude towards Cheng.

"He is a prig." Pyles remarked.

"Tut, tut, let's wait and see," Hogan suggested.

Brian Sims, Pringle's predecessor, wasn't exactly a boon companion, but he stood up for fairness and harmony, which he considered essential in an isolated outpost. Dr Sims was an old stager, blessed with experience, good judgement and impartiality. But after a treacherous fall he returned to Winnipeg for treatment.

From the day when Pringle arrived clouds of discord appeared on the horizon; they soon followed him wherever he went. The sight of Sun Cheng seemingly disturbed his equanimity. To his colleagues' chagrin he bridled before he reluctantly took the cook's outstretched hand, which he barely touched, with a mien marred by distaste, and a brow creased from temple to temple.

"The man is biased," both murmured under their breath.

Within a week the hitherto tranquil camp turned into a place of dissent that sapped one's strength and weakened everybody's mettle. Hardships, hitherto endured with shrugs and smiles, now evoked gloomy countenances and imprecations. The wind from the tundra sounded ominous; the nip in the air went to the core, despite their arctic clothes. The work, till recently carried out with deft hands and light hearts, became a burdensome task; performed sulkily, with feet of clay, and hands of lead. Their power of observation, crucial to the work, was dimmed by distracting thoughts.

A silent but acrimonious struggle ensued between the new leader and the cook, who seemed to gain the upper hand. Cheng's indifference, whether real or apparent, drove the thorn deeper in Pringle's side. When being rebuked, the man from Manchuria bowed respectfully, grinned sheepishly, and promised to improve himself. Locking horns with the chief seemed never to enter his mind. Was he play-acting, behaving naturally, or following traditional mores, nobody ventured to

say. Yet a lurking suspicion existed that the chief's carping
steeled Cheng's resolve.

Pringle couldn't leave well enough alone. Neither Hogan
nor Pyles understood this preoccupation with the factotum's
denigration. In their estimation he performed his tasks
admirably. They considered him good-natured, anxious to
please, and blessed with a wonderful sense of humour. For a
while they balked at the chief's unspoken invitation to toe the
line; in other words to support him in his effort to put the pesky
Manchurian in his place.

"I shall wipe that grin of his face yet," he promised all and
sundry.

Hogan's and Pyles' initial reluctance to join the chorus of
complaints and vilification soon weakened. Although they did
not take part in this relentless censure, disapproval directed at
Cheng evidenced itself in their countenances. Pringle's
intentions to freeze out their man Friday remained
unsuccessful. What his colleagues sensed he dared not to admit
in thought and words.

They were evenly matched in more than one way. Pringle,
towering over Cheng in rank and height, was upstaged by the
factotum's wit and resilience. His alien disposition, wrapped in
ancient wisdom, and gift for repartees, infuriated Pringle.
When Cheng hummed a tune, the chief clapped both hands
over his ears while shaking his head censoriously. No doubt
Clyde Pringle had bitten off more than he could chew, judging
by undeniable signs. One glance at his face sufficed to behold a
man in distress. The cheerful person of a month ago had
become an inveterate crosspatch. His colleagues were at sea by
the inexplicable hostile attitude towards Sun Cheng, which
affected them more and more unpleasantly. They wished that
one, or both, would simply disappear.

Strange to say, their rising animosity was chiefly directed
against Sun Cheng, who admittedly had nothing to answer for,
in contrast to Pringle, who pounced on every opportunity to
create a disturbance.

"Did you notice what he is doing now?"

"Who?" Pyles asked with tongue in cheek, meant to roil the
chief.

He succeeded alright.

"Who? Who else but that pesky Manchurian. He harangues the bears with monologues."

Hogan shrugged his shoulders as if to say:

"What of it?"

"In Mandarin," Pringle snorted.

Hearing neither words of rebuke, nor perceiving gestures of annoyance, he declared:

"That's not all. He plays that accursed pipa which excites and angers the bears."

Hogan, as much as Pyles, remained silent while gazing longingly across the bay, wishing that the ice would gain strength; it did, but not fast enough to please them. The same could be said for the bears who lingered and wandered about, getting hungrier and more ornery by the day. Their numbers increased as the ice on the bay thickened. It was now mid-November, snow lay on the ground; in fact, it had snowed every day of the week. Arctic air moved down from the Gulf; a bone-splitting cold gripped the land. Hogan, the wag, sniffed the air:

"I smell, what do I smell? Ah, fresh doughnuts in the pantry and fruit loaves on the table."

Pringle, who seemingly understood the hint, declared almost ruefully:

"Yes, our work will soon come to an end."

If the others noticed the tinge of disappointment in his voice, they did not let on. Whereas everyone else seemed to be yearning for the day of departure, Pringle gave the impression that he dreaded it.

"What's eating the chief?" Hogan asked his companion, who shrugged his shoulders:

"Search me, Simon, he is probable nursing a grievance again," Pyles suggested.

"By the way, have you noticed the change in Sun Cheng's deportment?"

"Not really," Pyles replied, then queried:

"What are you alluding to?"

"For one, his scowl is gone; two, I have never seen him so smug-faced before, nor so ingratiating," explained Hogan.

"Hm, now that you mention it, he does strike one as a man gaining decisiveness by the hour."

"Yes, like someone who found a solution to a nagging problem," Hogan agreed.

Those were also Pringle's thoughts who observed Cheng from the corners of his eyes. That fellow is up to something, the chief concluded. Whatever it was caused him scant concern however, far less than a disquieting fact: Sun Cheng was not brought to his knees by the relentless carping and chicanery directed at him for weeks on end; quite the contrary had happened. The man from Manchuria walked with head raised high, and a smirk that made the chief cringe. Hogan, as much as Pyles, sensed Cheng's growing resolve, attributable to impertinence, they thought, which must be stifled with harsh reprimands or withering looks. Yet they did neither, for Cheng, their factotum, had assumed an imperious air which none dared to challenge.

Corporal Sillery wished that he had more hands, heads, and feet. Despite working like a Trojan, many calls remained unanswered. This was the busiest time of the year. The bears were getting hungrier, more restive and intrusive. They brazenly walked through the town of Churchill, thereby alarming the residents, plus attracting outsiders; tourists in other words, whom the corporal called a pain in the neck. Thus, when calls from Winnipeg came in, which he considered extraneous, he took scant notice. Especially of the ones made by Ernie Novak, the owner of Nanook Resources. He was a farmer turned football player, and now wildlife researcher. Novak, a man given to pithy language, hard-headed and blunt beyond endurance, wasn't exactly the corporal's favourite. He was aware of Novak's undertaking at Button Bay on the other side of the Churchill River estuary. Observing polar bears in their natural environment, the government called it. A misnomer of grand proportion, others countered.

Corporal Sillery vaguely knew about the so-called research conducted by Nanook Resources on behalf of the Canadian Government. But he was neither aware of the crews names, nor the size of it. When most of the bears were on the ice, and the tourists had left, the corporal returned Novak's calls.

"I know, corporal, I am a nuisance, but listen to me."

"What's up, Mr Novak?"

"A premonition is up, officer," the fellow at the other end of the wire drawled, who sounded like a man in overalls with a pitchfork in his hand, and a blade of straw in his mouth.

"Premonition about what?"

"About my crew over at the Old Fort. I hear the tocsin ring, we haven't been in contact for over two weeks."

"Well, that's no cause for alarm," the corporal pointed out.

Rightly so, since in remote places like this, communication with the outside world is often interrupted for prolonged periods.

"True, officer, in normal circumstances I wouldn't give it another thought."

"Oh, is there something special going on at the fort?"

After hemming and hawing for a moment, Novak admitted that there could be, in a way of speaking.

"Hm, how shall I say it, we recently hired a new scientist."

Corporal Sillery wanted to hear nothing about Novak's problems, but promised to investigate within the next few days. Such an errand didn't exactly enthuse the policeman, for which reason he decided to send constable Fleury over, after his return from York Factory.

The same night it stopped snowing, after which a dreaded cold wave pushed down from the high Arctic that froze the tears in one's eyes, and made the spittle crack when it reached the ground.

Later in the day Sun Cheng showed up. Most locals knew him, which included the authorities, who universally liked the Chinese. They never missed an opportunity to exchange good-natured repartee with the man from Manchuria. But not this time, for one glance in his direction told the corporal otherwise. Banter seemed inappropriate under the circumstances, the man facing him seemed at the end of his tether. Officer Sillery, who knew Cheng for years, had never seen him so distraught. He was known throughout the town as Rosy Sun. When others huddled morosely in a fierce snowstorm, Cheng hailed them with a laugh and friendly words. Should people grumble on account of record-breaking cold snaps, he reminded them of the summer, just around the corner to be sure, when the land will be ablaze with profuse vegetation again. Yes, Sun Cheng always had a smile on his face, and friendly words on his lips. Even in oven-like heat, rendered unbearable by swarms of biting insects, he remained sanguine.

But not now, far from it. He bore no resemblance to a harbinger of good tidings. He impressed the corporal as someone in the grip of the horrors.

"What's up, Sun Cheng, have you seen a ghost?"

"They are not coming down."

"Who isn't coming down?" Sillery queried.

"The men on the lookout haven't come down for two days and nights," Cheng groaned.

Corporal Sillery, though considerable younger than Cheng, struck up an avuncular tone:

"Easy now, old boy, have a nip or two."

"No, no time, come quickly, it's cold."

Sillery needed not to be reminded of it. One glance at the ice-covered windows told him more than words. Corporal Sillery asked many questions to which few answers were forthcoming. Sun Cheng, reputed to be blessed with a sunny, calm disposition, made little sense; in fact, he was incoherent.

The policeman felt disinclined to walk three miles, in deep snow to boot, on someone's behest, who appeared to be unnerved. Stirred by Cheng's insistence, however, he decided to go. Corporal Sillery was a stalwart, judged by any yardstick, but the stubborn cold had sapped his strength. Probing as he might, Cheng could not be drawn out. Beyond the refrain:

"We must hurry, corporal," he hardly said another word.

What took place at the lonely windswept outpost, remained a riddle now as before.

The policeman put on warm clothes, slung a camera around his neck, then bid Cheng to come along. But the fellow didn't stir; he glanced from the officer to a rifle leaning in the corner.

"The rifle, corporal, you need a rifle," Sun Cheng urged.

"What for? the bears are gone."

The man from Manchuria shook his head slowly but emphatically:

"I tell you, Mr Sillery, a gun is needed."

Corporal Sillery observed the man standing opposite him closer. Although he had encountered him often in the past five years, he barely could place the distraught fellow. Sun Cheng came up to Churchill as an employee of Nanook Resources. His job consisted of maintaining the camp at the Button Bay promontory year round, plus be a factotum to the small crew from June to November. Nanook Resources were engaged by the Canadian Government to document the behaviour of polar bears in their natural habitation.

"It's a waste of money," quite a few locals averred.

"A chimerical scheme," people in the know called it with condescending chuckles.

Understandably so in view of an annoying reality: When the bears come on land in the early summer, they are haunted by visitors from every corner of the globe. These tourists, thrill seekers and whisky swillers, gape at the huge beasts from enclosed vehicles. It surely gives the lie to assertions that they are being observed in their wonted environment. Added the fact that these bears practically live near the local garbage dump, through which they rummage, draws the frame around the whole picture.

"Natural habitat? Don't make us laugh," the old-timers say.

Sun Cheng, being light-footed, walked several strides ahead of the policeman. Crossing the Churchill River at the narrowest point where it empties into the Hudson Bay, proved to be a chore; for corporal Sillery in any case. To be sure the narrow passage was frozen solid, yet the heavy blanket of snow, aggravated by drifts, caused the stocky policeman a great deal of trouble. Irritated, no less embarrassed, he bid Cheng, who nimbly skipped ahead, to slow down. Then he admonished:

"This better be worth my while."

It was. When they arrived at the spot, the corporal refused to trust his eyes. What he saw made him gasp. The ground surrounding the observation tower resembled a battlefield; it looked as if a massacre without quarter had taken place.

"I'll be hanged," corporal Sillery exclaimed.

Indeed, a charnel yard's aspect could not have been more gruesome than the sight that faced him. Blood and gore soaked the tamped down snow, bones were strewn around in all directions. He dared not think the unthinkable. Unconsciously he cast an inquiring glance at Cheng. Amid the sepulchral silence the corporal panted:

"Cheng, what happened?"

The Manchurian wordlessly shrugged his shoulders. Stung to the soul, the policeman pointed at the shambles ahead:

"This – this blood and gore, does it stem from...?"

Sun Cheng, baffled for an instant, sported a knowing grin; he understood.

"No, no, it's from the bears. They fought with teeth and claws for several days and nights," he averred.

Corporal Sillery frowned, it made little sense to the man who was stationed east and west, north and south above the sixtieth parallel. Besides, in all the years he had spent in Churchill he seldom, if ever, saw these huge beasts fight in earnest. No doubt, they cherish mock frays, but lacerating each other to the extend of drawing blood, copiously to boot, judging by appearances, the corporal found unusual.

Out on a promontory were old army barracks, unused for decades, which in part served Nanook Resources as temporary quarters. The observation tower, set back from the bay and the camp, overlooked a wide area. The little structure, sitting on two sturdy piles, resembled a large hunter's perch, totally enclosed with windows all around. Steel bars, traversing between the piles, functioned as a ladder. The bears' movement and their behaviour could be monitored from the raised hut.

Officer Sillery approached the lookout with utmost circumspection, contrary to Sun Cheng who showed no inclination to slow down. He turned around several times and beckoned the policeman to make haste. The corporal ignored Cheng's impatient signals; he proceeded like a hunter who sneaked up on a dangerous prey. While instinctively clasping his rifle, whose safety lock he pushed aside, he tiptoed forward. When he caught up with Cheng, he inquired with a measure of incredulity:

"Did I hear you say there are men up there?"

"Yes."

The curt reply made the officer grimace in annoyance. Cheng's taciturnity started to nibble at his forbearance. The fellow usually talked like an oracle, but for some reason he was closed as a clam today.

While they stood there staring at each other, amid the great white silence and bone-splitting chill, daylight waned rapidly. Corporal Sillery felt the tentacles of apprehension moving up his spine. He never before felt so alone; an ardent desire for company other than Cheng overwhelmed him. Nearby Churchill, across the narrow channel, seemed worlds away, beyond reach in fact. He felt plagued by a predicament. Darkness descended rapidly, thus rendering an investigation difficult, if not impossible. He felt an urge to turn back without making further inquiries. Yet a glance at the smirking Cheng set him right. He could have sworn to see sneering imps in the Manchurian's eyes. Was he mocking him, trying to lure him into a trap? Hardly, the police officer decided, as he called the Manchurian's irenic disposition to mind. But, nevertheless, keeping one's eyes open can do no harm he thought. In any case his intrinsic sense of duty gained the upper hand.

A glimpse at the setting sun spurred him into action; almost, that is, for another concern reared its head. Climbing up those rungs might be easy enough for a man not weighed down by indecision. Ascending with a loaded rifle invited a mishap, he realised, but leaving it behind could well prove injudicious under the circumstances. Yet one way or the other, he felt obliged to get up there, on the double to boot. Thus he emptied the chamber and put the cartridges in his pocket, while muttering:

"Police regulations, you know."

As Cheng asserted the three men were still in the tower, albeit dead as doornails, frozen to the marrow.

Daylight waned rapidly. Since heavy clouds obscured the sky, the range of vision became limited, thus not much could be achieved till tomorrow. Yet it was still early enough to notify the corporal's superiors in Winnipeg. Finding their way back of course presented no hurdle; the lights of Churchill guided them adequately. The police officer asked many questions, although answers were given haltingly, if at all.

"Sun Cheng, why did these men not come down?"

"I told you the reason. The bears were fighting below, they would have torn them to pieces."

Although the corporal pooh-poohed that notion, he did admit that stepping among enraged polar bears could be tantamount with suicide. No doubt they were hungry, but not starved, in his opinion. Granted, however, waiting for the ice to thicken must have taxed their patience, thereby making them fretful. Yet hurling themselves ferociously at any living being, seemed out of character, especially days before the start on their long journey due north.

As they approached the town, many notions raced through corporal Sillery's head. Some absurd, others plausible; yet one recurring thought he could not banish: Sun Cheng concealed more than he revealed. He harboured no wish to co-operate, thus he deserved the label of hostile witness.

When they arrived in Churchill, officer Sillery turned towards Sun Cheng, who had fallen back, and advised:

"You must come with me to make an official statement."

Annoyed, because he received no answer, he halted his steps and turned fully around. Sun Cheng could nowhere be seen or heard. It seemed that the frozen ground had swallowed him without leaving a trace. Was this one of the Manchurian's silly tricks for which he was known by young and old? Oh well, he had neither time, nor was he inclined to think about it, or run after him. In any case he would not be able to leave town till tomorrow afternoon. And even then, there are ways, legal or illegal, to prevent his departure. First and foremost his superiors must be notified. That done, the corporal went to look for Sun Cheng, whom he did not find.

The next morning by the first glimmer of daylight, Cheng showed up at the police station, which also served the officers as living quarters. Corporal Sillery's inquiries about yesterday afternoon's Houdini act, elicited a blank stare, a smile, and an expression of innocence; yet no reply. It should be noted that Cheng's comprehension of the English language could have been termed extraordinary. True, he spoke with an accent, but nevertheless talked loops around most native speakers, if so disposed, that is.

"I am ready, chief," he announced with scarcely concealed scorn in his voice, and sarcasm written all over his face, that probably originated in the mountains of Jehol thousands of years ago.

The policeman glowered at Cheng, he took umbrage at the Manchurian's levity, obviously directed towards him. Ready he was; for what? One glance through the window drove home an irrefutable reality. Venturing abroad a hundred yards beyond the town's perimeter would be worthy of the motley. Why? Because a full-blown blizzard was in the making. After a heavy snowfall that had lasted all night, a howling wind swept down from the tundra. Gathering strength by the minute it whistled passed the stunted trees, then roared through the village. Snow, whirled in the air by the screaming northern, obstructing the view almost totally. After signing a statement prepared by the corporal, and promising to return when the storm abated, Cheng went his way.

Instructions from Winnipeg had arrived; as expected they contained no surprises.

The blizzard raged for two days and nights. On the third day the storm petered out, then stopped suddenly. The ensuing silence had an eerie effect on man and beast. The bright sunshine amid a ghostly stillness disquieted more than it pleased, especially corporal Sillery, who was forced to tear himself from the grip of inertia.

Constable Fleury, who had meanwhile returned, understood his chief's sentiments, thus he took the reins in both hands. Men, equipment, and appropriate vehicles were organised. The corporal, still suffering from a lingering influenza, heaved more than one sigh of relief when he noticed his subordinate's selfless efforts. Sun Cheng was again nowhere to be found, thus the group set out without him.

The initial enthusiasm ended quickly; the outing proved to be anything but a cakewalk. A fairly thick blanket of snow, although tamped down somewhat by the wind, nevertheless encumbered men and equipment.

Upon arrival at the site, the corporal sent constable Fleury plus another man up to the tower, with ropes, pulleys, detailed instructions, and a camera. Then came a call that affected everyone like a bolt from the blue:

"There is nobody up here," constable Fleury yelled.

All eyes turned towards the corporal. A man, who harboured no predilection for the police in general, least of all for Sillery, snorted derisively. At first the corporal didn't react, but after Fleury repeated his words, he bellowed angrily:

"Stow it Rob, this isn't the time for shenanigans, fall to it, send them down, we are freezing."

The other fellow chimed in:

"The constable is right, there is nobody up here."

Corporal Sillery, chilled to the bones a moment ago, broke out in a steaming sweat. Speechless, assailed by doubts, no less angry at the two men in the lookout, whom he suspected of tomfoolery, he decided to assure himself. Of what? his inner voice demanded to know. Did he not see and touch the three men huddling for warmth, yet were stone cold with not another breath in their lungs? So how can they not be there anymore? Dead men don't walk, and climb even less. For an instant the corporal's imagination ran the gauntlet of weird notions. Did the lingering fever addle his brain and weaken the body, thus making him an easy prey for Sun Cheng's repeated assertions, bordering on hypnotic suggestions, that three men were in the observation tower continuously for two days and nights in that bone-splitting cold? Did he, Sillery, perceive them below the threshold of consciousness?

The corporal hesitated. Shuddering visibly, he looked around once, then twice, while uttering:

"Where is Sun Cheng, has anyone seen that blasted Chinese?"

Heads turned, glances were cast from one to the other amid head-shaking and gestures of denial. Then a man spoke up:

"Sun Cheng? He left."

"Left? When, whereto?" the corporal burst out.

The man, miffed by the officer's high-handedness, replied in the same vein:

"How should I know? He boarded the train this morning, more I cannot say."

Constable Fleury and the assistant had meanwhile descended. Judging by their demeanours they had much to say, but remained silent. While contemplating Corporal Sillery, the urge for reprove was stifled, as much as the intention to ask pointed questions. In a flash both men realised that the corporal deserved pity rather than rebuke. The upholder of law and order, known throughout the sub-arctic for boldness and backbone, displayed not a flicker of such sterling qualities. He stood there kicking his heels, while staring aghast into space, like a man uncertain of his own existence. Muttering to himself he started to walk towards the lookout. Constable Fleury followed him.

"Sean, you needn't bother, take my word for it, there is nobody up there," he pleaded.

"I must verify that myself, so don't interfere."

Gripping the rung with both hands, he turned his head towards his subordinate:

"Rob, there were three dead men up there a few days ago. I stake my life on it," Sillery declared.

Realising the futility of raising further objections, constable Fleury stepped back. Sillery tried to put up a brave front, but he deceived no one, probably not even himself. Craning and turning his head several times, he finally started to climb, slowly and painstakingly. When he stuck his head through the opening, he almost fainted. The place was empty, not a sign of the three corpses existed. The corporal's demeanour said more than his words:

"This must be a nightmare, the frozen bodies have disappeared," he moaned.

Then, staring defiantly, and no less deliberately at everyone present, he grumbled:

"Snicker on, fellows, sneer all you want, but mark my words, you will soon wear a dunce's cap. I shall see to it in due time."

The corporal's promise turned out to be an intemperance of the tongue, worthy of Lord Brag. Solving the mystery was not in the cards; it turned out to be an enigma wrapped in layers of puzzles.

Talking to Ernie Novak, the owner of Nanook Resources, shed no light on the murky affair; quite the contrary, it stuck another spoke in the authorities' wheel. The waspish farmer, turned scientific observer, didn't mince words:

"Did I not voice presentiments about that new scientist? As mentioned some time ago, I could hear the alarm bells ring from far away. You see, officer, Clyde Pringle, our temporary replacement for Brian Sims has, or should I say had, two strikes against him, as we discovered later. The first was:"

Corporal Sillery heard sounds but no words, for he had entered a trance-like state, where the mind informs the senses, instead of the senses the mind. In other words, he suffered from bouts of hallucinations. Had he really seen the frozen bodies or did he subconsciously perceive what Sun Cheng willed?

As Ernie Novak continued to voice his chagrin, the corporal's thoughts wandered across the river to the promontory where the greatest riddle of his career loomed large. While he lent Novak a perfunctory ear, the nearby lookout rose vividly before his eyes, as did a string of self-incriminations.

First and foremost he deplored his failure to photograph what he had encountered that afternoon. The excuse of duskiness held no water; in retrospect he execrated this inexplicable omission. Furthermore, he bemoaned his unprofessional handling concerning Sun Cheng, who should have been detained as a material witness, by legal or dubious means.

At the inquest the coroner, plus some of the jurors, hauled him over the coals on account of such negligence. No doubt he deserved to be criticised, but not pilloried, Sillery admitted. Using the raging blizzard as an excuse led nowhere; it just fanned the coroner's scorn:

"Corporal, according to your testimony there were three frozen bodies in the lookout. The least you should have done is photograph them," the coroner chided.

True enough, he silently granted, but nevertheless offered a vindication, albeit a limping one:

"In retrospect you are right, although the conditions weren't exactly ideal. Darkness was setting in rapidly, the sky took on

an ominous aspect, whereas the chill and moist air fogged up
the viewing windows in a split second. Therefore it seemed
prudent to return in the morning to conclude the investigation."

It was more than a white lie, he admitted to himself.

"But you didn't go back the next morning," a juror
reminded him.

Lowering his head he answered:

"No."

"Why not, corporal?"

The query, posed with a measure of reproof, discomfited
him. He vividly recalled his acerbic, and no less indignant
reply:

"A snowstorm started in the wee hours, which quickly
turned into a full-blown blizzard. Being abroad in that white
fury, besides risking one's life, would have served no purpose."

The verdict rendered, equivocal and no less inconclusive,
found no favour among the town's inhabitants, who felt
endangered by the sinister event.

"Presumptions of an accidental death is warranted although
no bodies were produced."

The jury recommended that no effort should be spared to
find Sun Cheng, the only witness, nor must the investigation
cease till the bodies of the three men, presumed to have
vanished, are found. Did some of the jurors' smirk when this
request was announced?

At the moment corporal Sillery gave not a hoot about
anybody's conjecture, whether blazoned abroad or hinted at
with significant glances. Least of all did he cherish Ernie
Novak's presence. That man sure knew how to make a
nuisance of himself. He talked nonstop in a loud emphatic
voice that tempted the corporal several times to cover his ears.
Ernie Novak had said enough for now, judging by his
demeanour. He rose in that lumbering fashion peculiar to a
farmer's wont, which neither the big city nor the synthetic life
of a businessman, managed to change.

"Well, corporal, I must go back to Winnipeg, you know
where to reach me," he remarked.

The police officer welcomed the bucolic's departure, it
revived his spirits somewhat.

"Before you leave, Mr Novak, there are a few vexing details you might help to explain."

"That's what I'm here for, go ahead."

"Sun Cheng has been employed by you for some time, I understand."

"Five years to be exact."

"You know him fairly well then," the officer suggested.

"Hm, come to think of it, he has been a sphinx to everyone from day one, but why do you ask?"

"I am puzzled by his behaviour."

Novak chuckled:

"You are not the only one, most of us find him annoyingly inscrutable. True, he speaks volumes, but most of it is nothing but talkie-talkie. Anyway, what baffles you?"

"In his own words the three men were in the lookout uninterrupted for two days and nights, yet Cheng never investigated."

"No mystery there, our man Friday suffers from vertigo. Climbing on a chair even makes him dizzy. Clambering up those vertical rungs? Not our Sun Cheng."

"Well, then he could have contacted them from the ground.

Novak bristled involuntarily. Sizing up the policeman with evident disdain, he blurted out:

"Did Sun Cheng not say that bears were fighting ferociously around the observatory, drawing blood even?"

"Quite so, but they could have been chased away."

"Oh, by what means? Polar bears don't cut and run at the sight of a diminutive man," Novak protested.

"Maybe not, but a rifle shot would have sent them scurrying."

Novak's brow puckered:

"Cheng wouldn't touch a gun even if his life depended on it."

Corporal Sillery said nothing, but he cast a quick, sideways glance at his visitor, which Novak deemed offensive. Stung by the presumed scoff, he advised acidly:

"Besides, discharging a gun at the site is forbidden, unless in cases of mortal danger. In our many years of operation the occasion hadn't arisen yet."

Corporal Sillery bristled up, he resented Novak's didactic way of speaking, as much as his cocksureness. He considered Novak closer, who met his gaze with eyes that mirrored the wide, open prairie, and a true but foolish heart. For he, Sillery, wasn't exactly born yesterday, extensive police work had taught him an irrefutable lesson: Take what you hear with a grain of salt, and pay attention to what you don't hear. He couldn't banish the notion that something was amiss here; his visitor deliberately obfuscated certain facts. Granted, Ernie Novak's credulity and alertness could not be refuted, but in this case both attributes were huddling under the mantle of sanctimony, the authorities believed. One and all of the officers involved confessed that they smelled a rat or two.

"Mr Novak is protecting Sun Cheng," chief Brent asserted.

"He called twice today already," Brent's assistant remarked.

"Demanding that his rifle be returned, I guess," the chief chuckled.

"Of course."

Chief Brent stroked his chin while pursing his lips:

"Hm, I wonder what endearing qualities that gun possesses for a man of ample means," he speculated.

"Don't we all, chief, don't we all?"

Corporal Sillery, feeling still under the weather, quite annoyed at his visitor's self-confidence, decided to take a string out of his bow:

"Mr Novak, you said a moment ago that your rifle at the site had not been discharged in years."

"I did."

"You would bet your bottom dollar on it, I heard you say."

"I would."

"Well, sir, consider yourself lucky that I am not a betting man."

"What are you implying?"

"The gun had been fired recently."

"Impossible," Novak burst out.

"Yet true," the officer insisted. "Our laboratory has ascertained that several shots were fired from the subject rifle about a week ago."

Instinctively Novak felt tempted to ask once more for the return of his rifle, but a quick glance at the smirking policeman suppressed the urge. Anyway, a desire to be away from there, far away, became uppermost. He took umbrage at the corporal's demeanour, marred with scepticism from temple to temple. His pursed lips and raised eyebrows made him, Novak, self-conscious.

"He doesn't think I am trustworthy," it flashed through his mind.

"Before you go, Mr Novak, explain one thing."

"I shall try."

"You stated at the inquiry that the cardinal rule, a must to adhere to, is this: There ought to be always one man, not counting Sun Cheng, on the ground. That wasn't observed, as I personally can attest to. Here is the clincher: Why were all three up in the lookout? Then of course the matter of the trampled down, blood soaked snow around the observatory, defies explanation, so far in any case."

"The gore on the ground? Didn't Sun Cheng tell you that the bears were fighting each other?"

"He did."

"Well, doesn't that answer your query?"

"Not really, Mr Novak. You see, in all these years I spent in the Arctic, at lonely outposts now and then, I never saw polar bears fighting with each other in earnest. Inquiries with colleagues, priests, and old-timers confirmed my finding."

"Maybe so, but that is not etched in stone from what I hear and read. A wounded polar bear for instance, I am told, turns into a ball of fury, and attacks anyone within sight with a diabolic ferocity to the last breath of this mighty body."

Corporal Sillery gasped. He sucked in his breath audibly, while staring at Novak as if thunderstruck. Feigning pressure of business, he sort of manoeuvred his visitor out of the station.

Afterwards corporal Sillery sat down to think. What had just come to his ears set the wheels of ratiocination in motion. Why did Novak mention that hawker's news concerning polar bears, who are avers to strife if unmolested, but once they feel threatened in a twinkle turn into snarling creatures of claws and teeth? The fact is known to every tundra dweller. So, for what reason did Novak try to enlighten him, with a sly smile to boot? No matter, whether he attempted to lead him astray or point his nose to a scent undetected so far, it made him prick up his ears and open his eyes.

The bleak landscape depressed him, yet not as much as the mystery of this unsolved case. Were they tilting at windmills? More likely than not, he concluded with a deep sigh. One thing remained irrefutable: The man who held the key to the riddle in his hands had vanished without a trace. Novak, Cheng's employer, deemed him a book written in hieroglyphics, who talked like an oracle, and revealed even less. No doubt, that straw-chewing descendent of prairie farmers knew more than he let on, corporal Sillery told himself. He also was not the fool he tried to portray. Had he been duped by the disclosure concerning the rifle? Hardly, judging by his reaction, and the query dripping with sarcasm:

"Corporal Sillery, why did you not tell the jury about the shots fired from the gun?"

Indeed, why not? Novak, with inclined head, had observed him with the mien of a slyboots with decades of practice.

"Was it a lapse of memory?" he prodded.

Not really, Sillery admitted to himself, yet despite Novak's insistent gaze, he made no reply. Telling the truth was out of the question; hemming and hawing would open the floodgates of doubt and scorn. The only expedient course seemed to be a pretext of urgent work needing immediate attention. Novak virtually fled at the first hint.

The long hard spell of winter came to an end; spring had arrived. The ice on the Churchill River broke up; it pushed onto the still solidly frozen bay. Snow buntings had returned; their soft purr and clear whistle filled the air amid stunted trees and the low growth of the sub-arctic. Ptarmigans exchanged their white plumage for the summer's rufous colours. Strong winds prevailed; gathering strength over the tundra farther north they relentlessly battered the shores. Days grew longer, the sun gradually climbed towards its zenith.

"Soon the barren land will come to life," people reminded each other.

Corporal Sillery neither heard the sweet song of the buntings, nor felt the sun's warming rays on his bowed head. Why bowed? For one thing, not a shimmer penetrated the darkness surrounding the mystery of the frozen bodies in the lookout. That, however, constituted only a small part of his chagrin, for he, as much as his superiors, had thrown in the towel; in other words the pertinent file had been pretty well closed. Albeit not in the corporal's mind, it continued to be the plague of his bosom, but for entirely different reasons. Was he chasing chimeras created by an inflamed mind? Or were these disquieting perceptions rooted in reality? Did the good folks of Churchill, not merely his detractors, see him as someone rummaging in a phantom world? It certainly looked like it, judging by the sideways glances and hastened steps when they encountered him. Gone were the days when nearly anyone over a certain age hailed and buttonholed him at every opportunity with a heart-warming glee. The favoured son of Churchill, paragon of the sub-arctic, was now observed with eyes peeled, and brows wrinkled

"He has gone off the rails," they told each other.

"Yes, he lost his grip on reality," kinder souls suggested.

"Trying to pull the wool over our eyes again, is he? backbiters insinuated.

Corporal Sillery divined the whispers, and perceived oblique comments with mixed feelings. Some called him a scheming scoundrel, others a man suffering from hallucinations. Either way, they declared, his efficacy as a policeman had come to an end; certainly in that rough-and-tumble area. When in the dumps, officer Sillery almost shared the townspeople's sentiments, who gave scant credence to his assertion about that grisly discovery at the lookout. Who could blame them! By the same token why should he do so in view of his own scruples? For if the truth be known, he was torn by opposing emotions, which swayed from assurance to nagging misgivings. Was he labouring under delusions induced by Sun Cheng's extraordinary powers, like hypnotism perhaps? At times he succumbed to such notions, but only briefly. For invariably the macabre image of the three corpses rose before his eyes. How could one ever forget those contorted shapes, frozen to the marrow, huddled together, embracing each other for warmth, but several days later they had vanished without a trace. Who removed them from the lookout, and why? Dead men do not walk, and climb even less. Sun Cheng?

"No! and no! again," the corporal exclaimed louder than intended.

The mere thought made him risible despite his grief. First and foremost, what possible motive would have induced Cheng to commit such a folly; second, how could a small man, albeit sinewy, carry out such a strenuous feat? The urge arose to let the seeds of self-doubt germinate again. But he managed to nip it in the bud. Those three men froze to death, and that's the end of it, he told himself. Why they stayed up there during a bone-cracking cold spell remained the darkest of mysteries which only Sun Cheng could shed light on. But he was conspicuous by his continued absence.

Corporal Sillery made an effort to forget the recent past, albeit quite unsuccessfully. The road to Calvary seemed forever to loom before his eyes. Try as he may, its lure was stronger than the will to resist. Imbued with hope that distance would cure his penchant for brooding, he applied for a transfer. The request found scant enthusiasm with his superiors, who reluctantly entered his name on the roster.

Igloolik, at the tip of Melville Island, where he previously held office, seemed an appropriate spot to court oblivion of the past. For despite the brave front, bordering on bravado at times, corporal Sillery had fits of anxiety, and pangs of guilt. The voice inside refused to be silenced:

"You were derelict of your duty," it whispered, rather hissed.

He could have endured these insinuations, but not the villagers' askance glances, oblique comments, and snickers, all pregnant with reminders that suspicion reigned. Many old-timers expressed their misgivings, not only under the rose, about his conduct. Whether on account of suspected villainy or of a temporary mental aberration, his standing in the community has suffered, they maintained.

Soon the first bombshell fell. Tourists, spurred by a thirst for adventure, arrived from every corner of the globe. Forever in a turmoil, they thronged the main street of Churchill. Their forced gaiety and unrestrained deportment made some residents self-conscious; it instilled the need to look in every direction prior to venturing from their abodes. They felt disinclined to encounter these revellers who rattled up the air with questions. Cameras poised, searching for stirring sights, the visitors seemed to be constantly on the move. Some were taken on tours to observe the migrating belugas from boats, whereas others, of a more daring disposition, snorkelled alongside of the sportive creatures.

One of them found a rifle on the river bed. The corporal, as much as his assistant, instinctively divined its significance. Their premonition proved to be justified when Ernie Novak positively identified it as his. Corporal Sillery, who had balked at the idea of consulting the bucolic, as he called the owner of Nanook Resources, quickly pulled in his horns. Chief Brent brooked no opposition to his wishes, certainly not from a subordinate.

On the next day Novak arrived, captious as ever, armed with pictures, serial number of his rifle, and a malicious grin. What the police feared held true; they were raked over the coals unmercifully. Pressed for a comment he declared:

"This is my gun alright."

When the corporal advised that two shots were missing from the magazine, Novak said nothing, yet his sideways glances left not much to the imagination:

"Why should I believe you now if you misled me before?" his mien seemed to imply.

"I take it that the gun in your laboratory is a case of mistaken identity then," Novak inferred in a tone dripping with mockery.

"Indeed, it is," the policemen answered in unison.

When Novak bristled in disbelief, both looked the other way and changed the subject.

"You haven't heard from Sun Cheng, I suppose?" constable Fleury inquired.

The question elicited a sardonic grin. Contemplating the officers with evident disdain in one eye, and malicious joy in the other, Novak declared:

"I shall let you know as soon as I do."

Then another surprise manifested itself. Corporal Sillery went on leave. It happened not a day too soon, for to say the least his nerves were frayed beyond the edges. The hitherto forthright and bold officer had turned into an equivocator whose former unflinching disposition now teetered between irresolution and deviousness. The measured stride, his badge as it were, had given way to a slouching shuffle. A desire to bind his wounds and salve his conscience overshadowed the sense of duty.

Gradually the signs of inner torment pervaded his being. Try as he may, they could no longer be subdued, as much as the moans of a conscience in revolt. Calgary, his hometown, gained allure by the hour. Though far away, he could smell the scent of wild roses, and see the alpenglow beyond the foothills. Pity that the spectacular stampede had ended, but the peculiar spirit of Cowtown should help mend his scarred ego, he hoped.

It proved to be idle speculation; events of the past nipped at his heels wherever he went. Anxiety, fuelled by doubts and remorse, hung around his neck like the proverbial millstone. Almost every day he walked through the Bow River Park, then invariably ended up in Chinatown. Ascribing it to mere coincidence, he shrugged his shoulders and chuckled to himself. Soon, however, he owned up to the fact that an irresistible force guided his steps.

On the way down from Churchill he inquired about Sun Cheng in Winnipeg's Chinatown. Yes, he was well known there.

"Where can he be found?"

"Not here, he left many months ago."

Of course these inquiries were made casually while clad in civil clothes.

"Try the Asian Cultural Centre in Calgary," some advised.

But after beating the bushes there for two weeks, he realised that he was trying to shoe the goose; besides, his presence raised eyebrows and turned heads.

One day, while sitting in his favourable haunt, the Silver Dragon, a man stepped up to his table, who extended a hand and offered salutations:

"Corporal Sillery, what a surprise. How are things?"

Not exactly enthused to have his cover blown, the policeman greeted him with a puckered face. He recognised the fellow immediately; it was Brian Sims, Nanook Resources' chief scientist.

"May I join you?"

The corporal nodded perfunctorily while anxiously turning his head in every direction. What he saw put him on edge. He neither liked the knowing smirks, nor the remarks which he didn't understand. They are laughing up their sleeves, it flashed through his mind. The reason? Any tomfool could have figured that out, he silently confessed.

"Still recuperating from your mishap?"

"In a way, yes," the scientist admitted.

"Shall we see you up our way again?"

"Most certainly. I will be at my post within the month."

They observed each other silently for a moment, as if trying to guess at the reason of their presence. There was no love lost between them; the officer found Sims aloof beyond endurance. He, a man of the people, preferred associating with hail-fellow-well-met types. They had a few run-ins over the years on account of trifles attributable to diverging personalities. As often happens when people of contrary perceptions enter into a conversation, it soon strikes the sands. The flow of words dries up quickly, yawning boredom sets in, as does awkwardness. But as luck had it the recent misadventure bridged the widening gap of self-consciousness.

Corporal Sillery broached the subject first. Dr Sims remained surprisingly noncommittal; he never expressed indignation nor apprehension. He appeared to be utterly unconcerned. When the corporal proclaimed it a mystery, most likely buried deep in the sands of time, the scientist responded quizzically:

"Hm, maybe so."

"What is that supposed to mean?" the officer blurted out, thoroughly taken aback.

Realising his indelicate slip of the tongue, corporal Sillery searched for words to appease the breach of etiquette. His

efforts were cut short by Dr Sims' question which made him sit
up:

"Do you know where I can find Sun Cheng?"

Shaking his head deliberately, the corporal advised that he
did not:

"I have attempted to locate him for weeks without success
myself."

The comment elicited a chuckle plus several ahas from
Sims. Seeing the corporal's puzzled look, he expounded:

"I was mystified by the unfriendly reception in a place
where smiles and banter were the norm so far. Even school-
boys acted like artful dodgers when confronted by my innocent
queries concerning Sun Cheng. After all they knew me, as
much as my honourable intentions; besides, what I have to
offer benefits one of their own."

"I deduce that you wish to extend Sun Cheng's
employment."

"Quite correct."

"But you are unable to find him."

"How can I if he is hiding from you!"

Dr Sims knew of course about the coroner's inquest,
including the open verdict, as much as the directive to produce
the Manchurian. When the scientist prepared to leave, officer
Sillery posed a question:

"You have known Sun Cheng for awhile, I understand."

"Yes," came a monosyllable reply, dripping with suspicion.

"Forgive me if I appear obtrusive, remember it's done in the
line of duty. Admittedly I, as much as my colleagues, are
thoroughly baffled."

"About the incident at the fort?"

"Decidedly. We keenly wish to talk to Sun Cheng."

"Well, should I find him we shall notify you."

With these words Brian Sims departed.

Being on tenterhooks corporal Sillery did not notice the
man sitting at a nearby table. Circumspection, central to his
line of work, had become subordinate to anxiety. Unwittingly
the absorbing subject had made them careless. Their voices,
restrained at the outset, had grown more intense and louder,
thus inviting unwelcome listeners, like the man alluded to, who

rose and approached corporal Sillery. Bowing respectfully, he said:

"Excuse the intrusion, sir, I couldn't help overhearing your conversation which awakened nostalgic feelings in an old man's heart."

Flustered, no less irritated, the corporal stared at the interloper, whom he was about to give a resounding tongue-lashing. But his intentions were forestalled by the eavesdropper's comments:

"I heard a name mentioned which opened the floodgates of haunting memories. I am referring to Sun Cheng, the Manchurian."

Observing the professed eavesdropper with a more lenient mien, brightened by interest, the corporal queried:

"Do you know him?"

"First let me introduce myself. Brad Hulbert is the name. Now to your question. Sun Cheng and I walked many a path strewn with thorns and fraught with dangers. Our standing of superior and subordinate quickly changed to a relationship of equals and friends. He proved to be a godsend, whose amazing presence of mind, strength and pluck, more than once saved our lives and limbs; in fact, I wouldn't be standing here were it not for his daredeviltry and dexterity with guns."

"Are we talking about the same man?" the corporal interrupted.

"Well. Let me describe his distinctive features."

After mentioning several physical traits and general bearings, the policeman nodded assent:

"That's him alright."

Observing the fellow with rising interest, corporal Sillery asked him to be seated, although he felt no affinity to the uninvited guest. He was small in stature, rather portly, and obviously revelling in self-confidence. Corporal Sillery did not like the man, whose studied aura was meant to flutter the dovecotes. Alone his Vandyke beard, neither in season nor in fashion, could easily disturb a man's equanimity.

"Are you implying that Sun Cheng is adept with a gun?"

"Adept is not the word. Cheng can make a bull's eye from a hundred yards. I have seen it more often than once."

"You spoke of strength."

"Call it brawn," Hulbert chuckled, "brawn and fortitude. True, at first sight one deems him irresolute and wizened, even fifteen years ago he looked that way. Yet appearances can be deceptive, as I discovered quickly."

Perceiving the policeman's attentiveness, he expounded:

"One day while sluicing for gold in the Selkirks we had visitors. Two men, evidently set to cause mischief, started to heckle us. Pesky they were, but seemingly not dangerous. In a derogatory way they alluded to our accents, and what not. My hope, that if we ignore them they would shuffle off, was dashed quickly.

" 'Look at the Chink, what a sight.'

"Barely were these words spoken, when Sun Cheng rushed upon the taunting marplot. Believe it or not, he lifted the heavy-set fellow off the ground, then hurled all two hundred pounds of him unto a pile of rocks nearby."

A heartfelt sigh escaped from Hulbert's breast, a rueful expression darkened his countenance. Corporal Sillery felt at sea; attracted on the one hand, repelled on the other by the astounding narration. Was he being hoodwinked by a fibber or piffled by a raconteur perhaps? Although slow on the uptake he sensed a connection between the mishap in Churchill and Hulbert's narration. Thus he perked up, but instantly slumped down again upon glancing at the fellow sitting across from him. Nevertheless, curiosity gained the upper hand.

"When did you part company with your friend?" he asked.

"About five years ago."

Pulling a long face he added in a tone of distaste:

"Friend you say? Adversary would be a more fitting label," Hulbert moaned.

"But didn't you just extol your mutual amity?"

"Indeed, indeed, but it wilted faster than it sprouted."

"What happened?"

A rueful smile stole around Hulbert's lips. Grimacing as if in pain, he bowed his head:

"Nothing really. Cheng's deportment just changed practically overnight. His amenity, while still present, lacked spontaneity. What seemed natural before became stiff and forced. When I asked what's bothering him, he scowled and turned away. I tell you, sir, our halcyon days were counted, discord set in. Not that we quarrelled, not openly anyway, yet a silent tug of war ensued. At one end I dug in my heels trying to prevent an inexorable draw towards a morass, though not visible, yet divined with every bone in my body. Sun Cheng had something up his sleeve, squarely aimed at my demise."

"But why?" the officer exclaimed.

"Hm, that's what I asked myself a hundred times, till finally it hit me like a bolt from the blue."

Noticing the other's raised eyebrows and knitted forehead, he hastened to continue:

"I shall explain it in a moment. First let me tell you the rest."

Leaning halfway across the table, Hulbert asked:

"Have you ever experienced sheer terror?"

"I cannot say that I have."

"Well, I did in that lonely expanse, surrounded by wild beasts, and an oppressive stillness where the fall of a pebble sounds like a gun report. All the way from Ungava Bay to Shefferville, where we parted company, I lay in the grip of mortal fear. Sun Cheng grew more taciturn by the hour. However, that in itself, though disquieting, was not the source of my dread."

The corporal, wishing to leave but equally wanting to hear more, made a gesture of impatience.

"What was it?"

Hulbert shifted uneasily, conveying a reluctance to say more.

"You may think me paranoid, go ahead, do so, but hear my words. At times I had an eerie sensation of being stabbed in the back. When I whirled around a gasp broke from my lips. Sun Cheng stood there observing me with eyes of a predator ready to pounce on his prey. He uttered not a word, not even a syllable crossed his lips when I expressed surprise and discomfort.

" 'Sun Cheng, what is eating you?' I asked in a voice pregnant with portent.

"I received no answer, but his gaze spoke louder than words. Like the fabled basilisk he tried to look me dead."

"You mentioned a moment ago that you puzzled out his arcane transformation."

"It wasn't arcane really, considering the Oriental's turn of mind, which contrasts our own to an amazing degree. To begin with, in the course of time I became too familiar, embarrassingly intimate it seemed to Cheng's intrinsic prosaic nature. Adding insult to injury, Cheng's that is, I started to carp. Never blessed with inordinate patience, our existence, aggravated by hardship, disheartened by loneliness, took its toll. I lost my composure, thus calling into being the Manchurian's silent wrath, who was bestowed with fortitude from cradle to grave; in short, I began to fear for my life.

"One morning, after a sleepless, harrowing night, tormented by a premonition, I approached Sun Cheng:

" 'Give me your rifle, Cheng,' I commanded.

"He just grinned while gripping it with both hands. Knowing his physical strength and stamina, as much as his dexterity with guns, I pulled in my horns."

"Why are you telling me all this?" officer Sillery queried, to no avail.

Hulbert convincingly digressed.

"I know who you are, corporal. I am also familiar with recent events in which Sun Cheng had a pivotal part."

Rising abruptly, Hulbert took his leave; not, however, before he made a puzzling remark:

"What I related serves a purpose, it might assist you to solve the riddle seemingly buried in the bog of eternity."

On the way back the corporal called on his superior. Chief Brent listened patiently, albeit not attentively to his subordinate's report, which he found pretty well irrelevant. He now as then harboured the belief that the three men wandered off in that raging blizzard, and, like others before them, lost their way and met a gruesome fate. He told his colleagues:

"True, we have corporal Sillery's assurance of the presence of three frozen men in the lookout, which according to eyewitnesses were not there a few days later. Something else.

These roving corpses had never been positively identified, since the corporal failed to take pictures," Brent stressed.

"Granted, yet these three men did vanish," reminded some.

"What about Brad Hulbert's story?" others inquired.

"It's a story, and there the matter ends. Drawing conclusions from it? Far be it from me."

Chief Brent was blessed with commendable attributes; imagination, however, was not one of them.

"I am not a man of motley," meaning a licensed fool, was one of his pet sayings.

High-flown theories were not to his liking. Corporal Sillery's latest report warranted nothing more than a chuckle and harrumph. Leaning back, closing his eyes, he went over the case once more, including Hulbert's insinuating narration. That seemingly chance encounter smacked of contrivance. The revealing remarks, allusive, tailored to impugn Sun Cheng's peaceable nature, rang false. Who should one believe; the respected, albeit somewhat clamorous farmer turned businessman, or a stranger imitating Vandyke's creations? Reaching for the folder named Nanook, he wrote on the cover in bold letters: File closed.

His decision was countermanded within the week; Sun Cheng showed up.

"I understand that you are looking for me," he said to the policeman manning the desk.

"What's your name?"

"Sun Cheng."

Of course everyone in the department knew about the Manchurian, who purportedly had the key in his hands to the riddle of riddles.

A second inquest was held which led nowhere. The coroner, as much as some of the jurors, assailed Cheng with insistent questions that were answered curtly and calmly. He had nothing more to say, nothing beyond what the authorities knew already, Cheng maintained with an air befitting Zeno the Stoic. Indeed, they could have directed their cajolery, menacing innuendoes, and attempts to browbeating at the centrepost of the room with equal success. His shrugs and raised eyebrows annoyed the coroner, more so the accompanying grins exuding condescension, and implying esoteric knowledge, stoked his punitory tendencies.

Inclining his head towards a juror, he whispered:

"Wouldn't the Scavenger's Daughter be a perfect tool for him?"

"Ah, those manly days will never return," the juror, locally known as: String-em-up, replied louder than necessary.

Did the snickers discompose Sun Cheng? Not a bit! Judging by his demeanour they amused him. Placid as ever he observed the jurors with a mien expressing pity rather than chagrin.

"You stated to corporal Sillery that the three men were still in the lookout."

"I did."

"How could you have known since you never investigated?" a juror inquired with a sideways glance and snug demeanour, which fazed the witness not a bit.

"They hadn't come down," Cheng explained indulgently as one does to a pesky child.

As already mentioned he spoke English fluently, yet one couldn't banish the feeling that he was struggling with the meaning of words. The coroner fell in with a scowl:

"Why did you not go up and check?"

"The bears were angry."

So it went. Sun Cheng never contradicted himself, nor did he waste words. Many questions were asked, few satisfactory answers were given. Attempts to ensnare the witness with words uttered in honeyed tones, evoked vacant stares and pouts. Cross-examination, conducted in part from the high horse of imagined superiority, elicited broad grins, interrupted by monosyllabic replies. Attempts at soft-soaping misfired:

"Can you explain what happened, in your opinion, would this or this be possible?"

Such inquiries aimed at Cheng's pliancy completely missed the mark. The case remained shrouded in darkness; the file was permanently closed.

Yet rumours persisted; they traversed the vast tundra and immense waters of Hudson Bay. Divergent opinions were offered concerning the occurrence at the Old Fort. Some clung to the idea that Sun Cheng, a foreigner, deemed inscrutable to western minds, had a hand in it. Others, however, proponents of Hegelean dialectics, pooh-poohed the notion, which could not stand up to the rigour of logic, they maintained. Emboldened by their acquaintance with metaphysics, the science that depicts depths in shallow water, they concluded as follows: Corporal Sillery, the only person who supposedly saw the frozen bodies in the observatory, had been a victim of subliminal persuasion, triggered by Sun Cheng's insistence that three men were up there. This assurance skewed his perception. In short, the corporal saw what he subconsciously expected to see.

Winter approached, nights turned bitterly cold, daylight diminished rapidly. Ice flowers formed on windows exposed to the biting wind from the north. The polar bears grew increasingly restive as the bay froze up. Nanook Resources were at their post as usual; minus the three missing men, plus Sun Cheng.

Corporal Sillery had quit the force. Assailed by self-doubts, weighed down by clouds of suspicion from every side, he disappeared one day without a word of farewell. About a month later a note arrived at the local newspaper office.

"Think what you like, but I repeat: Those men were up there. Dead as doornails, cold as blue ice, all three were beyond help. I shall never forget those frozen stares, never."

Well, the townspeople did forget, the authorities followed suite.

Sun Cheng was seen less and less in town, although crossing the river on solid ice entailed scant difficulties. His visits, of short duration now, served only one purpose: to replenish supplies. Muffled up to the ears, with lowered eyes, he scurried along. Something appeared to weigh on his mind. The buoyant spirit of passed days had forsaken him, it visibly yielded to dejection, caused by irresolution.

"Like Hercules at the crossroads," the schoolmistress declared.

"Racked by indecision," she corrected herself.

Yet one day towards the end of January, a change manifested itself. Sun Cheng's ill humour was clean gone; his animal spirits came back.

"He found a solution to his dilemma," the schoolmistress conjectured who, despite advancing years, had not lost her womanly perception; an intuition which the highest seat of learning cannot convey. She liked the Manchurian, whom she considered a denizen of her own world. True, they hailed from opposite corners of the globe, spoke entirely different languages, and embraced dissimilar cultures. Yet they were akin in spirit. When they met the old gal felt like a lass again. No doubt, the vital spark of past days crackled once more in the ageing Manchurian's breast. His strides had acquired its former bounce; the sallow face lit up as happens when a man finds inner peace. The solitary schoolmistress said it aloud:

"That little rascal is up to something."

In the spring when the ice started to thin on the bay, the whole town was astir with exiting news. A book had been published bearing the title: Churchill's mystery solved. Lorne Huffy, the author, depicted events at the Old Fort with audacious aplomb. The source of his information? With brazen effrontery he stated that it came straight from the horse's mouth. The horse? Who else could it be than Sun Cheng, the sole survivor of that fatal incident. But the Manchurian hee-hawed the notion with such fervour that it sounded not only convincing but outright asinine. Yet rumours gain veracity in proportion to their fatuity. Here is the tale in a nutshell:

Ming Huan, the factotum at an observation station near Churchill, Manitoba, suffered from the chief scientist's bias. At first he bore the bullying with equanimity which seemed to stoke the embers of Somers' inbred nastiness; in fact, it dilated his tyrant's vein. Ming Huan, trusted and appreciated by his employer, liked by everyone in town, shrugged his shoulders while performing the enjoined work with added zeal. He never complained, but when the other two members of the crew also started to ride him, he decided to seek redress. Walking away from his gadflies never entered his mind. The thought of submitting a grievance to his employer made his lips curl in distaste. The gauntlet had been thrown, thus rendering it an affair of honour. Once he decided to pick it up his tormentors didn't realise that their lives weren't worth a rush anymore. Blessed with the patience of Job, favoured with innate perseverance, Ming Huan got busy to devise a scheme that could neither fail, nor land him in hot water. The polar bears, he instinctively knew, played a pivotal part in his plans. The mighty beasts of the tundra held few secrets in Huan's mind. It could be stated that a certain affinity existed between the inscrutable man from the Kinghan Mountains and the rovers of the north.

Playful these bears can be, curious and peaceful if not crowded, but ferocious if threatened. Woe betide the person who is deemed a menace to them. Certain perdition is in store for someone taking a missing or wounding shot at the monarch of the great White Silence. They might as well turn the gun on themselves.

When the ice on the bay thickened, the bears' restiveness increased, as did their irritableness. The crew at the outstation was cognisant of the fact; circumspection became the order of the day, as did a rigorous regimen which, however, was not inscribed in stone, as intimated by the author.

Soon the hour arrived when Ming Huan had everything worked out, thus he waited for a propitious moment to act. Despite the lack of necessity, desisting from his intention never occurred to him. His torment would soon end since the seasonal work was done, thus making the crew's departure imminent. Somers, the leading scientist, thorn in his flesh, was not slated to return next year. Yet act he must, the demon embedded in the depth of Ming Huan's being commanded ceaselessly. The voice of honour spoke louder than good sense.

To Huan's dismay events rushed along unexpectedly. One early morning towards the end of November the bears, as if on cue, congregated at the edge of the bay. It was a sight to behold, but not for Ming Huan whose vision was blurred by disappointment. He realised that before the sun reached its meridian the bears would be on the ice and start to wander northward. His hopes were dashed, crushed by a sudden bone-chilling cold snap, which firmed up the ice. But all was not lost, providence smiled while nodding approval.

The two men on duty were still up in the lookout when their relief, Brad Somers, approached it. This was a serious breach of rules, his last one as it turned out. Despite Ming Huan's dwindling hope he watched the surrounding with keen eyes, albeit a pounding heart, not to mention silent prayers, which were seemingly answered, when he caught sight of three bears endeavouring to join the others beyond the river. To the factotum's chagrin they paid no attention to him or Brad Somers. Well, Ming Huan knew his bears; their inborn curiosity is proverbial, they seldom resist an impulse to investigate what arouses their interest.

Huan hesitated not even a second. He stepped forward, raised the rifle over his head and performed a few pirouettes. This immediately caught the bears' attention; they slowed down and cast glances in his direction. Two continued on their way, the other one, a huge specimen, veered to take a closer look. What happened next, the author declared, is difficult to recount, it boggles the pen, he intimated. Quick as lightning Huan ducked behind a wall. A shot rang out, followed by a second one. Hardly had the echo died away when an angry roar rent the morning air. In a twinkle the bear, a ball of fury now, hurled himself towards the man on the ground, who instinctively ran towards the lookout which he ascended just in time. Although anticipating a ferocious reaction, Huan slunk terror-stricken out of harms way. The sight of the ensuing spectacle made him fear for his life despite the safety of the camp. Bleeding profusely, the wounded beast flew into a towering rage. Pawing the air menacingly, digging up the frozen ground at intervals, he circled round the structure while emitting bloodcurdling growls. Several times he attempted to scale the vertical rungs. Failing to do so he bit the steel bars with gnashing teeth. Now and then he assailed the lookout which he tried to topple. The mighty hunter of the north was in a frenzy; not so much on account of shooting pains, Huan reckoned, but because his pride had been hurt. He visibly lost strength as much as ferocity, but not an ounce of determination.

The three men in the lookout became frantic, none harboured illusions about the cruel fate in store for them should they fall prey to the irate bear's formidable claws. None was armed, nor were they aware of Huan's amazing marksmanship. The author quoted freely what he was told:

"You should have heard their peremptory commands, uttered in a lordly manner:

" 'Hey there, fellow, get on the radio. Call the police. Be quick about it,' Somers the boss barked like a panjandrum vested with authority over lives and limbs.

"His orders, dripping with scorn, interspersed by expletives, were hurled at me, his butt of derision, the object of rampant abuse. They were wasting their breath. Even when these gruff directions acquired a conciliatory note, they were going in one ear, and out the other, contrary to the rampaging bear's menacing growls that grated on my nerves."

The sun sets early near the sixtieth parallel at this time of the year. Darkness descends quickly and totally. The bear maintained his grim vigil all night. The cries from the deck became frantic and outright wheedling, but also fainter. The chill in the air that made the spittle crack when it hit the ground took its toll; judging by the infrequent calls for help, that sounded more like death rattles. In the morning all was calm. The bear had left, the lookout was wrapped in eerie silence. The intense cold, aggravated by fear, had sent his tormentors to the realm of the majority.

Ming Huan tinkered with the radio to make it unusable. The rifle, carefully wiped down, he lowered through a hole in the ice, which took a while to make, then he made his report.

Subsequent events, well known and documented, were barely mentioned by the author, who implied that he will reveal in this very book the mystery of the three corpses.

"Read on, dear reader, be prepared for an amazing conclusion," he promised.

Huffy knew his trade, he divined people's predilection for melodrama. Cryptic remarks, he understood, could even whet a yawning sceptic's curiosity. Allusions appeared to be his strong points, begging the question followed close behind. What happened at that outpost prior to the season's first blizzard? Did the policeman really see three frozen corpses on that deck, or was he mesmerised by the wily factotum who had an axe to grind? In other words did the corporal fall prey to subliminal persuasion?

Some facts could not be doubted, the author declared. Three men had vanished without a trace. The officer in charge asserted that he saw three frozen corpses in the lookout, which a day or so later had disappeared. The coroner's jury's decision, known by everyone in town, granted that a presumption of accidental death existed, although the bodies were not produced. Small wonder, Huffy hinted, since they, rather their skeletons, lay at the bottom of the Churchill River. Wild assertions meant to titillate rather than to convince, some readers must have thought. Well, as mentioned previously, the author understood the art of stoking suspense.

This is what happened according to him:

After the officer's gruesome discovery Ming Huan decided to lie low for a while. A sojourn among his own people, he reckoned, should soothe his conscience. The Silk Road in Vancouver seemed like an ideal place to melt away till the dust had settled. But he hesitated, something held him back; an undefinable force riveted him to the spot. The notion to leave town on tonight's train as planned set his whole being on edge. His mind was unable to turn away from the looming outlook that conveyed a message which he couldn't puzzle out. Did guilt, the beast with deadly claws and ferocious appetite, hold him back? The mere thought elicited snorts and scowls, for the lives of his tormentors meant not a fig to him. They got their just dessert, and that's the end of it.

It wasn't. Ming Huan's dither waxed till he reached for the bottle. That helped to open the sluicegates of memory. In a flash he recognised the source of his disquiet. A custom of the Kinghan Mountains it was, which dictated that the dead must be buried promptly at the place of their demise. Ming Huan needed not another drop, the mores of his forebears spoke loud and clear, anxiety dissipated in a twinkle. A glance at the clock indicated that time was of the essence; he must act without delay. Wild horses couldn't have held him back. Buried they must be, it would soothe his conscience in more than one way. True, satisfying tradition to the letter was quite impossible, considering the frozen ground. Burying them Inuit fashion under piles of stones did not appeal to him. The river! There! that was the solution.

A man not plagued by convention of a strange, faraway land might have chuckled at the notion of risking life and limb to perform an unnecessary task, which broke the law to boot. Disturbing the dead is a delict, Huan realised, spiriting corpses away is a grave offence; besides, if caught, the dogs of suspicion will surely be unleashed. Why chance it? As the matter stood not a smidgen of guilt nor negligence can be imputed to him. Desist! his better judgement commanded. You must! you must! a distant voice urged, which drowned out reason's objections.

On the way to the outpost Ming Huan went over every detail. With determination and luck his plan should succeed. Luck? Gazing at the northern sky gave the answer; it looked ominous. The signs could not be mistaken, something was brewing over the tundra; the first blizzard of the season showed its grim face.

Huan hurried on, there was no time to deliberate. Reflecting on the run he concluded that everything he needed was on hand. Block and tackle were attached to the structure, picks and axes could be found at the camp. The walls were draped with ropes, thus handling the stiff corpses, a task he abhorred, should be easy enough. Hacking a hole, however, in the thick ice proved to be a Trojan's job; but he managed to do it. Then, with a triumphant "han" he pushed one after the other into the ice-cold, swift water of the Churchill River.

Five hours later he sat in the rumbling train, grinning from ear to ear. That would teach those petty tyrants to tangle with a man from the Kinghan Mountains, Huan muttered, more often than once.

"There you have it," the author concluded, "the mystery of the vanished corpses has been solved."

The schoolmistress read the book from cover to cover. When she laid it aside a smile flitted across her face. She instinctively guessed the identity of the author, whose pen name Huffy made her chuckle appreciatively.

# The Funeral

*I* have noticed your interest in Riverview," Joe Sifton remarked casually, he hoped, to his friend Gil Caron.

Did the younger man wince and move his head sideways in disgust, or was it an illusion? Anyway, Caron made no reply, he just shrugged his shoulders and indicated with a gesture that he wished not to talk about it. Judging by the surly look, the mere hint at his friend's possible connection with the Riverview Hospital annoyed him considerable. Sifton resolved not to mention that place again, certainly not within earshot of Caron.

What allurement those grounds exerted on a man on his way to fame and riches, Sifton, as much as others of their coterie, couldn't fathom. True, the facility possessed character and undeniable signs of splendour. The park-like setting high above the Coquitlam River housed mentally ill men and women, including the criminally insane, who remained securely locked up till their sanity returned, as determined by two psychiatrists. One could see them standing behind sturdy bars, grimacing at the outside world, glowering at passers-by as if they bore the responsibility for their plight.

Caron now as before undertook trips to Riverview, which he glossed over mind you, rather tried to, albeit with little success. Seeds of suspicion started to take root, thus these outings lost the blush of innocence. Friends, as much as acquaintances, imputed ulterior motives to the visits that defied admittance.

Sifton, overwhelmed by a desire to investigate, took a jaunt up the hill. What he saw there forced a smile onto his lips, and wrinkled the broad brow. The beauty of the sprawling property, well maintained, containing older, stately buildings, invited one to linger. But the sight of men and women loitering about induced him to hurry along. More so after he perceived countenances framed in abject misery, and clouded by resignation.

On the way back Sifton felt more confused than before. What the dickens is wrong with Gil? he asked himself. How could he be drawn to an environment disgraced by gaping, surly people, inveterate loafers, living in a world of doom? He would have liked to take him to task, help him perhaps to overcome that impulse, but Sifton desisted. Rather not, he thought, when he recalled the recent rebuff.

Sifton and Caron had known each other for some years. They referred to themselves as friends, which held not true under Aristotle's criterion of friendship. No, they were not a single soul dwelling in two bodies. Yet, they got along famously, perhaps on account of their dissimilar backgrounds. They used to meet almost every day, with the exception of Saturday, when Sifton supposed Gil travelled to Riverview.

As time passed their habits changed; they saw less and less of each other. Whether this happened by design, on account of latent tensions between them, or fortuitously, never came to light.

Gil Caron grew strangely restive on account of Leroy Montcalm's altered disposition. His cousin, whom he had visited regularly for the past year or so, improved by leaps and bounds. Whereas hitherto he accepted his presence grudgingly, he now seemed to enjoy it. An even more astounding fact manifested itself: Till recently his cousin perceived him as a stranger, but suddenly he remembered not only his name, but also their kinship and shared life.

Leroy was under medical and psychiatric treatment at a special unit somewhat distant from the other buildings. The diagnosis: Mental derangement caused by a traumatic shock. Gil Caron soon understood how the wind blew. He was not such a John-a-Nokes to be duped by masters of gobbledegook and geniuses in affectation. But he pretended to be awed by their knowledge of, and mastery over, the human mind. When he posed a question concerning cousin Leroy's convalescence or possible release, the doctor's countenance darkened, his brow furrowed, while his head moved from side to side as if saddened by such unthinkable notions.

At the beginning Caron felt tempted to inform the doctors what took place on that evening in the Chic-Choc Mountains of northern Quebec. But seeing their high and mighty behaviour concerning mental disorders, he withheld his knowledge.

Gil Caron, as much as Leroy Montcalm, both an only child, became orphans in their youth. They were born and raised in Gros-Morne on the spectacular north coast of the Gaspe Peninsula. It is a lonesome, wind-lashed region, dotted with small fishing villages for hundreds of miles. Winter arrives early there, particularly in the mountains. Snow can fall in October and remain on the ground till April. Cold temperatures seem to love the Chic-Chocs. Wind, reaching gale forces, gathers strength on the open stretch of water, a distance of more than a hundred miles, and whip sheets of rain or snow onto the coast.

As mentioned cousin Leroy's convalescence advanced rapidly; the same could be said about his memory, which returned at a miraculous rate. With one exception, however; the disastrous funeral several years ago appeared to have been purged from his mind. When Caron questioned his cousin with more then a trace of anxiety about his power of recollection:

"Leroy, how is your memory shaping up?" he received an unexpected assurance:

"Gil, old man, it couldn't be in better condition."

After beating about the bush for a moment or two, Caron put out a feeler:

"Is it as good as before?"

"Absolutely. I can recall the most trifling incidents since I outgrew my diapers."

Fidgeting uneasily, speaking deliberately, Caron put out another feeler:

"Hm, so you can remember the funeral, I suppose?"

"Funeral? Which one?"

"Jules Petand's."

"Oh, did the old man die? I didn't know," Leroy remarked indifferently.

If his cousin noticed Caron's heartfelt sigh of relief, he didn't let on.

"Well, Mr Caron, your cousin has made an amazing recovery," Dr Warren advised about a month later.

"Does that mean he can be released?"

"It does, sir."

"Can I collect him next Saturday?"

"Or any time before," Caron was assured.

Perceiving the doctor's quizzical glances, Caron inquired:

"Is there something I should be aware of?"

The psychiatrist chuckled:

"Not really, but I, rather we, would surely like to find out what caused your cousin's mental breakdown."

Waving a hand at Caron's anticipated response, the doctor hastened to remark:

"I know, I know, he was the sanest and healthiest man till he suddenly lost his mind. Some emotional shock, caused by a frightening experience, must have unsettled him."

Caron made for the door, he appeared to be anxious to leave. Dr Warren called after him:

"You don't know what happened, Mr Caron?"

"Doctor, I have told you before, the answer is no."

Dr Warren seemed to disbelieve him, judging by his ruffled demeanour.

Some weeks later Leroy started to get restless. Although he didn't say much, Caron sensed that something weighed on his mind. He hemmed, cleared his throat, and at times stared vacantly into space. Was he relapsing into that frightful state of stagnation coupled with amnesia? Caron needn't to have worried on that account, yet another source of concern manifested itself. An eerie feeling almost overpowered him that cousin Leroy's putative vacant stares were in reality directed at him. He was being sized up, like a victim chosen by a predator watching for a chance to pounce. When Leroy finally spoke, Caron heaved a sigh of relief.

"Gil, I'm going back home," he announced.

"Oh, I am sorry to hear it," Caron replied while drawing a deep breath.

It was understandable, he assured Leroy, that one's place of birth holds an irresistible attraction.

"I too have to dry many a tear when thinking about our childhood and youth, living among genuine folks in a natural environment. But homesick or not, I cannot pull up stakes now, no, old chap, this luxury is beyond my reach."

Yet Leroy did not budge; he appeared to have forgotten about the intention to move. Was he averse to undertake the journey for lack of resolve or pecuniary reasons? Caron wondered. But he quickly repudiated the notion, since he realised that his cousin possessed ample means to lead a life in revel and riot up in the back country. What kept him in this place where unpleasant memories must surely be present day and night? Life back home in northern Quebec is gentler, Caron knew, reminiscences are kinder to an errand soul. Surrounded by one's own sort who speak the same language, and adhere to ancestral mores, should affect Leroy beneficially. So why didn't he go back? In a fit of candour Caron admitted what he dared not mention aloud. Cousin Leroy's presence made him feel uneasier by the day. His stares grew more intrusive, less furtive, and outright worrisome. Caron perceived them as daggers honed with malevolence, dipped in bile and poison, and aimed at him.

What was going on? Were his eyes deceived by pangs of guilt which Schiller called an evil unexcelled? Maybe so, Caron granted, but just the same, cousin Leroy's creepy deportment entitled one to feel apprehensive. To begin with, he doggedly avoided him like someone infested with leprosy.

Suddenly everything began to change; rather Leroy's disposition did. He became chatty and obliging, yes, even jocular as in the days back home. To Caron's surprise, as much as annoyance, he started to play tricks on him again. Evidently anxious to make amends for his past misbehaviour, Leroy went out of his way to please Caron. He did everything but cut capers for his cousin's amusement.

One morning Leroy approached him with cap in hand, as it were.

"Gil, I have been sorely amiss in my duties."

Surprised, but no less leery, Caron raised his head.

"In what way, Leroy?"

"Let's call a spade a spade, and a fig a fig. I have conducted myself abominably lately."

"Oh well, Leroy, fate hasn't exactly been benign to you," Caron intimated.

"That's not your fault, cousin Gil."

"Yes, it is," Caron was about to blurt out, but he managed to mind his tongue.

If Leroy noticed his cousin's temporary discomfort, he glossed over it. He chuckled.

"Anyway it's all over now as you can see. So let me tell you, next week I am going home."

Seeing Caron's inadvertent pout, he hastened to add:

"This time I'm serious, the necessary arrangements have already been made."

When cousin Gil expressed regrets about the impending departure, Leroy's countenance acquired a sardonic aspect; yet only for an instant. Within the beat of a heart he beamed from ear to ear again.

"Gil, I have a request to make."

"Well?"

"Before I leave I would dearly love to hike up the Seymour Mountain once more; in your company of course."

"Most certainly. When would you like to go?"

"On the weekend."

"Alright. Any particular place?"

"The same as last time, if it suits you."

They set out on Saturday morning and never returned.

About a week later they were found at the bottom of a ravine with broken limbs. Of course both were dead. The authorities were unable to identify the corpses. Advertisement, as much as general inquiries, achieved no results. The compulsory coroner's inquest shed little light on the strange occurrence. Witnesses were not stepping forward. With the exception of the two hikers who discovered the bodies, none others showed up. The police presented disquieting evidence, thus confuting the notion of a straightforward accident.

Here are the investigator's words:

"They were locked in a dog-fall, meaning like combatants going down together. Even more significant, one of them had a hangman's halter around his neck. To sum up: Physical combat probably preceded the fatal fall.

The jury, evidently at sea, rendered a judgement:

"Accidental death under mysterious circumstances."

Life went on in the villages along the north shore of the Gaspe Peninsula. Since the closure of some mines in Murdochville, many younger men left, whereas the older ones reverted to the way of life their forebears practised; fishing, and hoping for a miracle. The town of Murdochville, where copper once reigned, had shrunk from five thousand inhabitants to less than eight hundred. But now even the die-hards whispered about pulling up stakes. Beyond the horizon the faraway town of Sept-Iles on the north shore of the Gulf was rumoured to be the next El Dorado. Eyes, filled with longing, gazed across the open stretch of water. Expectations, gradually diminishing, were rising again; dying dreams came to life once more.

Disquieting news reached Lucien Marteau in Gros-Morne. He advised Victor Nantes and Lionel Grafton of Gil Caron's letter addressed to him. They met at the local brasserie, where they huddled like thieves in the night, and whispered in each other's ears.

Marteau announced:

"Leroy is coming back."

They stared at each other uneasily.

"Does he – does he remember?" Nantes asked.

"Gil believes he does, but he is not certain."

"What of it?" snickered Grafton with a defiant pout.

"Don't be a fool, Lionel," hissed Nantes while giving him a kick in the shins.

"I agree, fellows, don't take it too lightly, we could be made criminally liable," suggested Marteau.

Seeing Grafton's smirk, he snapped:

"Grin all you want, but remember, caught together, hanged together."

Nantes concurred:

"Lucien is right. Leroy might reveal what we cleverly covered up so far, so let's discuss ways to save our necks."

"Save our necks?" Grafton mimicked.

"Ah, don't mind Victor, he always sees tomorrow's clouds in today's sunny sky," chuckled Marteau.

Nantes shook his head reprovingly:

"Don't delude yourselves, what we have done will hardly win us laurels."

"Perhaps not, but neither do we deserve wreaths of thorns," protested Marteau. "After all it wasn't done out of spite," he added.

Grafton concurred:

"I doubt that the law would step in."

Nantes remarked:

"Maybe not, but Father Therrier might. As we all know it is best not to tangle with him. He will curse us by bell, book, and candle, if our caper comes to his attention."

Grafton moaned:

"What a clown that Leroy is, why must he come back."

But of course neither Leroy nor Gil Caron returned. They couldn't, since both lay in nameless graves in North Vancouver's cemetery.

Work in the Murdochville mines grew scarcer by the week. Pink slips were handed out with promises:

"When circumstances improve you will be recalled."

The consolation offered, though well meant, became chilled before they died away. Miracles are difficult to achieve, even if invoked with religious fervour by professional enchanters. The hollowed out mountains had served a purpose; the devastated grounds were exploited, they contained little copper anymore. Men, born and raised in the villages, began to wander off; they were looking for greener pastures. Some made it to Montreal; others, impecunious or close to it, got stuck in Rimouski, where they laboured to earn enough money for a berth on the ferry to Sept-Iles.

Winter arrived early that year, soon the entire province lay under a carpet of snow. Childhood friends of the remote villages drifted apart. Since writing was never their long suit, they eventually lost track of each other. Most men, and women for that matter, who moved away from their ancestral villages, were haunted by heartbreaking nostalgia that brought tears to their eyes, and prayers to their lips. The young ones soon forgot their roots, whereas the older ones became entangled in them.

Lucien Marteau, being better off than most from the area, took it easy for awhile. He rambled upstream along the Saint Lawrence River, past Quebec, then westward to Montreal. The bustle of the city almost frightened the bucolic, used to a humdrum existence among congenial people aspiring to similar aspirations.

Awed by the reckless gaiety, and bewildered by the many languages spoken, he kept to himself at first. Whereas at home conformity was the measure of a man, variety in his new environment seemed to be a way of life. Marteau felt intimidated by the vitality of the people; especially the young ones appeared to be irrepressible.

On a warm, sunny day the atmosphere along Ste-Catherine Street crackled with exuberance, which he had never met before. After awhile he began to like the stir of his new surrounding, thus he decided to settle down; for some time in any case.

Being of a parsimonious turn he started to look for work immediately. At the beginning Marteau shied away from people. Being bashful by nature, especially towards strangers, he kept his distance. Yet after he had found employment, Marteau ventured to visit restaurants and places of entertainment. Although he could never be called a man about town, the fisherman, turned miner, gradually entered into the spirit of his new surrounding.

A fellow worker introduced him to the Hieronymus Club; a most extraordinary establishment. Keen-minded men and women gather there to relate tales reminiscent of those told by Baron von Münchhausen; in other words they were required to be high-flown, bizarre preferable, and short.

Marteau joined reluctantly. His co-worker almost had to take him by the seat of the trousers and walk him Spanish all the way. He instantly liked the place; not only the imaginative decor, but also the members. Concerning the stories offered, well, that was a horse of a different colour. But being an uneducated, meaning unschooled rustic, he voiced no judgement.

When one day someone looked at Marteau and said:

"It's your turn, sir," he almost jumped in the air.

"We did not bargain for that," his mien expressed.

"Yes, Lucien, old man, you are next. Don't forget the tale must be related in the first person," his co-worker reminded.

Marteau protested:

"I – I can't tell stories."

"Don't act coy, such are the rules. Every member must tell a tale when his or her turn comes," he was advised.

Marteau still balked, he simply felt not up to it. Realising that his back was against the wall, he tried to gain time.

"Give me time till I think of something," he requested.

It was a demand that caused brows to knit, and countenances to grimace, since everyone understood that tales ought to be concocted in advance. Heads turned towards each other, miens bespoke annoyance, but also a willingness to postpone the new member's citation till they meet again.

It proved unnecessary, for Marteau suddenly changed his stance. Sporting a foxy grin, he advised:

"Alright, I shall tell you a story."

Faces lit up, chairs were moved closer towards the dais where the narrator sat. Here is Lucien Marteau's tale:

"As you probably inferred from my accent and deportment I hail from the backwoods of Gaspe. Let me say this: We are a mischievous lot, inspired by a propensity for practical jokes. For a laugh we play the fool, for a guffaw we cut capers. From the day we rise onto our feet, horseplay is essential to us like air to breathe. As we grow older some of our pranks become legendary."

Marteau paused, then, after casting nondescript glances at his listeners, he continued:

"Leroy, Gil Caron's cousin was a consummate prankster, known between Ste-Anne-des-Monts and Petit-Cap. Playing tricks appeared to be endemic in that fellow. Rain, shine, sweltering heat, or bone-cracking cold, cousin Leroy was on the prowl for victims. Some of his capers were silly, others farcical, and more than a few bore the stamp of crudeness.

Believe me, there came a time when these escapades got under our skins."

Marteau took a breather. He glanced at his listeners to gauge their reaction, which seemed favourable, judging by demeanours all around.

"Hm, not bad for a clodhopper," they implied.

"One day I met Lionel Grafton and Victor Nantes at the local tavern, where we heaved more than a few. Gil Caron, Leroy's cousin, joined us later. Despite liberal elbow bending the wonted conviviality remained absent. Quite the contrary; after every clank of glasses our spirit sank. The reason? A weight lay on our minds which none wished to broach. Cousin Leroy, Gil Caron's relative, was the source of our inhibition. Deemed true as touch, generous to a fault, his absorption with practical jokes slowly became a mania squarely aimed at us.

" 'Gil, I can take no more,' Nantes burst out.

"Further explanations were superfluous, we knew what Victor meant. Grafton, who suffered more than anyone else from Leroy's escapades, spoke up:

" 'I have had it neck and crop with these larks,' he moaned.

"After lengthy discussions we still remained irresolute how to stave off Leroy's detested habits."

Marteau raised his head and turned in every direction, trying to take the pulse of his audience, who appeared to be attentive.

"Did I say that we wished to wean cousin Leroy from his vile practices? Well, we did it, and for good to boot. A week later we heard that old man Petand lay on his deathbed. That gave us an idea which served two purposes. Besides, being a pleasant diversion, it might teach cousin Leroy a lesson."

Marteau fell silent again, a peculiar glint entered his eyes that intrigued his listeners, who were all ears now and hung on his lips, expecting to miss not a single word. As often happens men from rural districts possess a narrator's gift; in fact, Lucien Marteau was a regular raconteur.

"Jean Proust, the local undertaker, possessed an old-fashioned, horse-drawn hearse, which in the past, and even then, was used at times to convey deceased men or women to their places of burial. The handcrafted hearse, a family heirloom, drawn by white horses rigged to the nines, was a wondrous sight. Gil Caron arranged everything. He told Jean Proust a cock and bull story about an outsider who wished to make a short film about funerals of times past. Mr Proust, old and gouty, readily agreed to hire out his hearse and all; even a coffin, for a certain recompense of course. Then Caron approached his cousin Leroy whom he inveigled to assist us. He advised him of old Petand's death, whose family had entrusted Mr Proust, the undertaker, with all funeral arrangements. He in turn, Leroy was told, asked that we perform certain tasks for him.

"We, Victor Nantes, Lionel Grafton, and I agreed to collect the deceased man from the hospital and convey him in Mr Proust's hearse to a designated place for burial preparations.

" 'Will you help us?' Cousin Leroy jumped with heart and soul at the suggestion to act as a deathwatch. In other words he declared his willingness to sit beside the coffin in the back of the enclosed hearse and guard the corpse.

"We set out after nightfall, hoping that in the cover of darkness notice would be avoided. Gil Caron played the coachman, Victor Nantes and Lionel Grafton assisted as co-drivers. Everything proceeded like clockwork. Words fail me to describe the beauty of the starlit night. We collected the corpse as arranged, laid it in the coffin, which we placed inside the hearse. I said there was no hitch but that changed quickly.

"Suddenly a shriek, neither human nor bestial, cleaved the stillness of the night. Cousin Leroy jumped up and retreated to the farthest corner of the hearse, where he stood wide-eyed, while alternating braking out in maniacal laughter and feral howls. As mentioned Leroy guarded the corpse, Gil Caron was the coachman, flanked by Nantes and Lionel Grafton, the co-drivers. Where was I, you may ask? Inside the coffin, prepared to rise from the dead at an appropriate moment. A death mask was hiding my face, whereas my body was clad in a shroud. Slowly, ever so slowly, I lifted up the lid, then rose from the coffin. Cousin Leroy kept screaming till he collapsed. This is the end of my tale. As I told you we cured him of his silly compulsion, but regrettably we also drove him out of his mind."

The audience, somewhat stunned, declared Marteau's story as one of the best ever narrated in the club. He was entreated to relate others in due time.

On the way home his co-worker paid tribute to Marteau's recital:

"My dear Lucien, that was quite a yarn," he praised.

"No, it wasn't."

"But almost everybody thought so," the co-worker protested.

"They thought wrong. It's a true story."

# The Hawks Are Circling

"Why did you come?" Gil Robson asked his brother.

"To see you, my dear brother."

"You are not welcome," the younger man was advised.

Raising his eyebrows in mock surprise, Brent Robson made a sweeping motion with his hand.

"Isn't this huge wilderness large enough for the two of us?"

"It isn't, and you understand me."

"Now, now, dear brother, aren't you a bit harsh with your brother-german whom you used to coddle and piggy-back around the farm?"

"That was a long time ago."

"Can I come in?"

"Tell me first what you want."

"Bruce has been found."

Gil Robson stepped back.

"Come in," he said gruffly.

They sat down. Eyeing his younger brother with pain in his heart, and suspicion etched on his forehead, he inquired:

"Did I hear you correctly, Bruce Holden has been found?"

"Exactly, I have it from the horse's mouth."

Gil stood up. Walking several times around the table, then stopping in front of his brother, he growled:

"Brent, is this one of your silly jokes?"

"It isn't. Of course Bruce wasn't found in body, but his bones were disinterred."

Shrugging his shoulders, pouting disdainfully, Gil chided:

"Did you come all this way to tell me about bleached bones that could be anybody's, even an animal's?"

He was ready to show his estranged brother the door, when a closer look made him desist. The plague of his bosom, a regular harum-scarum, had never looked so serious, nor less worried. Brent was not making this up; not wholly anyway, it flashed through his mind.

"They found his grave?"

"It was too shallow, Gil. You might recall that we had a fierce argument about it."

With a deprecating motion of the hand, Gil said:

"How could I remember when we bickered about everything under the sun in those days."

"So we did, so we did," the brother murmured, while grinning knowingly.

"Brent, are you sure it is Bruce, his skeleton I mean?"

"Quite sure. The place has been sufficiently described to pinpoint it. I went there myself, on the sly of course. The very spot had been dug up and back-filled loosely again."

"Has his name been mentioned?"

"Not yet officially, but wild rumours are flying up and down the Columbia. It must be Bruce Holden, more than a few know-it-all insist. Has he not disappeared suddenly without a trace? Somebody murdered and robbed him, then buried the poor man. That is pretty well the consensus in the area."

Both fell silent for a while, thinking, pondering about that fatal morning. They used to be devoted to each other, but it was no longer the case. They had grown apart over the years, mainly on account of the younger brother's arcane slide into a world of trickery, if not outright baseness, which affected both adversely. The incident with Bruce Holden turned Gil's waning sympathy into enmity and loathing for his kid-brother. For a long time they were inseparable, especially after their parents' death. The family endured a harsh life on the vast prairie that knew no mercy. It aged the parents prematurely; more so during the great drought when the cruel wind lifted the soil from their homestead, which bore seeds and seedlings already. Dejected in spirit, weakened in body, they lost their way in a howling dust storm and became victims of a pitiless fate. The brothers drifted westward, almost penniless, with growling stomachs and misery nipping at their heels. Their spirit rose at the sight of the Rocky Mountains. When they stood at the Continental Divide, an elation gripped them which they had never felt before.

"Gil, do you see what I see?"

"Yes, beauty that has no equal."

"Do you smell what I smell?"

"I think so, the sweet odour of happiness."

Luck was on their side. They staked a claim under the shadow of Tangle Peak in the Columbia Valley where, contrary to all predictions, they dredged gold from a creek forgotten long ago that was treated with disdain by the old-timers. They were contend with themselves, each other, and the world. But regrettably that ease of mind didn't last. The glue, habit and want which held their comradeship intact, became brittle and flaky. Soon they drank no longer from the same cup or ate from the same dish.

Gil asked his brother a plaguing question:

"Did the police contact you?"

"Not yet."

"You know what to say."

"We rehearsed it often enough," a reply followed, dripping with sarcasm.

Gil wanted to be rid of his brother's presence; for good to boot. But the wish from the heart of hearts was weakened by the mind that knew better. Like a vice, though abhorred, yet missed when unavailable, his sentiments towards Brent gnawed at his vitals. No doubt, Brent, as much as himself, would be questioned by the authorities. What will his fickle, treacherous brother say? Then again what could he say without implicating himself. As Brent rose and turned towards the door, Gil called out:

"Who discovered Bruce's grave?"

Brent, forever inclined to levity, sported a broad grin:

"The hawks, big brother, the hawks."

Gil bridled:

"Quit being frivolous," he demanded.

"In a way they did. You remember how they screamed and circled above us at the clearing?"

"They seemed annoyed alright, for reasons I couldn't understand," Gil concurred.

"We disturbed their peace in more ways than one," Brent reminded.

The oblique remark raised Gil's eyebrows, but he remained silent. His brother explained:

"Lou Sharkey set the ball rolling."

"The half-breed?"

"Yes. When he crossed the clearing on his way to our camp, he had what he called an encounter with those hawks. Do you know what he said?"

"I am not a clairvoyant," Gil said tartly.

"When he approached the open space he noticed four hawks circling in the sky, peacefully and majestically as ever. That lofty behaviour changed when he stepped onto the clearing. Uttering eerie cries they spiralled downwards, then circled around, low enough that his heart missed a beat or two. In his own words:

" 'They either wanted to scare me away or direct my attention to something.' "

Gil snorted:

"Sharkey isn't just a half-breed but also a halfwit."

"Maybe so, but he gave it no rest. I remember his parting remark:

" 'Brent, take my word, someone is buried within that clearing.'

"Of course I pooh-poohed the notion, but that moocher took no heed. He pestered the mayor, the newspaper editor, and the police, till they investigated. The rest you know."

He did now, but he would have preferred not to know. Why did Brent tell him anyway, in person to boot? A coded message by post would have sufficed.

On the way out his brother said something that cut him to the quick:

"I think our goose is cooked."

Gil jumped up, his face was a mask of anger. Rushing outside he bawled:

"Don't be a milksop, and don't ever forget we are in this together."

Two weeks passed in which nothing undue happened. Nevertheless, Gil felt that there was something in the wind which he couldn't explain. Yet a presentiment gnawed at his mind that made him think of the sword of Damocles. Inveighing against, ridiculing such wild notions led nowhere, it did not mitigate his fears.

Gil Robson, after an extensive search had found this spot where he intended to lie low for a while. He needed to find inner peace, and forget this recent past. This tract of land in the middle of nowhere suited him like a tee. Situated in the wilds of the Kootenays, across from Kaslo, it bordered on the lake. The land was undulating and forested, with the exception of a large clearing, and somewhat raised. A cabin stood in the middle of the grassy opening. In those days several hundred acres could be had for a song; especially if the property lacked road access, power supply, and telephone connection. The place was ideal for a man who sought seclusion. A small rowboat conveyed him to wherever he wished to go.

Once a week he rowed across the lake to replenish his larder, collect or send mail, plus take care of other matters. Kaslo had taken root in his heart, although one would have hardly thought so. For despite a pronounced courtesy shown to everyone, he wasn't exactly convivial. He liked the inhabitants of the quaint town. People seemed to be blessed with heart-warming insight. They never asked probing questions, thus he had to tell no lies. His name at the post office was registered as Gil Proust. Considering him a recluse, he was left alone by all and sundry.

A week later a message arrived: – Bruce identified – was written on a piece of paper, stuck in a sealed envelope. It bore neither name nor a return address. Puzzled, but also concerned, Gil frowned. How could that be? Who was able to guess a skeleton's identity? He went to the library to do some research. The best explanation he could find was this: A local dentist had Bruce's dental impression on file that showed irrefutable who the skeleton was in the flesh. The supposition was quicker refuted than made; it sounded far-fetched, if not improbable.

On his way back, while still pondering about the note concerning Bruce, an irresistible urge made him examine the sky. Chuckling in amusement, since he could not recall similar impulses before, he nevertheless scanned the firmament. Soon his eyes saw what the mind subconsciously sought: Four hawks were circling above the clearing. Gil murmured:

"How odd, I have never noticed them before."

Watching the birds soar with wonted grace stirred his spirit as always. Their silent presence never failed to instil lofty sentiments in his heart. Even the seldom uttered high-pitched screams, though eerie and feral, did not disturb his serenity. On the contrary, they made him feel strangely alive; always, until now, when they conjured up unpleasant memories, which he tried to forget.

A week later another notice arrived. – A witness has come forward.

Not another syllable was written on the piece of paper, enclosed in an envelope bearing neither a name nor a return address. Gil Robson was alarmed. Before his inner eye rose the spectre of doom, grinning, whetting its fangs. He repeatedly asked himself:

"What had been witnessed? Bruce's burial or–or his mishap?

All day Gil wrangled with reality. He deserved a black belt for bending and twisting the truth. Walking around the cabin, trying to keep his head to the ground, he went over the incident, as he preferred to call it, from every possible angle. That was his intention, yet success eluded him, for an invisible bridle-hand seemed to pull up his head at short intervals, for the sole purpose to observe the hawks. Watching them gliding through the air, effortless, like creatures meaning to assure rather than alarm, Gil's malice towards them grew by the minute. Their motion of harmony did not arouse inner smiles as in the past, nor did it awaken noble sentiments.

"Their days are numbered," he told the restless water below.

Tomorrow he would send these birds of ill omen to wherever birds go at the end. The rifle stood in the corner, ammunition lay nearby, all that he needed was a steady hand and a keen eye. The law? May the devil fetch the law.

On the next morning he loaded the rifle and went outside. The hawks, evidently unsuspecting of rocks ahead, untiringly and majestically soared. When he stepped onto the clearing a most astounding event took place. The hawks, emitting sounds he knew so well, descended rapidly towards him. Then hovering fairly low a minute or two, they dipped their wings and uttered cries he had never heard before. Ascending with lightning speed again, all four flapped their wings while filling the air with their characteristic cack-cack-cack. This exercise was repeated several times. Were they attempting to scare him away? Gripping the loaded rifle with both hands, he aimed to draw a bead at the nearest one when it dawned on him: They were saluting the man who wished to shoot them. Gil Robson wasn't exactly the flower of chivalry, but he did possess a code of honour. Prophets of doom or not, he vowed never to harm them.

He kept the promise, although just barely, for at the sight of these majestic birds he felt the sharp claws of dread at his throat. Their presence evoked a constant reminder of a nagging predicament: Should he act or wait? Not that temptation, the hussy that never shuts an eye, did not rush him occasionally. When this happened he beseeched heaven and earth to stand by him. Yet he foresaw the outcome; giving in was the norm.

With fury in his heart, and the song of vindication in his ears, he rushed in and out of the cabin. With the rifle in his hands, and curses on his lips, he took aim and pulled the trigger. Click, click, click it went. Nothing further happened, except that his brow smoothened, and a smile stole to his lips, aimed at the foresight that bid him to leave the gun unloaded, and put away the bullets.

For three days and nights a northwester blew down from the snow-covered mountains, tossing up the lake and bending treetops. Gil Robson never failed to be strangely affected by these storms. They stirred his soul and honed his mettle. Even a corn-levelling tempest did not daunt him. Quite the opposite happened; squally weather lifted his spirit. At such times he was ready to fight the gods. But not now, he felt on edge and intimidated. Should he take a chance and brave the churned water? A closer look at the foaming waves gave him the answer; better wait. The hawks were circling, seemingly undeterred by the furious wind. He watched them with envy in his heart. How easy it is with those mighty wings, and time immemorial skills to accomplish what, should he attempt it, might well signify a grave at the bottom of the lake.

Robson was on pins and needles, to say the least. Realising that he had no choice but to wait till the storm subsided, he went inside. The anticipated message weighed heavily on his mind. What would it be? Nothing agreeable, he surmised. More grief was pursuing him in full cry; namely, his brother's fickleness. Will he sing in tribulation? Talk out of school in exchange for expected rewards, or tell tales for the sole purpose to cadge flattery? Quite likely, Gil granted. He asked himself again and again: How much does Brent know? He was quite certain that he did not witness the …. the accident. But of course he was present at the burial.

Gil recalled vividly what took place on that cold afternoon. Clouds hung over the valley, the peaks were already covered with snow. On a clear day it was a sight to behold, but not on that day. An atmosphere of gloom lay in the air which, however, did not match the despondency pervading their camp. The brothers were quickly reaching a point of no return. Brent's behaviour, enigmatic for some time, became untenable. Moping, even though deemed detestable to Gil, he could have put up with, but not moroseness that culminated in morbidity. Besides, he had fits of delusions, like now for instance.

"Brent, what is bothering you?" Gil asked.

Lowering the binoculars with a censorious gesture, his brother snapped:

"Don't you see them?"

"See what?"

"The hawks, Gil, the hawks."

Did Gil blanch? He couldn't say, but his hands surely shook when he accepted the proffered binoculars. Brent chuckled:

"I notice you don't like what you see."

"Why should it upset me? It's a common enough sight."

"Not here, Gil, not here."

Shrugging his shoulders Gil walked away. Thirty minutes later he saw his brother walking towards the clearing some distance due north. Being hailed he turned angrily and hollered:

"Don't interfere, there is something amiss over there. I'm on my way to find out what it is."

Gil could have told him in two words what attracted the hawks' attention: Bruce Holden, or rather his remains. But he reined his tongue and waved Brent on.

Two hours later his brother returned in a veritable snit.

"Bruce is dead," he announced as soon as he came within shouting distance.

"So he is," Gil almost said, but he restrained himself.

Brent, whose deportment could have no longer been described with civil words, now became outright aggressive. Like a berserker of yore he raved and lamented, while several times shaking a fist almost in his brother's face. Gil feared for his safety, because Brent, of Herculean built, although being of two minds, was still of one strength. Yes, he would forever remember that clammy November afternoon when his reason took leave and his senses went blind. Laying the blame for his mistake of a lifetime at Brent's threshold salved his vanity for a while, but not anymore. All went to plan till then. Two months had passed since he pushed Bruce off a cliff. It was time to pull up stakes; for him to move on, for Brent to spend the winter in Invermere. They knew in their heart of hearts that this time the separation would be long, if not forever. They felt terribly lonely in each other's company, desolate, plus on edge. Clouds of rancour darkened the one-room cabin. Bitterness had built an impenetrable wall between them that rose and widened by the day. Of course a friendly smile or hearty embrace would have blown that barrier asunder. But it was not meant to happen. Both were ensnared in sentiments that deserve no mention.

Looking outside he moaned. The hawks, who circled high up in the sky, breasting the storm, awakened memories which he had intended to lay to rest. He must forget that shameful deed; forget or perish.

Gil rose and went outside while cursing Lou, the half-breed, along with his progenitors and descendants. What business did that snoop have so far up-river? As he walked on, watching the waves on the lake, listening to the rush of the wind, his brow furrowed and his countenance acquired a puzzled aspect. Pondering for awhile, he realised what bothered him. It was this: Lou Sharkey, a half-breed from Wilmer true to his tribe's tradition, would never co-operate with the authorities, let alone rubbing shoulders with them. Didn't Brent say that Lou not only advised the police, but insisted upon a thorough investigation. Hm, that does sound fishy, Gil allowed.

His thoughts reverted to their claim beyond the Purcell Mountains, more specifically to the day when enmity engulfed him and his brother. Brent grew violent, for reasons incomprehensible to anyone endowed with a grain of sense. He remained adamant; Bruce had to be buried without delay. He berated his brother, Gil that is, with such vehemence, in an ominous undertone which made Gil uneasy. An acrimonious argument ensued that widened the chasm between them; in fact, it made it unbridgeable.

"Listen to reason, Brent, we have no other responsibilities except notifying the authorities when we get back to town."

His brother wouldn't hear of it.

"We must bury him. We must! We must!" he yelled at the top of his lungs.

Exacerbated beyond endurance, Gil exhorted his brother:

"It's called tampering with a corpse, which is a felony to my knowledge."

But Brent paid no heed; he appeared to be in a frenzy that needed to run its course. To this day Gil did not understand why his brother insisted on a fool's errand of neither rhyme nor reason, that was a felony to boot, thus might result in dire consequences. He, Gil, had nothing to fear. The most prudent path to take was this: Do nothing, and pretend to know even less. He harboured no wish to partake in a perilous undertaking that might land him in a jail. As things stood then, should the authorities get wind of Holden's death, what of it? He worked a claim up-river from theirs, which they almost never visited. He probable had an accident and died, as many loners did, and still do. But he realised that before the end of the day he must make a decision: Either take part in Brent's irrational scheme or move on prior to sunset.

His brother was getting insufferable; he grew more hysterical by the minute. He shadowed him while lamenting with greater conviction than Jeremiah could ever have done. His conduct, piteous to be sure, downright menacing at times, engendered a feeling of anxiety in Gil.

"Bruce needs a Christian burial," his brother wailed.

"Maybe so, but not with my assistance."

Looking back he found it odd that his brawny brother begged for help to perform a rather easy task.

"Why don't you do the job alone?"

A bolt from the blue would have had less effect than these words. Shocked to the core, and surprise mixed with dismay reflecting on his face, Brent gasped. He didn't, probable couldn't, utter a syllable. It was frightening to behold; it made Gil wish to be elsewhere, to flee from the spot and never return. But as several times before he suppressed the temptation, for the mere thought conjured up silhouettes of their childhood and younger years, when they were one soul in two bodies. Finally Gil relented. They buried Holden, mangled and strangely contorted, without the benefit of clergy. It was a mistake, but seemingly unavoidable.

On the way back Brent's deportment changed drastically. A little while ago he acted like someone tormented by snarling fiends, yet now he appeared to be at peace with himself and the world. He smiled, spoke calmly, and seemed anxious to make amends.

"I gave you a rough time, Gil," he intimated.

"So you did," came an acerbic response, and then a question:

"Why were you bent on doing something that profits no-one, yet could harm us?"

"Bruce deserved a Christian burial."

"He did not," exclaimed Gil.

Being in a conciliatory mood, Brent offered no rebuttal. Gil, still annoyed on account of his compliance, grumbled discontentedly:

"We interfered with a corpse, I'm sure it is against the law."

A smile stole around Brent's pursed lips, his face acquired an expression Gil knew so well. It reminded him of the days when they wandered over the vast, windswept prairie, thanking heaven to be alive. Nodding, cocking his head, Brent said:

"We did, but who knows it?"

"What do you mean?"

Brent gave no answer; he didn't have to, his brother understood. There and then they vowed never to breathe a syllable to anyone concerning Holden's burial.

The gusts came more frequent during the night. Gil recognised the signs; the storm was blowing itself out.

In the morning he pushed the boat into the still choppy water. The crossing, while no longer life threatening, nevertheless did offer a degree of risk. Driven by an urge that overpowered reason, he panted and rowed on. Progress was slow; it could have been faster had he not lowered the oars every few minutes and scanned the sky. The hawks were circling, all four soared in that inimitable fashion; silently and ominously.

The expected note was there alright – The police are on our trail – it said. Plagued by conflicting feelings he rowed back. The more he neared the opposite shore, the heavier felt his oars. He stopped rowing; the need to reflect became overwhelming.

"What could happen to me?" he mused. "Not much," he decided.

Even if Brent talked out of school, the law could hardly touch him. Beyond giving him a slap on the wrist for failure to advise the authorities, he had nothing to fear. But what about the message that a witness had stepped forth?

"Balderdash," he snorted, "witnessing what? Bruce's tumble from the Cochran Cliffs? Not likely," he decided.

"There was no-one near to give testimony to what happened, and my lips are sealed," he promised once more.

"Forget about the witness who is probably a tattletale, a show-off seeking the limelight."

Viewing the situation rationally soothed his nerves and lent renewed strength to his arms. Soon he detected the shadows in the sky; the hawks were still circling. When he approached the shore Gil slowed down in order to observe them a bit closer. As his eyes followed their inimitable flight, contradictory sentiments assailed him. One moment the sight of those graceful birds, from the bosom of an untamed wilderness, lifted his mind to the gates of elation. The next instant he felt drawn into a Serbonian bog. The cause of this feeling of dread he dared not name yet, although deep down he divined what made his life a sea of misery. Fear from the law? Hardly, he admitted, since not even sufficient circumstantial evidence existed to lay charges against him. No, that wasn't the source of Gil's discomfort, a much greater antagonist beset him; his conscience was on the prowl. Did he commit a dastardly deed without justification? Lately he catechised himself increasingly concerning an act that ceased to bestow satisfaction. Revenge is sweet, the saying goes, but his was turning sour.

Bruce Holden, a man on the wrong side of middle age, over twenty years his senior, had been a neighbour on the prairie, where anyone within three miles is deemed as such. They hardly associated with each other. For some reason their parents avoided him assiduously. Should his name be mentioned, they exchanged glances pregnant with meaning. Something untoward must have happened years ago, the brothers surmised, that wasn't dead and buried yet. While no overt enmity existed, the parents seemed rather wary of their neighbour.

"Oh well, you know how old folks are. They either trust wholeheartedly or not at all," Gil advised his younger brother.

One day his father became unwontedly chatty; he talked about the Holden homestead. What stirred him Gil couldn't have said. The blue sky over the sunlit country perhaps, or the feral calls of coyotes that greeted the day? That was neither here nor there. Gil was more than eager to learn about his parents' relationship, rather lack thereof, with their enigmatic neighbour, known as the man about town. They could see the farm in the distance near a gravel road. Even from afar the place looked run-down, forsaken, and forgotten.

"It wasn't always like that," his father explained. "The previous owners kept it in shipshape. They worked the land, made improvements, and were an asset to the community.

Knowing that someone like them lived nearby, made one rise early in the morning, and fall into bed with a thankful sigh in the evening."

"Why did they sell?"

"They didn't."

"Oh?'

His father, a man buffeted by the winds of fate, fighting windmills at times, fell silent. He lived by the tenets of the three wise monkeys.

"What happened, father?" Gil prodded.

"Holden tricked them. They took out a mortgage with the Royal Bank in Regina, which he managed. In short, he somehow contrived to obtain the property with unethical, albeit legal means. It is a sad story, best to be forgotten."

"The story or the man?"

"Both."

Gil and his brother were not keen on husbandry. Both worked and lived in Moose Jaw. After the death of their parents they decided to sell the property and move on. They realised that farms of less than a quarter section changed hands but sporadically. Thus they harboured scant hope for a speedy sale and gain. Since they sensed more than a whiff in the air that their jobs were on the line, they started packing. Then fortuity intervened; not only once, but twice.

Gil met Arnold Metzner in town, who was known far and wide as a trader with a shady reputation. He never seemed to work, yet was always sitting pretty.

"How is he doing it?" folks asked.

The older, hard-bitten farmers took to their heels at the sight of him. If asked why, they shrugged and went their way. Did they take exception to his glibness or affability? Gil didn't think so, for country people can be quite talkative, and prone to spread the news, meaning rumours. Then what quickened their steps when they saw him coming? His generosity, so to speak, for he always had something to give away. That in itself made these tight-fisted plainsmen suspicious, though not resentful. Such sentiments were attributable to the strings attached, which unfailingly accompanied these gratuitous offers. Mere gossamers they were, in Metzner's words. Who can take

umbrage at trifles like unpaid taxes or smidgens of a fee, when
fortunes can be made overnight?

"There he is, my old buddy, Gil Robson, just the man I want
to see," Arnold hollered.

Since it was too late to duck, Gil acknowledged Metzner
with a wave of the hand, but walked on.

"Stop right here, Gil, I got something for you."

They went to a nearby tavern to talk things over. Metzner
had a lot to say; many projects were on the roster, numerous
bargains waited to be scooped up.

"I hear you are heading out."

"Yes."

"Is Brent going with you?"

"He is."

Metzner lowered his head, while glancing in every
direction. Observing his opposite with simulated indifference,
he reached in his pocket. The gesture made Gil vigilant, he
divined what was coming. True enough Metzner fished out a
paper, which he held up as if it were a page from the book of
books.

"Did I hear you say you aim to move farther west?"

"Yes, to British Columbia," Gil replied.

"Hm, what a coincidence."

Tapping the paper with a finger, Metzner advised:

"You are in luck, old boy, I own a placer claim in the
Kootenais."

"I am not interested."

"Said ignorance, but sense boxed her ears," Metzner said,
then changed the subject.

"I am sorry to hear what happened to your parents."

"Yes, it is sad," Gil agreed.

Arnold Metzner couldn't be called a Thessalian, meaning
deceitful or fraudulent, but just an inveterate salesman. True,
he resorted to tricks of the trade at times, but his conscience
was never pricked by remorse. I am providing a service,
necessary and no less entertaining, he told himself and the
world. He liked the Robsons, they were cut from a similar cloth
as his forbears. He contemplated Gil with sympathetic eyes and
an expression that signified compassion.

"What happened exactly?"

Gil, though reluctant to talk about it, commented:

"They lost their way in that early, unexpected sandstorm, which everyone will remember, be it only on account of the sudden drop in temperature. That's all I can tell you."

Metzner shifted uneasily while hemming and hawing as if undecided whether to say something that weighed on his mind. Annoyed by his stare, Gil grumbled:

"Something wrong with me?"

"No, no, I'm just debating with myself whether to tell you about an experience I had."

Chuckling, Gil advised:

"Decide quickly, because I'm on my way out."

"Well then. About a week ago Bruce Holden stumbled in here."

Seeing Gil's raised eyebrows he hastened to add:

"Yes, stumbling is the word, he was obviously in the wind. When he saw me, he waved and approached my table. He evidently was looking for a father confessor. Hardly had he sat down when I noticed his muddled condition; he wanted to get something off his chest."

Gil interrupted:

"Arnold, get to the point."

"Patience, cry the lepers. But anyway, here is what I learned. Bruce beat about the bush for awhile. Pouting one moment, grimacing the next, he finally blurted out:

" 'Those stuck-up pretenders got their comeuppance.'

" 'Who are you referring to,' I asked?

" 'The Robsons,' he exclaimed.

" 'Oh, you dislike them?'

" 'Yes, the whole clan is hateful to me,' he admitted. I laughed in his face.

" 'You are drunk, Bruce, go home and sleep it off,' I advised.

" 'I am drunk? Maybe, maybe not.' Leaning forward he sneered:

" 'But let me tell you they got their just dessert. And you know what?'

"After he had turned in every direction he looked straight at me:

" 'I served it to them,' he sputtered.

"I was about to rise and walk away, when something in Holden's demeanour stopped me."

"Oh, what was it?" Gil asked.

"A diabolical grin, dripping with malicious glee, spread across his face. Give him horns, I mused, and there sits the devil and something worse. I was consternated, to say the least. If the truth be told, I felt a compulsion to cut and run, but I lacked the strength to rise. An awful notion overwhelmed me which I could not have named then, yet now I can."

"What is it?"

"Let me explain first what happened next. I asked Bruce what he meant by: 'I served them their just dessert.' He started, then looking at me sideways, muttered in his beer:

" 'Did I say that?'

" 'You sure did. In fact, you said more.'

"Quite cowed now, trying to sober up, struggling with emotions, he stared at me.

" 'Those stuck-up pretenders got their comeuppance,' I remember him saying. Strange, I thought, that he would gloat over someone's cruel fate, who have never harmed him, by his own admission. You asked about my notion? Let me explain. I suddenly realised that Holden harboured a grudge against your parents, which rankled like a worm that feeds on itself. An opportunity arose to satisfy this craving."

"Do I understand you correctly?" Gil asked somewhat amused.

"I think you do. Holden refused to shelter your parents, thereby causing their death."

"Nonsense, he was not even at home during the storm."

"So he stated at the inquiry, I am told. But listen to this. After concluding a deal, we wet our whistle a bit more. Then I casually referred to the sandstorm, which missed me by miles, since I was out of town. I asked Holden if it wouldn't be more sensible to board up the house and stay inside at the first sign of a sandstorm."

" 'Most certainly, that's what I did when the last one ravaged our area,' he answered.

" 'You were at home when the Robsons knocked?'

" 'That's what I just said,' he growled, then sucked in his breath."

Gil frowned as if trying to connect loose ends.

"He was drunk you said," he commented.

Chuckling, Metzner remarked:

"When Holden realised his mistake he became cold sober. Anyway, I sold him a gold claim before we parted."

"You did?"

"Yes."

"Where? if I may ask."

"Some distance upriver from the one I offered you."

"A hundred dollars you want for it?"

"Not a cent more, not a penny less."

After the transfer was duly notarised, they parted company.

That occurred over a year ago. Subsequently Gil and Brent took possession of the newly acquired placer claim. The yield was sparse, but luck proved plentiful. After the dollar went off the gold standard, the value of gold rose fifteen-fold. The brothers were in clover. They accumulated a small fortune within several months. Bruce Holden must have got wind of the transaction, for he showed up right after. His appearance changed their lives; it was the second fateful coincidence.

Presently Gil stood outside of his cabin and watched the circling hawks, who kindled his uneasiness. He tried to forget the past, overshadowed by fears. Live in the presence, enjoy the beauty of the land, unspoiled and soul-lifting, reason urged. But her well-meaning advice was tossed to the winds by portents that refused to yield.

Night fell. Gil went inside, lit a candle and sat down to read. All in vain; concentration proved elusive, images rising from the depth of a tormented mind blotted out the lines before him.

In the morning clouds started to form. Although being nothing more than fleece, Gil recognised their significance; the squally months were approaching. He hesitated no longer; a trip to Invermere became imperative. Brent's silence seemed inexplicable; no further notes had been received. Thoughts he couldn't stave off raced through his mind. Some rather wondrous, like the one whether he should make a confession.

Snow hadn't fallen yet in the Columbia Valley, but the northeaster, pushing down from the high mountains, bearing the icy breath of the glaciers, made people muffle up and hurry along. Gil was on his toes, he avoided people as much as possible. It was no small feat in a town where life takes place on one street. Somebody hailed him:

"What do you know, the rustic from the prairie," someone shouted.

Before he could make himself scarce, Gil felt a heavy hand on his shoulder. It was Lou Sharkey, the half-breed, from nearby Wilmer, the last man he wished to see; after all he was deemed the author of his grief. Sharkey showed no signs of embarrassment. He shook his hand and said:

"Am I glad to see you."

Gil, in a flutter, blurted out:

"See me, why?"

"Because I am thirsty, but broke."

Looking at Gil, who seemed to have lost his tongue, he put a hand to his ear as if straining to listen.

"Did I hear an invitation?"

Gil, despite his consternation, grinned, while jerking his head towards the hotel.

After customary exchanges about the weather and local gossip, Sharkey asked:

"Where have you been? I haven't seen you for a while."

"I was on the road. How about you?"

"Stuck to the soil as ever."

Gil frowned, then commented:

"You were busy, I hear."

"Busy? Not that I could say."

Lou Sharkey, though thick-skinned, appeared to be miffed.

"Is something bothering you, Gil?" he asked in a rebuking tone.

"Yes, and you know what it is."

Squinting, cocking his head, Lou considered his host closer.

"I do not, so why not tell me?" he suggested.

As Gil expounded, Lou listened attentively, while gradually his face broke out in a flush of anger and disappointment. Raising his hand he declared:

"Call me what you want, but hear this: I have never set a foot on the place you mentioned; in fact, I couldn't even find yours, nor the other fellow's claims."

"What about the co-operation with the police?"

Sharkey made no reply; he broke out in a hearty horselaugh. Slapping his thighs he sang out:

"This is capital, Lou Sharkey snuggling up to the police. Ha, ha, ha, and again, ha, ha, ha."

Lou shook his head so vigorously that his neck creaked.

"Lou Sharkey in cahoots with the police. What a canard! Who put that idea in your head? I would climb mountains, cross torrential rivers, and fight mountain lions in order to circumvent the police. Anybody within a hundred miles knows that."

Gil had heard and seen enough; he took leave from Sharkey and stepped outside. Thorough confused he rubbed his eyes and wiped his brow. Despite the sharp wind that nipped his ears, he broke out in a cold sweat. Thanking his lucky star for the chance encounter with Sharkey, he directed his steps towards the police station; not to give himself up, but to test the waves. He knew the sergeant who greeted him unaffectedly, thus mitigating the pangs of anxiety. Just the same, caution is the mother of wit, he had learned a long time ago. Gil spoke about this and that, while endeavouring to avoid the subject close to his heart. He gingerly steered towards the purpose of his visit:

"Sergeant, I am looking for Bruce Holden, he has a claim up-river from ours."

The sergeant turned to the policeman at the desk, who shook his head:

"I have never heard of him," he remarked disinterestedly.

Gil, a firm believer in the adage about angel visits, thanked the policeman and left.

There we go, he thought, things are shaping up, the clouds were dispersing, albeit not wholly. The messages sent him, bogus from start to finish, were now as before wrapped in layers of mystery. True, Brent's penchant for pranks, innocent at times, but mostly mischievous, had always been a bone of contention between the brothers. But upon those messages adhered neither a trace of mischief, nor a tinge of tricks. They were meant to erect a castle of fear in his mind that would be his companion forever. Why? Well, he intended to find the answer to that perplexing question; tomorrow, and not later.

In his room at the hotel, Gil started to reminisce, not with a forgiving heart, and even less with a culpable one. The time had arrived to look reality in the face. He and brother Brent, their relationship to be exact, stood at the crossroads. With these latest machinations Brent had crossed the Rubicon. Although the reasons for his brother's despicable behaviour were no longer deemed worthy of consideration, curiosity still lurked in the back of Gil's mind. He rapidly lost the compulsion to unriddle Brent's slide into a morass of morbidity. He was not always treacherous and churlish; the opposite was true. But since the death of their parents he gradually became an unconscionable lout. What possible joy or benefit could someone derive from lifting up the heel against his own brother, who coddled him when a child, and guided his way later. Something dreadful must be gnawing at his vitals. An uncontrollable grudge perhaps, that he felt compelled to nurture yet never dared to name?

Midnight had passed, most lights in the village were out. Below, the still ice-free lake shimmered unruffled in the dim light of the moon. Gil couldn't sleep; the sight in the silence of the night awakened tender memories. In the heart of his hearts he pined for the past.

"Brent, what has happened?" he asked no one in particular.

In retrospect he saw himself and his brother as two tiny spots wandering over the boundless plain, whose silence was broken by the eerie calls of coyotes, and the whistling and yapping of prairie dogs. The never-failing wind tussled their hair, joy mirrored in their faces. He felt homesick. Prairie fever, that feeling which invigorates the spirit and endows one with new life, overwhelmed him.

"I am going back," he informed the snow-capped mountains beyond the valley.

At sunrise the next morning he set out. He arrived at their camp four hours later. The cabin was boarded up; Brent had left. Bruce Holden's had also been carefully barricaded. The hawks were no longer circling over the clearing, frozen now, waiting for the first snow of the season. Bruce Holden's burial spot had not been disturbed by the looks of it. Gil couldn't help mumbling:

"Rest in peace, Bruce Holden."

Gil headed homeward to the farm, which had not yet been sold. There were too many on the market, one agent told him. Another advised to stay the sale till further notice.

After a long dreary train ride he arrived, weary and on pins and needles. As expected Brent was there. At the sight of Gil he shrunk back, while scowling like a man cornered. Without any preamble, Gil took the bull by the horns:

"Why, Brent, why?" he asked in a sepulchral voice.

Recovering his self-possession, his brother countered:

"You fool, you pushed the wrong man off the cliffs."

Caught unawares, Gil offered neither a denial nor a confirmation, he just managed to stutter:

"The wrong man, you say?"

"Yes, brother, decidedly so."

As often happens, Gil, trying to jump out of the smoke hopped into the fire. He incriminated himself:

"I hurled the wrong man to his death, who should it have been?"

"I, dear brother. You should have pushed me off the cliffs," Brent advised with a devilish sneer.

"Realising his mistake, Gil played dumb.

"I don't know what we are talking about," he declared.

"Of course you do. Arnold Metzner's narrative fired you up, didn't it?"

Gil was losing his composure fast. Tossing caution into the wind, he protested:

"What do you know about it?"

"More than you think."

Dumbfounded, Gil queried:

"Did Arnold tell you anything?"

"He did, but not the truth."

"Which of course you know," Gil mocked.

There was that leer again, peculiar to a man beset by malevolence directed at himself, borne of fear and shame.

"I do, brother, I do," Gil was told.

Then Brent's countenance changed. While relaxing visibly he leaned back and said:

"I guess you are aware that Arnold Metzner's parents once owned the farm acquired by Bruce."

"I wasn't, but father told me that Holden gained ownership by trickery."

"Perhaps, perhaps not. What is certain is this: Arnold had, probably still has, an axe to grind."

"With Holden?"

"Exactly. For which reason he intended to set us against him. In other words, Arnold invented the entire episode. Yet strange enough something like it happened."

Gil observed his brother with eyes almost well-disposed.

"Brent, you are talking in riddles again," he remarked.

"It's some riddle, you want to hear about it?"

"Of course."

Brent chuckled, then said:

"You are not going to like it."

Gil shrugged as if to say, we shall see.

Brent, evidently loath to call suppressed memories to life, told a hair-raising story.

"Bruce wasn't at home that afternoon when the storm struck."

Gil bridled up:

"Who told you that?" he cried.

Brent darted a withering glance at him that crackled with hate, and dripped with wretchedness.

"No need to be told by anyone. I was the only person in the house during that time."

A bolt from the blue couldn't have disconcerted Gil as much as his brother's utterance.

"Brent, have you lost your mind, are you suffering from delusions?" he cried.

As if transfixed with emotions he didn't understand, Brent stared into space, while murmuring:

"I wish it were true. Here is what happened: I was inside, alone, to be exact, when someone knocked at the door and rattled at the barricaded windows. Bruce, who was out of town, had sent a message to be so good and secure the buildings in case of an approaching sandstorm."

"Somebody wanted to get in? Who was it?"

Brent, looking daggers at his brother, seemed twice on the verge of saying what lay on the tip of his tongue. Twice he desisted. Finally he blurted out:

"How should I know?"

Taken aback, Gil frowned. For an instant he was speechless, since an unwritten law of the plain required that anyone must be offered shelter in a blizzard or dust storm. His frown deepened when something occurred to him.

"Brent, couldn't that have been our parents?" he gasped.

Touched to the quick, Brent's countenance mirrored abhorrence mingled with defiance. He reminded Gil of an animal cornered, yet too perplexed to run away or fight. In a flash Gil realised an awful truth.

"Those were our parents, weren't they?" he moaned.

Brent rose, then staggered backwards. His face turned into a mask of malevolence. Flying into a rage, he bawled at his brother:

"You were always their darling, who was never scolded, but forever right.

" 'Why can't you be like your brother?' I was reminded a dozen times a day.

"They neither wanted to see nor hear me.

" 'Gil, Gil,' all day long. 'Look, how clever he is, how well behaved our boy is,' they praised. Whereas I, the fifth wheel, got smothered with torrents of rebuke."

Gil, walking towards the door, shook his head; then turning and facing his cowering, snarling brother, he had this to say:

"Brent. You are beyond help. This is my lasting farewell."

Two days later he was back at his lonely cabin. The hawks were nowhere in sight. He never felt so forlorn in his life.

# The Sick Father

*H*ow is he, Miss Sklar?" Dr Wisborne asked.
A superfluous question that was, judging by her grief-framed countenance.

"Worse, doctor, he is sinking visibly," she replied.

A painful expression whisked across Dr Wisborne's face. Shaking his head in bafflement, he said:

"I don't understand it, I surely don't. I and my colleagues find nothing wrong on the outside, nor internally for that matter."

"Yet he is wasting away," Judith Sklar, the daughter lamented.

Jake Sklar, the son, chimed in:

"I regret to say it, our dear father's days are numbered."

A deep sigh escaped from the doctor's breast as he climbed the stairs leading to his patient's sumptuous quarters.

"How are you, Mr Sklar?" the doctor queried with pretended exuberance.

Marvin Sklar, a man in his sixties, looked like death's head on a mopstick. Nothing could describe him better than this figure of speech.

"Can you sit up, sir?"

Sklar shook his head with little gusto.

"Not easily," he lamented.

After a perfunctory examination, performed with the conviction of futility, the doctor remarked:

"The prescribed medicine doesn't help, it seems."

"It makes it worse," the patient moaned.

Dr Wisborne chuckled good-humorously, he had heard such assertions hundreds of times. Human nature is such, he knew, that an outstretched helping hand quickly loses its sheen if it does not assuage misery invited by the sufferer, to which he clings determinately. Surely this is what happened here. He, as much as his colleague Dr Berthold Schlier, could find nothing wrong with Sklar; not physically anyway. Consulting a well-known psychiatrist shed no light on the matter. His, Dr Baruch's, diagnosis, spiritual emptiness, made no sense to either one.

"My dear colleague, you mean grief of course," Dr Schlier intimated.

"After all his wife died not too long ago," declared Dr Wisborne.

The psychiatrist considered them with a wise man's scorn:

"Not grief, but chagrin, to be exact."

"Chagrin?" the doctors echoed in one voice.

The psychiatrist's face acquired an oracular aspect. It was his trademark, the mainstay of reputed wisdom that bestowed fame, deference, plus a steady income.

"Exactly. I know the symptoms. The patient has lost the reason for being, his thunder has been stolen, the zest for life no longer exists."

"Because of the loss of his wife?" Dr Wisborne suggested.

It earned him a rebuking glance from the psychiatrist.

"Indirectly, yes."

Dr Schlier frowned:

"How is that to be taken, doctor?"

"Mr Sklar is more vexed than aggrieved on account of his wife's death," they were informed.

That conversation took place several weeks ago, the situation had changed drastically since then. His patient, Dr Wisborne acknowledged, had entered the path of no return. He cradled his chin, as was his habit when perplexed. Sklar, he realised, needed encouragement. But how does one hone the mettle of a man stuck in an oppressive environment? One cannot, was the short of it.

"Cheer up, Mr Sklar, I shall see you again a week from now, at the same time," Dr Wisborne declared.

As he walked out the door, the patient stirred. He expelled a tone that sounded like a cry, rather a moan of distress.

"Doctor, doctor Wisborn, please," he groaned.

It was too late to be heard, the doctor had already closed the door behind him. After giving a short report to Jake the son, and Judith the daughter, he stepped outside.

Later in the day he met Dr Schlier at a restaurant for lunch. His colleague sat already at their favourite table. After exchanging a few preliminaries Dr Schlier inquired:

"How is your patient?"

"Which one?"

Cocking his head as if to say:

"You know whom I mean," he replied:

"Marvin Sklar."

Dr Wisborne shook his head slowly, he wasn't at all pleased.

"That whole affair reeks of an ill omen. I understand less and less of it," he admitted.

Leaning back, he added:

"That sure is an odd family."

"I dare say," concurred his colleague.

"Neither the father, nor son and daughter fit any mold. Certainly scant affection exists between them. That is one of the reasons why Mr Sklar is not convalescing, I should think. Anyway, that whole place makes me feel uncomfortable."

"Now that you mention it, I too felt apprehensive in that house."

"I noticed it," Dr Wisborne acknowledged.

"Why don't you move your patient to a hospital, far away from that place which is evidently haunted by spectres of the past."

"I suggested it, more often than once."

"And?"

Mr Sklar seemed willing at first, but the son, as much as the daughter, balked strenuously at the idea."

"Citing filial concern, of course," Dr Schlier conjectured with tongue in cheek, it seemed.

"Yes, they laid it on heavily, even to the extent of questioning my dedication and medical competence. The son implied that perhaps they should look for another doctor."

"You should have jumped at the suggestion," Dr Wisborne's colleague intimated.

"That thought never took root. I can't tell you why, but I have my reasons."

"I shall not pry, dear colleague, but tell me this: You said a moment ago that Mr Sklar was willing to be transferred at first, but not anymore, I take it?"

"That's correct. He now refuses to budge from that house."

Before the doctors parted they touched on Dr Baruch's perplexing diagnosis.

"Dying of chagrin on account of his wife's death?"

Dr Wisborne chuckled:

"That's his conclusion."

Grimacing, Dr Schlier declared:

"I find that to be a strange assessment; to fret, but not mourn on account of one's wife untimely death."

A week later Dr Wisborne made another sick call. When he stepped into the hall he instantly became aware of the changed atmosphere. Jake and Judith Sklar looked different; unusually subdued it deemed him. The bravado of former days no longer manifested itself; it had given way to diffidence. A peculiar languor adhered to one as the other; their wan faces and awkward movements compelled the doctor to ask:

"What happened, are you sick?"

"No, no, just a bit indisposed," Jake Sklar explained.

When the doctor entered the sickroom he was thunderstruck. His patient sat up and greeted him with raised hands and a smile. The pallor, while still lingering on Sklar's face, no longer reminded one of death's wrap at the door.

"You look better," Dr Wisborne remarked.

"I feel a bit better," Sklar admitted, not exactly enthusiastically.

After a superficial examination, a discussion ensued; about this, that, and the other. Dr Wisborne, preparing to leave, made some encouraging remark:

"Well, Mr Sklar, you will soon be up and about."

"Oh, not so soon, I fear. I still lack the strength to walk more than a few steps, even on a level floor," the patient protested.

Was the doctor mistaken, or did Sklar take measure of him with a shy glance and a cunning smile? Prior to leaving the doctor commented:

"By the way, your son and daughter seem to have caught a virus."

"Virus? Well, the biter will be bitten," Sklar said with a devilish grin that came to haunt Dr Wisborne for a long time.

Two weeks later Dr Wisborne rang the bell at Sklar's mansion. As if struck by lightning he shrunk back. Marvin Sklar, his supposed laid up patient, greeted him effusively:

"Surprised, doctor?"

Seeing his beaming face and jaunty demeanour, Dr Wisborne declared:

"Flabbergasted would be a better description."

"There now, doctor, it shows you what proper medicine can achieve. But do come in."

Dr Wisborne hesitated, since he saw no reason to enter. His patient, hale and hearty now, no longer required medical attendance. Besides, patients were waiting for him at his praxis.

"Come in, doctor, come in," Sklar repeated with more urgency.

"I am a bit pressed for time, Mr Sklar, is there something special?"

Then it occurred to him. Looking every which way, he inquired:

"Where are the youngsters?"

"They are sick. The virus you divined is squeezing the life out of them."

"Oh, are they in the hospital?" the doctor inquired with concern in his voice.

With an inviting gesture Sklar remarked:

"I shall lead you to their sick quarters."

Not quite certain whether he was being made sport of, the doctor followed hesitantly. Sklar knocked at a door, then showed Dr Wisborne in.

"Jake's room is at the end of the hall. Should you need me, I am downstairs or out in the garden," Sklar advised.

One glance at Judith Sklar manifested a simple fact: She was wasting away. Like her father, who miraculously regained health and mental acuity, she was befallen by a frightening lassitude. The sap of life seemed to ebb rapidly from her body. An examination, accompanied by questions, revealed almost identical symptoms afflicting the siblings. Like their father before, they had difficulty speaking clearly; neither one could walk more than a few halting steps. Physical pain, according to them, was totally absent. Yet mental anguish, a feeling of utter despair racked their very being. Not willing to pussyfoot again, Dr Wisborne announced:

"Both of you are going to the hospital."

To his astonishment they consented.

Amazingly their condition improved almost instantly. Three days ago Judith and Jake stood at death's threshold, now they walked without assistance through the halls. The colour of youth returned visibly, as did their gift of the gab.

One morning while eating an early breakfast, Dr Wisborne mulled over the recent past, more specifically he reflected about the Sklar family, whom he found a bizarre tribe. No doubt that mansion had more than one closet occupied by skeletons. Ghosts of the past appeared to be haunting its halls and chambers, whose very atmosphere reeked of malice. Every time Dr Wisborne stepped inside, perceptions of bitter strife, if not smoldering hate, assailed him. The psychiatrist's finding flashed through his mind. He never rightly understood his colleague's diagnosis. The nebulous terms, while gripping his imagination, failed to illuminate his pragmatic intellect. He decided to pay him a visit.

"Dr, do you remember Marvin Sklar, a patient of mine whom you examined?"

Sporting that unfailing grin of a sage sitting on the well of wisdom, Dr Baruch replied:

"I do indeed."

"If it is not to much to ask, could you explain something to me?"

"I can try," he promised, then called out:

"Rosemarie, will you bring the file of Mr Marvin Sklar, please?"

They waited in silence till the documents were laid out, and Dr Baruch had glanced at them.

"What would you like to know?"

Seeking for words to state his request succinctly, Dr Wisborne hesitated for a moment.

"This: Your conclusion that Sklar's morbidity ensued on account of his wife's untimely death, not because of grief but vexation, is unclear to me."

"Simply put Sklar's marriage was not made in heaven. Their mutual resentment, which gradually turned to hate, though for awhile abhorred by Sklar, eventually became his stuff of life; a vital force essential to his existence. Thus her death, probably prayed for many times, he considered to be a dastardly betrayal."

"In other words, vexation, relentless and corrosive, pushed him over the edge?" questioned Dr Wisborne.

"Sort of. You see, he felt abandoned, left in distress. As often happens in such cases he took flight into an illness possessing neither name nor remedy."

Outside, Dr Wisborne, pragmatic from head to toe, pooh-poohed his colleague's notion. He muttered:

"As the fool thinks, so the bell clinks. No, my esteemed colleague, Sklar was sick alright, seriously so, quickly approaching moribundity, my friend. How he managed to recuperate, as if by magic, is a riddle which I intend to solve. The prescribed medicines, pills mostly, could hardly have been a contributing factor towards his rapid convalescence, since they consisted almost solely of placeboes."

At the next hospital visit Dr Wisborne gave Judith and Jake Sklar a clean bill of health; they could go home in other words.

More than a year had past. Old patients fell into oblivion, new ones visited his praxis. The puzzle surrounding the Sklars remained unsolved. Dr Wisborne hardly thought about them anymore. He went to the mansion twice, but each time the place was locked up, and his knocks were not answered.

Spring waned, summer approached. Dr Wisborne got into the habit to wander around Mount Royal, situated in the centre of Montreal. Every Sunday afternoon, swinging his cane jauntily, he enjoyed the 'Music on the Mountain' concert.

One day in late August, whom should he met but Marvin Sklar. He was exuberant with health. Grinning from ear to ear he called out from afar:

"Ah, Dr Wisborne, what a pleasant surprise. How is trade?"

"Good, Mr Sklar, how are things with you?"

"Couldn't be much better, after all the biters were bitten, weren't they?"

Casting a questioning glance at Sklar, the doctor chuckled:

"You made that remark before, what exactly do you mean?"

"You know the adage, I presume?"

"I do, but I can't fathom the connection."

Sklar contemplated the doctor with a look reminiscent of the demon of Cathay; half leer, half anticipated joy over a forthcoming tasty meal.

"One day you will, doctor."

With these words he took his leave.

The encounter not only dampened Dr Wisborn's spirit, but also ruined his day. Growing more listless by the minute, he halted his steps, then walked to a bench where he sat down. Thoughts whisked through his head, some speculative, others unworthy. He never cottoned on to the Sklars, particularly the youngsters, whom he deemed deceptive. The twain never failed to ruffle his composure. Reflecting on incidents of the past, something suddenly occurred to him. Although the siblings resembled each other noticeable, they shared no traits with the father, neither in physical aspects nor in demeanour.

Some months later Dr Wisborne had a visitor. Glancing at the calling card presented, he read aloud:

"Farley Spragg, investigator. Hm, I wonder what he wants," he murmured, then gestured to the secretary to bring him in.

"I won't take much of your time, doctor."

Looking at a clock on the wall, Dr Wisborne advised:

"Ten minutes is the most I can dedicate to you."

"Very well. I am engaged by Marvin Sklar to inquire into the matter of his late sickness, to which you attended."

"Quite so, Mr Spragg."

"You had prescribed medicine to alleviate his almost fatal ailment."

"Yes, yes, come to the point, Mr Spragg."

"The point? It is this: Mr Sklar claims that the pills were killing him by degrees."

"Oh, come now. Are you insinuating that I attempted to poison my patient?"

Farley Spragg considered the doctor with eyes of a picture book sleuth.

"Doctor, do you remember his miraculous recovery?"

"How could I forget."

"Have you a notion what caused it?"

"To be honest, no."

Looking at the doctor with an accusatory mien, Spragg explained, emphasising every syllable:

"He stopped taking your pills."

Dr Wisborne stiffened. Staring at the investigator for an instant, he rose from his chair and walked through the door. When he returned with a file in his hand, he informed the visitor that the scheduled patient agreed to postpone her appointment. Sitting down the doctor said:

"Now, what did you tell me a moment ago?"

"Mr Sklar swears by the bell, book, and candle when he stopped taking the pills, lo and behold, the drying-up sap of life started to gush again."

Dr Wisborne seemed at the verge to say something, but he held his tongue. What he heard could not be denied; the patient's almost sudden mysterious convalescence was inexplicable. Within two weeks the seemingly doomed man had returned into a twittering, prancing wag who thumbed his nose at fate.

"Anything else you wish to tell me?" Dr Wisborne inquired.

Nodding his head the investigator replied:

"Mr Sklar, who realised that the pills were the source of his malady, not only stopped taking them, but he hoarded each and everyone."

Did Dr Wisborne perk up in surprise or alarm? Spragg wasn't sure, but the doctor seemed undoubtedly concerned; even more so at the next words.

"We sent samples to three laboratories."

"Did the results come back yet?"

"One as the other concluded that the samples contained substances which defied analysis. In other words, though potent and pernicious, these components could not be defined."

Shaking his head in disbelief, Dr Wisborne stated categorically:

"Impossible, simply impossible!"

Annoyed at the imagined rebuke, Spragg reached in his briefcase from which he removed an envelope.

"Here are the reports, doctor, convince yourself. You may keep the copies if you wish."

"Don't be cross with me, Mr Spragg, I did not question the veracity of the reports."

Looking up sharply, the investigator exclaimed:

"Didn't I hear you say, impossible, simply impossible?"

"Yes, yes, but I alluded to something entirely different. You see, the prescribed pills were nothing but placeboes."

"Placeboes?" the investigator echoed.

"You know what these are, I presume?"

"Dummies, meant to deceive," suggested Spragg.

"Just that. They contain no medical value, absolutely none," the doctor asserted.

Since the investigator seemed not so fast on the uptake, Dr Wisborne explained:

"Either the prescriptions were wrongly filled…"

"Or?" Spragg cut the doctor short.

"They were exchanged," assured Dr Wisborne.

"By whom?" the investigator called out.

"You are the investigator, Mr Spragg," the doctor reminded his visitor with a tinge of sarcasm.

"So I am, so I am," Spragg muttered while handing a phial containing two pills to the doctor.

"They are from the same lot that were sent to the laboratories. By the way, I understand there was no nurse in attendance."

"No. Mr Sklar never asked for one. Besides, the children were loath to the idea."

"Thus the medicine was dispensed by them?"

"I should think so."

Farley Spragg, who evidently divined more than he knew, spoke those parting words:

"Doctor, you have my card, please feel free to contact me, should you think it necessary."

After the investigator had left, Dr Wisborne read the reports, then examined the pills. His consternation grew visibly. He frowned, telltale creases appeared around his eyes, his mien expressed concern. After all, this whole affair reeked not only of skulduggery, but of attempted murder. Leafing through the file he found what he sought. Checking and crosschecking Sklar's prescriptions confirmed what he had told Spragg; the pills mentioned were each and all placeboes, quite innocuous in other words. Consequently either the prescriptions were wrongly filled or the pills were exchanged. Wrongly filled? Hardly, considering the test reports. Any laboratory worthy of its name would have unfailingly identified the ingredients of any approved medicine. Yet three opinions given by reputable chemists state clearly that the pills are composed of unknown substances, which drug manufacturers are unable to identify. Thus, the placeboes prescribed were exchanged. By whom, and why? Another unsolved riddle sprung up again; namely, the curious incident regarding Jake and Judith Sklar. Both, like their father before, were befallen by that inexplicable lethargy, approaching moribundity, from which they wholly recovered after being transferred to a hospital. Questions supplanted questions. Conjectures made one moment were repudiated the next. Heaving a sigh, leaning back, he promised himself:

"I must stop thinking about it."

A few Sundays later, up on the mountain, he encountered Marvin Sklar again. A woman walked on his side whom he had not seen before. They seemed quite intimate, judging by their dallying behaviour. Sklar appeared to be in a sporting mood.

"Meet my wife, doctor," he said with a prankish mien.

"Your wife? I thought she was dead."

"Tut, tut, doctor, a man is allowed to remarry, isn't he?"

Flushing a bit on account of his perceived tactlessness, Dr Wisborne shook hands with them while he uttered a few inanities. They parted quickly. Sklar couldn't resist turning around while still within earshot and call out:

"Don't forget, doctor, the biter will be bit, ha, ha, ha."

Dr Wisborne, a confirmed bachelor, although having looked at Mrs Sklar, didn't see her. Had one ask him to describe her, the answer would most likely have been:

"Hm, she is a nondescript person in man's attire."

Dr Wisborne vowed to curb or cease his interest in what he called a labyrinth where even thoughts lead nowhere. Promises of course are broken at times, like this one. Wrestling with one's conscience is often a match stacked in favour of temptation.

"Should I?" he asked himself one moment.

"No, and never!" he answered the next instant.

"Why not?" a voice from somewhere taunted.

And so it went till he subconsciously started to pack the pills, then vindicate his intent to send them to a chemist he knew quite well.

The ensuing report coincided on the whole with the others. A postscript, however, made Dr Wisborne perk up. Here it is: The chief chemist, Dr Vincent Duval, had this to say:

"While we cannot identify all ingredients, I harbour a strong suspicion that these pills contain substances that can cause paralysis, if not death, if taken in excess or too long. One should be aware, however, that suspicion often negate facts."

"Dr Duval is trying to tell me something which he dares not state in writing," Dr Wisborne concluded.

A visit to the laboratory confirmed his conjecture.

"What I am going to tell you is off the record of course."

Dr Wisborne nodded:

"That's understood."

Perusing the letter accompanying the samples, the chemist said briefly:

"Your patient's condition deteriorated rapidly."

"Yes. He became indifferent, then torpid, and finally inanimate."

"Despite the fact that you, and your colleagues could find nothing amiss with him?"

"Not physically, beyond signs of lethargy, as mentioned."

Dr Duval contemplated his visitor hesitantly, as if not certain to say what lay on his tongue. He overcame his reluctance.

"Doctor, did you ever hear of the Bizango Society?"

"Never. Who are they?"

"A small group of people that dwell in the Black Mountains of Haiti. This society, maroons mostly, practises one cult or another. They produce a powder which can induce suspended animation."

Noticing a tinge of a sardonic smile hover around the doctor's lips, Dr Duval raised a hand.

"Not so fast, doctor, they can make it, I vouch for it. You see, I lived and worked in Haiti a number of years. Being younger then, plus endowed with a roving nature, I spent many an hour among these furtive people, where I witnessed more than once extraordinary incidents. I am convinced that members of that society, older women mostly, can produce concoctions that induces lifeless conditions."

Dr Wisborne had heard enough, he took his leave.

Contacting Marvin Sklar proved a bit difficult, yet he finally managed it. They met at a restaurant. Dr Wisborne faltered not a moment, he came right to the point:

"Why did your children want to harm you?" he asked.

"They are not my children."

Noticing Dr Wisborne's astonishment, he added:

"I am their stepfather."

Chuckling he said more:

"By the way, they didn't want to harm me."

"They exchanged the placeboes with pills that could prove fatal."

"Quite so, doctor. But saying they wanted to harm me, palliates the truth."

Looking fully at the doctor, Sklar moaned:

"They wanted to kill me."

"But why, sir, why?"

Sklar had a habit when uncertain what to say, to incline and tilt his head sideways.

"To inherit my fortunes, why else?"

The doctor, a delicate man, didn't pursue the matter, which hardly concerned him. His interest lay elsewhere; namely, to ward off blame. His former patient's intentions, admittedly somewhat hazy, nevertheless where a source of discomfort to him. No doubt Sklar was gearing up for mischief. Why now, over a year after the fact, made little sense, but neither did anything else about that unsavoury family.

Sklar appeared to be anxious to get something off his chest, judging by his edginess. With one eye lit up by roguery, the other brimming with malice, he started to talk:

"Remember what I said about the biters will be bit?"

"I do, but now as then I find your words cryptic, to say the least."

"I shall explain. Those two brats got their comeuppance."

"Brats?" echoed Dr Wisborne.

"Jake and Judith."

Hearing someone who approached middle age called brats, evoked a grin on the doctor's part. Sklar paid no heed to it, he got into his stride.

"You see, after the announcement of my impending marriage with a woman no longer young, but far from being old, they, Judith and Jake, were alarmed. There will be less for us, their covetous eyes seemed to say. We must act, we must act quickly, their pinched countenances silently proclaimed. To tell the truth, doctor, I became apprehensive. A week later I was laid up. The rest you know."

The doctor shook his head.

"Not really," he advised.

"Oh, what's missing?"

"The explanation of your stepchildren's inexplicable, as much as sudden, illness."

"You are the doctor," Sklar let it be known.

"So I am, so I am."

Casting a long deliberate glance at Sklar, Dr Wisborne spoke with emphasis:

"Mr Sklar, quit beating about the bush, you are evidently eager to tell me something; so, out with it. Who is the biter that has been bitten?"

"Bitten to the bones, doctor, down to the bones," Sklar snorted.

"What is that supposed to mean?"

"Jake and Judith hoisted their own petard."

"In what respect?" the doctor wanted to know, for after all they were at one time under his care.

"Two weeks ago both were committed to Centre de Crise."

"The mental hospital?"

Sklar nodded, dripping with glee.

"The mental hospital," he confirmed.

Dr Wisborne shrunk back in utter amazement. He offered condolences:

"I am sorry to hear it."

Marvin Sklar, preparing to leave, had this to say:

"Gradually, upon their return from the hospital, the one you had sent them, they changed drastically. More ornery beings I had never encountered. True, I was at no time enamoured with their characters, though they conducted themselves fairly well. Now I began to loathe one as much as the other. I tell you, doctor, the air inside the house, and all around it, was soon saturated with bile and venom. They started to follow me around, literally spitting and hissing and hurling profanities in every direction."

"Had they gone mad?" the doctor wondered.

"To all appearances, yes. At times they calmed down. But all of a sudden another burst of dementia, as I called it, broke out in one or the other, thus infecting the one untouched, who in the twinkling of an eye fell in tune."

Sklar paused for a moment while looking every which way, except at Dr Wisborne. He took up the thread of his report again:

"You may think that I have an axe to grind. In a way, yes, but such sentiments were rapidly supplanted by fear. They had changed not only in demeanour, but even in body. Anyway, my wife eventually gave me an ultimatum: 'Either they go, or I start packing.' "

"I can't blame her," the doctor commiserated.

"I had no choice, they had to move."

"To the mental hospital?" the doctor suggested.

"Eventually, yes, the situation became insufferable."

A few days later Dr Wisborne visited his erstwhile patients at the Centre de Crise. Judith and Jake Sklar were living in a world of their own making; both had lost their equilibrium. They had difficulties remembering their names, let alone anything else. Dr Wisborne went back to his office, or rather his study at the foot of Mount Royal.

Spring had arrived with a suddenness peculiar to this part of the country. Street musicians appeared in the city, a festive mood lay in the air, unequalled far and wide, which never failed to stir the doctor's mettle. The free and easy deportment of the people touched the strings of his heart. He liked to wander up and down Ste-Catherine Street, savouring the music, enjoying that nameless uplifting force rising within him. The atmosphere, made delightful by laughing faces, sporting lovemaking, banter, and dallying glances, was ambrosia for his body, and nectar for his soul. Today, however, his spirit did not soar. Laden with vexation it stayed on the ground.

Another visit at the chemist's did not entirely unveil the mysteries, but it gathered them up. Dr Duval listened patiently to what his visitor had to say. His brow wrinkled in annoyance, like that of a man assailed by unpleasant memories.

"Doctor, what is the purpose of your visit?"

"To be enlightened," Dr Wisborne replied.

"I may not be able to do that, but I have a theory," the chemist hinted.

"Let's hear it," the doctor prompted.

"Here it is: Marvin Sklar, an unmitigated rascal, is suddenly laid up. No physical signs of an ailment were present, yet he sank rapidly into a torpor. The old rogue caught on quickly, he heard the bells ring backwards. He stopped taking the medicine and started thinking, while hoarding every single pill, which he ground into powder. Gaining health and mobility by the hour, he sneaked down at night and added the mind-robbing powder to his stepchildren's diet. He measured amply, in the hope to harm them as much, or more, than they had harmed him. After all, he must have figured: What can happen to me?"

"Not much, considering the circumstances," the doctor granted.

Chuckling the chemist said:

"Yet you wrecked his plans, which must have caused him a measure of chagrin."

"Oddly enough it didn't. When I suggested that Jake and Judith be immediately transferred to a hospital, he agreed with alacrity."

Evidently surprised to hear it, Dr Duval responded:

"Hm, that is strange, inexplicable, in fact."

After a short pause, he said something that made his visitor sit up and take notice.

"Anyway it was too late, the seeds of a tragedy were sown."

"Meaning?"

Jake and Judith had already been affected, irrevocably so, by the drug, as I learned from you. A metamorphosis had begun, imperceptible at first, but in time hip and thigh; it cannot be reversed. The Bizango powder justified its reputation, and fulfilled all expectations."

"Frankly, my esteemed colleague, I do not follow you."

"You will in a moment."

Dr Duval smiled almost imperceptibly. He divined his visitor's scepticism, concerning matters outside his realm of experience or comprehension, but he went on:

"You needn't to believe what I'm going to relate, but here it is: The Bizango powder, although being seldom fatal, can have devastating after-effects."

"Like causing dementia, as happened in the case of the Sklars?" Dr Wisborne suggested.

The chemist pursed his lips:

"It may be called thus in our society. But the locals, the maroons of Haiti and other places, pay little heed to such notions; they simply perceive it as a change of personality, to which they attune their minds. To them it is merely a new, albeit different, reality."

Dr Duval said no more. He observed his visitor with eyes that have seen beyond the horizon of western civilisation. Dr Wisborne weighed in his mind his host's tangled tale, which he accepted with considerable reservation. Though these notions did not unwrap the enigma, they served as the skein within a maze.

"What I don't understand is this: Marvin Sklar took enough of this putative medicine to send him on the way to kingdom come; yet after he stopped taking them he recovered quickly and wholly. Besides, his personality did not change," Dr Wisborne declared.

"In all due respect, doctor, the old fox flimflammed you."

"In what way?"

"He never ingested these pills beyond one or two, I maintain, if any at all."

"But the symptoms," Dr Wisborne protested.

"Simulation, doctor, patent simulation. I bet when he got a taste of the pill, he not only had the wind up, but he also concocted a plan how to rid himself of his onerous stepchildren."

"Well, he evidently succeeded," affirmed Dr Wisborne.

The chemist cocked his head and knit his brow. He wondered aloud:

"What baffles me is from where Jake and his sister obtained the powder, which they rolled into pills?"

"That might be easily explained, considering the fact that they were borne and raised in Haiti. Their father, a French architect, managed a construction company in Port-au-Prince till his premature death. His wife, their mother, returned to Quebec a few years after, where she married Sklar."

Silence reigned for a few minutes; each man followed his own thoughts. Dr Wisborne felt an urge to rise and flee. Instinctively his hands moved towards his shirt collar, which seemed to contract. The whole episode with the Sklars had unnerved him. Even Dr Duval, an innocent bystander, made him uneasy. He knew too much, and believed even more concerning matters that made the down-to-earth physician uncomfortable.

"Give me reality," was his motto. He rued his zeal, which once more outran good judgement, and discretion.

When he shook the chemist's hand to thank him and say goodbye, the doctor couldn't ward off an impression that across the chemist's face whisked a sardonic smile. Dr Wisborne didn't like it; neither the smile nor his bow, but he grit his teeth and left.

# Help Wanted

Wilf Williamson was in a snit; he snorted and puffed into his wife's ears about one complaint after another.

"No luck again?" Agnes Williamson asked with a troubled mien.

"I haven't seen a single suitable man," her husband asserted.

What he meant by suitable, his wife instinctively knew, was a true Canadian, for her husband of three years harboured sentiments of rampant prejudism; it made him blind, and dimmed his perception.

For over a week he went to Tillsonburg every morning, driving up and down Brock Street where employment seekers congregated. Most spoke broken English, plus dressed outlandish, and behaved un-Canadian. They furthermore possessed a looseness that repulsed Williamson. Strangers from Mars, he called them, who made him feel utterly uncomfortable.

Two years ago he had hired a man from Sweden, the homeland of his parents, whose very presence caused his stomach to revolt, and whose double Dutch made him cringe. That in itself would have been bearable, but never the singing which he not only deemed un-Canadian, but also outright unmanly. The fellow's work could not be reproached; his demeanour, however, made Wilf see red. To begin with, his veiled smile stung like a personal insult. Melodies, even if only hummed, cut him to the quick. Despite Wilf's covert and overt bullying and fault-finding, the Swede endured the onerous treatment for over two months.

This morning Wilf's demeanour had shed its swagger; he was in a conciliatory mood.

"Tell me, Agnes, what am I doing wrong? The two men I have hired so far turned out to be regular duds."

"And drunks," Agnes added.

"Tell me straight, am I unlucky or is my judgement skewed?"

Agnes was no fool. Guided by experience, plus a womanly instinct, she had learned how to dissemble. Telling Wilf the truth, she knew invariably resulted in domestic discord. She therefore cloaked her answer with praise:

"Don't fret, Wilf, no one can fault you for acting in good faith. How could anybody, almost in an instant to boot, judge a man's worth?"

Wilf's face lit up; he liked what he heard. Yet a glance through the windows quickly darkened his features again. The tobacco seedlings were growing at an alarming rate, thus they must be hoed. The grass had to be mowed soon, the hay season approached rapidly.

Agnes knew the problem, as much as the remedy, but she dared not mention it. Year after year, since their holdings increased, they were faced with similar difficulties. Although men thronged to the area in order to find work, the Williamsons obtained scant benefit from this labour pool. For some arcane reason they invariably ended up with men who seldom walked like they talked. This was a thorny subject with Wilf, whose notion in that respect, the inability to judge men, drove his wife to distraction. For reasons already mentioned she kept her own counsel; so far that is.

For weeks now anger made itself felt, for she envisioned another season of drudgery, aggravated by bickering, recriminations, and reciprocal fault-finding. Yes, she would take Wilf to task; today, and no later. Let him sulk and withdraw once more to his narrow cage, where bigotry reigns, and intolerance blurs perception. She would tell him the truth once and for all.

Agnes Bagnell, once a dutiful daughter, now a compliant wife, did not enjoy her present status. To tell the truth, she almost never did. Some months after the wedding she realised that the envisioned conjugal magic proved to be a mirage, which edged away as time passed. True, she never felt a grand passion for Wilf, but the little bit present at the beginning petered out quickly. Soon he became a stranger at her gate. Affection, as often happens with marriages, did not replace the initial ardour. Billing and cooing turtledoves they were not, but they managed to get along, although Agnes had to endure trying moments. Wilf, stolid to the marrow, wrapped in thick layers of chauvinism, had never been warmed by the sacred flame of imagination. But she had learned to lower her threshold of expectations, while keeping the spark of her earlier days alive. To her husband's dismay her heritage was a shrine to which she fled in times of grief.

While Agnes remained irresolute whether, and when, to approach Wilf for a serious talk, an unexpected event occurred. A man showed up who sought work. Wilf instinctively drew himself up; annoyance was written all over his face. The job-seeker had two strikes against him: He spoke with an accent, and possessed an aura inherent in foreigners. Wilf was about to reject him gruffly, when he noticed his wife's odd behaviour. She stepped back. Visibly apprehensive she held up a hand as if attempting to repulse an attack. The fellow, still fairly young, observed her with a strange glint in his eyes. Wilf's initial inimical attitude softened somewhat; why, he couldn't have said. Perhaps Agnes' baffling deportment, deemed defiant, was the not so gentle nudge that changed his mind. But the manifestations of necessity might have influenced him.

"What's your name?" Wilf asked.

"Luc Boisvert."

"Aha, one of those," Wilf thought.

"Experience?"

"Plenty. I grew up on a farm in Quebec, agriculture is in my blood."

Wilf vacillated. Loyalty to inherited tenets dictated that he should send the fellow on his way. Necessity, however, urged: hire him. Before he decided he cast a glance at Agnes. To his surprise she shook her head. Either Wilf misunderstood the signal or he ignored it. Observing Boisvert with a withering look, he declared:

"Alright, I will give you a try. Remember the rules: One serious breach and you are back on the road."

Later, when he and Agnes discussed Luc Boisvert, Wilf wondered:

"Hm, something is odd here."

"Oh, what?" Agnes inquired.

"That fellow never asked about wages."

His wife pursed her lips and turned on her heels.

The long hot summer days drew closer; the fields were parched, the farmers prayed for rain. The Williamsons, as much as other planters in the area, had suffered reverses lately. The cause was twofold: Shortage of suitable labour, plus a decreasing number of smokers. Wilf and Agnes, being childless and endowed with foresight, were seriously considering to sell out and move westward. They were advised and even exhorted:

"Stay, hold on to your land, things will improve," friends and neighbours declared.

Some spoke of branching out into fields more profitable. Others mentioned government plans, which they couldn't rightly name, but nevertheless lauded them unstintingly.

"Help will soon come," starry-eyed old-timers professed.

Agnes, the lass from the stormy Gaspé coast, saw the handwriting on the wall; besides, she wished to lay a distance between her and the prosaic locals, who were not only spiritless, but also maddeningly conventional.

"How is your new man working out?" Lars Sandvik inquired.

His property adjoined the Williamsons, thus they were ranked as next door neighbours, despite the considerable distance that lay between their houses. Wilf frowned, as he did habitually when answers were not readily found.

"Not bad," he admitted, albeit reluctantly.

"That doesn't sound too convincing," Sandvik observed.

Wilf shifted his peaked cap from side to side. To his wife's chagrin he wore that hated headgear in and outside of the house.

"He would wear it in bed should I not balk," she asserted.

"Well, really, I cannot complain about the work, but remember, he is not one of us."

"Oh, were is he from?

"Quebec of all places," came a surly reply.

"French," Sandvik suggested.

"Annoyingly so."

Wilf was about to raise lamentations concerning people who cannot be like everybody else, when he remembered that Sandvik, a second generation Canadian, hadn't entirely conformed yet. He still spoke Swedish fluently and openly. To make matters worse he showed no compunction to do so in the presence of seasoned Canadians. Wilf reined his tongue and said goodbye.

As often before, he vented his anger on Agnes.

"Why can't people learn to speak English properly," he fumed.

"Are you referring to Luc Boisvert?"

"Who else," he barked.

"How good is your French? Remember, Canada is bilingual."

In a flash she realised her transgression, and no less the consequences. Her inner eye could see the dark clouds of discord approaching. Sure enough the expected severance of hearts took place once more. Wilf drew himself up, snorted a few times, then spun around and left the house. This happened on a Sunday, the day of rest. Boisvert had gone to Tillsonburg, thus Agnes was left alone at the isolated farm. She felt a bit dispirited, not lonesome, but walled in by gloomy thoughts. As on most Sundays, being the day of rest, she intended to read a book. Luc Boisvert had gone to Tillsonburg, her husband, probably still recuperating from his conniption fit, went somewhere, perhaps to the land of the Little Sticks, she hoped. She chose a volume from her meagre collection and went outside, where she sat down under a nearby cheery tree. She quickly regained her wonted optimistic disposition. A smile stole around her lips, which always occurred when she reminisced. Without realising it she walked out onto the country road. Soon she saw Boisvert approaching at a good clip. Agnes waited till he stood opposite her.

"Why did you come?" she asked in a reproachful tone.

"To see you," he replied.

"You promised, Luc, you promised not to follow me," she complained.

"So I did," he agreed.

When she noticed the pained expression on his face, her mien softened. Not for long, however, considering what happened next. Boisvert's doleful bearing, depicting a man laden with misfortune, changed in a wink. The lines of distress were supplanted by wrinkles of amusement. When he started to speak in French, Agnes' blood seemed to freeze. Had a viper bitten her, the reaction would probably have been less vehement. Looking in every direction, she moaned:

"Don't do that."

"Agnes, you are being childish. French is my native tongue, you speak it with equal ease, so what's amiss?"

"More than you think. Wilf doesn't like it."

"Well. He can lump it then," Boisvert snapped, and terminated the conversation.

Several days later Agnes and Wilf sat outside under the cherry tree. Darkness set in gradually, as did an eerie silence. Their conversation became halting, then died out. Both squirmed in embarrassment. An invisible wall seemed to loom up between them, which good intentions were unable to pull down. It happened every time after a tiff, and that wall grew, into the bargain. Suddenly Wilf started:

"What is that?" he cried.

From the upper story of the house could be heard the sweet sounds of a flute. Wilf jumped up:

"Can you not hear it?" he demanded to know.

She did, and would have liked to hear it all evening. Yet, what made her play possum, neither a clairvoyant nor a mind-reader could have divined; even less what prompted her to keep up the dissimulation. Yes, she wasn't averse to improvise on it.

"Hear what, the crickets behind the house?" she asked.

"No, no," he barked.

"Then you must be referring to the frogs in the ponds," she suggested.

Bewildered, somewhat intimidated, Wilf's voice faltered:

"Listen, Agnes, listen closer. It's that confounded Frenchman playing a flute, I bet," he exclaimed, albeit with less conviction.

Agnes affected a motherly tone:

"It's your tinnitus acting up again," she consoled.

To her surprise Wilf did not rush inside and stomp upstairs to berate Boisvert. Either he didn't think of it, or more likely felt apprehensive to be his usual impulsive self. For Boisvert hardly gave the impression of a pushover in a wrangle. He possessed a ready wit, plus pluck and brawn to spare. Besides, considering the remoteness of the farm, prudence was advisable. The loneliness, not particularly onerous during the daytime, can be burdensome after darkness. The awareness of being dependant on one's own resources, dampens anybody's desire for strife.

Wilf began to walk back and forth, while clapping both hands over his ears. Doubts weakened his resolve to storm inside, indecision angered him. Added fear from his recurring ring in the ears, Agnes was not surprised that he lost his composure.

"I will go up there and send him packing, this instant," he threatened. Yet he made no move to carry out the promise.

Agnes smiled. She knew her man who blustered readily, but proceeded cautiously. Wilf stopped, then lowered his hands while listening intently.

"He is still at it," he moaned.

Staring at his wife accusingly, he was about to say more, but she forestalled him:

"It's the crickets, Wilf, they are having a field day this evening," she observed soothingly.

What occurred next caused Agnes to sit up, and Wilf to stiffen.

"It's gone, Agnes, he stopped playing," he cried loud enough to be heard some distance away.

The truth of Wilf's observation could not be contested, but Agnes wouldn't let well enough alone. A prankish spirit seemed to have her in tow; whether willing or not it dragged her along. Despite the nips of compunction, she felt no inclination to desist from stoking her husband's consternation. Once she got a whiff of deception's bittersweet aroma, invisible imps urged to enjoy it to the full. Shaking her head as one does when trying to enlighten a contrary child, she pointed something out:

"Listen closer, Wilf."

He did, and he noticed:

"The frogs and crickets are silent," he muttered.

"So they are, so they are."

Raising her head, observing her husband almost dolefully, she asked:

"Do I need to say more?"

Wilf understood. She was alluding to his tinnitus, that recurring plague, ignited by anxiety, and fanned by droning noises. The inference was plain:

"No one plays on a musical instrument, Wilf. What you hear, or rather want to hear, is a capricious product of your mind."

But when the natural sounds of the night resumed, Agnes reaction astonished her husband. She bolted upright and blurted out:

"What on earth."

Wilf heard it too; the flute was being played again. When he prepared to investigate, Agnes, as if in a trance, followed him. They walked around the house and listened under Boisvert's bedroom window. Silence reigned upstairs, silence, and darkness.

On the following evening the same thing happened again. As darkness set in the crickets chirped lustily, the frogs quickly followed suite. And there was the flute. This time Wilf made no bones about his intentions. After a defiant glance at Agnes' mocking face, he hastened towards the house, which he entered in a huff. Emboldened by nebulous motivations he rushed up the stairs and towards Boisvert's room. Then something restrained his steps. As if riveted to the floor, Wilf listened in disbelief. What his ears perceived the mind refused to acknowledge. Then it dawned on him: A flute, somebody played with a flute. But not in the farm hand's room as expected, but outside near the house.

Wilf retreated silently, then tiptoed down the stairs, and scurried out of the house. The sound of the flute had died down, yet the mighty serenade of the frogs and crickets continued undiminished.

By now Wilf felt thoroughly perplexed, and no less sheepish. The ringing in his ears grew more intense by the second, thereby muffling his hearing, and impairing reasoning. He did not immediately return to his wife, who must have been anxiously waiting for him, he reckoned. Although darkness had now fully set in, the waxing moon shed enough light that enabled one to recognise contours easily. When he saw his wife standing at the picnic table, a thought rushed through his mind: Agnes had made no attempt to mollify him; neither with words nor gestures. Strange to say she never alluded to that cursed tinnitus, the bane of his life, previously held responsible for this flute hallucination, as she called it. In fact, did she not emit gleeful chuckles when he set out to light into Luc Boisvert?

These contemplations were rudely interrupted by the sounds of a flute, coming from upstairs again. Wilf listened in disbelief and rising distress. What was going on? Did his mind play him tricks anew? He shuddered, while recalling the past when noises made by a flute, full of dread and fury, almost drove him insane. Did his nemesis of old, drowned in the maelstrom of daily life, resurface once more, to haunt him forever? A terrible thought struck him. Had the new farm hand got wind of that unfortunate incident many years ago, which for some reason he wished to exploit? Hardly, Wilf decided. He felt quite sure that his terrible secret lay safely buried in a place thousands of miles away. He hadn't breathed a word to Agnes about it, nor to anyone else.

For an instant he felt tempted to unburden his heart concerning the stigma which no amount of rubbing could efface. Agnes knew about his intermittent tinnitus, but not the reason for it. Even less could she divine his abhorrence to flute playing. But he repudiated the notion quicker than it had entered his mind. True, Agnes was his wife, but not his confidant. Marriage, the knot meant to unite, had turned into a wedge that separated bodies and souls. Although they toiled side by side, broke bread countless times, friendship had eluded them. They no longer laughed together, but at each other. A force which neither one rightly understood, kept them an arm's length. They felt more estranged today as at the time when they embraced the first time.

The tobacco plants grew amid ample rain and sunshine; so did Wilf's irritation which was fanned by irresolution. Boisvert must go, his instinct demanded; we need him, good sense rebutted. Wilf had to admit that he was the best farm hand ever. Strong, hardy, and willing, he did the work of two men.

"Well and good," Wilf admitted, " but is the game worth the candle?" he asked himself, for he perceived Boisvert as an ill omen, a harbinger of mischief directed at him.

Besides, there were onerous matters that needed to be weighed; like the flute playing, and his approach to his wife.

"You must have known Boisvert in the past," he observed casually one morning.

"I have never seen him before," she lied.

Taken aback by the gruff retort and flash in her eyes, he stammered:

"Sorry, sorry, I didn't mean to upset you."

But he believed he did, judging by her distraught look, and combative pose.

"What gives you that idea?" she wanted to know.

Wilf had no ready answer. Aside from suspicion stoked by jealousy, no other indication existed; certainly not compelling ones. He realised that Agnes would presume upon an answer. Thus he ransacked his mind for justification concerning his supposition. He found none offhand, yet deep down, below the threshold of consciousness, he saw, rather divined, their common past. True, Agnes seemingly felt uncomfortable in the farm hand's presence, which under the circumstances wasn't easy to avoid. They worked together, ate at the same table, and surprisingly got entangled in interminable debates about every thing under the sun; after work of course.

Wilf would never have owned up to the fact that these dialogues were the main source of his discontent. They conjured up the demons envy and jealousy over a woman he did not love. The Williamsons' conversations invariably consisted of monosyllables and grunts. The ardour needed to exchange ideas had fizzled out a long time ago. Yawns bridged the gaps now which indifference had created. Yes, Wilf Williamson was annoyed. But what rankled most could be explained in one sentence: The apparent affinity of souls between the presumed antagonists. No matter how heated their arguments became, Wilf never detected a whiff of acrimony between them.

"Ahem, ahem," Agnes signalled while looking squarely at her brooding husband.

"I asked you a question, Wilf," she reminded.

"Oh, what was it again?"

"What makes you think that I know Boisvert from the past?"

"Well, first you speak French with each other at times."

"So we do." For good reason, she almost added, but chortled instead as if trying to amuse a child.

"Is this an indictment?" she asked with pursed lips and raised eyebrows.

Wilf knew of no retort, he just walked away while muttering to himself.

Circumstances soon took their toll. Fate was on the march. The past, laden with ugly memories, started to cast a pall over the lives of the three inhabitants. Boisvert must go, Wilf decided once more, yet his resolve wavered when he cast a glance across the fields which flourished at an alarming rate. What did Agnes say?

"Whatever you do, Wilf, don't dismiss Luc till a replacement has been found. I mean a suitable replacement, not another tough talker, but lame walker. We understand each other, I hope."

They did, for she had laid down the law in no uncertain terms.

"I shall not toil again like in the past years," were her exact words.

Wilf knew that tone quite well, and the pose even better. Her Scottish heritage spoke loud and clear: Leave things as they are, or be prepared to take the consequences.

But nevertheless he had gone to Tillsonburg almost every morning for the past days.

"Just looking around," he told Agnes who reminded him of a few things. Tacitly he concurred with her view, but he just couldn't let well enough alone. The desire to mingle among his own kind was overwhelming, especially since the arrival of that strange fellow from Quebec. He could barely resist the temptation to hire one of those rough talking men lining both sides of Brock Street. But the looming shadow of his wife dampened this desire.

This morning on the road back to the farm, Wilf felt like a man crossing the Bridge of Sighs on the way to his execution. Contradictory notions plagued his unsophisticated mind.

"Where, oh where shall it end?" he repeatedly moaned.

Well, he needed no soothsayer to predict what would happen if Boisvert remained and continued to play on the flute.

"A calamity would happen," he told himself.

While still tossing thoughts from pillar to post, Wilf arrived at the farm. Agnes and Boisvert were out in the fields hoeing side by side.

"There is your opportunity, Wilf, get that flute," the voice that never rests urged.

In a twinkle Wilf quickened his steps. Up he went in a hurry. Without a moment's hesitation he entered the farmhand's room. Although he searched everywhere, except between the walls, he found no trace of a musical instrument. At first he ascribed scant importance to Boisvert's secretiveness, nor did he suspect an ulterior motive.

"Must be one of that peculiar fellow's idiosyncrasies," Wilf advised to no one in particular.

Later in the day, however, he was struck by a disquieting thought.

"He knows, or suspects," Wilf moaned.

Common sense, however, quickly overshadowed the idea, for no one within a thousand miles could have possibly been privy to an episode that he had cleverly hushed up. His tracks were covered with subterfuge, white lies, and masterly dissimulation. He even had changed his name.

"So, quit worrying," he urged his conscience.

Yet worry he did, for guilt, stoked by fear, nipped at his heels once more. Sometimes he woke up in the middle of the night when he felt icy fingers, stiffened by apprehension, grope at his spine. Oppressive memories, believed to have been swept by high winds far into the Atlantic Ocean or swallowed by the mighty tides of the Bay of Fundy, had traversed westward over the land and water to find him again. The fault lay squarely with Luc Boisvert, deemed to be an impostor by Williamson. Even a dolt could see that with half an eye, Wilf concluded. A regular day labourer he was not, even less a country boy, judging by his manners and language. He, the boss, felt like an underling in the presence of this putative migrant worker.

The man was ill equipped for such rural areas; but come to think of it so was his wife, who underwent a curious transformation since the arrival of Boisvert. No doubt, they were acquainted with each other in the past. Why Agnes tried to gloss over the fact puzzled him as much as her attempt to hush up Boisvert's flute playing. Or did she really? Granted, the din made by the frogs and crickets could divert one's attention or drown out other sounds. But in his experience not sounds made by a flute which, however faint they are, affected him like a dozen tambours played nearby.

Something else came to his mind. Dr Ludwig's assertion that even the keenest sense of hearing cannot perceive at times certain noises, be they ever so loud or near.

Came evening, the frogs and crickets were at it again; so was Boisvert with his flute. Wilf stared at his wife suggestively. She returned his gaze with a knowing grin. Without bashing an eyelash she advised:

"I can hear it."

Wilf, visibly shaken, made no reply. Agnes, who expected another outburst from her husband, heaved a sigh of relief when he moved not a muscle to protest, let alone confront Boisvert. He sat there as if chilled to the bones, despite the sweltering summer heat. He is being chased again by ghosts of his own creation, Agnes surmised.

In the waning twilight distant objects began to disappear.
They obtained grotesque shapes before the darkness swallowed
them wholly. Wilf and Agnes, both wrapped in their own
thoughts, could still see each other's countenances effortlessly.
The big house took on the appearance of a looming giant
whose bowels emitted lovely music, which bewitched Agnes,
but judging by his grimaces caused Wilf mental suffering.
Agnes felt increasingly intrigued by her husband's behaviour.
How could a man be so perturbed by music, neither loud nor
disharmonious, especially if played on a flute? It struck her as
very odd, knowing his predilection for blaring, dissonant
renditions, which he called tunes of our time. This penchant of
his, juvenile she called it, caused considerable discord between
them. Something else Agnes noticed: Luc played certain tunes
over and over again, with added intensity, and a livelier
rhythm, as if conveying a message, she thought. Whenever this
happened Wilf displayed a singular deportment. Every muscle
in his face started to twitch, both hands flew at his ears, while
he bounced from his chair and started a regular prison walk.
Striding to-and-fro he declared:

"I can't take it anymore, go and tell that man to keep quiet.
Better yet tear that flute away from him, smash it over his head
a hundred times," he commanded.

Normally Agnes would have pooh-poohed his request, but
upon considering Wilf closer, she winced instead. No doubt, he
was completely going out of his head. She never knew, nor
suspected, that the homely man she had married had so much
fire in his veins, which awed and repulsed her simultaneously.
One thing, however, couldn't be denied. If this situation
prevails for any length of time, a disaster was in the offing.

"Wilf, do sit down for a moment," Agnes urged for the third
time.

She might as well have addressed the sky above and obtain
the same results. He neither replied, nor stopped walking to-
and-fro. Agnes gave up. She rose and walked into the house.
Upstairs in their bedroom she positioned herself at the window.
In the dim light of the stars and moon she was able to make out
Wilf's shadowy outlines, moving one way, then turning and
retracing his steps.

Meanwhile Luc had ceased playing; silence reigned in the house. Outside the crickets and frogs continued their serenade. All nature appeared to be attuned with itself; except Wilf, her distressed husband. What stung him to the soul Agnes could guess, why this happened she was unable to make out. For some arcane reason tunes played on a flute got Wilf on the raw. More likely, Agnes corrected herself, this inner turmoil could be attributed only to certain melodies depicted by Luc. She knew these particular airs well, which Luc had played often in her presence. She always found them lovely, albeit strangely sad. Whenever Luc struck up these mournful melodies, his demeanour changed. He appeared to have difficulties holding back tears. Why these soul-stirring melodies, played by dexterous hands, affected Wilf like salt rubbed into an open wound, filled Agnes with outright misgivings. She instinctively realised that this will not end in smiles and laughter.

Agnes slept in fits and starts. Haunted by one nightmare after another she found no rest. In one uneasy dream she vividly saw an image of the Pied Piper of Hamelin, leading the town's children to their graves. When she heard the sounds of a flute, she started up. The dream had called a wild fancy into life; in other words it gave her an idea.

When Agnes rose Wilf had already left. She could easily guess what he was up to. She wished him success, for in her innermost being she suspected that Luc had come to stir the pot of mischief.

At the breakfast table Agnes remarked:

"You never were a convincing liar, Luc."

Perhaps not, but he always was a good dissembler. Screwing up his face, looking left and right, raising his eyebrows in astonishment, he grimaced innocently. The pantomimes elicited a guffaw from Agnes.

"Quit pretending, you didn't come to see me," she declared.

Boisvert's feelings appeared to be hurt.

"Now, Agnes dear, I did undertake the trip to see you, after all weren't we engaged once?"

"Cut the cackle, Luc, confess. What's your motive?"

"Well, if you must know, I was itching to meet your husband."

"For what reason?"

"Jealousy, my dear, pure jealousy."

A pause ensued which Agnes interrupted:

"It's no secret, Wilf is looking for a replacement," she advised.

Luc chuckled:

"I don't blame him," he declared.

"Would that not thwart your scheme?" Agnes remarked casually.

Luc's reply followed in a flash:

"Not really."

She looked at him somewhat baffled, for she hadn't expected a response to her off the cuff comment. Realising his slip of the tongue, Luc hastened to add:

"What I mean is that work is easy to obtain."

"Yes," she granted, "for a steady, diligent man, and woman for that matter, jobs can be had with ease in and around Tillsonburg."

Shortly after Wilf returned with a new helper, who impressed Agnes as a man who had just stepped off the boat.

"Aha, my husband is learning," she thought.

Luc was summarily dismissed with the words:

"You are not suitable."

Boisvert shrugged his shoulders unaffectedly, since those days were still free and easy in Canada, where one could find work from sea to sea with little effort. Without a word he packed his belongings in a knapsack and said goodbye.

"Agnes, we shall see you again."

"Wilf, give my regards to Ethel, will you?"

"Ethel?" Wilf exclaimed as if cut to the quick.

"Yes, mon ami, Ethel Malraux, your first wife. Don't you remember her?"

Then producing his flute from somewhere, Boisvert walked towards the road, while playing the tunes Agnes knew so well. But with a difference that gave Agnes a jolt. Yes, she recognised the tunes, but not the timbre, which was strikingly bold, like a bugle's call to arms. Not a whiff of melancholy adhered to them anymore. Every note sounded bellicose, like an avenging angel's trumpet.

Agnes felt curiously touched by Luc's dramatic departure; it
raised her spirit, despite its theatrical aspect. But that changed
in a twinkle when she glanced at Wilf. He stood there like
someone about to draw his last breath. Shock mirrored in his
eyes, his mouth quivered while he gaped at Boisvert, who
walked with stately steps towards the road, while playing with
gusto on his flute. The sight of the spectral figure, her husband
in other words, made Agnes turn away. The misery etched on
his face elicited more revulsion than pity in the dispassionate
wife.

When Boisvert reached the road, he turned around, bowed
like a Spanish grandee, then played a rousing tune reminiscent
of a pibroch. The effect on Wilf startled Agnes, who observed
him from the corners of her eyes. Wilf trembled from head to
toe, like someone suffering from palsy, she thought.

After Boisvert had disappeared behind a bend in the road,
Agnes confronted Wilf to obtain some answers. Yet noticing
the unabated convulsions that shook his entire body, she
desisted. Every time thereafter when she alluded to Luc's
strange, significant references, he started to shake from head to
toe.

Life on that lonely farm became a slough of despair. The
new farmhand worked out well, but he soon left. Agnes could
easily guess the reason. For a poisonous vapour, caused by
rancour and inimical behaviour, soon engulfed house and yard.
She too suffered, since the oppressive silence felt like choking
hands at her throat.

After the farmhand's departure, Agnes fortitude plummeted;
she had never been so downcast in all her life. She harboured
not a moment's doubt that Wilf had entered a road which led
nowhere else but onto the hills of Golgatha. She had no
intention to accompany him. Agnes wanted to talk, clear the
air, then start afresh. Yet Wilf balked strenuously. At first she
graciously refrained from being importune, but ultimately she
demanded to be heard and answered. She practically
buttonholed him one morning:

"Wilf, we must discuss what can be no longer glossed
over."

But, lo and behold! the husband stiffened, than gaped, and ultimately succumbed to an uncontrollable tremor.

"It's a ruse," Agnes thought while turning disgustedly away.

Right there and then she decided to have the long planned conversation with Dr Ludwig, who should know what to do. He didn't, but nevertheless he offered some advice:

"My dear, according to your description Wilf is suffering from epileptic fits."

"They seem contrived to me," she countered.

"It could well be. For like many sicknesses they often serve as a sanctuary for battered minds."

"I don't understand," Agnes intimated.

"It's not necessary. Send Wilf to see me, and we shall go from there."

Wilf adamantly refused to visit the doctor, claiming there was nothing amiss with him. He pooh-poohed Boisvert's insinuating remarks, which he called darts of a silly, scheming Frenchman. He roundly accused Agnes of pestering him about something a lunatic had invented; with malice aforethought to boot. Perceiving her husband's surprising calm, Agnes felt encouraged to say more:

"If that is so, why do you have conniption fits whenever I touch on the subject? So tell me. Where you married to Ethel Malraux or not?"

Wilf gave no reply; he couldn't, for another attack of palsy prevented it. Did Agnes' ire surpass a nascent loathing or went it the other way? It would have been difficult to affirm, but one thing was plain as pikestaff; her cup was overflowing with a woman's fury.

The situation grew dire, yet Agnes, a descendant of unbowed Highlanders, proud in defeat and adversity, did not knuckle under. True, the circumstances were grim, but not hopeless, she found. Yet there came moments when pangs of discouragement assailed her. The fields cried for attention, the harvest became endangered unless stout hearts and eager limbs tackled the rank weed. Time, precious by now, could no longer be wasted by the pursuit of vindictive thoughts, and plots meant to harm each other. They weakened their resolve, and rendered muscles and limbs flaccid. Agnes had no illusions;

they were up the creek with broken paddles, which must be mended, or they will soon be beggars on the road. To her amazement Wilf didn't seem to care, judging by signs that couldn't be overlooked.

"He cherishes our looming ruin," she told herself.

Perhaps he did. In any case he showed scant interest in the property of the farm. He talked about selling this albatross around their necks, even at a fire sale price. Agnes wanted no part of it; besides, what good would it do. For whatever they did, wherever they went, misery would be their companion. The problem was not the farm, she realised, but the nagging demons within them.

Something else manifested itself: Wilf Williamson was no longer the man she had married, or the fellow he pretended to be. As the veneer flaked off, the unvarnished husband was not a sight to her liking; in fact, he frightened her. True, shortly after the marriage they started to drift apart, but Agnes had hoped that time and patience will eventually unite them. It turned out to be a daydream; the gap turned into a gulf.

Agnes understood the situation. A neglected farm lost not only its value, but was also difficult to sell. Clouds of discord were accumulating at an alarming rate. Wilf's disregard for the farm's welfare had become a controversial issue. She finally confronted her husband:

"Either you do your part or I shall advertise for suitable help."

In the midst of a furious argument Wilf stormed out while swearing with full lungs. This was news to her, for although he had a predilection for men, and women for that matter, who used four-letter words, he refrained from following suit, within her earshot anyway.

Later on Agnes heard him hammer and file in the shed. Curious to find out what he was doing, she walked over to investigate. To her surprise Wilf was reshaping and sharpening the hay rake's spikes. The wheel of the rake was raised to avoid stooping down. This, the work on the machine, astounded her for two reasons: First, he had assured her some days ago that the machine was in excellent shape; second, all maintenance had so far been performed in the barn some distance from the shed. When Wilf saw her standing there on the elevated ramp, he waved. Agnes couldn't have said why she stared as if transfixed at the piece of equipment. Suddenly a dreadful notion raced through her mind.

"My goodness," she thought, "anyone stumbling and falling would surely be skewered by these pointed spikes. Still shuddering, she perceived Wilf mounting the few steps and coming towards her, smiling of all things. Agnes instinctively turned and walked away.

Then something totally unexpected happened. Luc Boisvert showed up again.

On a Saturday after sunset sounds of a flute were heard, loud and clear. Wilf froze in his tracks, Agnes bolted from her chair to gain a better view. Stunned, like Balaam must have been when his ass spoke to him, he started ahead. Then, in the twilight, Luc Boisvert marched along the road, playing the tunes that enlivened Agnes' spirit, but hurled Wilf into the jaws of ungovernable rage. He completely lost his composure. While running towards the road, then stopping abruptly, he turned on his heels and ran into the house, swearing worse than a fishwife. In a twinkle he came rushing out again, holding a rifle in both hands, which he aimed at Boisvert; then pulled the trigger. Click, click, click it went. The magazine was empty, or not inserted. Throwing it to the ground, he was going to rush upon the flute player, crying:

"No!" Shrieking, "I will show that Frenchman, if it's the last thing I do."

It proved to be a prophetic promise. Overcome by emotions he stumbled and collapsed, while crying out in anguish. Within hours he was transported to the local hospital.

Luc Boisvert stayed on. He found additional help the next day. All three literally spat in their hands, and rolled up their sleeves. The neglected fields soon became a shining example of husbandry. Agnes smiled again. Her probing inquiries were initially evaded by Boisvert, but ultimately she succeeded to unriddle the puzzle; quite by accident it seemed.

"To bad what happened to Wilf," she said with a deep sigh.

As if stung to the marrow Boisvert burst out:

"First, his name is not Wilf; second, he got his dessert."

"What do you mean?" she queried.

"His name is, or was, Eric Ludmil."

"I don't believe it," Agnes protested.

It earned her a withering glance containing pity and gloating. He asked her to sit down:

"I will tell you the whole story," he promised. "About five years ago an event took place that touched my heart of hearts. I wasn't in Canada at the time, otherwise Eric Ludmil would be behind bars, where he belongs."

"Luc, this is not one of your tales of the tub, is it now?"

"No. Every word you are going to hear is true."

Raising his head, trying to suppress a woeful smile, he exclaimed:

"Ethel was murdered."

"Ethel? Oh, Ethel Malraux, whom you mentioned once before."

"The same. She was Wilf's first wife whom he foully murdered."

Agnes shook her head in disbelief. Her husband, who deferred to women almost cringingly, doing violence to his own wife seemed inconsistent with logic. As a matter of course she asked:

"What happened exactly?"

"Exactly? That we will never know for sure. The coroner's jury declared it an accident; I call it willful murder. She stumbled and fell onto a hay rake, they decided. I say that Wilf lured her onto the ramp and pushed her."

Agnes bolted from her chair. Pressing both hands against her chest, she groaned:

"No, oh no."

Mistaking her exclamation for an expression of shock and pity, Luc declared:

"Impaled on those razor sharp spikes, Ethel died a slow agonising death."

Agnes winced at the thought that she could have shared Ehtel's fate, had she not walked away in time.

Her attitude changed. Luc's narration, till now taken with a grain of salt, took on an entire different aspect. Choked by emotions that she could no longer hide, Agnes buried her head in her hands and moaned. The notion about breathing one's last, pierced by those sharp spikes, made her flesh creep. She sat down again, her interest was aroused.

"Luc, you said a moment ago that you were out of the country when the accident occurred."

"The murder," Luc cut her short.

"As you wish. Anyway, how can you arrive at the conjectures under these circumstances?"

"The letters told the tale."

"Letters?" she echoed.

"Yes. When I returned from an extensive trip, my postal box was cramped with letters; mostly from Ethel Malraux."

"Did you know each other well?"

Casting a sideways glance at her, he explained:

"We both were flutists with the Montreal Philharmonics for several years."

"The letters convinced you of Wilf's culpability then?"

"Yes. They, plus inquiries I made."

"Tell me more, Luc," Agnes prompted.

Boisvert observed her with a mien, appalling, yet strangely attractive. His eyes mirrored a soul defiled. She wondered how close he and Ethel Malraux had been.

"What I said before is true. Wilf's actual name is Eric Ludmil. He changed it to Wilf Williamson after Ethel's death."

"Forgive me for interrupting. Did you say Ethel died a slow death?"

"Slow and agonising."

"Wasn't anybody around to come to her assistance?" Agnes queried.

"Most certainly," Boisvert declared.

"Who?"

Boisvert chuckled derisively.

"Your doughty husband, my dear. But he fled the place of the crime, right after he had committed it."

"This was brought to light at the inquiry, I presume."

Boisvert shook his head:

"No."

"So how do you know it?"

Leaning back, contemplating Agnes steadily, he remarked:

"Agnes, how long have you known Wilf?"

"For about five years."

"In those years have you ever seen him touch liquor?"

Surprised at the question, she cocked her head and raised her eyebrows.

"Come to think of it, I haven't."

"Would it surprise you to learn that Wilf used to be a regular toper?"

"It sure would, for I never saw him take a drop of liquor."

"Do you wonder why?"

"Not really. He said it weakens the body and confuses the mind."

"And loosens the tongue," Boisvert added with a knowing grin.

Agnes' inquiring look prompted him to expound:

"Wilf, it seems, suffers from a compulsion. It's this: After a few draughts of beer, or a sip of hard liquor, he turns into a regular Jack Brag, impelled to tell all, I was told by several locals."

"Locals?" Agnes repeated.

"Wilf was born and raised in Cape Breton Island," Luc declared.

That was news to Agnes, who was let to believe that he hailed from a rural district south of Regina.

"Anyway, let me continue. Having read Ethel's disquieting letters, I set out to her place of ordeal, as she described it. Alarmed at what I heard, appalled by the letters in my pockets, I visited the crown attorney's office."

"What did you hear?"

"Pretty well what I had suspected. Shortly after the inquest Wilf, far and wide known as Eric Ludmil, visited a tavern at the other side of Canso Strait. Soon the bragging started. As if on command every man nearby either turned or moved away, except one who didn't know your husband yet. This did not deter Wilf who, after a few copious quaffs, commenced to swagger:

" 'Ha, death by misadventure. Ha again. What a bunch of dolts. Yokels they are pretending to be jurors.'

"Believe it or not, he bragged about his cleverness in planning and carrying out his wife's murder.

" 'Yes, I have done her in. Does anyone want to know why?'

"Nobody, except the man who still sat at his table, appeared to be interested. Grinning sheepishly he commented:

" 'Let's hear it.'

" 'Because she played the flute.'

"A patron nearby turned around and ordered Wilf roughly to shut up.

" 'Shut up yourself,' the man was told.

"Wilf, in his stride now, kept going:

" 'I advised her in no uncertain terms: 'One more peep out of that blasted instrument, and I break it over your head.' But you know women, they never learn to let well enough alone.'

"Well, neither could your husband, the dyed-in-the-wool fanfaron. He was unable to resist an urge to show off. In short, he blustered openly mind you, goaded by his demon alcohol, how his wife was sent to kingdom come, by his own hands.

" 'One push and she lay on the hay rake's sharpened spikes. Ha, ha, ha, that taught her a lesson.' "

Both fell silent. Agnes, trying to digest what she had heard, cleared her throat several times before she said another word:

"You know, Luc, I just cannot believe that we are talking about the same man."

"Yet we are. But let me say something else. When Wilf's flesh-creeping trumpeting came to my attention, I sat up and took notice. For in one of Ethel's letters, desperate letters I should add, his irrational hate for her flute-playing was decried almost word for word, and letter for letter matching the man's narration."

Agnes drew a deep sigh. Beset by doubts, perturbed by her own experience, which increasingly looked like a close call, she felt at sea.

Boisvert picked up the threat again:

"One of the letters bewailed Wilf's threat that he would break the flute over her head, should he hear another peep out of that blasted instrument."

"But why, Luc, why?"

"I shall come to that in a moment. Hear me out. A subsequent letter arrived, in my absence of course, wherein Ethel lamented: 'Luc, he has done it, my husband broke my flute. I fear for my life, he threatened to settle my hash, once and for all.' "

Boisvert's countenance acquired an aspect of a blood avenger on the prowl. Agnes had never seen such a forbidding face. It made her shrink back and lower her eyes. When his mien relaxed somewhat, she commented:

"You said that Wilf bragged openly about being the author of Ethel's demise."

"That's what I was told."

"Didn't the authorities show interest in – in Wilf's confession?"

"It seems they did. But deeming it just another one of Wilf's fanfaronades, their inquiries were rather cursory. But it induced your husband to refrain from imbibing alcohol thereafter."

"Did you inform the police of Ethel's letters?"

"No. But I visited the crown attorney's office in Sydney, were I reported what was told me, plus left copies of Ethel's relevant letters."

"What happened?"

"Not much so far, although they promised to investigate."

Agnes could imagine the rest. Boisvert for unknown reasons decided to take matters in his own hands. Strange to say, she felt closer to the man from Quebec than to her husband of some years, whom she never loved, and now loathed. Did he get his just dessert? Yes, she granted, be it only for his chauvinistic attitude, called in these parts a man's burden. Wilf, according to her, plucked the strings of maleness beyond endurance. Like a golem of old, he was an automaton lacking a soul, hiding behind a mask.

"Luc, I asked you before why a man should vehemently object to his wife's musical pursuits?"

"He felt threatened."

"By a flute?"

"No, by his wife's independence. You see, when Ethel played the flute she was beyond his reach and control. His male ego suffered. Eventually the sound of a flute drove him berserk."

They were sitting at the small picnic area under an enormous cherry tree, still bearing fruit. Evening had come and was almost gone; night set in. The frogs and crickets seemed to vie with each other to be heard.

Agnes, riven by conflicting sentiments, tried to collect her thoughts. She had visited the hospital, where she received dismal news. The doctor who treated her husband diagnosed his condition as grand mal, epilepsy in other words, accompanied by severe convulsions, and loss of consciousness.

"Every bit of excitement will trigger these seizures," she was advised.

Dr Ludwig joined them, he was in a sombre mood.

"Dr Ludwig, will my husband eventually recover again?" she inquired.

The doctor, who could be brutally honest at times, answered with a mournful smile:

"Not if he goes back to the farm."

Agnes, never slow on the uptake, nodded; she understood.

"Back to me, in other words," she acknowledged.

"Sad to say, that's the situation," she was advised.

Shrugging her shoulders, inwardly that is, Agnes left the hospital without going near her husband.

"I shall be back," she promised with scant conviction.

Anyway, for now Wilf must be left to the tender mercies of fate. The well-being of the farm comes first, she decided.

Meanwhile Luc had fetched his flute, but he hesitated to play on it. It was getting late for early risers, but neither Agnes nor Boisvert felt sleepy. An ominous silence ensued, which neither one wanted to interrupt, although both had much on their minds. But as mentioned it was getting late. Midnight approached, minds were overwrought with emotions only the truth could soothe.

Agnes spoke first:

"Luc, I had asked you before, why did you come?"

Boisvert hemmed and hawed like someone wishing to speak, yet dared not. Agnes divined more than what she knew. He replied:

"Reading Ethel's letters, belatedly mind you, I felt an obligation to investigate."

"To meet Wilf, in other words."

"That too," he admitted.

Agnes cocked her head and smiled amusedly at the man she was once engaged to. Their betrothal did not endure. Why, Agnes understood in time. After her marriage to Wilf, the puzzle unriddled itself. The man whom she never loved, she possessed wholly; the man whom she once deeply loved, was never completely hers. That, her vain heart considered to be an affront; thus she broke the engagement.

Agnes appreciated fully that Luc knew more than he wished to reveal. Wilf's bizarre attitude towards sounds from a flute, he was cognisant of. Agnes reckoned that thereby hung a tale, which in all likelihood would never be told. Could Ethel have been aware of Wilf's phobia to the sounds of a flute? Had she intentionally stoked the embers into destructive flames with the help of her flute? Anyway, strange forces were at work that reason alone could not explain. Curiosity gained the upper hand with Agnes.

"Luc, weren't you taking a chance by flaunting yourself out on the road?" she queried.

"On account of Wilf's anticipated reaction, you mean?"

"Yes."

"Wilf is a weakling, if I may say so," Boisvert asserted with a measure of disdain.

"Well, he had a rifle, as you found out."

"That posed no danger," Agnes was assured.

"I don't follow you."

"The chamber proved empty, as you heard."

"But you could not have known that," Agnes protested.

"Yet I did. For on the same afternoon when you were out in the fields, I removed not only the magazine, but also stuck a splint into the chamber; just to be on the safe side."

Agnes became pensive. She managed to comprehend most of the bizarre events, yet not rightly why Luc enmeshed himself with threatening difficulties on account of a colleague that once played the flute beside him. She could not resist the temptation to asked:

"Luc, Ethel Malraux was someone special to you, I reckon?"

"She was my first love."

The next question Agnes rued for some time.

"First and only love?"

Boisvert didn't answer. He raised his flute and started to play.

# The Wag

Spring arrived early that year. The relentless high winds, which lift the soil and limit visibility, had not yet begun. Taking advantage of the lull, Roger Brisco and Max Rinaldo took a morning stroll through Regina's Wascana Park. As usually they were at loggerheads about everything under the sun. With kindly tempers mind you, but nevertheless with might and main. Opinions voiced by one or the other elicited chuckles or guffaws that made the ducks on the water raise their heads. They quickly became enmeshed in an argument about subliminal persuasion. Brisco derided the very notion:

"Are you implying that fancies of one's own making or evoked by others can alter a man's psyche, and even his behaviour and looks?"

"Yes. Thoughts and beliefs instilled by yourself or others can shape you mentally as much as physically."

"In other words, what you believe long enough you shall become."

"Exactly."

"Piffle to that, and two pshaws as an encore," Brisco cried.

A smile flitted across his good-natured face. Pointing to a man sitting at a nearby bench, he challenged his friend:

"You see that fellow, old and used up? Go, persuade him that he is really a youngster in the finest of fettle."

Scarcely had Rinaldo cast a glance at the shrivelled figure, when Brisco sensed that there was something wrong; terribly wrong. Rinaldo stopped, then bridled while gaping at the wisp of a man. Brisco was about to crack a joke, but his friend's demeanour dissuaded him from doing so. Rinaldo's puckered brow deterred him, his distended eyes did the rest. What bewildered him most, however, was the old fellow's sudden gesture. He raised a hand which he cocked into a pistol, then aimed it squarely at Rinaldo. Even years later Brisco maintained that images of the old man's devilish grimace made him shudder.

Rinaldo stood there as if rooted to the spot. Bewildered beyond description, his face mirrored uncertainty first, then astonishment, and finally confusion mixed with fear.

"No, no, it's impossible," he moaned.

"What is impossible, Max?" his friend demanded to know, somewhat snappishly.

Brisco's insistent questions remained unanswered; his demands to continue their walk fell on deaf ears. Rinaldo appeared to have been transported with utter confusion by the sight of the shrivelled fellow, who sported a fiendish grin. He turned abruptly:

"It's time to go to work," he muttered as he walked towards the Legislative Building.

Quite annoyed, Brisco, undecided what to do, cast another glance towards the prankster on the bench. He wasn't there anymore.

Max Rinaldo and Roger Brisco worked almost side by side at the provincial government building. Both were newcomers, still looked at with sideways glances by old-timers. They, Brisco and Rinaldo, had drifted towards an uneasy friendship, that proved to be not as firm as a rock. Endeavour as he may, Brisco couldn't hide his ill-feelings on account of his friend's silly behaviour, deemed unseemly for a middle-aged professional engineer. How could that decrepit loiterer's antics discompose one to such an extent to lose self-control?

Brisco's huff was soon overshadowed by curiosity. Rinaldo, anxious to mend the slight kink in their relationship, showed an eagerness to talk; not, however, about the recent incident in the park. Both were early risers and avid walkers. They invariably met at the gates of the nearby art gallery for a brisk stroll through the park.

"Shall I see you at the usual place in the morning?" Brisco asked at quitting time.

The innocent query appeared to disconcert his friend; but only for an instant.

"Of course," he answered.

Brisco, blessed with a quick ear and a discerning mind, did not fail to notice the catch in Rinaldo's voice.

Rinaldo didn't show up in the morning, not on time anyway. Brisco waited ten minutes, then set out alone. Following their customary route, he briskly walked on. When he crossed the raised footbridge his eyes turned involuntarily towards the spot where he supposed the old wag to be. Sure enough, there he sat again, craning his neck to obtain a better view. The fellow is expecting us, he conjectured correctly, as it turned out. Although not squeamish in the matter of people's physiognomies, Brisco recoiled when he obtained a closer look at the man who seemingly had an axe to grind with his friend. The sneer on his face he could have borne with a measure of equanimity, but not the scowl oozing with malicious intent.

"Where is your friend?" Brisco was asked.

Against his better judgement he replied:

"He couldn't make it, I guess."

"You guess, you guess," the queer fellow snarled.

Brisco was averse to chat, he walked briskly away. Being quite close to the old prankster this time, he noticed two things: The fellow's native Indian features, and his surprising unlined face. What made him look like Methuselah must have been that menacing frown.

Rinaldo did not show up for work. He advised the office that he had a bout of spring fever. All day Brisco felt beset by a premonition of an impending disaster. That loiterer in the park had a sinister message to convey which Rinaldo did not want to hear. This foreboding took root when he glanced through the windows, which overlooked the park. As suspected, the half-breed had come closer; he walked, rather shuffled, to and fro, while keeping a sharp eye at his surrounding. He is waiting for Max, Brisco surmised, with whom he has an axe to grind, judging by appearances.

Rinaldo remained off work the following day. When he failed to show up for a whole week, Brisco made discreet inquiries. What he learned surprised and upset him. He was advised that Rinaldo had asked to be transferred to another location. Since this proved unfeasible, he gave his notice to be effective immediately. Somewhat peeved on account of the perceived snub, Brisco decided to wash his hands of Rinaldo and that pesky half-breed lurking about. It was easier resolved than adhered to. Roger Brisco, while not possessing the traits of a lone wolf, kept to himself. He had burned his bridges decades ago, thus twinges of loneliness assailed him at times. He seemed forever to be the odd man out, a thorn in everyone's side, an intruder who hampered the customary self-confidence of others. As far back as he could remember, Brisco sought congenial company, that became more elusive as he grew older. Max Rinaldo, although pricked at times by orneriness, nevertheless satisfied his craving for men of his own ilk. For two whole days, and half nights, Brisco grappled with vanity, who held a brief for haughtiness and sense, but who dictated otherwise. He didn't know where Rinaldo lived; not exactly anyway. But since they had patronised a club downtown, he was confident to find him.

The half-breed gave it no rest.

"Where is your friend?" he asked at every opportunity. "I have a message for him," he sneered.

When the fellow became more restive, Brisco told him roughly where to go.

Curiosity won out. Brisco, more intrigued than annoyed over the putative slight, visited the club alluded to. At the sight of him his friend prepared to slip out through the back door.

"Wait, Max, I have news for you," he shouted loud enough to be heard by everyone within the lounge.

Feigning surprise, Rinaldo stopped and turned around. Grinning sheepishly, he greeted his friend. After they sat down at a private table, Rinaldo asked:

"What's the news?"

"You can stop running."

"Who is running?"

"You are fleeing from that half-breed lurking about in the park. Why, Max, why?"

Starting aside as if trying to fend off a blow, Rinaldo panted:

"I can't, Roger, I can't."

Brisco had no mind to relent.

"Max, that fellow is nothing but a wag searching for dupes."

"No, Roger, he is a ghost risen from his grave."

Brisco was taken aback for an instant. He was about to make a sarcastic remark when his eyes perceived the distress etched on Rinaldo's face. His next words, however, uttered by his friend, tore the strands of sympathy asunder. Bending halfway across the table, Rinaldo panted:

"The wag, as you call that apparition, was named Chadwick Michelson."

"What do you mean – was?" Brisco protested.

Falling back onto his chair, Rinaldo moaned:

"It's his ghost, Max, we buried Michelson two years ago."

Believing that his colleague was halfways over, Brisco prepared to rise and leave. Rinaldo laid a soothing hand on his friend's arm.

"Don't leave, Roger, calm down, remain seated, and listen. I shall tell you about an event that might change your mind about subliminal persuasion."

Leaning back, drawing a deep breath, Rinaldo started to narrate:

"Remember our discussion concerning the subconscious?"

"How could I forget? My head still throbs, and my ears ring from the echo of your assertions which you tried to drum into me."

"Well said, dear colleague, well said," Rinaldo chuckled, then continued:

"Let's call for another bottle, then I shall relate events that prove my theory. As you know I am a professional engineer."

Brisco nodded assent.

"But I am also a justice of the peace, registered in the Northwest Territories. A few years ago I was stationed in Snowdrift, a small settlement at the south shore of Christie Bay."

Noticing his colleague's inquiring gaze, Rinaldo expounded:

"Christie Bay lies at the eastend of Great Slave Lake, above the sixtieth parallel. The settlement is chiefly inhabited by

Chippewa Indians. The place is remote and quite inaccessible, since neither a roadway nor a rail line exists.

"One day a group of Indians arrived from Yellowknife. They were a noisy lot, full of mischief, and generally bothersome. The leader, Chadwick Michelson, proved to be insufferable in more than one way. He was vain, mouthy, and brash, but surprisingly vigorous and handsome. I guessed his age to be nearing seventy, judging by telltale signs, such as arteries, skin texture, and bone structure. Yet his spirited bearing told another story, it made him look at least ten years younger. Indeed, he professed to be fifty-nine years old.

"The group's intentions soon manifested themselves."

"What were they up to?"

"Start and run an outfitters camp. Anyway, complaints about them were soon the order of the day. However, since no laws were broken, there wasn't much I could do."

Brisco raised a hand. He wanted to say something.

"Yes, Roger?"

"This Chadwick Michelson, I presume, is the fellow who loiters in the park," Brisco suggested.

Had he stuck a dagger in his friend's back his reaction couldn't have been more dramatic. He winced like someone in agony, his eyes mirrored reproach as much as distress when he complained:

"Roger, I witnessed Michelson's burial. Indeed, I read the funeral rites, and threw the first shovel of earth onto his lowered casket. Tell me, how in the name of the lord could that wag, as you call him, be Michelson in the flesh?"

Brisco appeared to be cornered for an instant. But then his face lit up.

"He might be his Doppelgänger, as the Germans say," he suggested.

"That's what I thought at first, till my eyes fell on his disfigured hand. You might have noticed that the little finger of his left hand is severed at the joint."

"Yes, I did."

"Well, so was Michelson's."

This information, while not absolutely decisive, nevertheless made Brisco sit up and take notice. Chuckling under his breath, Rinaldo continued his narration:

"Chad, as he wished to be called, was not liked outside his coterie. Almost every adult in the community urged me to take him to task; on what grounds none of us knew. As it so happened I was deeply immersed in the studies of subliminal persuasion."

Brisco stopped yawning, he pricked his ears.

"An idea took hold of me which I prepared to test forthwith. Remember, Michelson was not only vainglorious, but also proud of his youthful looks. He believed to be fascinating to women. Something else I became aware of."

Feeling obliged by his friend's inquiring glance to respond, Brisco asked:

"What was that?"

"He had a morbid fear of ageing."

"Haven't we all?" Brisco intimated.

"More or less. But you see, Michelson didn't really know how old he was."

"That's strange," Brisco suggested.

"Not really under the circumstances. He was a waif who had drifted from place to place all his life."

Rinaldo paused for a moment, he observed his colleague with shrewd eyes.

"What is it, Max?"

"Before I tell you the rest you must give me your word never to repeat a syllable of it."

"You can rely on it."

"I started a rumour that Michelson's age is closer to eighty than sixty years. A few days later he knocked at my door.

" 'Judge, I need a favour,' he said.

" 'Let's hear it,' I encouraged.

" 'Could you find out my date of birth?'

"Feigning surprise about something I knew already, I promised to investigate."

"You knew what, Max?"

"That he was ignorant of his chronological age. Anyway, I made inquiries in Yellowknife and surrounding settlements which, as expected, led nowhere."

"Chadwick Michelson's birth wasn't registered, in other words."

Rinaldo shook his head, an enigmatic smile hovered around his lips.

"No. Thus I recognised the chance to test this theory of subliminal persuasion."

"I don't follow you."

"You will in a moment. The seeds sown, the rumour about Michelson's advanced age were already sprouting; he started to look and act like an elderly man. I, as much as others, couldn't hide my amazement concerning this rapid transformation. The swagger of former days was gone; his bouncy step had deteriorated to a regular slouch. The erstwhile unlined, handsome face, showed signs of decrepitude."

"In a few short weeks?" Brisco questioned with a frown.

"Yes, in a few short weeks," Rinaldo echoed.

"Upon my return, Michelson waited for me at the wharf, anxious beyond description.

" 'Judge, what did you find out?'

" 'You should have let well enough alone,' I replied with a measure of regret. Pulling a piece of paper from my pocket, I handed it to him.

" ' I can't read, what does it say?'

" 'That you were borne in the Old Town, near Yellowknife.'

" 'When?'

" 'Seventy-nine years ago,' I advised.

" 'No, no,' he quailed, and stumbled off.

"When I met him again several weeks later I had to tax all my faculties to recognise the chap. Before me stood a care-worn man looking twice his age, whatever it was."

Brisco interjected:

"Max, I like to call a spade a spade."

"And a fig a fig, isn't that how it goes?"

"How old, in your estimation, was Michelson?"

"Near sixty, on the wrong side. That was the spade. How about the fig?" Rinaldo queried.

"Did you draw up that birth certificate?"

"I was the justice of the peace, wasn't I?"

If Brisco was shocked, he didn't show it, aside from a wry smile.

"What happened next?" he inquired.

"After a short while news reached me that Michelson was confined to bed. He wanted to see me. Feeling guilt nipping at my heels, I started our boat and drove across the bay to the outfitters' camp. Michelson appeared to be on his last legs. My suggestion to call a doctor was roundly rebuffed; not only by Michelson, but even more vigorously did his cronies object."

"That sounds strange," intimated Brisco.

"Exactly my sentiments then, and now. But knowing these people, I didn't insist."

Rinaldo paused. Shaking his head in a way suggesting surprise and consternation, he declared:

"I shall never forget the mood in that camp, which defies description, despite the lasting impression it made upon me."

"Were they antagonistic?"

"Not at all. On the contrary, everybody seemed pleased to see me. Yet I had a distinct feeling of being mocked. Not openly mind you, but through sideways glances, full of meaning. I couldn't help thinking that every man jack gloated over something connected with me."

"They were a puckish lot, I heard you say," interjected Brisco, who became fidgety. His friend's narrative bored, rather than entertained him. Suppressing a yawn, his eyes wandered to the clock on the wall. However, Rinaldo's next words perked him up again.

"Two weeks later I was invited to Michelson's funeral, where I performed the burial rites, and threw the first shovel of earth on the lowered casket. It's the end of my experience in that lonely, windswept settlement."

Brisco prepared to say something, but a closer look at his friend made him swallow his words. Dread was etched on his face, the sight of that half-breed in the park had set his teeth on edge. Brisco wondered why a loafer with a penchant for clownery should upset a man known to be calm to a fault.

Looking at it from every direction his colleague's panic made no sense.

"Max, you shouldn't have resigned," he remonstrated.

"I had to, for I am leaving in a few days."

"But why, Max, why?"

"I am a haunted man, I must flee."

"Haunted by your conscience?" Brisco queried.

"No, by a spectre," Rinaldo said with a wry smile.

Brisco leaned halfway across the table. Squinting, vexation darkening his face, he remonstrated:

"You are not serious. Tell me, and yourself, that you are not serious."

Heaving a deep sigh, drawn from the bottomless well of fear and despair, Rinaldo replied:

"I am, Roger, I am."

Brisco, baffled to the core, at a loss for words, felt not only his hackles rise but an overwhelming desire to leave.

"Max, what's your game?" he queried with a deprecating grin.

"Game?" his colleague echoed, visibly surprised.

"What else is it? Tell me, Max, what else could it possibly be? Here is how I see your predicament, non-existent predicament in my opinion. In order to test a half-baked theory, called subliminal persuasion, you tricked a man into believing that he was much older than he really was. He died, as we all do eventually. Fine and good. Repent and forget, I say, don't put your conscience through fire and water the rest of your days. My advise, Max? Quit being a milksop, come back to work, ignore that wag in the park. If he accosts you in any way, give him tip for tap, he will soon leave you in peace."

Brisco prepared to go his way, when something dawned on him. Striking the table with an open hand, he exclaimed:

"Why didn't I think of that before?"

Astonished, and no less vexed at his colleague's spirited outburst, Rinaldo snapped:

"Think of what?"

"The man you buried and the wag in the park are identical twins."

"Nonsense, Michelson had no siblings, and besides, twins or not, both couldn't have the self-same deformities," Rinaldo protested.

"Fiddlesticks, old chap, this happens quite often. Identical twins are exactly that, the same in every respect."

Rising abruptly, Brisco said:

"I shall see you in the morning, at the same place and time."

Rinaldo moved as if to make a comment, but he resigned himself to remain silent.

Rinaldo did not show up the next morning, or any other time thereafter. The wag was nowhere to be seen.

Three days later a message arrived, addressed to Brisco. Rinaldo wrote.

"My dear friend, we shall probably never see each other again. By the time you receive this communication, I shall be on my way to Europe. By the way, your conjecture about identical twins holds no water in this case. Why, is easily explained. I am quite certain that Michelson had no siblings, let alone a twin brother with the same infirmities. Should one exist, whom Michelson never met nor was aware of, how do you explain this: That character in the park, whoever or whatever it is, cocked his left hand like a pistol at me, while sporting a devilish grin. Well now, Michelson went through the same motion whenever we met. I can assure you that the gesture and grimace are unmistakably identical. Added the mangled small finger on his left hand, as in Michelson's case, what can one conclude? The character in the park must either be Chad Michelson, which is impossible, or his reincarnation on the loose."

Brisco read the short letter twice. He couldn't make head or tail out of it, despite several attempts. Many questions arose, few answers were found. Was Rinaldo delusional? Had some bleak experience left a wound on his psyche which refused to heal? Be that as it may, Brisco decided to distance himself from the whole affair, deemed more contrived than mysterious. But resolutions have a habit to lose force, and start yielding to curiosity.

May had arrived, a steady wind swept over the prairie. Clouds of dust hung around Regina, whose location had almost be guessed from afar. Brisco's promise to forget Rinaldo and his wild notions of spectres intent to haunt him to his grave, got caught in a web of excuses.

After talking things over with his wife, he prepared to make a trip. He asked his employer for a week's vacation, which was granted.

Reaching Yellowknife proved easy enough. Proceeding to Snowdrift, two hundred miles farther east, involved some difficulties. When he arrived at the outfitters' camp, whom should he meet, but the wag of the Wascana Park. The moment when he laid eyes on him, up came his left hand, cocked like a pistol, squarely aimed at him:

"Where is your friend?" he called out.

Brisco, not normally at a loss for words, stared at him silently. When the fellow introduced himself as Chadwick Michelson, he involuntarily echoed:

"Chadwick Michelson, aren't you supposed to be...?"

"Dead and buried?" the other mocked.

Meanwhile a small crowd of Native Indians started to congregate. They were a hardy, unkempt lot who evidently welcomed his presence. All were armed with formidable knifes and guns which they raised above their heads while uttering something unintelligible. They spoke Athapascan with surprising fluency, but English haltingly. No one except Michelson spoke to him. It was still early in the season. Thus not a single customer, adventurers, and thrill seekers had shown up yet.

Michelson said something in Athapascan after which the small crowd dispersed. Turning to Brisco he remarked:

"You are a long way from home."

"So I am."

Chuckling under his breath, the half-breed smirked as only he could. Malicious delight lit up his entire being.

"How did you do it?" Brisco asked.

"It's the wrong question."

"Oh, what should it be?"

"This: How could a man in an official position be so deceitful."

"I am not quite certain that I follow you," Brisco protested.

Could mockery kill, he would have been an instant corpse. Could disdain lame, he would have limped the rest of his days.

Michelson declared:

"I believe you do. Rinaldo, a justice of the peace, forged a document, which is a criminal offence, and an abuse of power to boot."

Brisco did not respond, he was preoccupied with disconcerting notions, presentiments really of an impending evil. The atmosphere crackled with oracular prophecies that bid him to flee.

"Run, Roger, run," an inner voice urged.

Something unpleasant lay in the air which he could not name, but whose sting he felt.

Michelson had more to say:

"Adding insult to injury, Rinaldo, the local magistrate, made a fraudulent report."

"About your death?"

"Exactly, he signed a document to which he affixed his seal."

Vexed, thoroughly confused, Brisco considered the other with unconcealed consternation and nascent loathing. What a nasty character stands before me, he thought, whose pretence of annoyance at Rinaldo's dereliction of duty reeked of unmitigating sanctimony. Brisco wasn't that slow on the uptake. The purpose of the exercise no longer baffled him. The tables were turned on his colleague, his vaunted subliminal persuasion had passed the test. Michelson, with the help of followers, succeeded beyond anyone's dreams. Their aim to scare him out of his wits had been achieved. Michelson, dead and buried, had risen from his grave to haunt him day and night. The scheme worked, but not wholly as intended, since Rinaldo left unexpectedly two days after the interment.

Looking fully at Michelson, Brisco remarked:

"You set Rinaldo up, didn't you? Tell me why and how."

That fiendish leer, found repulsive, and no less disquieting by Brisco, wasn't long in coming. A soul, rising from the well of spite, darkened Michelson's face. It made him look old and vicious, like the proverbial demon of Cathay. Brisco shuddered, it was time to leave, yet something held him back.

Curiosity came to mind, but he quickly rejected the notion. What he felt went far beyond mere desire to become informed. The mysterious urge to tempt fate bid him to stay. Before his inner eye rose Rinaldo's distraught face, signifying uncertainty about his sanity. In his ears rang the words that compelled him to undertake a perilous journey.

"Roger, that experience in the untamed wilderness, not far below the tree line, left a scar on my mind. When I arrived at the outfitters' camp I was shown an open coffin, wherein lay Chad Michelson, dead as a doornail, ready to be buried. Make no mistake, I had an impression that something was out of kilter there."

When asked what induced him to think so, he explained:

"The corpse was rigged up to the nines, meaning dressed full Chippewan regalia."

"Like a warrior?" Brisco asked.

"More like a chief, I should say. Which in itself astonished me, since Michelson lacked the status of even a full blood Chippewan. Something else caught my eye, the corpse's odd disjointedness."

Brisco asked no further questions then, his colleague offered no other explanations thereafter.

His friend Rinaldo had been duped; how exactly, Brisco could not have said, to what purpose he understood. Michelson faked his death, co-workers prevailed upon Rinaldo to preside at and help out with the burial. Thus making sure that Michelson's death was forever anchored in his mind. Therefore when the man he had buried suddenly appeared before his eyes, his friend and colleague concluded that it could be nothing but a spectre, bent on haunting him to his grave.

Michelson's expectations were being fulfilled. Max Rinaldo, stung to the soul, suffering from pangs of guilt, fell for it. He fled hell-bent for a sanctuary which, like Utopia, will never be found. With remorse nipping at his heels, and fear fingering his throat, Brisco reckoned that even in the fortress Impregnable, his worthy colleague would find no inner peace, for a conscious pitted by remorse and dread is a millstone around one's neck.

Brisco had seen and heard enough. Rinaldo's scheme had boomeranged, the theory of subliminal persuasion had passed the acid test alright, but the result was not as anticipated by Rinaldo who, in Brisco's estimation, should have chosen a less rancorous and inventive medium. His friend was tricked, no doubt about it, by an artifice he couldn't comprehend. Michelson, with the support of his assistants, convinced Rinaldo of his death, who witnessed and certified the subsequent interment. Who or what lay in that coffin inspected by his colleague, sealed before his eyes and lowered with his help? Not Chad Michelson, to be sure, since the coffin with its nailed down lid never left his friend's sight. Therefore whoever lay in there remained buried in the ground. Insinuations that his colleague could have been deceived by a stuffed-out figure resembling Michelson were roundly rejected.

"Roger, Chad Michelson lay in that casket, I recognised him, warts and all. Granted, he did look younger, more relaxed than two weeks ago. Think what you want, say what you like, those features, remarkable in some ways, belonged to no one else but Chadwick Michelson."

Brisco made no attempt at rebuttal, for he realised that approaching death often smoothers careworn countenances, and loosens limbs.

On the way back Brisco decided to stay overnight in Yellowknife. Daylight above the sixtieth parallel lasted almost till midnight now, twilight extended up to dawn. Streets were enlivened by strollers and bargain hunters past the wee hours.

Brisco walked up and down the main street while keeping an eye peeled at the show windows. Stores hadn't closed yet, some merchants displayed their wares on the sidewalk. What he sought exactly Brisco couldn't have named, what he found lifted the veils of uncertainty; it explained the vexing mystery in a flash. Before his eyes on a well-lit shelf stood several busts whose sight made him smile appreciatively. They were spitting images of Chad Michelson. His friend had been hoodwinked by experts.

# The Suitors

Elisabeth St. Clair arrived in style, it should be said, on a rainy March afternoon. Reaching the hamlet of Bamfield in those days could hardly be called a pleasure trip. The word was soon out:

"Spruce up, young men, a belle is among us."

Her appearance caused a flutter in the small community with fewer than two hundred residents. In no time did she thrill the hearts of men, married mostly, and put a crimp in the women's hold over them.

"Let's look at her in the bright sunshine," they snickered among themselves, while keeping both eyes peeled at their husbands who might harbour unseemly notions.

No two ways about it, Elisabeth St. Clair was an eye-catching woman, born and raised in nearby Victoria, thirty years ago.

Jeremy Scahill, the head of the Marine Centre, Elisabeth's employer, compared her, not so silently mind you, to Spenser's amoret. Gentle as a dove, chaste as a lily, disposed like a seraph.

"What fools men are," Ruth Scofield informed everyone, including the fish in the sea.

She owned a small general store, the only one within a day's journey. She had renounced love some thirty years ago, which to her was a game not worth the candle. An early marriage wasn't exactly made in heaven. Kisses behind the garden gate soon yielded to nagging and scolding. One stormy night her husband left the pit that dug itself deeper by the day, and vowed never to return.

"That's the only promise he ever kept," Mrs Scofield proclaimed with that peculiar cackle known in the region.

She harumphed Jeremy Scahill's notions:

"An epitome of womanly grace she is? What fools men are. That female is as hard-boiled as they come. Mark my words, she is up to no good, this Miss St. Clair is."

Two months later the boats started to arrive. Soon the government wharves were occupied from end to end. Summer at the West Coast is invariable sunny and warm, albeit somewhat stormy.

Barry Lasco was already ensconced at his summerhouse across the Bamfield inlet. He was locally known as the millionaire, and no less as a dyed-in-the-wool bachelor, who gave women a wide berth. Those sentiments underwent a change, however, when he encountered Miss St. Clair. Although she kept to herself, meeting one another in this small community proved unavoidable. Invitations, rather scarce it must be said, were treated by Elisabeth with consummate adroitness. Visibly touched, blushing in appreciation, she managed to decline with words and gestures that amused rather than offended. The men's compliments, as much as their admiring glances, she answered with frowns, and nothing else. The women's appraising looks she met with a beguiling smile and a hearty greeting.

"She is a recluse," some declared.

"She is a Jezebel," Mary Sartos asserted, whose husband of thirty years had suddenly acquired a roving eye.

Miss St. Clair made no attempt to entice the menfolk, nor did she try to antagonise the women, who observed her with Argus-eyes. Their female intuition told them that she was anything but a Zuleika: pure, dutiful, and innocent.

"Why did she come to this out-of-the-way place?" it was said.

"Surely not for her health, nor the low paying, seasonal work."

Curiosity breathed new life into the hearts of some locals, rumours enlivened their workaday routine. Gossip, unkind and sensational at times, made the grapevine hum.

"May I invite you for tea, or coffee perhaps, Miss St. Clair?" Lasco, standing at the gate, called out.

Elisabeth started, turned, and seemed prepared to bound.

"No, thank you," she replied, visibly annoyed at the unsolicited salutation.

"Oh, well, maybe another time," he chuckled, while raising his hand in a chipper way.

Barry Lasco, a man past fifty, the inveterate bachelor, was not a misogynist; far from it, but marriage he eschewed strenuously, he deemed it eternal purgatory where both sides stoke the fire, hoping that the other felt the heat more. Anyway, foregoing liberties he cherished, or changing entrenched habits? Not for the sweetest of kisses, he vowed, nor for that divinest of love, Venus on the mountain promises.

Antonio Ricci, Lasco's friend of many years, usually spent the month of July at his retreat. For inexplicable reasons he harboured a desire that Antonio should skip his visit this year. He neither understood nor questioned why this should be so. Yet the notion recurred, although he deemed it wishful thinking in view of the message that was sent:

"Will be at your gate as usual. Unlimber the liquor."

They were friends in accordance with the mores of modern days. Two minds of a single thought? Not Barry Lasco and Antonio Ricci, who was blessed with mercurial wit, thus contrasting sharply the other's morose disposition. Their temperaments were forged in different smithies. What induced one to smile made the other frown. Words of wisdom uttered by Lasco were deemed fatuous by Ricci. Yet they referred to each other as friends, affectionate friends, in fact.

"How was the trip?" Lasco, who stood at the wharf, called out.

"A bit rough past Port Renfrew, but otherwise bearable."

They greeted each other with hugs and friendly words, then settled down in the garden, which had no equal far and wide. The estate, spread out on the west side of the inlet, had a charm of its own. A wondrous tranquillity permeated that spot; the wind appeared to convey a message: All is well, all is well. The waves, rolling in from the open sea, though breaking noisily on the rocky shore, augured an enchantment that put one's heart at ease.

"Halcyon reborn," Antonio informed the mountains beyond.

Ricci saw her first, the sight made him lift his head and crane his neck.

"What do you know, Barry, one of your conquests?" he chaffed.

When Lasco looked up he recognised Miss St. Clair who stood at the boardwalk, evidently lost in thought. Noticing the men's attention accorded her, she tiptoed away.

"Who is she, Barry?"

"Elisabeth St. Clair, a seasonal worker at the Marine Station."

"Married?"

"Unattached and unapproachable," Antonio was informed.

Ricci pooh-poohed the notion, his quick eye discerned what Lasco couldn't even divine. He wasn't quite the gay Lothario of Rowe's 'The Fair Penitent', but he did appreciate the fair sex, who in his opinion deserved a man's homage. He started to whistle one of his catchy tunes, while a roguish expression framed his countenance:

"Hm, unattached and unapproachable, you say? Hm, hm."

Three days later Ricci presented Miss St. Clair at the Lasco estate.

"She deigns to have a glass of wine with us," he declared with a bow befitting a Spanish nobleman.

The courtship was on; not in earnest mind you, but Miss St. Clair harboured no doubts how the bells tinkled. She neither welcomed the idea, nor decried their effort to be pleasant. At first Lasco felt sheepish in the roll of a cavalier, which he deemed unbecoming for a man of affairs. Amorous sentiments, neglected and suppressed for some time, raised their heads again. Many years ago he had vowed that no woman's shadow shall darken his threshold again.

"Love bears a whiff of ill repute, if not an odour of indignity," he declared.

Anyway, aspiring to wealth and esteem seemed more dignified than billing and cooing, thus making a fool of oneself. Besides, he felt too old to fit into the mould of a beau. In addition he balked at the idea to tie a knot with his tongue, which the best set of teeth are unable to untie.

However, the proximity of Elisabeth St. Clair, coupled with Antonio's boldness, spurred him on. Ricci's ardour became his hone. He peeled off priggishness in a hurry, gave primness a shove, and showed himself in a light that no other suitor could match, he reckoned.

The end of July drew near, yet not a syllable was spoken concerning Antonio's departure. Miss St. Clair, who initially frowned, than smiled at the antics of the wooers, began to enjoy their attention. The homage of two men, pleasant to look at, blessed with engaging manners, obviously well off, could but quicken a woman's heartbeat. When she sensed their serious intentions, it also brightened the colour on her face, subdued, however, by a nagging thought: Would Lasco propose? Observing the staid businessman's inner struggle brought a smile to her lips. He appeared to be riven by opposing emotions, unseemly desires, and embarrassment. The whispering campaign of scandalised women, parroted by their browbeaten husbands, she treated with pursed lips and unladylike snorts.

Antonio spoke first:

"Barry, the situation becomes untenable, one of us must bow out."

"Well, Antonio, start bowing."

"Not so fast, not so fast. Remember, Elisabeth is enamoured of me."

"Perhaps so, but we only have your word for it, don't we?"

Ricci looked his friend full in the face. He remained silent for a moment. Significant thoughts appeared to course through his mind. Thrusting out his chin, cocking his head, he queried:

"What are your intentions concerning Elisabeth?"

"Matrimony, and yours?"

"The same."

"Hm, there seems to be a bridegroom too many then. Since neither one wants to step back voluntarily, what now?"

"The game," Ricci declared.

Lasco nodded.

"Yes, it's the only solution," he agreed.

"Fetch the board and don't forget the pebbles," Antonio requested.

Lasco returned in a twinkling with the warri board in one hand, and the bag of counters in the other. He wasn't too enamoured of the notion to make such a momentous decision hinging on a game of chance, yet it seemed to be the only honourable way out. The winner of two matches out of three proposes to Elisabeth, while the loser decamps.

Barry Lasco, the prosaic man of affairs' perception of 'The Game of Houses' held no water, it is anything but a contest of chance. Something else he didn't know; namely, that Antonio had spent many years in the Lesser Antilles, where warri matches are being played at almost every street corner, especially in Antigua and Barbados. There, squatting beneath the blue sky, fanned by the cooling trade wind, surrounded by awed natives, he learned from the old masters how to move nickars with lightning speed.

Lasco knew nothing about Ricci's extended sojourn in the Caribbean Islands, thus his skill at the ancient Game of Houses remained a secret. It should be noted that while his friend possessed a chatty bent, he could be tight-lipped about certain matters. For instance, to Lasco's chagrin, Antonio consistently mystified the sources of his income.

Some time ago Ricci gave his friend a finely crafted warri board, and taught him how to play. Antonio won the first match, but lost the second and third one.

The wedding took place two months later.

Ricci left the country for a while. When he returned a frantic message awaited him:

"Antonio, contact me at once, I need help," it read.

Antonio smiled from ear to ear. Why, no one could have guessed. They met in Port Alberni. At the sight of his friend, Antonio stepped back involuntarily; a ghostlier face he had never seen. Misery was etched on every inch of the once broad, serene countenance. The hitherto dark full head of hair, besides getting sparse, had acquired a grizzled hue. Ricci gasped:

"Barry, what happened, are you sick?"

"Sick of life, Antonio, and even sicker of matrimony," the friend groaned.

"Now, now, tell me all about it."

His friend did. He related a pitiful tale of woe, which he concluded with a prediction:

"Either I have to commit suicide, go insane, or accede to her demands, " he declared

While not understanding every word of Lasco's dirge, Ricci got the gist of it. It seemed that Elisabeth proved to be a fortune huntress of the vilest sort.

"She is a profligate with a streak of meanness running from head to toe, and a scold to boot."

"How about a divorce?" Antonio queried.

Lasco winced, his whole body appeared to be in pain:

"Tomorrow wouldn't be too soon."

"So, what's the hold-up?"

"Silly laws, and a woman's avarice."

Signs of impatience became evident in Antonio's demeanour. He raised, then lowered his head, turned it sideways and grimaced as if annoyed. He appeared to be on edge.

"Did you broach the subject?" he inquired.

"I did."

"And?"

"She is amenable to a divorce," Antonio was advised.

"Well, cheer up, then."

"How can I when her demands are usurious and by far exceed the limits of my generosity."

Antonio almost swallowed the wrong way. Calling his friend generous stretched credibility a bit too wide. How often did he tell him in jest:

"Barry, are you sure that your middle name isn't thrifty?"

Skinflint would have described his sentiments more accurately. For separating a man from his shadow might have proved easier than wangling a dime out of his tight-fisted friend.

"What does she want?"

"Half of my possessions, plus alimony for ten years."

"Hm, that does sound exorbitant," Ricci granted with a strange gleam in his eyes.

"Indecent, I call it. Making such demands for a year's misery," Lasco confirmed.

On the way out his steps became halting before he stopped, then raised a hand to his brow and turned around.

"Do you know, Antonio, what puzzles me most?"

"How could I?"

"It's a curious fact, Elisabeth knows almost to a dollar the value of my assets. Isn't that odd?"

Did Ricci flinch while lowering his head? Lasco wasn't sure, yet he noticed his friend's peculiar behaviour. From the moment they had set eyes on each other again, Antonio appeared to be on pins and needles. Telltale signs of uneasiness were noticeable in words, gestures, and demeanour.

"It's this: Elisabeth has an uncanny ability to assess my assets almost to the dollar. I am perplexed, to say the least."

The anticipated news reached Antonio three months later:

"The coast is clear: Maid of the mist," the short communication read.

Ricci understood, the code name said it all. Elisabeth would tell him what he so anxiously wanted to know. He dawdled not a moment. After a glance in the mirror, a tug here, followed by pats and strokes there, and off he went.

They met as arranged in Toffino at one of the hotels whose main attractions were the winter storms, accompanied by an incomparable surf. They had avoided all contact from the time when he and Lasco played for Elisabeth's hand; till now.

"We don't want to raise even a whiff of suspicion," Antonio had cautioned, for their escutcheons were anything but clean.

After all they did plot to trick his friend Barry Lasco, known as the Croesus of Barkley Sound.

Two surprises awaited Antonio: The presence of Barry Lasco, and Elisabeth's mien. She looked like a woman ennobled. The harshness, which the most ingenious make-up could not hide, had vanished. The hard-bitten appearance of the past existed no more. Even the telltale signs of strain, caused by inner strife, were no longer visible. Elisabeth, the aloof, calculating woman, exuded an air that thoroughly confused

Antonio. He smelled a rat, something was not going according to plans, caution had to be used. Lasco's strident voice, dripping with sarcasm, tore him from his observations.

"What's the matter, ganelon, are you nonplussed?"

Turning to Elisabeth, he mocked:

"Ha, ha, ha, our Judas is struck dumb."

Looking daggers at Antonio, he snarled:

"Coming to celebrate?"

Ricci fell back a few steps, irresolution clouded his face. Should I leave or should I stay? the question seemed to be.

He looked inquiringly at Elisabeth, who sat in the anxious seat. True, she was embarrassed, but also relieved, and no less determined to make a break from her sordid past. Antonio's quick mind took it all in, even before Elisabeth rose and said in a quiet voice:

"I have told Barry everything."

Wincing in disbelief, then shrugging his shoulders as only a man from the Abbruzzese can, he informed her and the walls:

"I haven't a clue what you are alluding to."

Lasco, stung by such unmitigated cheek, sprung up:

"Bold as brass, aren't we? But let me tell you, the jig is up, unless…"

"Unless what?"

"You leave the country forthwith, and never return."

Brazen-faced Ricci could be called, worthy of the motley he was not. In a twinkle he assessed the situation, circumstances spoke against him. In a criminal procedure Elisabeth, a material witness no doubt, though guilty by association, would surely be offered immunity if she testified. Antonio smiled as he signified agreement with a gentleman's bow.

More at ease now, yet still visibly miffed at Elisabeth's turnabout, Antonio prepared to leave, when Lasco cleared his throat. Fearing that his erstwhile friend was going to shower him with abusive language, he raised a hand while hurrying towards the exit.

"Easy, easy, Antonio, let bygones be bygones. After all we had some good times together," Lasco reminded him.

Though suspecting a trap, Ricci halted his steps. When Elisabeth chimed in with conciliatory words, he turned around.

There he stood like someone whose mind received pushes and tugs simultaneously. Should he or should he not break a vow given some time ago?

"What have you got in mind?" he asked in a menacing tone.

They looked at each other with eyes that mirrored resolve weakened by trepidation. Ricci glanced sideways at Elisabeth, who divined what was in the offing. There it was: When Antonio moved towards her, Lasco rose and raised a hand. Ricci snorted:

"Don't worry, I won't harm her, but there is something you ought to know."

Elisabeth's transformation touched on the supernatural. The aspect of a duteous, loving woman existed no more. The Amelia of a moment ago resembled a spitting cobra, ready to strike. Antonio stepped back instinctively, he knew what the posture meant. Lasco, the husband, stopped as if rooted to the floor. Did he gape? Perhaps, yet he did not remember. But the incident proved too strong a fare for the prim man of affairs, who asked:

"What should I know?"

Antonio, still tense, daunted by Elisabeth's familiar posture, gave no answer. He shook his head and left. But not before he asked in disbelief:

"Am I to understand that you are still married?"

"Happily so," they answered in unison.

Ricci intended to leave the country soon. Not because he gave his word to do so, but solely for selfish reasons. He might likely be punished somehow should his erstwhile pal decide to pursue the matter. With Elisabeth's connivance his chances were slim to walk away unscathed. What an enigma she turned out to be, a riddle even to his sophisticated mind. He did manage to have a chat with her in private, which proved to be short and evasive, plus acrimonious besides.

"Yes, I would tell all, truthfully so," she advised.

"But – but, could that not be tantamount with harming yourself?" Antonio protested.

"Even so, should it end up in court I shall sing," she vowed.

Yes, Elisabeth St. Clair puzzled Antonio, who was plagued by a nagging suspicion that she had lost her sanity.

"But, if I too decide to tell all, what then?"

Could scorn kill, Antonio Ricci would have been a dying man, writhing on a side walk of Ucluelet. A smile stole around her lips. It bore strains of disdain, traces of defiance, and tinges of bravado.

"You would be laughed out of the courtroom," she hissed, then turned on her toes and walked away, huffing and puffing like only an irate woman can.

Antonio returned to his old haunts, where he felt safe from prosecution and sheltered from Elisabeth's mocking eyes. He could not forget that chance meeting in Ucluelet. Even today, thousands of miles distance, he shuddered in the heat of the Windward Islands, at the thought of that encounter. Her strange bearing had made him uneasy. The face, normally placid, exuded emotions he could not fathom. It shone with evil delight, a triumphal gloating marred the countenance so painstakingly groomed. The feeling obtruded itself that she had, or intended to outwit him adroitly, and no less thoroughly.

A year or so later he met Barry Lasco at the Crane Hotel in Barbados. His surprise could hardly be described. Yet not on account of the presumed fortuitous encounter, but because of his former pal's battered air, which implied that he was on his last leg. Indeed, an aura of dejection adhered to the man that made Antonio turn instinctively aside. The term, a dead man walking, flashed through his mind. He almost cracked a fatuous joke, like:

"Are you on your way to your own funeral, Barry?"

But a closer look bid him to bite his tongue. Lasco's grief seemed not only to be profound but quite genuine. No, he wasn't being hoodwinked again, the man before him was evidently halfway to Golgatha.

"Have you got some time, Antonio?"

"As much as you need."

"Then be my guest, I must talk to you."

"Let's sit out on the balcony," Antonio suggested.

The sight, incomparable even in the Caribbean, seemed to leave Lasco cold. The roar of the foaming water breaking over distant reefs, affected him as little as the constant trade wind that lifted one's spirit and cooled one's brow. The cries of the seagulls, wild and free, that never failed to make short work of Antonio's penchant for moping, elicited neither a remark from Lasco nor a look.

Antonio spoke first:

"Where is your wife, is she not with you?" he asked.

Had he plunged a dagger in Lasco's heart, his reaction could have been hardly more remarkable. He groaned, put a hand at his throat, then wiped his forehead with the other one, as if to chase away dark memories. Sighing once more, he declared:

"We are no longer together."

Antonio, who misunderstood the moaning, heavy breathing and Lasco's words, lowered his voice:

"Is she – did Elisabeth die?" he asked.

"Ha, I should be so lucky," Lasco snorted.

Taken aback, Antonio remonstrated:

"I don't understand, Barry."

Casting a withering glance at Antonio, Lasco rasped:

"I believe you do."

"Man alive, what are you talking about?"

The ensuing scowl, meant to be murderous, might have worried Antonio back home in Canada, but not here. Sitting high above a beach that knows no equal, washed by the surf of a windswept ocean, amid the rustle of palm trees, Lasco's threatening posture possessed no edge. It tickled one's fancy rather than stoke one's apprehensions.

"Dissemble all you want, it won't do any good," Lasco admonished.

Quite irate now, he continued:

"What I am talking about is this: Elisabeth finally managed to ease me out of my assets, under your tutelage, of course."

"My tutelage?" Antonio echoed.

Leaning back he observed the breaking waves far out. His brow puckered, he appeared to be wrestling with thoughts that were difficult to disentangle. His eyes lit up, he raised both hands in an attempt to soothe Lasco, who appeared to be cut to the quick.

"Wait a minute, Barry, just wait a minute," he urged, while a smile illuminated his face.

Then, without another word or sign, he broke out in hee-haws that made bathers below raise their heads. Lasco, though still angry on account of the presumed plot, nevertheless found Antonio's hilarity contagious. While not in the mood to chime in, he couldn't suppress a chuckle. That belly laugh, sprouting from a vivacious heart and a puckish soul, reminded him of many an elbow bending session and merrymaking. But those were happier times which would never return in his lifetime. Feeling self-conscious, he protested:

"Restrain yourself, people are staring at us."

"Let them stare, they have nothing better to do," Antonio retorted.

Although he seemed to be still amused, he toned down the raucous laughter. Between bouts of merriments Antonio burst out:

"From one dupe to the other, tell me what happened."

Irritated to the hilt, Lasco snapped:

"I wouldn't dream of explaining my distress to the very author of it."

Antonio shook his head vigorously:

"You are confusing the issue, Barry. I remember what happened about a year ago at our meeting in Tofino. You and Elisabeth were billing and cooing like newlyweds, while practically chasing me out of the country. You hinted that all was forgotten and forgiven as long as I left the country and didn't come back."

"Quite true, but things have changed drastically," Lasco declared.

"I kept my end of the bargain, so why rake up the event again? Wasn't our motto always: Let's sleeping dogs lie?"

"Perhaps so," Lasco agreed reluctantly, but also somewhat pacified.

Knitting his brow, stroking his chin absent-mindedly, he asked:

"You haven't been back, I heard you say?"

"Not so far."

"Does Elisabeth know your whereabouts?"

"Not likely," came an answer accompanied by a withering look. "Get to the point, Barry, get to the point," Antonio requested.

"I will in a moment. Just one more thing: Were you in contact with Elisabeth since our meeting in Tofino?"

Antonio was about to expel an angry no, when he recalled that short encounter in Ucluelet."

"Hm, come to think of it, a week prior to my departure we accidentally came upon each other on the streets of Ucluelet."

"Aha," Lasco exclaimed.

"Save your breath, Barry, nothing untoward was said or done. Elisabeth, annoyed to the core at the sight of me, reiterated her stand: Should I not leave the country permanently, you were ready to go to the police. Come what may, she emphasised again, she would testify against me in court."

Barry Lasco possessed a forgiving heart and forgetful mind. He could not be called a rancorous man, unless his wallet became endangered. He realised below the threshold of consciousness that Antonio was telling the truth. He had no hand in Elisabeth's ultimate scheme to enrich herself with the lion's share of his assets, which caused him much anguish. The signs of bitterness were etched on his face; his limbs bore witness of a man weighed down by rancour. His eyes, dull now, had lost their former lustre. To Antonio's annoyance he seemed to be oblivious of the bewitching surrounding; peaceful and uplifting. The lively but nevertheless unruffled souls and minds of the natives, left the man of wealth untouched. Judging by his demeanour he paid no heed to the rush of waves breaking over the far reefs. His fortune had decreased, thus his spleen grew, excessive bile had transformed him into an old man, in less than a year.

"You asked what my point is? Nothing less than this: I have been gypped with your help."

Antonio's puckered lips expressed disappointment and irritation.

"I thought that this was settled. You forgave me, provided I accepted banishment, " he protested, then continued:

"I am not aware of what Elisabeth told you. Yes I helped weaving the net that caught the fish. But let me assure you, not for pecuniary consideration."

"For what then?" Lasco wanted to know.

Antonio hesitated, he grinned as if in pain. Irresolution, that debilitating emotion, appeared to be uppermost in him. He made an attempt to sidestep the question by diverting Lasco's attention. Pointing towards the open sea, he remarked:

"Look, what some fool is trying to do. There he is, fighting the waves to reach the reefs."

"Never mind, let him drown. You were going to reveal the reason why you teamed up with Elisabeth to get your hands on my fortune."

"Not so, not so at all. I was only guided by one motive."

"Which is?"

"To part company with Elisabeth."

Puzzled, Lasco stared at him inquiringly, then said:

"That's a cryptic remark alright."

"Not once you know the truth. You see I wanted to be rid of her; once and for all."

"I am still confused," admitted Lasco.

"Let me enlighten you then. When Elisabeth walked past your property you perked up, or am I mistaken?"

"Not particularly."

Did Antonio titter? Yes, inwardly. After a significant glance, accompanied by a sardonic smile, Antonio explained:

"It was all part of the plan."

"Plan? Whose plan?"

"Mine. She played her roll well. A professional actress could hardly have trumped her performance."

Lasco bounded from his chair with such vehemence, that for an instant Antonio feared he would jump over the railing.

"You speak of a plan, a plot even, directed at me. Why, Antonio, why did you want to betray me?"

"I didn't wish to betray you, I just saw a way to disentangle me from Elisabeth," came a laconic explanation.

"But you hardly knew her, I thought," protested Lasco.

"You are wrong. I was married to her once."

Had a bolt from the blue just struck, Lasco's reaction could hardly have been more violent. He literally doubled up, then straightening himself flailed his arms and spoke under his breath:

"You are off the deep end. Elisabeth had never been married before; she told me everything."

"Not quite, Barry, not quite. Remember our encounter in Tofino when I wanted to speak up?"

Lasco did. He also recalled Elisabeth's bizarre conduct. She resembled a tigress, ready to spring.

"We were married in Mexico six months before you tied the knot. Yes, we joined hands in March. In April I fled from her. Divorce? Not Elisabeth St. Clair, unless she found another man. I decided to help her, plus let her have all my possessions; except the boat."

He did not, however, allow to have been a partner to defraud him of his fortune.

Lasco looked down at the almost deserted beach below, then scoured the open sea for no particular reason. His mien changed, he gave the impression of a man whose subconscious raced ahead of his thoughts. Questions entered his mind, which one side of him was tempted to ask, but every time he stood on the verge of doing so, an admonishing voice from within urged him to desist.

"Let bygones be bygones," that little voice whispered.

He slowly turned towards Antonio:

"You know the expression: 'my friends, the enemy,' I take it?"

"I do, but if you impute to me enmity towards you, I protest. True, I helped Elisabeth, whom I did not cherish as a wife, to find another husband. But no one forced you to marry her. So I tricked you in some small way, letting you win the two warri games, for instance, just to help things along. That can hardly be called treachery."

Lasco let it be at that. The dastardly deed, as he liked to call Antonio's betrayal, started to lose its sting shortly after he stepped onto the island. The sneak, whose punishment he sought, had turned into a harum-scarum amid the soft air and lilting voices of the natives. Now, after two hours, surrounded

by an atmosphere that must be experienced, since it defies
description, he saw in Antonio a companion again, albeit not a
trustworthy one, but worthy of acquaintanceship. Barry Lasco,
the staid businessman's demeanour relaxed, the spell of the
Caribbean was upon him. He smiled despite an irresistible
hunch: Antonio and Elisabeth were still husband and wife
when he married her.

www.ingramcontent.com/pod-product-compliance
Lightning Source LLC
Chambersburg PA
CBHW020619260626
47157CB00003B/1079